A Little, Aloud

An anthology of prose and poetry
for reading aloud to someone
you care for

Edited by Angela Macmillan
Foreword by Blake Morrison
Illustrations by Mary Lundquist

Chatto & Windus
LONDON

Published by Chatto & Windus 2010

4 6 8 10 9 7 5 3

We are very grateful to Mary Lundquist for
providing illustrations free of charge
www.marylundquist.com

The publisher is donating all royalties in full from this book
to The Reader Organisation.

First published in Great Britain in 2010 by
Chatto & Windus
Random House, 20 Vauxhall Bridge Road,
London SW1V 2SA

www.rbooks.co.uk

Addresses for companies within The Random House Group Limited
can be found at: www.randomhouse.co.uk/offices.htm

The Random House Group Limited Reg. No. 954009

A CIP catalogue record for this book
is available from the British Library

ISBN 9780701185633

The Random House Group Limited supports The Forest Stewardship Council (FSC), the leading international forest certification organisation. All our titles that are printed on Greenpeace approved FSC certified paper carry the FSC logo. Our paper procurement policy can be found at www.rbooks.co.uk/environment

Contents

Foreword

'Poetry makes nothing happen,' Auden wrote in his famous elegy to W. B. Yeats, and those who believe that literature and the arts are a sideline or an indulgence have been all too quick to agree. But Auden was careful to qualify his position. Poetry might not overthrow dictators but it can still have a value as 'a way of happening, a mouth,' he suggested. And for the benefit of readers, he urged poets to sing on – 'With your unconstraining voice/Still persuade us to rejoice'. If poetry can persuade us to rejoice, or even just to keep going, then it serves an important purpose. I have never forgotten the man who came to a writing workshop I ran, many years ago, who said that he'd been about to kill himself – had the bath running, and the razor on the side – when he sat down to write a poem instead and, having finished it, decided life was worth living after all. It's an example of how poetry *does* make things happen: of its power to inspire, console, heal and transform.

'One sheds one's sicknesses in books,' D. H. Lawrence said, and a growing number of teachers, readers and health professionals seem to share that view. 'Bibliotherapy' might be a new word but the idea behind it has a long history. In Ancient Greece, Apollo was god of both poetry and healing: as Pindar puts it (in his Pythian odes), he's the god

Who sends
Mortal men and women
Relief from grievous disease. Apollo,
Who has given us the lyre.
Who brings the Muse
To whom he chooses, filling the heart
With peace and harmony.

In similar vein, the Bible tells the story of David calming Saul by playing music to him on a harp: 'so Saul was refreshed, and was well, and the evil spirit departed from him'. By the Renaissance, the idea that poetry and song could 'banish vexations of soul and body' was well-established, with the effects of tragedy thought to be just as therapeutic as comedy. In *The Art of English Poesie* (1589) George Puttenham advises the poet to use 'one dolour to expel another', the sad cadence in a line of poetry allaying the burden of pain or depression in the reader, 'one short sorrowing the remedy of a long and grievous sorrow'.

Readers down the ages have testified to literature's capacity to make us feel better – better *in* ourselves and better *about* ourselves – by immersing us in the lives of others, or articulating eternal truths ('what oft was thought but ne'er so well expressed'), or by speaking of feelings so deep and complex that they're almost impossible to put into words. Some of these readers have themselves been writers. They range from George Eliot (who recovered from the grief of losing her husband George Henry Lewes by reading Dante with a young friend, John Cross, whom she subsequently married) to John

Stuart Mill, who, thanks to a passage in the memoirs of Jean-François Marmontel, recovered from a 'crisis in my mental history [when] I seemed to have nothing left to live for . . . A vivid conception of the scene and its feelings came over me, and I was moved to tears. From this moment my being grew lighter. The oppression of the thought that all feeling was dead within me was gone. I was no longer hopeless: I was not a stock or a stone.'

The reasons for it may not be clear, but literature in general and poetry in particular do seem capable of raising the human spirit; one of the most elaborate descriptions of the process comes in Anne Brontë's *Agnes Grey*:

When we are harassed by sorrows or anxieties, or long oppressed by any powerful feelings which we must keep to ourselves, for which we can obtain and seek no sympathy from any living creature, and which yet we cannot, or will not, wholly crush, we often naturally seek relief in poetry – and often find it, too – whether in the effusions of others, which seem to harmonise with our existing case, or in our own attempts to give utterance to those thoughts and feelings in strains less musical, perchance, but more appropriate, and therefore more penetrating and sympathetic, and, for the time, more soothing, or more powerful to rouse and to unburden the oppressed and swollen heart.

To unburden her oppressed heart, Anne Brontë wrote about the natural world she saw around her, in all its bleakness:

'Blow on, wild wind; thy solemn voice,/However sad and drear,/Is nothing to the gloomy silence/I have had to bear.' Better a solemn voice than a gloomy silence. And poets' voices aren't always solemn, of course, even when their subject matter is grave. If you listen to Seamus Heaney read his poem 'Digging' (a poem included in this anthology) you can't miss the sheer enjoyment of the performance, despite the serious questions he raises about loyalty, work and staying true to one's family. It's a poem about finding one's way in life and, by finding the right words, rhymes and rhythms he shows us how that's done and includes us in the process.

We tend to think of reading as a solitary activity and for most of us, most of the time, it probably is. But we read, in part, in order to feel less alone in the world, and a great novel or poem will put us in good company, even when we're on our own. Books are inclusive: they invite us in and help us belong. It's especially heartening when a poet or novelist expresses emotions and ideas that we thought, till we saw them written down, were unique to us: at such moments, as Hector, the schoolteacher in Alan Bennett's play *The History Boys* puts it, it's as if a hand has reached out and taken our own. Literature has traditionally been presented as an individualist enterprise. But in reality it's communal and collaborative. A book might exist as an object without anyone ever opening it. But it only exists as a text by being read.

And reading isn't necessarily a silent activity. As children we are read to by others (parents, grandparents, teachers): it's aurally rather than visually that we first encounter books. And though it's said that people flock to literary festivals in order to *see* famous authors, the opportunity to *hear* them read from their work is part of the attraction, too. I know couples who read books aloud to each other in preference to watching television. And then there are books we read to friends in hospital or to relations in care homes. To share a book in this way can bring insights not available when we read alone. It's as if the author acts as an intermediary, allowing us to broach subjects that there isn't the time or space or intimacy for in the normal pattern of our lives.

Milton knew that reading had its limits, that a man could be 'deep-versed in books and shallow in himself'. But at best, literature touches something deep within us and, because of that, makes our dealings with the world deeper too. What moves us in literature isn't just seeing the words, on the page, but hearing them resonate, in the air. Try it yourself, with the poems and prose passages in this anthology: speak them aloud, to yourself or someone close to you, and (to quote Auden again) 'In the deserts of the heart/Let the healing fountain start'.

Blake Morrison

Introduction

❧

SHARED READING, SHARED MEANING

Nearly thirty years ago I was putting the Nobel prize-winning novelist Doris Lessing on a train at the end of her first visit to Liverpool. I was in a state of great awe, this beautiful and distinguished writer was my hero, and old enough to be my mother. She was a storyteller who had captivated and deeply affected me; I had invited her to visit and talk, and now in these final moments at Lime Street Station, I wanted some last and meaningful remarks from her – I demanded this of her. So I asked her something childishly unanswerable along the lines of 'What does it all mean?' Ridiculously unanswerable, and yet she did answer – with a question fired right back at me.

'What are human beings *for*?' she said, giving me that gimlet eye contact of hers.

Her question stayed with me, and has woven itself into the nature and fabric of The Reader Organisation, and, indirectly, into this book.

It is not a question with one single answer. But part of the answer is about making meaning. Form follows function, great designers tell us, and when we think about what we do, as human beings, what function we perform in the world, one of the key things that we do all the time, each and every one of us, is to discover, invent, construct, or make meaning. Listen to any two people talking on the Tube or in a bar or as they stand in a supermarket queue and what you will hear are stories, interrogations, people using language to prod reality and see what can be made of it.

'Did she?'

'She did! You wouldn't believe it.'

'What a cheek!'

'I know! So I said . . .'

We find it fascinating. We *are* stories; we exist to make meaning. Even when we are alone, that insistent narrative voice is telling stories about what we are doing, thinking, feeling, and commentating on it all, too: now I am entering the train station, there's a man who looks like a banker, ridiculously affected red scarf; here's a girl going home for the holidays; now I am stepping onto the train; there's a woman who looks very smart and very nervous, perhaps she is going for an interview . . . and so on and on and on, the inner voice that talks to us, at us, in us, all the time – individual consciousness.

We have what amounts to a biological need to make meaning. It starts in us, not in books. And while it begins in individual experience, this consciousness needs to make social connections. A solitary experience is intuited as valuable largely by the sense of the impact it will have when we get back home again and can share it with friends and family. The act of sharing the story – letting the story out into the world – confirms to us our inward sense of self, and lays the groundwork for self-worth and our personal relation to the world. When we can't make meaning – because life is too hard, or too barren, or because we are too emotionally or psychologically damaged, or because physical degeneration makes memory-connection impossible – we tend to break down, physically, mentally or spiritually. Some doctors now think that the way in which we each understand our own 'story' contributes to our health or the lack of it: *narrative medicine* is taught in the most forward-looking medical schools. And this is one reason why we find dementia frightening: without cohesive stories the nature of our individual identity seems deeply threatened.

If the impulse to make or listen to stories is, as it were, natural, then written language – literary stories and poetry – capture this natural function and harness it in ways that make it more obviously useful, just as cultivation has made wild plants more useful and productive. When human beings created written language, about 4,000 years ago, we invented a system for keeping track of actual things: the first writings, scratched in clay, were lists of objects: bushels of corn, pitchers of wine. But, almost as soon as this mind-expanding, economy-growing invention had come about, a great natural storyteller – the first *anon* – realised that this new technology could be used to shape and record (perhaps also to grow) the inner life as well as the material world. The *Epic of Gilgamesh*, written on clay tablets in Sumer around 3,000 BC, tells the story of Enkidu and his battle against the trials of life and the gods. Human beings have been writing stories and poems down ever since. For most of human culture stories, and in particular written stories, have been connected to spiritual understanding. The first great books were religious books, and in many cultures, writing itself was seen as God-given. People read these books aloud and shared the meanings they created. From the start, reading was about creating meaning.

READING ALOUD

People who were lucky enough to be read to as children know that listening to someone read is one of the deepest sources of comfort humans have. Nourishing and replenishing, there's a sense – as with physical food – that someone is looking after you, that you can relax into a more passive state, trusting that another creature will care for you. It is a different experience to that of reading to oneself. Being removed from the need to take in and translate the marks on the page gives an immense freedom and ease: the mind and imagination can move freely and at leisure. Part of this comes from the slowness of the human voice, operating at perhaps a quarter of the speed of the competent silent reader. When we read privately the eye goes too quickly, is too greedy for what happens next and what it all means. On the one hand we have the excitement of narrative pull; on the other, things are happening so fast we hardly know what's going on. But when we are engaged at the pace of the speaking voice, we feel more the consequence of the story. It grows deeper and more real. Being part of the creation of meaning through text and voice develops a powerful human connection between reader and listener. There are times for all adults when the security of knowing that someone else will help with the most basic needs – human sustenance – is an incomparable comfort and form of trust. We need meaning, and shared reading offers us a form by which that biological function can naturally take place.

But adults, and sadly also many children, are rarely read to. This is a two-sided loss, for while being read to may be comforting, relaxing and sustaining for the listener, for the reader it can also be a source of generous delight. You'll enjoy it! And that's good for you. In devising the 'Five Ways to Well-being', the New Economics Foundation[i] has formulated the mental equivalent to five portions of fruit and vegetables: to keep healthy, we are reminded, we need to remember to connect, be active, take notice, keep learning and to give. Reading aloud ticks at least four of these five boxes, and for both parties.

THE READING REVOLUTION

The Reader Organisation – as I write, a national charity with 30 staff – was born in the spring of 1997 with the first issue of *The Reader* magazine. My colleagues Sarah Coley, Angela Macmillan and myself had been teaching Continuing Education literature classes at the University of Liverpool for some time. We were reading across the literary spectrum from Chaucer to Philip Roth via Dostoevsky, George Eliot, Seamus Heaney, A. S. Byatt and the Brontës, not as academic experts, but as people sharing a reading experience; we were reading aloud to bring the books to life in the room, and talking about what we were reading with groups of people who typically weren't literature students but who were willing and adventurous readers. We felt something exciting was happening in our classes but we didn't know what. We decided we wanted to share the excitement with a wider audience. The idea was that *The Reader* magazine could be a written version of what we were experiencing in class and it was an attempt to get that kind of experience out of Liverpool and into the wider world of readers. At the very moment that many within the literary and academic establishment were mourning the loss of the 'general reader', we seemed to be finding that mythical creature in new ways.

We still publish *The Reader* magazine[ii] but these days the main work of The Reader Organisation is to run more than 200 weekly shared reading groups in the UK and to support the developing movement in the rest of the world. We work with GPs, care assistants, firefighters, youth workers, psychiatrists, teachers, prison officers, and many other people, to get reading into places where it's currently not much experienced. This is what we call 'the reading revolution', bringing great writing to life and putting good reading into the hands of people who need it – pretty much most of us, in my experience. We are building the revolution with a project called Get Into Reading, which uses a shared reading model – reading aloud together and talking about it – based on that early work at the University of Liverpool.

Our work has always had a 'great books' flavour to it: we are not just about developing literacy, or getting more people reading, but also about opening access to a great tradition of literature: what Doris Lessing, in her Nobel Prize acceptance speech called 'the great treasure house of literature'. There it is, thousands of years of great writing! This treasure house is an amazingly rich resource, but it has become increasingly cut off and esoteric for many readers, as if it was meant for others, or is simply too difficult, or not immediate enough to claim and keep our ordinary attention. Often, in the name of an attempt at liberal inclusivity, educators and literacy promoters have looked to 'relevance' as a way of identifying books more suitable for the people they teach: there has long been an anti-canon feeling among the educated classes, as if great writing is not, by definition, relevant. This is a terrifying waste of human capital. Can you imagine food experts who told us not to bother with fresh vegetables because fast food was more relevant to most people? It was not always so. In his great history, *The Intellectual Life of the British Working Classes* Jonathan Rose records the feelings of many people, first-time readers, as they experienced the great richness that reading has to offer. Richard Hillyer, a cowman's son, born in 1900, writes:

Education began for me (with the poets). I was fascinated. My mind was being broken out of its shell. Here were wonderful things to know. Things that went beyond the small utilities of our lives, which was all that school had seemed to concern itself with until then. Knowledge of this sort could make all time, and places, your own. You could be anybody, and everybody, and still be yourself all that time. It was like coming up from the bottom of the ocean and seeing the universe for the first time.

That is the reading revolution we want to bring about: to break the shells that contain us, to free our minds, to come up from the bottom of the ocean. Richard Hillyer's brilliant phrase is so revealing, 'And still be yourself all that time'. You meet all this wonder with yourself, and a self that is all the time growing. Books of all sorts can help us do that: great writing gives us access to the multifarious forms of meaning. But let's not just talk about it, let me give some examples from real life.

Tennyson and 'Ulysses' in a Care Home

A project worker in Get Into Reading had been reading with a group of people in a care home. After some weeks she decided to read Tennyson's great poem on old age, 'Ulysses', which ends:

> Come, my friends.
> 'Tis not too late to seek a newer world.
> Push off, and sitting well in order smite
> The sounding furrows; for my purpose holds
> To sail beyond the sunset, and the baths
> Of all the western stars, until I die.
> It may be that the gulfs will wash us down;
> It may be we shall touch the Happy Isles,
> And see the great Achilles, whom we knew.
> Tho' much is taken, much abides; and tho'
> We are not now that strength which in old days
> Moved earth and heaven; that which we are, we are:
> One equal temper of heroic hearts,
> Made weak by time and fate, but strong in will
> To strive, to seek, to find, and not to yield.

In the group are people who have serious, life-ending diseases, who have suffered the indignities and disablings of strokes or other serious illnesses, whose life-partners have died, who no longer have the identity of their work or family life, who are 'made weak by time and fate'. In this context, the poem feels huge and rather dangerous: close to the bone. As the poem sinks in and discussion develops, Molly says the poem is about being old but not giving in and thinking this is the end and that's that. Asked which lines she thought most true she says 'that which we are, we are'. 'You can't change things,' she says. 'This is it now, you just have to get on with it.' Tommy, a man in his nineties, now barely able to speak, but decorated as a Spitfire pilot in the Second World War, agrees with her. He says, 'You need courage and willpower and love to go on facing life.' Penny (who had been delighted to find that Ulysses' wife was called Penelope), on understanding that the poem was written in response to the death of Tennyson's friend Arthur Hallam, says that having lost her husband two years ago she could understand the line 'tho' much is taken, much abides'.

Wordsworth and the new baby

A professional woman in her thirties has just had her first baby. She's spent months in conversation on Mumsnet and thought she knew what having a baby would mean. She is not surprised by lack of sleep and the chaos of objects this new creature has brought to her living room. But no one had touched on the emotional and psychological, perhaps even spiritual, truths that Wordsworth offers about a new baby[iii]. Yes, there is much

screaming and anxiety but also there is the sense of wonder.
The new mum lies on a sofa as her own mother reads:

>   blest the Babe,
>   Nursed in his Mother's arms, who sinks to sleep
>   Rocked on his Mother's breast; who with his soul
>   Drinks in the feelings of his Mother's eye!
>   For him, in one dear Presence, there exists
>   A virtue which irradiates and exalts
>   Objects through widest intercourse of sense.
>   No outcast he, bewildered and depressed:
>   Along his infant veins are interfused
>   The gravitation and the filial bond
>   Of nature that connect him with the world.
>   . . . Emphatically such a Being lives,
>   Frail creature as he is, helpless as frail,
>   An inmate of this active universe:
>   For, feeling has to him imparted power
>   That through the growing faculties of sense
>   Doth like an agent of the one great Mind
>   Create, creator and receiver both.

'"An inmate of this active universe",' says the new mother,
looking into her son's blue eyes. '"Creator and receiver both"
is right – you can see he is already learning things.' Mother
and grandmother watch the baby wave his frail arms, violently
kick his skinny legs. '"Emphatically such a Being lives": I like
that,' says the mother. 'He is really, really here.'

A Stroke and *The Secret Garden*

A woman lies on a bed. She has suffered a stroke and nine months on is unable to move her limbs or to speak. Her sister sits in an armchair by the window. She is sewing under a lamp as the darkness gathers outside. A Get Into Reading project worker sits by the bed reading aloud from *The Secret Garden* by Frances Hodgson Burnett. All three are intent upon the old children's story. The atmosphere is warm and calm and when the reader finishes reading for the day, all three have gained something from this simple, pleasurable activity – relaxation, comfort, mental simulation, a general sense of well-being. For twenty minutes in a difficult day the book has brought three people close in shared experience of the story.

'Invictus' and Domestic Violence

Kelly had been meeting weekly with Barbara, who is barely literate and who has suffered a difficult and undermining relationship with her long-term partner. Each week, following their shared reading, Kelly would ask, 'Did you like that, Barbara?' and Barbara would always reply, 'I don't know.' One day Kelly took W. E. Henley's poem 'Invictus' and she and Barbara each took a turn to read this determinedly affirmative piece of English literature.

> Out of the night that covers me,
> Black as the pit from pole to pole,
> I thank whatever gods may be
> For my unconquerable soul.

In the fell clutch of circumstance
I have not winced nor cried aloud.
Under the bludgeonings of chance
My head is bloody, but unbow'd.

Beyond this place of wrath and tears
Looms but the Horror of the shade,
And yet the menace of the years
Finds and shall find me unafraid.

It matters not how strait the gate,
How charged with punishments the scroll,
I am the master of my fate:
I am the captain of my soul.

After they had read the poem together a few times, Kelly asked Barbara if she liked the poem and this time she replied that yes, she did. Asked if there were any particular lines that she especially liked and she again said yes, proceeding to read them out again of her own accord – 'I am the master of my fate/I am the captain of my soul.' Kelly asked her why she liked those lines. At first Barbara reverted to her familiar response of 'I don't know.' But when Kelly asked her how reading those lines made her feel, she said, 'It makes me feel happy.' Through this poem Barbara had discovered, probably for the first time in her life, a genuine interest in and personal enjoyment of a piece of literature which she not only read but also had the confidence and desire to express an opinion about. Many readers will know that the poem was one that supported and encouraged Nelson Mandela during his years of imprisonment on Robben Island.

IS THIS BOOK FOR ME?

So is this the book for you? If you have a friend or relative or someone you care for, personally or professionally, with whom you have or want to have good fun and serious conversation, or share memories, fantasies and feelings, then the answer is yes, it's a good place to start. You might not be into poetry – statistics tell us there are actually more writers of poetry than readers of it – but the fact that you've picked this book up is a sign that you may be open to the possibility. Poetry is easier than you think – just start reading in your normal voice and keep going . . . then ask yourself if you liked it at the end. Whatever the answer is, read it again!

The Reader Organisation's shared reading model brings people together to share the making of meaning, and this book is a piece of equipment that will enable you to do that in your own individual way. Going back to the story has been a catch-phrase with The Reader Organisation since its inception. Because, as Mrs Lessing taught me all those years ago, that's what we do, that's what we naturally do.

Jane Davis, The Reader Organisation

[i] http://www.neweconomics.org/projects/five-ways-well-being
[ii] www.thereader.org.uk/publications
[iii] From *The Prelude*

How to Use this Book

We chose all the short stories, novel extracts and poems for this anthology because they have been read and enjoyed by Get Into Reading groups of all ages and backgrounds.

None of the prose pieces take longer than 30 minutes to read aloud, making them particularly appropriate for reading with the elderly, people in hospital or in circumstances when it is not possible to make a long-term commitment. We have given very approximate reading times, which will of course vary from reader to reader and depend on the number of times you pause to talk about what is happening.

The anthology is divided into reading sessions consisting of a story and a poem brought together under a loose theme. Hopefully one piece will resonate with another and enhance the experience of reading and thinking about both.

Each reading session concludes with suggestions for talking points. We were anxious that this should not resemble something that might be found in a school textbook or even a reading group guide. The Reading Notes briefly recount conversations, anecdotes, observations and questions about that session from existing reading groups. They might relate what a group in a residential home made of *A Doll's House*, or what a group of carers found in a poem by Wordsworth, or the connection one young single mother made between her own life and the life of another young single mother 150 years ago. These are personal responses to reading, outside the classroom or the seminar and their purpose is to prompt ways of talking about the literature.

How might you decide which of the sessions to read? Well, you could of course simply begin at the beginning, or even flick through until you come to something that catches your attention and begin there; be it a poem, a story or a whole session. The book is like a tool; *you* decide the best way to use it. But it may be helpful to start by thinking about the interests of the person you are going to read to. If you think that they might enjoy hearing about young children, any of the first five sessions might be suitable. Charles Dickens' story of Pip and Miss Havisham, in the session 'Strange Ladies', is a memorable encounter between an unworldly boy and a very eccentric old woman. The sense of shame this instills in Pip will taint the rest of his life. In contrast, the legacy of the meeting between a child and an old woman in Eleanor Farjeon's poem, is a lasting memory of light and wonder. The reading session called 'The Unloved', pairs a poem and story about children who do not have enough love in their lives while 'Ghastly Children' offers readers high class fun and entertainment. The session called 'Clamorous Wings' has a memoir of an Irish boyhood and an Irish poem about memory. If you want something to make you laugh, try the hilarious episode from *Pickwick Papers*, or Joanne Harris's wonderful, life-affirming story, *Faith and Hope Go Shopping* or Thomas Hood's timeless poem, *A Parental Ode to My Son*. Many of the stories give the reader a problem to grapple with: *The Necklace* or the American story, *Silk Stockings,* will both

provoke the question 'what would *I* do in these circumstances?' Some stories and poems provide the opportunity to
talk about difficult things: 'The Paths of Our Lives' is a reading
session that deals with life choices, providence and free will,
while 'Unjust Life' teams a light story which has a serious
underlying theme, together with a difficult, rewarding poem.
Both ask the questions, why do bad things happen to good
people? Why isn't life fair?

Some of the poems will be familiar from school days: *The
Charge of the Light Brigade*, or *The Listeners*. These may provide
a good starting point for people who are wary of poetry. There
are a couple of ghost stories: *An Adventure in Norfolk* is light-
hearted and traditional while *The Demon Lover* is darkly terrifying. There are some gorgeous love stories and heart-stopping
love poetry and finally there are two reading sessions for Christmas,
which is, of course, traditionally a time for gathering round the
fire and the telling of tales.

Don't rush your reading and try not to be self conscious;
just concentrate on the meaning of the words on the page.
Something special happens when we share the experience of
reading together. As one voice reads aloud, the book is brought
to life again, becomes a strong reality, a binding force. We
hope this book will bring hours of pleasure to readers and
listeners alike so that they might afterwards say, as Wordsworth
says in one of our poems: 'joy it was for her, and joy for me!'

Angela Macmillan, The Reader Organisation

A Child's World

❧

THE DOLL'S HOUSE
Katherine Mansfield

(approximate reading time 18 minutes)

When dear old Mrs Hay went back to town after staying with the Burnells she sent the children a doll's house. It was so big that the carter and Pat carried it into the courtyard, and there it stayed, propped up on two wooden boxes beside the feed-room door. No harm could come of it; it was summer. And perhaps the smell of paint would have gone off by the time it had to be taken in. For, really, the smell of paint coming from that doll's house ('Sweet of old Mrs Hay, of course; most sweet and generous!') – but the smell of paint was quite enough to make anyone seriously ill, in Aunt Beryl's opinion. Even before the sacking was taken off. And when it was . . .

There stood the doll's house, a dark, oily, spinach green, picked out with bright yellow. Its two solid little chimneys, glued on to the roof, were painted red and white, and the door, gleaming with yellow varnish, was like a little slab of toffee. Four windows, real windows, were divided into panes by a broad streak of green. There was actually a tiny porch, too, painted yellow, with big lumps of congealed paint hanging along the edge. But perfect,

perfect little house! Who could possibly mind the smell? It was part of the joy, part of the newness.

'Open it quickly, someone!'

The hook at the side was stuck fast. Pat prised it open with his penknife, and the whole house-front swung back, and – there you were, gazing at one and the same moment into the drawing-room and dining-room, the kitchen and two bedrooms. That is the way for a house to open! Why don't all houses open like that? How much more exciting than peering through the slit of a door into a mean little hall with a hat-stand and two umbrellas! That is – isn't it? – what you long to know about a house when you put your hand on the knocker. Perhaps it is the way God opens houses at dead of night when He is taking a quiet turn with an angel . . .

'O–oh!' The Burnell children sounded as though they were in despair. It was too marvellous; it was too much for them. They had never seen anything like it in their lives. All the rooms were papered. There were pictures on the walls, painted on the paper, with gold frames complete. Red carpet covered all the floors except the kitchen; red plush chairs in the drawing-room, green in the dining-room; tables, beds with real bedclothes, a cradle, a stove, a dresser with tiny plates and one big jug. But what Kezia liked more than anything, what she liked frightfully, was the lamp. It stood in the middle of the dining-room table, an exquisite little amber lamp with a white globe. It was even filled all ready for lighting, though, of course, you couldn't light it. But there was something inside that looked like oil, and that moved when you shook it.

The father and mother dolls, who sprawled very stiff as

though they had fainted in the drawing-room, and their two little children asleep upstairs, were really too big for the doll's house. They didn't look as though they belonged. But the lamp was perfect. It seemed to smile to Kezia, to say, 'I live here.' The lamp was real.

The Burnell children could hardly walk to school fast enough the next morning. They burned to tell everybody, to describe, to – well – to boast about their doll's house before the school-bell rang.

'I'm to tell,' said Isabel, 'because I'm the eldest. And you two can join in after. But I'm to tell first.'

There was nothing to answer. Isabel was bossy, but she was always right, and Lottie and Kezia knew too well the powers that went with being eldest. They brushed through the thick buttercups at the road edge and said nothing.

'And I'm to choose who's to come and see it first. Mother said I might.'

For it had been arranged that while the doll's house stood in the courtyard they might ask the girls at school, two at a time, to come and look. Not to stay to tea, of course, or to come traipsing through the house. But just to stand quietly in the courtyard while Isabel pointed out the beauties, and Lottie and Kezia looked pleased . . .

But hurry as they might, by the time they had reached the tarred palings of the boys' playground the bell had begun to jangle. They only just had time to whip off their hats and fall into line before the roll was called. Never mind. Isabel tried to make up for it by looking very important and mysterious and by whispering behind her hand to the girls near her, 'Got something to tell you at playtime.'

Playtime came and Isabel was surrounded. The girls of her class nearly fought to put their arms round her, to walk away with her, to beam flatteringly, to be her special friend. She held quite a court under the huge pine trees at the side of the playground. Nudging, giggling together, the little girls pressed up close. And the only two who stayed outside the ring were the two who were always outside, the little Kelveys. They knew better than to come anywhere near the Burnells.

For the fact was, the school the Burnell children went to was not at all the kind of place their parents would have chosen if there had been any choice. But there was none. It was the only school for miles. And the consequence was all the children of the neighbourhood, the Judge's little girls, the doctor's daughters, the store-keeper's children, the milkman's, were forced to mix together. Not to speak of there being an equal number of rude, rough little boys as well. But the line had to be drawn somewhere. It was drawn at the Kelveys. Many of the children, including the Burnells, were not allowed even to speak to them. They walked past the Kelveys with their heads in the air, and as they set the fashion in all matters of behaviour, the Kelveys were shunned by everybody. Even the teacher had a special voice for them, and a special smile for the other children when Lil Kelvey came up to her desk with a bunch of dreadfully common-looking flowers.

They were the daughters of a spry, hardworking little washerwoman, who went about from house to house by the day. This was awful enough. But where was Mr Kelvey? Nobody knew for certain. But everybody said he was in prison. So they were the daughters of a washerwoman and a jailbird. Very nice company for other people's children! And they looked it. Why Mrs Kelvey made them so conspicuous was hard to understand. The truth was they were dressed in 'bits' given to her by the people for whom she worked. Lil, for instance, who was a stout, plain child, with big freckles, came to school in a dress made from a green art-serge table-cloth of the Burnells', with red plush sleeves from the Logans' curtains. Her hat, perched on top of her high forehead, was a grown-up woman's hat, once the property of Miss Lecky, the post-mistress. It was turned up at the back and trimmed with a large scarlet quill. What a little guy she looked! It was impossible not to laugh. And her little sister, our Else, wore a long white dress, rather like a nightgown, and a pair of little boy's boots. But whatever our Else wore she would have looked strange. She was a tiny wishbone of a child, with cropped hair and enormous solemn eyes – a little white owl. Nobody had ever seen her smile; she scarcely ever spoke. She went through life holding on to Lil, with a piece of Lil's skirt screwed up in her hand. Where Lil went our Else followed. In the play-ground, on the road going to and from school, there was Lil marching in front and our Else holding on behind. Only when she wanted anything, or when she was out of breath, our Else gave Lil a tug, a twitch, and Lil stopped and turned round. The Kelveys never failed to understand each other.

Now they hovered at the edge; you couldn't stop them listening. When the little girls turned round and sneered, Lil, as usual, gave her silly, shamefaced smile, but our Else only looked.

And Isabel's voice, so very proud, went on telling. The carpet made a great sensation, but so did the beds with real bedclothes, and the stove with an oven door.

When she finished Kezia broke in. 'You've forgotten the lamp, Isabel.'

'Oh, yes,' said Isabel, 'and there's a teeny little lamp, all made of yellow glass, with a white globe that stands on the dining-room table. You couldn't tell it from a real one.'

'The lamp's best of all,' cried Kezia. She thought Isabel wasn't making half enough of the little lamp. But nobody paid any attention. Isabel was choosing the two who were to come back with them that afternoon and see it. She chose Emmie Cole and Lena Logan. But when the others knew they were all to have a chance, they couldn't be nice enough to Isabel. One by one they put their arms round Isabel's waist and walked her off. They had something to whisper to her, a secret. 'Isabel's *my* friend.'

Only the little Kelveys moved away forgotten; there was nothing more for them to hear.

Days passed, and as more children saw the doll's house, the fame of it spread. It became the one subject, the rage. The one question was, 'Have you seen Burnells' doll's house?' 'Oh, ain't it lovely!' 'Haven't you seen it? Oh, I say!'

Even the dinner hour was given up to talking about it. The little girls sat under the pines eating their thick mutton sandwiches and big slabs of johnny cake spread with butter. While always, as near as they could get, sat the Kelveys, our Else holding on to Lil, listening too, while they chewed their jam sandwiches out of a newspaper soaked with large red blobs.

'Mother,' said Kezia, 'can't I ask the Kelveys just once?'

'Certainly not, Kezia.'

'But why not?'

'Run away, Kezia; you know quite well why not.'

At last everybody had seen it except them. On that day the subject rather flagged. It was the dinner hour. The children stood together under the pine trees, and suddenly, as they looked at the Kelveys eating out of their paper, always by themselves, always listening, they wanted to be horrid to them. Emmie Cole started the whisper.

'Lil Kelvey's going to be a servant when she grows up.'

'O-oh, how awful!' said Isabel Burnell, and she made eyes at Emmie.

Emmie swallowed in a very meaning way and nodded to Isabel as she'd seen her mother do on those occasions.

'It's true – it's true – it's true,' she said.

Then Lena Logan's little eyes snapped. 'Shall I ask her?' she whispered.

'Bet you don't,' said Jessie May.

'Pooh, I'm not frightened,' said Lena. Suddenly she gave a little squeal and danced in front of the other girls. 'Watch! Watch me! Watch me now!' said Lena. And sliding, gliding, dragging one foot, giggling behind her hand, Lena went over to the Kelveys.

Lil looked up from her dinner. She wrapped the rest quickly away. Our Else stopped chewing. What was coming now?

'Is it true you're going to be a servant when you grow up, Lil Kelvey?' shrilled Lena.

Dead silence. But instead of answering, Lil only gave her silly, shame-faced smile. She didn't seem to mind the question at all. What a sell for Lena! The girls began to titter.

Lena couldn't stand that. She put her hands on her hips; she shot forward. 'Yah, yer father's in prison!' she hissed, spitefully.

This was such a marvellous thing to have said that the little girls rushed away in a body, deeply, deeply excited, wild with joy. Someone found a long rope, and they began skipping. And never did they skip so high, run in and out so fast, or do such daring things as on that morning.

In the afternoon Pat called for the Burnell children with the buggy and they drove home. There were visitors. Isabel and Lottie, who liked visitors, went upstairs to change their pinafores. But Kezia thieved out at the back. Nobody was about; she began to swing on the big white gates of the courtyard. Presently, looking along the road, she saw two little dots. They grew bigger, they were coming towards her. Now she could see that one was in front and one close behind. Now she could see that they were the Kelveys. Kezia stopped swinging. She slipped off the gate as if she was going to run away. Then she hesitated. The Kelveys came nearer, and beside them walked their shadows, very long, stretching right across the road with their heads in the buttercups. Kezia clambered back on the gate; she had made up her mind; she swung out.

'Hullo,' she said to the passing Kelveys.

They were so astounded that they stopped. Lil gave her silly smile. Our Else stared.

'You can come and see our doll's house if you want to,' said Kezia, and she dragged one toe on the ground. But at that Lil turned red and shook her head quickly.

'Why not?' asked Kezia.

Lil gasped, then she said, 'Your ma told our ma you wasn't to speak to us.'

'Oh, well,' said Kezia. She didn't know what to reply. 'It doesn't matter. You can come and see our doll's house all the same. Come on. Nobody's looking.'

But Lil shook her head still harder.

'Don't you want to?' asked Kezia.

Suddenly there was a twitch, a tug at Lil's skirt. She turned round. Our Else was looking at her with big, imploring eyes; she was frowning; she wanted to go. For a moment Lil looked at our Else very doubtfully. But then our Else twitched her skirt again. She started forward. Kezia led the way. Like two little stray cats they followed across the courtyard to where the doll's house stood.

'There it is,' said Kezia.

There was a pause. Lil breathed loudly, almost snorted; our Else was still as a stone.

'I'll open it for you,' said Kezia kindly. She undid the hook and they looked inside.

'There's the drawing-room and the dining-room, and that's the the—'

'Kezia!'

Oh, what a start they gave!

'Kezia!'

It was Aunt Beryl's voice. They turned round. At the back door stood Aunt Beryl, staring as if she couldn't believe what she saw.

'How dare you ask the little Kelveys into the courtyard!' said her cold, furious voice. 'You know as well as I do, you're not allowed to talk to them. Run away, children, run away at once. And don't come back again,' said Aunt Beryl. And she stepped into the yard and shooed them out as if they were chickens.

'Off you go immediately!' she called, cold and proud.

They did not need telling twice. Burning with shame, shrinking together, Lil huddling along like her mother, our Else dazed, somehow they crossed the big courtyard and squeezed through the white gate.

'Wicked, disobedient little girl!' said Aunt Beryl bitterly to Kezia, and she slammed the doll's house to.

The afternoon had been awful. A letter had come from Willie Brent, a terrifying, threatening letter, saying if she did not meet him that evening in Pulman's Bush, he'd come to the front door and ask the reason why! But now that she had frightened those little rats of Kelveys and given Kezia a good scolding, her heart felt lighter. That ghastly pressure was gone. She went back to the house humming.

When the Kelveys were well out of sight of Burnells', they sat down to rest on a big red drain-pipe by the side of the road. Lil's cheeks were still burning; she took off the hat with the quill and held it on her knee. Dreamily they looked over the hay paddocks, past the creek, to the group of wattles where

Logan's cows stood waiting to be milked. What were their thoughts?

Presently our Else nudged up close to her sister. But now she had forgotten the cross lady. She put out a finger and stroked her sister's quill; she smiled her rare smile.

'I seen the little lamp,' she said, softly.

Then both were silent once more.

THE LITTLE DANCERS
Laurence Binyon

Lonely, save for a few faint stars, the sky
Dreams; and lonely, below, the little street
Into its gloom retires, secluded and shy.
Scarcely the dumb roar enters this soft retreat;
And all is dark, save where come flooding rays
From a tavern-window; there, to the brisk measure
Of an organ that down in an alley merrily plays,
Two children, all alone and no one by,
Holding their tattered frocks, thro' an airy maze
Of motion lightly threaded with nimble feet
Dance sedately; face to face they gaze,
Their eyes shining, grave with a perfect pleasure.

READING NOTES

A woman in a residential home for the elderly was delighted to remember that she had once owned a doll's house with a beautiful set of sweet jars with real sweets in them. Another remembered that her cat used to like to sleep squashed into the doll's house. The group talked about how children can often be cruel to one another and thought about why it was that some children were picked on more than others. James thought that the Kelveys were picked on because their mother was a washerwoman; he blamed parents for teaching their children to be snobs. The children in the poem reminded Molly of the Kelveys at the end of the story: 'face to face they gaze, / Their eyes shining, grave with a perfect pleasure.' Then the group talked of pubs and barrel organs, of the monkeys that sometimes belonged to organ grinders and how children never used to be allowed in public houses. Everyone remarked on the special atmosphere of the poem and the children in a world of their own.

Strange Ladies

GREAT EXPECTATIONS
(EXTRACT FROM CHAPTER 8)
Charles Dickens

(approximate reading time 18 minutes)

Pip is a young orphan living with his much older sister and her husband, the village blacksmith. In this extract he has been summoned to Satis House by Miss Havisham, a wealthy old woman who, having been jilted by her fiancé on the very day of her wedding, has lived out the rest of her life as if in a state of suspended animation, never leaving the room in which she received her terrible news . . .

I knocked and was told from within to enter. I entered, therefore, and found myself in a pretty large room, well lighted with wax candles. No glimpse of daylight was to be seen in it. It was a dressing-room, as I supposed from the furniture, though much of it was of forms and uses then quite unknown to me. But prominent in it was a draped table with a gilded looking-glass, and that I made out at first sight to be a fine lady's dressing-table.

Whether I should have made out this object so soon, if there had been no fine lady sitting at it, I cannot say. In an armchair, with an elbow resting on the table and her head leaning on that hand, sat the strangest lady I have ever seen, or shall ever see.

She was dressed in rich materials – satins, and lace, and silks – all of white. Her shoes were white. And she had a long white veil dependent from her hair, and she had bridal flowers in her hair, but her hair was white. Some bright jewels sparkled on her neck and on her hands, and some other jewels lay sparkling on the table. Dresses, less splendid than the dress she wore, and half-packed trunks, were scattered about. She had not quite finished dressing for she had but one shoe on – the other was on the table near her hand – her veil was but half arranged, her watch and chain were not put on, and some lace for her bosom lay with those trinkets, and with her handkerchief, and gloves, and some flowers, and a Prayer-book, all confusedly heaped about the looking-glass.

It was not in the first few moments that I saw all these things, though I saw more of them in the first moments than might be supposed. But, I saw that everything within my view which ought to be white, had been white long ago, and had lost its lustre, and was faded and yellow. I saw that the bride within the bridal dress had withered like the dress, and like the flowers, and had no brightness left but the brightness of her sunken eyes. I saw that the dress had been put upon the rounded figure of a young woman, and that the figure upon which it now hung loose, had shrunk to skin and bone. Once, I had been taken to see some ghastly waxwork at the Fair, representing I know not what impossible personage lying in state. Once, I had been taken to one of our old marsh churches to see a skeleton in the ashes of a rich dress, that had been dug out of a vault under the church pavement. Now, waxwork and skeleton seemed to have dark eyes that moved and looked at me. I should have cried out, if I could.

'Who is it?' said the lady at the table.

'Pip, ma'am.'

'Pip?'

'Mr Pumblechook's boy, ma'am. Come – to play.'

'Come nearer; let me look at you. Come close.'

It was when I stood before her, avoiding her eyes, that I took note of the surrounding objects in detail, and saw that her watch had stopped at twenty minutes to nine, and that a clock in the room had stopped at twenty minutes to nine.

'Look at me,' said Miss Havisham. 'You are not afraid of a woman who has never seen the sun since you were born?'

I regret to state that I was not afraid of telling the enormous lie comprehended in the answer 'No.'

'Do you know what I touch here?' she said, laying her hands, one upon the other, on her left side.

'Yes, ma'am.' (It made me think of the young man.)

'What do I touch?'

'Your heart.'

'Broken!'

She uttered the word with an eager look, and with strong emphasis, and with a weird smile that had a kind of boast in it. Afterwards, she kept her hands there for a little while, and slowly took them away as if they were heavy.

'I am tired,' said Miss Havisham. 'I want diversion, and I have done with men and women. Play.'

I think it will be conceded by my most disputatious reader, that she could hardly have directed an unfortunate boy to do anything in the wide world more difficult to be done under the circumstances.

'I sometimes have sick fancies,' she went on, 'and I have a sick fancy that I want to see some play. There, there!' with an impatient movement of the fingers of her right hand; 'play, play, play!' But, I felt myself so unequal to the performance that I stood looking at Miss Havisham in what I suppose she took for a dogged manner, inasmuch as she said, when we had taken a good look at each other:

'Are you sullen and obstinate?'

'No, ma'am, I am very sorry for you, and very sorry I can't play just now. If you complain of me I shall get into trouble with my sister, so I would do it if I could; but it's so new here, and so strange, and so fine – and melancholy –' I stopped, fearing I might say too much, or had already said it, and we took another look at each other.

Before she spoke again, she turned her eyes from me, and looked at the dress she wore, and at the dressing-table, and finally at herself in the looking-glass.

'So new to him,' she muttered, 'so old to me; so strange

to him, so familiar to me; so melancholy to both of us! Call Estella. You can do that. Call Estella.

To stand in the dark in a mysterious passage of an unknown house, bawling Estella to a scornful young lady neither visible nor responsive, and feeling it a dreadful liberty so to roar out her name, was almost as bad as playing to order. But, she answered at last, and her light came along the dark passage like a star.

Miss Havisham beckoned her to come close. 'Let me see you play cards with this boy.'

'With this boy! Why, he is a common labouring-boy!'

I thought I overheard Miss Havisham answer – only it seemed so unlikely – 'Well? You can break his heart.'

'What do you play, boy?' asked Estella of myself, with the greatest disdain.

'Nothing but beggar my neighbour, miss.'

'Beggar him,' said Miss Havisham to Estella. So we sat down to cards.

It was then I began to understand that everything in the room had stopped, like the watch and the clock, a long time ago. I noticed that Miss Havisham put down the jewel exactly on the spot from which she had taken it up. As Estella dealt the cards, I glanced at the dressing-table again, and saw that the shoe upon it, once white, now yellow, had never been worn. I glanced down at the foot from which the shoe was absent, and saw that the silk stocking on it, once white, now yellow, had been trodden ragged. Without this arrest of everything, this standing still of all the pale decayed objects, not even the withered bridal dress on the collapsed form could have looked so like grave-clothes, or the long veil so like a shroud.

So she sat, corpse-like, as we played at cards; the frillings and trimmings on her bridal dress, looking like earthy paper. I knew nothing then, of the discoveries that are occasionally made of bodies buried in ancient times, which fall to powder in the moment of being distinctly seen; but, I have often thought since, that she must have looked as if the admission of the natural light of day would have struck her to dust.

'He calls the knaves, Jacks, this boy!' said Estella with disdain, before our first game was out. 'And what coarse hands he has! And what thick boots!'

I had never thought of being ashamed of my hands before; but I began to consider them a very indifferent pair. Her contempt for me was so strong, that it became infectious, and I caught it.

She won the game, and I dealt. I misdealt, as was only natural, when I knew she was lying in wait for me to do wrong; and she denounced me for a stupid, clumsy labouring-boy.

'You say nothing of her,' remarked Miss Havisham to me, as she looked on. 'She says many hard things of you, but you say nothing of her. What do you think of her?'

'I don't like to say,' I stammered.

'Tell me in my ear,' said Miss Havisham, bending down.

'I think she is very proud,' I replied, in a whisper.

'Anything else?'

'I think she is very pretty.'

'Anything else?'

'I think she is very insulting.' (She was looking at me then with a look of supreme aversion.)

'Anything else?'

'I think I should like to go home.'

'And never see her again, though she is so pretty?'

'I am not sure that I shouldn't like to see her again, but I should like to go home now.'

'You shall go soon,' said Miss Havisham, aloud. 'Play the game, out.'

I played the game to an end with Estella, and she beggared me. She threw the cards down on the table when she had won them all, as if she despised them for having been won of me.

'When shall I have you here again?' said Miss Havisham. 'Let me think.'

I was beginning to remind her that to-day was Wednesday, when she checked me with her former impatient movement of the fingers of her right hand.

'There, there! I know nothing of days of the week; I know nothing of weeks of the year. Come again after six days. You hear?'

'Yes, ma'am.'

'Estella, take him down. Let him have something to eat, and let him roam and look about him while he eats. Go, Pip.'

I followed the candle down, as I had followed the candle up, and she stood it in the place where we had found it. Until she opened the side entrance, I had fancied, without thinking about it, that it must necessarily be night-time. The rush of the daylight quite confounded me, and made me feel as if I had been in the candlelight of the strange room many hours.

'You are to wait here, you boy,' said Estella; and disappeared and closed the door.

I took the opportunity of being alone in the court-yard, to look at my coarse hands and my common boots. My opinion of those accessories was not favourable. They had never troubled me before, but they troubled me now, as vulgar appendages. I determined to ask Joe why he had ever taught me to call those picturecards, Jacks, which ought to be called knaves. I wished Joe had been rather more genteelly brought up, and then I should have been so too.

She came back, with some bread and meat and a little mug of beer. She put the mug down on the stones of the yard, and gave me the bread and meat without looking at me, as insolently as if I were a dog in disgrace. I was so humiliated, hurt, spurned, offended, angry, sorry – I cannot hit upon the right name for the smart – God knows what its name was – that tears started to my eyes. The moment they sprang there, the girl looked at me with a quick delight in having been the cause of them. This gave me power to keep them back and to look at her: so, she gave a contemptuous toss – but with a sense, I thought, of having made too sure that I was so wounded – and left me.

But, when she was gone, I looked about me for a place to hide my face in, and got behind one of the gates in the brewery-lane, and leaned my sleeve against the wall there, and leaned my forehead on it and cried. As I cried, I kicked the wall, and took a hard twist at my hair; so bitter were my feelings, and so sharp was the smart without a name, that needed counteraction.

IT WAS LONG AGO
Eleanor Farjeon

I'll tell you, shall I, something I remember?
Something that still means a great deal to me.
It was long ago.

A dusty road in summer I remember,
A mountain, and an old house, and a tree
That stood, you know,

Behind the house. An old woman I remember
In a red shawl with a grey cat on her knee
Humming under a tree.

She seemed the oldest thing I can remember.
But then perhaps I was not more than three.
It was long ago.

I dragged on the dusty road, and I remember
How the old woman looked over the fence at me
And seemed to know

How it felt to be three, and called out, I remember
'Do you like bilberries and cream for tea?'
I went under the tree.

And while she hummed, and the cat purred, I remember
How she filled a saucer with berries and cream for me
So long ago.

Such berries and such cream as I remember
I never had seen before, and never see
Today, you know.

And that is almost all I can remember,
The house, the mountain, the grey cat on her knee,
Her red shawl, and the tree,

And the taste of the berries, the feel of the sun I
    remember,
And the smell of everything that used to be
So long ago,

Till the heat on the road outside again I remember
And how the long dusty road seemed to have for me
No end, you know.

That is the farthest thing I can remember.
It won't mean much to you. It does to me.
Then I grew up, you see.

READING NOTES

One group talked about Dickens' description of Miss Havisham's room and what it must have been like for a small boy to find himself in such an extraordinary place with people he could never have imagined in his wildest dreams. Someone picked out the line 'I saw that the bride within the bridal dress had withered like the dress, and like the flowers, and had no brightness left but the brightness of her sunken eyes.' What were Miss Havisham's reasons for going on living in such a pitiful state? Estella's cruel treatment of Pip concerned people, especially the way in which Pip is made to feel ashamed.

In the poem, as in the story, a small child comes across a strange old woman. Somebody remarked that the poem is about memory; meeting the woman that day had such a powerful effect that it became part of her life and the group wondered what lifelong effect the meeting with Miss Havisham would have on Pip. They wondered why we remember some things and not others, and discussed how, in the poem, the memory is more than just a picture in the narrator's head – it is constructed of smells, tastes and the feel of things as well.

What do you make of the line 'It won't mean much to you. It does to me'?

The Unloved

❧

AT THE END OF THE LINE
Penny Feeny

(approximate reading time 14 minutes)

She'd been laying the fishing tackle out on the table when they arrived: the lengths of the rod to be fitted together, a box of cruelly barbed hooks, a choice of floats and weights, a fine translucent coil of line.

Roger pushed the boy over the threshold, kept his own feet firmly on the step. 'Very good of you to have him,' he said. 'What with Frank away on his honeymoon and no other relatives the least bit handy.'

'I'm on holiday too,' said Grace, though she knew it wouldn't make any difference. Clearly her function as Roger's step-mother was to be available to mind his girlfriend's child.

Within minutes he was back in his car, his hand flapping goodbye out of the rolled-down window, leaving Grace and the boy staring at each other.

Stubby fingers reached for a reel and began spinning it.

'Put that down, it's not a toy,' snapped Grace.

He tugged at the handle. 'How does it work?'

'I'll show you later. Don't you want to unpack?'

He kicked his brand new sports bag with its shrieking yellow flash and said sullenly 'I didn't want to come.'

She'd given him the big bedroom, the one she used to share every summer with Frank. She'd chosen to sleep instead in a room so shaded it seemed as if it were underwater. No memories here, only an old bevel-edged mirror casting silvery pools of reflection around the walls. He wasn't going to stop her coming back, but he wasn't going to hover at her shoulder like a ghost either, especially when in reality he was idling about the French countryside with wife number three.

The boy turned the key in the lock, excluding her.

She shrugged and went outside, sat in the back garden in her slippers, swatting away the wasps with the Sunday newspaper. A long humid July afternoon: flies settling on the unwashed necks of milk bottles, aphids buried in the creases of rose petals – one touch and the entire bloom would scatter slowly to the ground. The fish would be sluggish until evening, gathering in the cool dark pouches of the river bed, around the footings of the arched stone bridge. Grace glanced through the paper and waited for the boy to leave his locked room. He'd surely come out when he was hungry.

At five she made a pot of tea and some corned beef sandwiches and called up the stairs.

Ryan, his name was. The first time she had met him, when Roger had brought the girlfriend round for display, she'd thought it was Brian – a solid, ordinary kind of name. God knew what the two of them would call the baby when it arrived.

At six when the tea was cold and the sandwiches had stiffened he came down.

'You got a television here?' he asked.

'No. Are you hungry?'

'What's in them?'

'Corned beef.'

'Yuk. I don't eat that.'

With her sharpest knife she began cutting the remaining sandwiches into tiny dice and he had to ask her why.

'It'll do for the fish.'

She was pleased with the look of incredulity he could not disguise. 'Fish eat sandwiches?'

'Some do.'

Ryan pointed at her box of flies, gleaming and iridescent, like the most fragile of jewels, glowing subtly in deceit. 'Then what are they for?'

'Oh, they're just to fool the trout. I'll be going out shortly. You can come if you want.'

Ryan kicked the table leg. Was there anything he didn't kick? 'Women don't fish,' he said.

'Well I do.'

'Roger says that's only because of his dad.'

'He got me started,' acknowledged Grace. 'But who's holding the rod now, I'd like to know.' Viciously she swept the chunks of bread and meat into a paper bag and slammed them into the fridge.

The glaring whiteness of the sky had softened, the cloud had lifted a little and a golden fringe of evening sunshine appeared around the edges of the trees. Each of Ryan's passing kicks released the dry and dusty scent of flowering grasses.

Grace, ignoring him, swung her arm in a long languourous arc and cast her line across the current so that gradually, naturally, it began to flow back towards her and the glossy green fly slid rapidly through the water. She felt a slight ache across her back and shoulders, an ache which made her wonder how much longer she would have the strength and stamina for the sport and how much of her passion for it stemmed from her urge to hold on to something she had shared with Frank. As she reeled in and cast again she was aware of a silence behind her. No boy was snapping twigs, stamping puffballs to powder, or carving his name on a tree.

Later, much later, a leap, a tug, a trout slipping and jerking at the end of her line. Steadily she wound it in, gently feeling in its mouth to pluck out the hook, swiftly tossing it back into the deepest part of the river.

'What d'you do that for?'

She began to pack up her things. 'It's what we usually do. Give it another chance.'

'What's the point of fishing then?'

'The point is the hunt. Now, where have you been?'

His face was petulant, his voice quivered. 'Wanted to ring me mum. Didn't have no change.'

His pockets were stuffed with notes and nowhere to spend them. Grace lent him some coins and took him to the phone box along the main road, by the bus stop, but there was no reply.

'She'll be in hospital now,' she told him. 'They're going to cut the baby out tomorrow because it's the wrong way round.'

'Babies,' snorted Ryan. 'They just poo and puke all day.'

Grace agreed. 'Don't care for them much myself.'

She gave him bread and jam when they got back to the cottage and an angling magazine to read. Peered into his room on her way to bed to see his bag still zipped to bursting and one hand poking from the cover of the satin eiderdown, stroking its silky finish for comfort. Then she lay down on her own narrow bed, stiff as a board, staring at the watery shadows on the ceiling while unpruned forsythia tapped at the window.

He disappeared again the next morning. I don't see why, muttered Grace to herself, I should be responsible for some child I hardly know. Why hasn't his mother any relations to send him to? Irritably she took up her position on the shady side of the bridge where the water swirled deep and silent and there was nothing to disturb her solitude.

A soft imploding thud distracted her. Then another. The boy was kicking to pieces a rotten tree stump; stringy white fibres of decaying wood hung in the air.

'Stop that,' she hissed.

When she turned around he was gone.

Hoping he might be tempted, she brought her catch home for lunch. After she had filleted and grilled the fish, her hands still speckled with dark spots of blood, he merely picked at his plate and left a mess of flesh drowned in ketchup.

'What's the matter with you then? Why can't you make the best of it?'

His large angry eyes were red where he had rubbed them. Once again he locked the door against her, lay with the smooth satin against his cheek.

Later she discovered why he never ate anything she put in front of him: he'd found his way to the post office and was spending his pocket money on crisps and chocolate bars. She came across him, scuffling disconsolately down the lane, shoulders hunched, laces trailing and pockets bulging with supplies. He was still wearing the clothes he had arrived in; thoroughly doused in dust and sweat they were now beginning to steam like an old tramp's. Damned if I'm going to do his washing, thought Grace, greeting him, half-heartedly. It was too late in her life for this: playing a fish on the end of a line was one thing, coping with small moody boys quite another.

Blowsy with angels, trumpets and pink ribbon a greetings telegram arrived, announcing the birth of baby Laurelle and her weight of four pounds twelve ounces.

Grace got through to Roger at home. 'The hospital want to keep her in for a bit,' he said. 'Can you hang onto Ryan for a couple more days?'

She was watching him through the misty glass of the phone

booth, head bent, the back of his neck red from the sun. 'I'm leaving on Friday.'

'Even better. You can bring him with you. Come and see my wonderful daughter. She's an absolute beauty. No one ever told me I would feel like this – it's fantastic, it's—'

'I wouldn't know,' said Grace. 'And I'm running out of change.'

'Friday?' said Ryan in anguish. 'What am I supposed to do?'

'We could get the bus into town,' she offered, dreading the plod around the shops and the mocking windows of the restaurant she and Frank used to go to.

But Ryan picked a café garish with jukebox and fruit machines, where he could have chips and a banana split sprayed with something pink and sticky.

Grace stirred her tea and had a brainwave. 'Why don't you buy a football?' she suggested.

'Nah. No point. Can't play on me own.' He hesitated. 'Did he tell you what the baby was like? Does she look like me?'

Less pasty in the past few days, thought Grace, appraising him. Probably a nice smile if it ever came. 'Well, actually yes,' she said. 'Coincidence, what?'

'Same hair and eyes and nose and stuff?'

'I think so. She's pretty small though.'

'How small?'

'She was born early, so she's not even five pounds.'

'How much is five pounds?'

Grace thought for a moment. 'A couple of good size fish, I suppose.' She might get him interested yet.

*　*　*

The day stretched ahead, the pair of them in their separate pockets of existence. Grace was doing the crossword, willing herself to complete an anagram; Ryan was pushing the buttons of his Game Boy. The air was heavy with pollen, thunderflies and a sense of resignation. He went over to the fridge, in futile search of a fizzy drink, and spotted a crumpled paper bag. Suddenly he announced he wanted to see how fish ate sandwiches.

Hiding her astonishment, Grace got out her coarse-fishing tackle and encouraged him to set up the line himself. His small unfamiliar fingers trying to thread the shot, front teeth sinking deep into his bottom lip. Slow down, she would insist, every time a bubble of irritation threatened to break the surface: fishing cannot be hurried.

They sat side by side on a pile of old newspapers. Ryan clung to the rod as if it might somehow slip from his grasp, his face fierce with tension. Even so, it was Grace who noticed his float bobbing first.

'Turn the handle gently,' she said. 'Gently as you can.'

'I can feel something,' he yelled, jerking backwards. 'I got a fish.' He wound cautiously and then more rapidly, but there was nothing.

His jaw set sulkily again.

'You have to be patient,' she told him. 'It might take hours. Days.'

All of his last day he spent by the riverside. Grace, unfamiliar with the sudden whims of childhood, couldn't believe the determination with which he sat there. Packing up her things, pushing all her unworn clothes and unread books to the bottom of the suitcase, she wondered where the week had disappeared, whether she would ever come again.

She heard him screaming when she was still several yards away, a bag of apples and a flask tucked under her arm. She thought at first he was being attacked: the 'Help me!' sounded so urgent she considered running back to the cottage for the poker. But when she saw him straining against the arching rod, trying to keep his footing on the slope of the bank, she rushed forward, gathering him into her embrace, squeezing his bony shoulders between her own.

His voice was squeaky with excitement. 'I was just sitting there. Didn't think I'd get a nibble. And it's so strong. How can it be so strong?'

Already they could see its tail, thrashing furiously, sparking showers of spray like fireworks. Grace kept her arms tightly around his – so long since she had held anybody. She could feel his heart pounding behind his ribs, his shirt sticking to hers, wet with effort and the splashing. She spooled out a little to give them all a breathing space.

'In a minute,' she said. 'We're going to pull him in. Get the net ready to catch him.'

In a streaming silver arc the fish rose, wavered in the air, but as Ryan pushed forward the net, the line snapped abruptly, plunging it back into the water.

Grace was afraid he would break from her, feared great shuddering sobs of disappointment. Keeping her voice even she said: 'Too heavy for the line that one, never seen such a monster here before.'

Ryan, however, stayed within her encircling arms, seemed surprisingly content. 'It was huge, wasn't it?'

'Five pounds at least.'

Now, as he twisted round to look at her, she could watch his smile come, see how his face shone.

INCENDIARY
Vernon Scannell

That one small boy with a face like pallid cheese
And burnt-out little eyes could make a blaze
As brazen, fierce and huge, as red and gold
And zany yellow as the one that spoiled
Three thousand guineas' worth of property
And crops at Godwin's Farm on Saturday
Is frightening – as fact and metaphor:
An ordinary match intended for
The lighting of a pipe or kitchen fire
Misused may set a whole menagerie
Of flame-fanged tigers roaring hungrily.
And frightening, too, that one small boy should set
The sky on fire and choke the stars to heat
Such skinny limbs and such a little heart
Which would have been content with one warm kiss
Had there been anyone to offer this.

READING NOTES

This story never fails to get people talking. Conversation has
ranged from the delights or otherwise of fishing; to the effects of
divorce; to the nature of loneliness; to children of broken homes;
to junk food. It is the awkwardness of the pair, the suppressed
anger, that usually interests people. What might happen to these
two after they return to their own homes?

The poem prompts further talk of children in trouble – the
James Bulger case for example or the effect of neglect on children's behaviour or the reasons children end up in trouble with
the law. The word 'frightening' is used twice in the poem and the
boys in both the story and the poem are unattractive: 'with a face
like pallid cheese' or 'sullen' and 'pasty'. What does that do to
our sympathies for them?

Ghastly Children

🌿

THE LUMBER ROOM
Saki

(approximate reading time 14 minutes)

The children were to be driven, as a special treat, to the sands at Jagborough. Nicholas was not to be of the party; he was in disgrace. Only that morning he had refused to eat his wholesome bread-and-milk on the seemingly frivolous ground that there was a frog in it. Older and wiser and better people had told him that there could not possibly be a frog in his bread-and-milk and that he was not to talk nonsense; he continued, nevertheless, to talk what seemed the veriest nonsense, and described with much detail the colouration and markings of the alleged frog. The dramatic part of the incident was that there really was a frog in Nicholas' basin of bread-and-milk; he had put it there himself, so he felt entitled to know something about it. The sin of taking a frog from the garden and putting it into a bowl of wholesome bread-and-milk was enlarged on at great length, but the fact that stood out clearest in the whole affair, as it presented itself to the mind of Nicholas, was that the older, wiser, and better people had been proved to be profoundly in error in matters about which they had expressed the utmost assurance.

'You said there couldn't possibly be a frog in my bread-and-milk; there *was* a frog in my bread-and-milk,' he repeated, with the insistence of a skilled tactician who does not intend to shift from favourable ground.

So his boy-cousin and girl-cousin and his quite uninteresting younger brother were to be taken to Jagborough sands that afternoon and he was to stay at home. His cousins' aunt, who insisted, by an unwarranted stretch of imagination, in styling herself his aunt also, had hastily invented the Jagborough expedition in order to impress on Nicholas the delights that he had justly forfeited by his disgraceful conduct at the break-fast-table. It was her habit, whenever one of the children fell from grace, to improvise something of a festival nature from which the offender would be rigorously debarred; if all the children sinned collectively they were suddenly informed of a circus in a neighbouring town, a circus of unrivalled merit and uncounted elephants, to which, but for their depravity, they would have been taken that very day.

A few decent tears were looked for on the part of Nicholas when the moment for the departure of the expedition arrived. As a matter of fact, however, all the crying was done by his girl-cousin, who scraped her knee rather painfully against the step of the carriage as she was scrambling in.

'How she did howl,' said Nicholas cheerfully, as the party drove off without any of the elation of high spirits that should have characterised it.

'She'll soon get over that,'

said the *soi-disant* aunt; 'it will be a glorious afternoon for racing about over those beautiful sands. How they will enjoy themselves!'

'Bobby won't enjoy himself much, and he won't race much either,' said Nicholas with a grim chuckle; 'his boots are hurting him. They're too tight.'

'Why didn't he tell me they were hurting?' asked the aunt with some asperity.

'He told you twice, but you weren't listening. You often don't listen when we tell you important things.'

'You are not to go into the gooseberry garden,' said the aunt, changing the subject.

'Why not?' demanded Nicholas.

'Because you are in disgrace,' said the aunt loftily.

Nicholas did not admit the flawlessness of the reasoning; he felt perfectly capable of being in disgrace and in a gooseberry garden at the same moment. His face took on an expression of considerable obstinacy. It was clear to his aunt that he was determined to get into the gooseberry garden, 'only,' as she remarked to herself, 'because I have told him he is not to.'

Now the gooseberry garden had two doors by which it might be entered, and once a small person like Nicholas could slip in there he could effectually disappear from view amid the masking growth of artichokes, raspberry canes, and fruit bushes. The aunt had many other things to do that afternoon, but she spent an hour or two in trivial gardening operations among flower beds and shrubberies, whence she could keep a watchful eye on the two doors that led to the forbidden paradise. She was a woman of few ideas, with immense powers of concentration.

Nicholas made one or two sorties into the front garden, wriggling his way with obvious stealth of purpose towards one or other of the doors, but never able for a moment to evade the aunt's watchful eye. As a matter of fact, he had no intention of trying to get into the gooseberry garden, but it was extremely convenient for him that his aunt should believe that he had; it was a belief that would keep her on self-imposed sentry-duty for the greater part of the afternoon. Having thoroughly confirmed and fortified her suspicions Nicholas slipped back into the house and rapidly put into execution a plan of action that had long germinated in his brain. By standing on a chair in the library one could reach a shelf on which reposed a fat, important-looking key. The key was as important as it looked; it was the instrument which kept the mysteries of the lumber-room secure from unauthorised intrusion, which opened a way only for aunts and such-like privileged persons. Nicholas had not had much experience of the art of fitting keys into keyholes and turning locks, but for some days past he had practised with the key of the schoolroom door; he did not believe in trusting too much to luck and accident. The key turned stiffly in the lock, but it turned. The door opened, and Nicholas was in an unknown land, compared with which the gooseberry garden was a stale delight, a mere material pleasure.

Often and often Nicholas had pictured to himself what the lumber-room might be like, that region that was so carefully sealed from youthful eyes and concerning which no questions were ever answered. It came up to his expectations. In the first place it was large and dimly lit, one high window opening on to the forbidden garden being its only source of illumination. In the second place it was a storehouse of unimagined treasures. The aunt-by-assertion was one of those people who think that things spoil by use and consign them to dust and damp by way of preserving them. Such parts of the house as Nicholas knew best were rather bare and cheer-less, but here there were wonderful things for the eye to feast on. First and foremost there was a piece of framed tapestry that was evidently meant to be a fire-screen. To Nicholas it was a living, breathing story; he sat down on a roll of Indian hangings, glowing in wonderful colours beneath a layer of dust, and took in all the details of the tapestry picture. A man, dressed in the hunting costume of some remote period, had just transfixed a stag with an arrow; it could not have been a difficult shot because the stag was only one or two paces away from him; in the thickly growing vegetation that the picture suggested it would not have been difficult to creep up to a feeding stag, and the two spotted dogs that were springing forward to join in the chase had evidently been trained to keep to heel till the arrow was discharged. That part of the picture was simple, if interesting, but did the huntsman see, what Nicholas saw, that four galloping wolves were coming in his direction through the wood? There might be more than four of them hidden behind the trees, and in any case would the man and his dogs be able to cope with the four wolves if they made an attack? The man had only two arrows left in his quiver, and he might miss with one or both of them; all one knew about his skill in shooting was that he could hit a large stag at a ridiculously short range. Nicholas sat for many golden minutes revolving the possibilities of the scene; he was inclined to think that there were more than four wolves and that the man and his dogs were in a tight corner.

But there were other objects of delight and interest claiming his instant attention: there were quaint twisted candlesticks in the shape of snakes, and a teapot fashioned like a china duck, out of whose open beak the tea was supposed to come. How dull and shapeless the nursery teapot seemed in comparison! And there was a carved sandal-wood box packed tight with aromatic cottonwool, and between the layers of cottonwool were little brass figures, hump-necked bulls, and peacocks and goblins, delightful to see and to handle. Less promising in appearance was a large square book with plain black covers; Nicholas peeped into it, and, behold, it was full of coloured pictures of birds. And such birds! In the garden, and in the lanes when he went for a walk, Nicholas came across a few birds, of which the largest were an occasional magpie or wood-pigeon; here were herons and bustards, kites, toucans, tiger-bitterns, brush turkeys, ibises, golden pheasants, a whole portrait gallery of undreamed-of creatures. And as he was admiring the colouring of the mandarin duck and assigning a life-history to it, the voice of his aunt in shrill vociferation of his name came from the gooseberry garden without. She had grown suspicious at his long disappearance, and had leapt to the conclusion that he had climbed over the wall behind the sheltering screen of the lilac bushes; she was now engaged in energetic and rather hopeless search for him among the artichokes and raspberry canes.

'Nicholas, Nicholas!' she screamed, 'you are to come out of this at once. It's no use trying to hide there; I can see you all the time.'

It was probably the first time for twenty years that anyone had smiled in that lumber-room.

Presently the angry repetitions of Nicholas' name gave way to a shriek, and a cry for somebody to come quickly. Nicholas shut the book, restored it carefully to its place in a corner, and shook some dust from a neighbouring pile of newspapers over it. Then he crept from the room, locked the door, and replaced the key exactly where he had found it. His aunt was still calling his name when he sauntered into the front garden.

'Who's calling?' he asked.

'Me,' came the answer from the other side of the wall; 'didn't you hear me? I've been looking for you in the gooseberry garden, and I've slipped into the rain-water tank. Luckily there's no water in it, but the sides are slippery and I can't get out. Fetch the little ladder from under the cherry tree—'

'I was told I wasn't to go into the gooseberry garden,' said Nicholas promptly.

'I told you not to, and now I tell you that you may,' came the voice from the rain-water tank, rather impatiently.

'Your voice doesn't sound like aunt's,' objected Nicholas; 'you may be the Evil One tempting me to be disobedient. Aunt often tells me that the Evil One tempts me and that I always yield. This time I'm not going to yield.'

'Don't talk nonsense,' said the prisoner in the tank; 'go and fetch the ladder.'

'Will there be strawberry jam for tea?' asked Nicholas innocently.

'Certainly there will be,' said the aunt, privately resolving that Nicholas should have none of it.

'Now I know that you are the Evil One and not aunt,' shouted Nicholas gleefully; 'when we asked aunt for strawberry jam yesterday she said there wasn't any. I know there are four jars of it in the store cupboard, because I looked, and of course you know it's there, but she doesn't, because she said there wasn't any. Oh, Devil, you *have* sold yourself!'

There was an unusual sense of luxury in being able to talk to an aunt as though one was talking to the Evil One, but Nicholas knew, with childish discernment, that such luxuries were not to be over-indulged in. He walked noisily away, and it was a kitchenmaid, in search of parsley, who eventually rescued the aunt from the rain-water tank.

Tea that evening was partaken of in a fearsome silence. The tide had been at its highest when the children had arrived at Jagborough Cove, so there had been no sands to play on – a circumstance that the aunt had overlooked in the haste of organising her punitive expedition. The tightness of Bobby's boots had had disastrous effect on his temper the whole of the afternoon, and altogether the children could not have been said to have enjoyed themselves. The aunt maintained the frozen muteness of one who has suffered undignified and unmerited detention in a rain-water tank for thirty-five minutes. As for Nicholas, he, too, was silent, in the absorption of one who has much to think about; it was just possible, he considered, that the huntsman would escape with his hounds while the wolves feasted on the stricken stag.

REBECCA, WHO SLAMMED DOORS FOR FUN AND PERISHED MISERABLY
Hilaire Belloc

A trick that everyone abhors
In Little Girls is slamming Doors.
A Wealthy Banker's Little Daughter
Who lived in Palace Green, Bayswater
(By name Rebecca Offendort),
Was given to this Furious Sport.

She would deliberately go
And Slam the door like Billy-Ho!
To make her Uncle Jacob start.
She was not really bad at heart,
But only rather rude and wild:
She was an aggravating child . . .

It happened that a Marble Bust
Of Abraham was standing just
Above the Door this little Lamb
Had carefully prepared to Slam,
And Down it came! It knocked her flat!
It laid her out! She looked like that.

Her funeral Sermon (which was long
And followed by a Sacred Song)
Mentioned her Virtues, it is true,
But dwelt upon her Vices too,

And showed the Dreadful End of One
Who goes and slams the door for Fun.

The children who were brought to hear
The awful Tale from far and near
Were much impressed, and inly swore
They never more would slam the Door.
– As often they had done before.

READING NOTES

Is Nicholas a 'ghastly child'? Would you want to know him? Aunts, bad behaviour, childhood punishments, attics, outings to the sea and the darkness of the story were some of the other things a library reading group talked about, but the subject that interested them most of all was the power of the imagination in childhood. As Nicholas explores the things stored away in the lumber room his imagination soars in a way that is so hard fully to experience as an adult. The group talked about their own capacity as children to daydream in fantastic and imaginative worlds; the trouble it got them into as well as the delight it brought about.

Is the poem 'Rebecca' simply a poem for children? What is its appeal for adults?

Innocence and Experience

❧

A MESSAGE FROM THE PIG-MAN
John Wain

(approximate reading time 17 minutes)

He was never called Ekky now, because he was getting to be a real boy, nearly six, with grey flannel trousers that had a separate belt and weren't kept up by elastic, and his name was Eric. But this was just one of those changes brought about naturally, by time, not a disturbing alteration; he understood that. His mother hadn't meant that kind of change when she had promised, 'Nothing will be changed.' It was all going to go on as before, except that Dad wouldn't be there, and Donald would be there instead. He knew Donald, of course, and felt all right about his being in the house, though it seemed, when he lay in bed and thought about it, mad and pointless that Donald's coming should mean that Dad had to go. Why should it mean that? The house was quite big. He hadn't any brothers and sisters, and if he had *had* any he wouldn't have minded sharing his bedroom, even with a baby that wanted a lot of looking after, so long as it left the spare room free for Dad to sleep in. If he did that they wouldn't have a spare room, it was true, but, then, the spare room was nearly always empty;

the last time anybody had used the spare room was *years* ago, when he had been much smaller – last winter, in fact. And, even then, the visitor, the lady with the funny teeth who laughed as she breathed in, instead of as she breathed out like everyone else, had only stayed two or three nights. *Why* did grown-ups do everything in such a mad, silly way? They often told him not to be silly, but they were silly themselves in a useless way, not laughing or singing or anything, just being silly and sad.

It was so hard to read the signs; that was another thing. When they did give you something to go on, it was impossible to know how to take it. Dad had bought him a train, just a few weeks ago, and taught him how to fit the lines together. That ought to have meant that he would stay; what sensible person would buy a train, and fit it all up ready to run, even as a present for another person – *and then leave?* Donald had been quite good about the train, Eric had to admit that; he had bought a bridge for it and a lot of rolling-stock. At first he had got the wrong kind of rolling-stock, with wheels too close together to fit on to the rails; but instead of playing the usual grown-ups' trick of pulling a face and then not doing anything about it, he had gone back to the shop, straight away that same afternoon, and got the right kind. Perhaps that meant *he* was going to leave. But that didn't seem likely. Not the way Mum held on to him all the time, even holding him round the middle as if he needed keeping in one piece.

All the same, he was not Ekky now, he was Eric, and he was sensible and grown-up. Probably it was his own fault that everything seemed strange. He was not living up to his grey flannel trousers – and perhaps that was it; being afraid of too many things, not asking questions that would probably turn out to have quite simple answers.

The Pig-man, for instance. He had let the Pig-man worry him far too much. None of the grown-ups acted as if the Pig-man was anything to be afraid of. He probably just *looked* funny, that was all. If, instead of avoiding him so carefully, he went outside one evening and looked at him, took a good long, unafraid look, leaving the back door open behind him so that he could dart in to the safety and warmth of the house . . . no! It was better, after all, not to see the Pig-man; not till he was bigger, anyway; nearly six was quite big but it wasn't really *very* big . . .

And yet it was one of those puzzling things. No one ever told him to be careful not to let the Pig-man get hold of him, or warned him in any way; so the Pig-man *must* be harmless, because when it came to anything that *could* hurt you, like the traffic on the main road, people were always ramming it into you that you must look both ways, and all that stuff. And yet when it came to the Pig-man no one ever mentioned him; he seemed beneath the notice of grown-ups. His mother would say, now and then, 'Let me see, it's today the Pig-man comes, isn't it?' or, 'Oh dear, the Pig-man will be coming round soon, and I haven't put anything out.' If she talked like this Eric's spine would tingle and go cold; he would keep very still and wait, because quite often her next words would be, 'Eric, just take these peelings,' or whatever it was, 'out to the bucket, dear, will you?' The bucket was about fifty yards away from the back door; it was shared by the people in the two next-door houses. None of *them* was afraid of the Pig-man, either. What was their attitude? he wondered. Were they sorry for him, having to eat damp old stuff out of a bucket – tea-leaves and eggshells and that sort of thing? Perhaps he cooked it when he got home, and made it a bit nicer. Certainly, it didn't look too nice when you lifted the lid of the bucket and saw it all lying there. It sometimes smelt, too. Was the Pig-man very poor? Was he sorry for himself, or did he feel all right about being like that? *Like what?* What did the Pig-man look like? He would have little eyes, and a snout with a flat end; but would he have trotters, or hands and feet like a person's?

Lying on his back, Eric worked soberly at the problem. The Pig-man's bucket had a handle; so he must carry it in an ordinary way, in his hand – unless, of course, he walked on all fours and carried it in his mouth. But that wasn't very likely, because if he walked on all fours what difference would there be between him and an ordinary pig? To be called the Pig-man, rather than the Man-pig, surely implied that he was upright, and dressed. Could he talk? Probably, in a kind of grunting way, or else how could he tell the people what kind of food he wanted them to put in his bucket? *Why hadn't he asked Dad about the Pig-man?* That had been his mistake; Dad would have told him exactly all about it. But he had gone. Eric fell asleep, and in his sleep he saw Dad and the Pig-man going in a train together; he called, but they did not hear and the train carried them away. 'Dad!' he shouted desperately after it. 'Don't bring the Pig-man when you come back! Don't

bring the Pig-man!' Then his mother was in the room, kissing him and smelling nice; she felt soft, and the softness ducked
him into sleep, this time without dreams; but the next day
his questions returned.

Still, there was school in the morning, and going down to
the swings in the afternoon, and altogether a lot of different
things to crowd out the figure of the Pig-man and the questions connected with him. And Eric was never farther from
worrying about it all than that moment, a few evenings later,
when suddenly he came to a crisis.

Eric had been allowed, 'just for once', to bring his train
into the dining-room after tea, because there was a fire there
that made it nicer than the room where he usually played. It
was warm and bright, and the carpet in front of the fireplace
was smooth and firm, exactly right for laying out the rails on.
Donald had come home and was sitting – in Dad's chair, but
never mind – reading the paper and smoking. Mum was in
the kitchen, clattering gently about, and both doors were open
so that she and Donald could call out remarks to each another.
Only a short passage lay between. It was just the part of the
day Eric liked best, and bed-time was comfortably far off. He
fitted the sections of the rail together, glancing in anticipation at the engine as it stood proudly waiting to haul the
carriages round and round, tremendously fast.

Then his mother called: 'Eric! Do be a sweet, good boy,
and take this stuff out for the Pig-man. My hands are covered
with cake mixture. I'll let you scrape out the basin when you
come in.'

For a moment he kept quite still, hoping he hadn't really

heard her say it, that it was just a voice inside his head. But Donald looked over at him and said: 'Go along, old man. You don't mind, do you?'

Eric said, 'But tonight's when the Pig-man *comes*.'

Surely, *surely* they weren't asking him to go out, in the deep twilight, just at the time when there was the greatest danger of actually *meeting* the Pig-man?

'All the better,' said Donald, turning back to his paper.

Why was it better? Did they *want* him to meet the Pig-man?

Slowly, wondering why his feet and legs didn't refuse to move, Eric went through into the kitchen. 'There it is,' his mother said, pointing to a brown-paper carrier full of potato-peelings and scraps.

He took it up and opened the back door. If he was quick, and darted along to the bucket *at once*, he would be able to lift the lid, throw the stuff in quickly, and be back in the house in about the time it took to count to ten.

One – two – three – four – five – six. He stopped. The bucket wasn't there.

It had gone. Eric peered round, but the light, though faint, was not as faint as *that*. He could see that the bucket was already gone. *The Pig-man had already been.*

Seven – eight – nine – ten, his steps were joyous and light. Back in the house, where it was warm and bright and his train was waiting.

'The Pig-man's gone, Mum. The bucket's not there.'

She frowned, hands deep in the pudding-basin. 'Oh, yes, I do believe I heard him. But it was only a moment ago. Yes, it was just before I called you, darling. It must have been that that made me think of it.'

'Yes?' he said politely, putting down the carrier.

'So if you nip along, dear, you can easily catch him up. And I *do* want that stuff out of the way.'

'Catch him up?' he asked, standing still in the doorway.

'Yes, dear, *catch him up*,' she answered rather sharply (the Efficient Young Mother knows when to be Firm). 'He can't possibly be more than a very short way down the road.'

Before she had finished Eric was outside the door and running. This was a technique he knew. It was the same as getting into icy-cold water. If it was the end, if the Pig-man seized him by the hand and dragged him off to his hut, well, so much the worse. Swinging the paper carrier in his hand, he ran fast through the dusk.

The back view of the Pig-man was much as he had expected it to be. A slow, rather lurching gait, hunched shoulders, an old hat crushed down on his head (to hide his ears?), and the pail in his hand. Plod, plod, as if he were tired. Perhaps this was just a ruse, though; probably he could pounce quickly enough when his wicked little eyes saw a nice tasty little boy or something . . . did the Pig-man eat birds? Or cats?

Eric stopped. He opened his mouth to call to the Pig-man, but the first time he tried nothing came out except a small rasping squeak. His heart was banging like fireworks going off. He could hardly hear anything.

'Mr Pig-man!' he called, and this time the words came out clear and rather high.

The jogging old figure stopped, turned, and looked at him.

Eric could not see properly from where he stood. But he *had* to see. Everything, even his fear, sank and drowned in the raging tide of his curiosity. He moved forward. With each step he saw more clearly. The Pig-man was just an ordinary old man.

'Hello, sonny. Got some stuff here for the old grunters?'

Eric nodded, mutely, and held out his offering. What old grunters? What did he mean?

The Pig-man put down his bucket. He had ordinary hands, ordinary arms. He took the lid off. Eric held out the paper carrier, and the Pig-man's hand actually touched his own for a second. A flood of gratitude rose up inside him. The Pig-man tipped the scraps into the bucket and handed the carrier back.

'Thanks, sonny,' he said.

'Who's it for?' Eric asked, with another rush of articulateness. His voice seemed to have a life of its own.

The Pig-man straightened up, puzzled. Then he laughed, in a gurgling sort of way, but not like a pig at all.

'Arh Aarh Harh Harh,' the Pig-man went. 'Not for me, if that's whatcher mean, arh harh.'

He put the lid back on the bucket. 'It's for the old grunters,' he said. 'The old porkers. Just what they likes. Only not fruit skins. I leaves a note sometimes, about what not to put in. Never fruit skins. It gives 'em the belly-ache.'

He was called the Pig-man because he had some pigs that he looked after.

'Thank you,' said Eric. 'Good night.' He ran back towards the house, hearing the Pig-man, the ordinary old man, the ordinary, usual, normal old man, say in his just ordinary old man's voice, 'Good night, sonny.'

So that was how you did it. You just went straight ahead, not worrying about this or that.

Like getting into cold water. You just *did* it.

He slowed down as he got to the gate. For instance, if there was a question that you wanted to know the answer to, and you always just felt like you couldn't ask, the thing to do was to ask. Just straight out, like going up to the Pig-man. Difficult things, troubles, questions, you just treated them like the Pig-man.

So that was it!

The warm light shone through the crack of the door. He opened it and went in. His mother was standing at the table, her hands still working the cake mixture about. She would let him scrape out the basin, and the spoon – he would ask for the spoon, too. But not straight away. There was a more important thing first.

He put the paper carrier down and went straight up to her. 'Mum,' he said. 'Why can't Dad be with us even if Donald *is* here? I mean, why can't he live with us as well as Donald?'

His mother turned and went to the sink. She put the tap on and held her hands under it. 'Darling,' she called.

'Yes?' came Donald's voice.

'D'you know what he's just said?'

'What?'

'He's just asked . . .' She turned the tap off and dried her hands, not looking at Eric. 'He wants to know why we can't have Jack to live with us.'

There was a silence, then Donald said, quietly, so that his voice only just reached Eric's ears, 'That's a hard one.'

'You can scrape out the basin,' his mother said to Eric. She lifted him up and kissed him. Then she rubbed her cheek along his, leaving a wet smear. 'Poor little Ekky,' she said in a funny voice.

She put him down and he began to scrape out the pudding-basin, certain at least of one thing, that grown-ups were mad and silly and he hated them, all, all, *all*.

FOR A FIVE-YEAR-OLD
Fleur Adcock

A snail is climbing up the window-sill
into your room, after a night of rain.
You call me in to see, and I explain
that it would be unkind to leave it there:
it might crawl to the floor; we must take care
that no one squashes it. You understand,
and carry it outside, with careful hand,
to eat a daffodil.

I see, then, that a kind of faith prevails:
your gentleness is moulded still by words
from me, who have trapped mice and shot wild birds,
from me, who drowned your kittens, who betrayed
four closest relatives, and who purveyed
the harshest kind of truth to many another.
But that is how things are: I am your mother,
and we are kind to snails.

READING NOTES

A young mothers' group was interested in the line 'Why did grown ups do everything in such a mad, silly way', as it suggests there might be lessons to be learnt from looking at a situation from the opposite point of view. Sometimes the gulf of understanding between the world of childhood and the adult world appears too wide to cross. On the other hand, readers have been interested in the way in which the lines between adult and childish behaviour are blurred in this story and have talked about the imaginative way that Ekky sees things in comparison to his mother. What will her failure to answer his final question do to the boy, and to their future relationship? How much damage do we cause through failure of imaginative sympathy?

People have wanted to talk about the feeling of closeness between mother and child in the poem despite the fact of the divide between innocence and experience. 'I see, then that a kind of faith prevails' has proved to be an important line in this train of thought. How does the phrase 'that is how things are' make you feel?

Love's Lonely Offices

❧

ALL THE YEARS OF HER LIFE
Morley Callaghan

(approximate reading time 14 minutes)

They were closing the drugstore, and Alfred Higgins, who had just taken off his white jacket, was putting on his coat and getting ready to go home. The little gray-haired man, Sam Carr, who owned the drugstore, was bending down behind the cash register, and when Alfred Higgins passed him, he looked up and said softly, 'Just a moment, Alfred. One moment before you go.'

The soft, confident, quiet way in which Sam Carr spoke made Alfred start to button his coat nervously. He felt sure his face was white. Sam Carr usually said, 'Good night,' brusquely, without looking up. In the six months he had been working in the drugstore Alfred had never heard his employer speak softly like that. His heart began to beat so loud it was hard for him to get his breath. 'What is it, Mr Carr?' he asked.

'Maybe you'd be good enough to take a few things out of your pocket and leave them here before you go,' Sam Carr said.

'What things? What are you talking about?'

'You've got a compact and a lipstick and at least two tubes of toothpaste in your pockets, Alfred.'

'What do you mean? Do you think I'm crazy?' Alfred blustered. His face got red and he knew he looked fierce with indignation. But Sam Carr, standing by the door with his blue eyes shining brightly behind his glasses and his lips moving underneath his gray moustache, only nodded his head a few times, and then Alfred grew very frightened and he didn't know what to say. Slowly he raised his hand and dipped it into his pocket, and with his eyes never meeting Sam Carr's eyes, he took out a blue compact and two tubes of toothpaste and a lipstick, and he laid them one by one on the counter.

'Petty thieving, eh, Alfred?' Sam Carr said. 'And maybe you'd be good enough to tell me how long this has been going on.'

'This is the first time I ever took anything.'

'So now you think you'll tell me a lie, eh? What kind of a sap do I look like, huh? I don't know what goes on in my own store, eh? I tell you you've been doing this pretty steady,' Sam Carr said as he went over and stood behind the cash register.

Ever since Alfred had left school he had been getting into trouble wherever he worked. He lived at home with his mother and his father, who was a printer. His two older brothers were married and his sister had got married last year, and it would have been all right for his parents now if Alfred had only been able to keep a job.

While Sam Carr smiled and stroked the side of his face very delicately with the tips of his fingers, Alfred began to feel that familiar terror growing in him that had been in him every time he had got into such trouble.

'I liked you,' Sam Carr was saying. 'I liked you and would have trusted you, and now look what I got to do.' While Alfred watched with his alert, frightened blue eyes, Sam Carr drummed with his fingers on the counter. 'I don't like to call a cop in point-blank,' he was saying as he looked very worried. 'You're a fool, and maybe I should call your father and tell him you're a fool. Maybe I should let them know I'm going to have you locked up.'

'My father's not at home. He's a printer. He works nights,' Alfred said.

'Who's at home?'

'My mother, I guess.'

'Then we'll see what she says.' Sam Carr went to the phone and dialed the number. Alfred was not so much ashamed, but there was that deep fright growing in him, and he blurted out arrogantly, like a strong, full-grown man, 'Just a minute. You don't need to draw anybody else in. You don't need to tell her.' He wanted to sound like a swaggering, big guy who could look after himself, yet the old, childish hope was in him, the longing that someone at home would come and help him. 'Yeah, that's right, he's in trouble,' Mr Carr was saying. 'Yeah, your boy works for me. You'd better come down in a hurry.' And when he was finished Mr Carr went over to the door and looked out at the street and watched the people passing in the late summer night. 'I'll keep my eye out for a cop,' was all he said.

Alfred knew how his mother would come rushing in; she

would rush in with her eyes blazing, or maybe she would be crying, and she would push him away when he tried to talk to her, and make him feel her dreadful contempt; yet he longed that she might come before Mr Carr saw the cop on the beat passing the door.

While they waited – and it seemed a long time – they did not speak, and when at last they heard someone tapping on the closed door, Mr Carr, turning the latch, said crisply, 'Come in, Mrs Higgins.' He looked hard-faced and stern.

Mrs Higgins must have been going to bed when he telephoned, for her hair was tucked in loosely under her hat, and her hand at her throat held her light coat tight across her chest so her dress would not show. She came in, large and plump, with a little smile on her friendly face. Most of the store lights had been turned out and at first she did not see Alfred, who was standing in the shadow at the end of the counter. Yet as soon as she saw him she did not look as Alfred thought she would look: she smiled, her blue eyes never wavered, and with a calmness and dignity that made them forget that her clothes seemed to have been thrown on her, she put out her hand to Mr Carr and said politely, 'I'm Mrs Higgins. I'm Alfred's mother.'

Mr Carr was a bit embarrassed by her lack of terror and her simplicity, and he hardly knew what to say to her, so she asked, 'Is Alfred in trouble?'

'He is. He's been taking things from the store. I caught him red-handed. Little things like compacts and toothpaste and lipsticks. Stuff he can sell easily,' the proprietor said.

As she listened Mrs Higgins looked at Alfred sometimes

and nodded her head sadly, and when Sam Carr had finished she said gravely, 'Is it so, Alfred?'

'Yes.'

'Why have you been doing it?'

'I been spending money, I guess.'

'On what?'

'Going around with the guys, I guess,' Alfred said.

Mrs Higgins put out her hand and touched Sam Carr's arm with an understanding gentleness, and speaking as though afraid of disturbing him, she said, 'If you would only listen to me before doing anything.' Her simple earnestness made her shy; her humility made her falter and look away, but in a moment she was smiling gravely again, and she said with a kind of patient dignity, 'What did you intend to do, Mr Carr?'

'I was going to get a cop. That's what I ought to do.'

'Yes, I suppose so. It's not for me to say, because he's my son. Yet I sometimes think a little good advice is the best thing for a boy when he's at a certain period in his life,' she said.

Alfred couldn't understand his mother's quiet composure, for if they had been at home and someone had suggested that he was going to be arrested, he knew she would be in a rage and would cry out against him. Yet now she was standing there with that gentle, pleading smile on her face, saying, 'I wonder if you don't think it would be better just to let him come home with me. He looks a big fellow, doesn't he? It takes some of them a long time to get any sense,' and they both stared at Alfred, who shifted away with a bit of light shining for a moment on his thin face and the tiny pimples over his cheekbone.

But even while he was turning away uneasily Alfred was realizing that Mr Carr had become aware that his mother was really a fine woman; he knew that Sam Carr was puzzled by his mother, as if he had expected her to come in and plead with him tearfully, and instead he was being made to feel a bit ashamed by her vast tolerance. While there was only the sound of the mother's soft, assured voice in the store, Mr Carr began to nod his head encouragingly at her. Without being alarmed, while being just large and still and simple and hopeful, she was becoming dominant there in the dimly lit store. 'Of course, I don't want to be harsh,' Mr Carr was saying. 'I'll tell you what I'll do. I'll just fire him and let it go at that. How's that?' and he got up and shook hands with Mrs Higgins, bowing low to her in deep respect.

There was such warmth and gratitude in the way she said, 'I'll never forget your kindness,' that Mr Carr began to feel warm and genial himself.

'Sorry we had to meet this way,' he said. 'But I'm glad I got in touch with you. Just wanted to do the right thing, that's all,' he said.

'It's better to meet like this than never, isn't it?' she said. Suddenly they clasped hands as if they liked each other, as if they had known each other a long time. 'Good night, sir,' she said.

'Good night, Mrs Higgins. I'm truly sorry,' he said.

The mother and son walked along the street together, and the mother was taking a long, firm stride as she looked ahead with her stern face full of worry. Alfred was afraid to speak to her, he was afraid of the silence that was between them, so he only looked ahead too, for the excitement and relief was still pretty strong in him; but in a little while, going along like that in silence made him terribly aware of the strength and the sternness in her; he began to wonder what she was thinking of as she stared ahead so grimly; she seemed to have forgotten that he walked beside her; so when they were passing under the Sixth Avenue elevated and the rumble of the train seemed to break the silence, he said in his old, blustering way, 'Thank God it turned out like that. I certainly won't get in a jam like that again.'

'Be quiet. Don't speak to me. You've disgraced me again and again,' she said bitterly.

'That's the last time. That's all I'm saying.'

'Have the decency to be quiet,' she snapped. They kept on their way, looking straight ahead.

When they were at home and his mother took off her coat, Alfred saw that she was really only half-dressed, and she made him feel afraid again when she said, without even looking at him, 'You're a bad lot. God forgive you. It's one thing after another and always has been. Why do you stand there stupidly? Go to bed, why don't you?' When he was going, she said, 'I'm going to make myself a cup of tea. Mind, now, not a word about tonight to your father.'

While Alfred was undressing in his bedroom, he heard his mother moving around the kitchen. She filled the kettle and put it on the stove. She moved a chair. And as he listened there was no shame in him, just wonder and a kind of admiration of her strength and repose. He could still see Sam Carr nodding his head encouragingly to her; he could hear her talking simply and earnestly, and as he sat on his bed he felt a pride in her strength. 'She certainly was smooth,' he thought. 'Gee, I'd like to tell her she sounded swell.'

And at last he got up and went along to the kitchen, and when he was at the door he saw his mother pouring herself a cup of tea. He watched and he didn't move. Her face, as she sat there, was a frightened, broken face utterly unlike the face of the woman who had been so assured a little while ago in the drugstore. When she reached out and lifted the kettle to pour hot water in her cup, her hand trembled and the water splashed on the stove. Leaning back in the chair, she sighed and lifted the cup to her lips, and her lips were groping loosely as if they would never reach the cup. She swallowed the hot tea eagerly, and then she straightened up in relief, though her hand holding the cup still trembled. She looked very old.

It seemed to Alfred that this was the way it had been every time he had been in trouble before, that this trembling had really been in her as she hurried out half-dressed to the drugstore. He understood why she had sat alone in the kitchen the night his young sister had kept repeating doggedly that she was getting married. Now he felt all that his mother had been thinking of as they walked along the street together a little while ago. He watched his mother, and he never spoke, but at that moment his youth seemed to be over; he knew all the years of her life by the way her hand trembled as she raised the cup to her lips. It seemed to him that this was the first time he had ever looked upon his mother.

THOSE WINTER SUNDAYS
Robert Hayden

Sundays too my father got up early
and put his clothes on in the blueback cold,
then with cracked hands that ached
from labor in the weekday weather made
banked fires blaze. No one ever thanked him.

I'd wake and hear the cold splintering, breaking.
When the rooms were warm, he'd call,
and slowly I would rise and dress,
fearing the chronic angers of that house,

Speaking indifferently to him,
who had driven out the cold
and polished my good shoes as well.
What did I know, what did I know
of love's austere and lonely offices?

READING NOTES

In a group of carers, this story and poem prompted thoughtful discussion about the idea of unconditional love: people were interested in the lengths that a parent might be prepared to go to to protect their child. One woman wondered what it must be like to be the mother of a serious offender, given what it cost the mother in the story to stand up for the son she already knew to be guilty and weak. In the story, Alfred discovers things about his mother that he had never realised: the group were divided in their sympathy for him.

The line 'love's austere and lonely offices' from Robert Hayden's poem will often make people think about and recall things their parents did for them, which they had not properly understood until they were grown up with children of their own. The poem provokes a wide range of talking points, from fathers who find it difficult to show love, to the delight and hard work involved in a coal fire.

Father and Son

❧

POWDER
Tobias Wolff

(approximate reading time 9 minutes)

Just before Christmas my father took me skiing at Mount Baker. He'd had to fight for the privilege of my company, because my mother was still angry with him for sneaking me into a nightclub during his last visit, to see Thelonious Monk.

He wouldn't give up. He promised, hand on heart, to take good care of me and have me home for dinner on Christmas Eve, and she relented. But as we were checking out of the lodge that morning it began to snow, and in this snow he observed some rare quality that made it necessary for us to get in one last run. We got in several last runs. He was indifferent to my fretting. Snow whirled around us in bitter, blinding squalls, hissing like sand, and still we skied. As the lift bore us to the peak yet again, my father looked at his watch and said, 'Criminey. This'll have to be a fast one.'

By now I couldn't see the trail. There was no point in trying. I stuck to him like white on rice and did what he did and somehow made it to the bottom without sailing off a cliff. We returned our skis and my father put chains on the Austin-

Healey while I swayed from foot to foot, clapping my mittens and wishing I were home. I could see everything. The green tablecloth, the plates with the holly pattern, the red candles waiting to be lit.

We passed a diner on our way out. 'You want some soup?' my father asked. I shook my head. 'Buck up,' he said. 'I'll get you there. Right, doctor?'

I was supposed to say, 'Right, doctor,' but I didn't say anything.

A state trooper waved us down outside the resort. A pair of sawhorses were blocking the road. The trooper came up to our car and bent down to my father's window. His face was bleached by the cold. Snowflakes clung to his eyebrows and to the fur trim of his jacket and cap.

'Don't tell me,' my father said.

The trooper told him. The road was closed. It might get cleared, it might not. Storm took everyone by surprise. So much, so fast. Hard to get people moving. Christmas Eve. What can you do?

My father said, 'Look. We're talking about five, six inches. I've taken this car through worse than that.'

The trooper straightened up, boots creaking. His face was out of sight but I could hear him. 'The road is closed.'

My father sat with both hands on the wheel, rubbing the wood with his thumbs. He looked at the barricade for a long time. He seemed to be trying to master the idea of it. Then he thanked the trooper, and with a weird, old-maidy show of caution turned the car around. 'Your mother will never forgive me for this,' he said.

'We should have left before,' I said. 'Doctor.'

He didn't speak to me again until we were both in a booth at the diner, waiting for our burgers. 'She won't forgive me,' he said. 'Do you understand? Never.'

'I guess,' I said, but no guesswork was required; she wouldn't forgive him.

'I can't let that happen.' He bent toward me. 'I'll tell you what I want. I want us all to be together again. Is that what you want?'

'Yes, sir.'

He bumped my chin with his knuckles. 'That's all I needed to hear.'

When we finished eating he went to the pay phone in the back of the diner, then joined me in the booth again. I figured he'd called my mother, but he didn't give a report. He sipped at his coffee and stared out the window at the empty road. 'Come on,' he said, though not to me. A little while later he said it again. When the trooper's car went past, lights flashing, he got up and dropped some money on the check. 'Okay. *Vamanos.*'

The wind had died. The snow was falling straight down, less of it now and lighter. We drove away from the resort, right up to the barricade. 'Move it,' my father told me. When I looked at him he said, 'What are you waiting for?' I got out and dragged one of the sawhorses aside, then put it back after he drove through. He pushed the door open for me, 'Now you're an accomplice,' he said. 'We go down together.' He put the car into gear and gave me a look. 'Joke, son.'

Down the first long stretch I watched the road behind us,

to see if the trooper was on our tail. The barricade vanished. Then there was nothing but snow: snow on the road, snow kicking up from the chains, snow on the trees, snow in the sky; and our trail in the snow. Then I faced forward and had a shock. The lay of the road behind us had been marked by our own tracks, but there were no tracks ahead of us. My father was breaking virgin snow between a line of tall trees. He was humming 'Stars Fell on Alabama.' I felt snow brush along the floorboards under my feet. To keep my hands from shaking I clamped them between my knees.

My father grunted in a thoughtful way and said, 'Don't ever try this yourself.'

'I won't.'

'That's what you say now, but someday you'll get your license and then you'll think you can do anything. Only you won't be able to do this. You need, I don't know – a certain instinct.'

'Maybe I have it.'

'You don't. You have your strong points, but not this. I only mention it because I don't want you to get the idea this is something just anybody can do. I'm a great driver. That's not a virtue, okay? It's just a fact, and one you should be aware of. Of course you have to give the old heap some credit, too. There aren't many cars I'd try this with. Listen!'

I did listen. I heard the slap of the chains, the stiff, jerky rasp of the wipers, the purr of the engine. It really did purr. The old heap was almost new. My father couldn't afford it, and kept promising to sell it, but here it was.

I said, 'Where do you think that policeman went to?'

'Are you warm enough?' He reached over and cranked up the blower. Then he turned off the wipers. We didn't need them. The clouds had brightened. A few sparse, feathery flakes drifted into our slipstream and were swept away. We left the trees and entered a broad field of snow that ran level for a while and then tilted sharply downward. Orange stakes had been planted at intervals in two parallel lines and my father steered a course between them, though they were far enough apart to leave considerable doubt in my mind as to exactly where the road lay. He was humming again, doing little scat riffs around the melody.

'Okay then. What are my strong points?'

'Don't get me started,' he said. 'It'd take all day.'

'Oh, right. Name one.'

'Easy. You always think ahead.'

True. I always thought ahead. I was a boy who kept his clothes on numbered hangers to ensure proper rotation. I bothered my teachers for homework assignments far ahead of their due dates so I could draw up schedules. I thought ahead, and that was why I knew that there would be other troopers waiting for us at the end of our ride, if we even got there. What I did not know was that my father would wheedle and plead his way past them – he didn't sing 'O Tannenbaum' but just about – and get me home for dinner, buying a little more time before my mother decided to make the split final. I knew we'd get caught; I was resigned to it. And maybe for this reason I stopped moping and began to enjoy myself.

Why not? This was one for the books. Like being in a speedboat, only better. You can't go downhill in a boat. And

it was all ours. And it kept coming, the laden trees, the
unbroken surface of snow, the sudden white vistas. Here and
there I saw hints of the road, ditches, fences, stakes, but not
so many that I could have found my way. But then I didn't
have to. My father was driving. My father in his forty-eighth
year, rumpled, kind, bankrupt of honor, flushed with certainty.
He was a great driver. All persuasion, no coercion. Such subtlety
at the wheel, such tactful pedalwork. I actually trusted him.
And the best was yet to come – switchbacks and hairpins
impossible to describe. Except maybe to say this: if you haven't
driven fresh powder, you haven't driven.

DIGGING
Seamus Heaney

Between my finger and my thumb
The squat pen rests; snug as a gun.

Under my window, a clean rasping sound
When the spade sinks into gravelly ground:
My father, digging. I look down

Till his straining rump among the flowerbeds
Bends low, comes up twenty years away
Stooping in rhythm through potato drills
Where he was digging.

The coarse boot nestled on the lug, the shaft
Against the inside knee was levered firmly.
He rooted out tall tops, buried the bright edge deep
To scatter new potatoes that we picked,
Loving their cool hardness in our hands.

By God, the old man could handle a spade.
Just like his old man.

My grandfather cut more turf in a day
Than any other man on Toner's bog.
Once I carried him milk in a bottle
Corked sloppily with paper. He straightened up
To drink it, then fell to right away

Nicking and slicing neatly, heaving sods
Over his shoulder, going down and down
For the good turf. Digging.

The cold smell of potato mould, the squelch and slap
Of soggy peat, the curt cuts of an edge
Through living roots awaken in my head.
But I've no spade to follow men like them.

Between my finger and my thumb
The squat pen rests.
I'll dig with it.

READING NOTES

'Powder is a very short story but it is deep and intense,' remarked a member of an ex-offenders' reading group. Indeed the group went on to talk at length about some of the issues it raised. They wanted to know more of the family's story before and after the slice given by Tobias Wolff. The relationship between the boy and his father felt real and the group looked closely for the parts in the story that backed up their feeling. There were lots of questions to explore: who was the more responsible of the two? What made the boy the sort of boy 'who kept his clothes on numbered hangers to ensure proper rotation'? Have your feelings for the father changed by the end of the story? What does the final paragraph make you feel and what does 'bankrupt of honor' mean?

Seamus Heaney's poem always moves people and affirms loving relationships. You don't have to have had the same experience yourself. 'The poem,' one man said, 'makes you feel the pride and the love and the strength of these three men. You have it as if it were yours.' They group went on to talk of potato growing, and memories of grandfathers and what the poet is digging with his pen at the end.

Real Gold

🌿

SILAS MARNER

(EXTRACT FROM PART I, CHAPTER 12)

George Eliot

(approximate reading time 14 minutes)

Silas Marner, a weaver, has been forced to leave his hometown and religious community after being wrongly accused of theft and betrayed by his best friend. Marner suffers from a form of epilepsy which causes him to experience cataleptic fits from time to time. In his anger, bitterness and loss of faith in everything he once held dear, he now lives alone, taking pleasure only in the gold he is accumulating. One evening, he returns to his house and is devastated to discover his precious hoard has been stolen from its hiding place.

Molly Farren is secretly married to the local squire's son with whom she has a baby daughter. She is an opium addict and as our extract opens she is attempting to walk to the squire's New Year party through the snow, carrying her baby . . .

She had set out at an early hour, but had lingered on the road, inclined by her indolence to believe that if she waited under a warm shed the snow would cease to fall. She had waited longer than she knew, and now that she found herself belated in the snow-hidden ruggedness of the long lanes, even the animation of a vindictive purpose could not keep her spirit from failing. It was seven o'clock, and by this time she was not very far from Raveloe, but she was not familiar enough with those monotonous lanes to know how near she was to her journey's end. She needed comfort, and she knew but one comforter – the familiar demon in her bosom; but she hesitated a moment, after drawing out the black remnant, before she raised it to her lips. In that moment the mother's love pleaded for painful consciousness rather than oblivion – pleaded to be left in aching weariness, rather than to have the encircling arms benumbed so that they could not feel the dear burden. In another moment Molly had flung something away, but it was not the black remnant – it was an empty phial. And she walked on again under the breaking cloud, from which there came now and then the light of a quickly veiled star, for a freezing wind had sprung up since the snowing had ceased. But she walked always more and more drowsily, and clutched more and more automatically the sleeping child at her bosom.

Slowly the demon was working his will, and cold and weariness were his helpers. Soon she felt nothing but a supreme immediate longing that curtained of all futurity – the longing to lie down and sleep. She had arrived at a spot where her footsteps were no longer checked by a hedgerow, and she had wandered vaguely, unable to distinguish any objects, notwithstanding the wide whiteness around her, and the growing starlight. She sank down against a straggling furze bush, an easy pillow enough; and the bed of snow, too, was soft. She did not feel that the bed was cold, and did not heed whether the child would wake and cry for her. But her arms had not yet relaxed their instinctive clutch; and the little one slumbered on as gently as if it had been rocked in a lace-trimmed cradle.

But the complete torpor came at last: the fingers lost their tension, the arms unbent; then the little head fell away from the bosom, and the blue eyes opened wide on the cold starlight. At first there was a little peevish cry of 'mammy', and an effort to regain the pillowing arm and bosom; but mammy's ear was deaf, and the pillow seemed to be slipping away backward. Suddenly, as the child rolled downward on its mother's knees, all wet with snow, its eyes were caught by a bright glancing light on the white ground, and, with the ready transition of infancy, it was immediately absorbed in watching the bright living thing running towards it, yet never arriving. That bright living thing must be caught; and in an instant the child had slipped on all-fours, and held out one little hand to catch the gleam. But the gleam would not be caught in that way, and now the head was held up to see where the cunning gleam came from. It came from a very bright place; and the little one, rising on its legs, toddled through the snow, the old grimy shawl in which it was wrapped trailing behind it, and the queer little bonnet dangling at its back – toddled on to the open door of Silas Marner's cottage, and right up to the warm hearth, where there was a bright fire of logs and sticks, which had thoroughly warmed the old sack (Silas's greatcoat) spread

out on the bricks to dry. The little one, accustomed to be left
to itself for long hours without notice from its mother, squatted
down on the sack, and spread its tiny hands towards the blaze,
in perfect contentment, gurgling and making many inarticulate communications to the cheerful fire, like a new-hatched
gosling beginning to find itself comfortable. But presently the
warmth had a lulling effect, and the little golden head sank
down on the old sack, and the blue eyes were veiled by their
delicate half-transparent lids.

But where was Silas Marner while this strange visitor had
come to his hearth? He was in the cottage, but he did not see
the child. During the last few weeks, since he had lost his
money, he had contracted the habit of opening his door and
looking out from time to time, as if he thought that his money
might be somehow coming back to him, or that some trace,
some news of it, might be mysteriously on the road, and be
caught by the listening ear or the straining eye. It was chiefly
at night, when he was not occupied in his loom, that he fell
into this repetition of an act for which he could have assigned
no definite purpose, and which can hardly be understood
except by those who have undergone a bewildering separation
from a supremely loved object. In the evening twilight, and
later whenever the night was not dark, Silas looked out on
that narrow prospect round the Stone-pits, listening and gazing,
not with hope, but with mere yearning and unrest.

This morning he had been told by some of his neighbours
that it was New Year's Eve, and that he must sit up and hear
the old year rung out and the new rung in, because that was
good luck, and might bring his money back again. This was

only a friendly Raveloe-way of jesting with the half-crazy oddi-
ties of a miser, but it had perhaps helped to throw Silas into
a more than usually excited state. Since the on-coming of
twilight he had opened his door again and again, though only
to shut it immediately at seeing all distance veiled by the
falling snow. But the last time he opened it the snow had
ceased, and the clouds were parting here and there. He stood
and listened, and gazed for a long while – there was really
something on the road coming towards him then, but he
caught no sign of it; and the stillness and the wide trackless
snow seemed to narrow his solitude, and touched his yearning
with the chill of despair. He went in again, and put his right
hand on the latch of the door to close it – but he did not
close it: he was arrested, as he had been already since his loss,
by the invisible wand of catalepsy, and stood like a graven
image, with wide but sightless eyes, holding open his door,
powerless to resist either the good or the evil that might enter
there.

When Marner's sensibility returned, he continued the action
which had been arrested, and closed his door, unaware of the
chasm in his consciousness, unaware of any intermediate
change, except that the light had grown dim, and that he was
chilled and faint. He thought he had been too long standing
at the door and looking out. Turning towards the hearth,
where the two logs had fallen apart, and sent forth only a red
uncertain glimmer, he seated himself on his fireside chair, and
was stooping to push his logs together, when, to his blurred
vision, it seemed as if there were gold on the floor in front of
the hearth. Gold! – his own gold – brought back to him as

mysteriously as it had been taken away! He felt his heart begin to beat violently, and for a few moments he was unable to stretch out his hand and grasp the restored treasure. The heap of gold seemed to glow and get larger beneath his agitated gaze. He leaned forward at last, and stretched forth his hand; but instead of the hard coin with the familiar resisting outline, his fingers encountered soft warm curls. In utter amazement, Silas fell on his knees and bent his head low to examine the marvel: it was a sleeping child – a round, fair thing, with soft yellow rings all over its head. Could this be his little sister come back to him in a dream – his little sister whom he had carried about in his arms for a year before she died, when he was a small boy without shoes or stockings? That was the first thought that darted across Silas's blank wonderment. *Was* it a dream? He rose to his feet again, pushed his logs together, and, throwing on some dried leaves and sticks, raised a flame; but the flame did not disperse the vision – it only lit up more distinctly the little round form of the child, and its shabby clothing. It was very much like his little sister. Silas sank into his chair powerless, under the double presence of an inexplicable surprise and a hurrying influx of memories. How and when had the child come in without his knowledge? He had never been beyond the door. But along with that question, and almost thrusting it away, there was a vision of the old home and the old streets leading to Lantern Yard – and within that vision another, of the thoughts which had been present with him in those far-off scenes. The thoughts were strange to him now, like old friendships impossible to revive; and yet he had a dreamy feeling that this child was somehow a message come to him from that far-off life: it stirred fibres that had never been moved in Raveloe – old quiverings of tenderness – old impressions of awe at the presentiment of some Power presiding over his life; for his imagination had not yet extricated itself from the sense of mystery in the child's sudden presence, and had formed no conjectures of ordinary natural means by which the event could have been brought about.

But there was a cry on the hearth: the child had awaked, and Marner stooped to lift it on his knee. It clung round his neck, and burst louder and louder into that mingling of inarticulate cries with 'mammy' by which little children express the bewilderment of waking. Silas pressed it to him, and almost unconsciously uttered sounds of hushing tenderness, while he bethought himself that some of his porridge, which had got cool by the dying fire, would do to feed the child with if it were only warmed up a little.

He had plenty to do through the next hour. The porridge, sweetened with some dry brown sugar from an old store which he had refrained from using for himself, stopped the cries of the little one, and made her lift her blue eyes with a wide quiet gaze at Silas, as he put the spoon into her mouth. Presently she slipped from his knee and began to toddle about, but with a pretty stagger that made Silas jump up and follow her lest she should fall against anything that would hurt her. But she only fell in a sitting posture on the ground, and began to pull at her boots, looking up at him with a crying face as if the boots hurt her. He took her on his knee again, but it was some time before it occurred to Silas's dull bachelor mind that the wet boots were the grievance, pressing on her warm ankles.

He got them off with difficulty, and baby was at once happily occupied with the primary mystery of her own toes, inviting Silas, with much chuckling, to consider the mystery too. But the wet boots had at last suggested to Silas that the child had been walking on the snow, and this roused him from his entire oblivion of any ordinary means by which it could have entered or been brought into his house. Under the prompting of this new idea, and without waiting to form conjectures, he raised the child in his arms, and went to the door. As soon as he had opened it, there was the cry of 'mammy' again, which Silas had not heard since the child's first hungry waking. Bending forward, he could just discern the marks made by the little feet on the virgin snow, and he followed their track to the furze bushes. 'Mammy!' the little one cried again and again, stretching itself forward so as almost to escape from Silas's arms, before he himself was aware that there was something more than the bush before him – that there was a human body, with the head sunk low in the furze, and half-covered with the shaken snow.

RICH
R. S. Thomas

I am a millionaire.
My bedroom is full of gold
light, of the sun's jewellery.
What shall I do with this wealth?
Buy happiness, buy gladness,
the wisdom that grows with the giving
of thanks? I will convert
a child's holding to the estate
of a man, investing the interest
in the child mind. Beyond this
room are the arid sluices
through which cash pours and the heart
desiccates, watching it pass.
Men draw their curtains against
beauty. Ah, let me, when night
comes, offer the moon
unhindered entry through trust's
windows so I may dream
silver, but awake to gold.

READING NOTES

A group of young mothers were impressed to find that a nineteenth-century novel could have such contemporary subject matter. When it came to the part in the story where Molly, the young drug-addicted mother, loses the fight with herself and takes the drug, one mother was shocked and unequivocally condemned Molly, while others took a more understanding position. There was talk of how Silas felt 'the sense of mystery in the child's sudden presence' and someone remarked how that sense of mysteriousness was quickly forgotten when the child begins to make her real presence felt. Everyone had experienced that!

In *Silas Marner* the portrayal of the child is very realistic and it is interesting to think about this in relation to the poem. The moment when Marner touches the soft curls is especially vivid and perhaps this is the moment when he becomes a real millionaire. Somebody said they believed that children are riches but that you had to have something to live on, too. The group wanted to discuss the meaning of 'trust's windows' and what 'the heart desiccates' might mean. That took ages.

Blessed Be the Infant Babe

SILAS MARNER

(EXTRACT FROM PART I, CHAPTER 14)

George Eliot

(approximate reading time 14 minutes)

After Molly Farren's death, Silas is determined he will keep her baby and look after it on his own, with occasional help from one of the local village women . . .

Among the notable mothers, Dolly Winthrop was the one whose neighbourly offices were the most acceptable to Marner, for they were rendered without any show of bustling instruction. Silas had shown her the half-guinea given to him by Godfrey, and had asked her what he should do about getting some clothes for the child.

'Eh, Master Marner,' said Dolly, 'there's no call to buy, no more nor a pair o' shoes; for I've got the little petticoats as Aaron wore five years ago, and it's ill spending the money on them baby-clothes, for the child 'ull grow like grass i' May, bless it – that it will.'

And the same day Dolly brought her bundle, and displayed

to Marner, one by one, the tiny garments in their due order of succession, most of them patched and darned, but clean and neat as fresh-sprung herbs. This was the introduction to a great ceremony with soap and water, from which Baby came out in new beauty, and sat on Dolly's knee, handling her toes and chuckling and patting her palms together with an air of having made several discoveries about herself, which she communicated by alternate sounds of 'gug-gug-gug', and 'mammy'. The 'mammy' was not a cry of need or uneasiness: Baby had been used to utter it without expecting either tender sound or touch to follow.

'You'll happen be a bit moithered with it while it's so little; but I'll come, and welcome, and see to it for you: I've a bit o' time to spare most days. So, as I say, I'll come and see to the child for you, and welcome.'

'Thank you . . . kindly,' said Silas, hesitating a little. 'I'll be glad if you'll tell me things. But,' he added, uneasily, leaning forward to look at Baby with some jealousy, as she was resting her head backward against Dolly's arm, and eyeing him contentedly from a distance – 'But I want to do things for it myself, else it may get fond o' somebody else, and not fond o' me. I've been used to fending for myself in the house – I can learn, I can learn.'

'Eh, to be sure,' said Dolly, gently. 'I've seen men as are wonderful handy wi' children. You see this goes first, next the skin,' proceeded Dolly, taking up the little shirt, and putting it on.

'Yes,' said Marner, docilely, bringing his eyes very close, that they might be initiated in the mysteries; whereupon Baby seized his head with both her small arms, and put her lips against his face with purring noises.

'See there,' said Dolly, with a woman's tender tact, 'she's fondest o' you. She wants to go o' your lap, I'll be bound. Go, then: take her, Master Marner; you can put the things on, and then you can say as you've done for her from the first of her coming to you.'

Marner took her on his lap, trembling with an emotion mysterious to himself, at something unknown dawning on his life. Thought and feeling were so confused within him, that if he had tried to give them utterance, he could only have said that the child was come instead of the gold – that the gold had turned into the child. He took the garments from Dolly, and put them on under her teaching; interrupted, of course, by Baby's gymnastics.

'Well, Master Marner,' said Dolly, inwardly rejoiced, 'you must fix on a name for it, because it must have a name giv' it when it's christened.'

'My mother's name was Hephzibah,' said Silas, 'and my little sister was named after her.'

'Eh, that's a hard name,' said Dolly. 'I partly think it isn't a christened name.'

'It's a Bible name,' said Silas, old ideas recurring.

'Then I've no call to speak again' it,' said Dolly. 'But it was awk'ard calling your little sister by such a hard name, when you'd got nothing big to say, like – wasn't it, Master Marner?'

'We called her Eppie,' said Silas.

As the weeks grew to months, the child created fresh and fresh links between his life and the lives from which he had hitherto shrunk continually into narrower isolation. Unlike the gold which needed nothing, and must be worshipped in close-locked solitude, which was hidden away from the daylight, was deaf to the song of birds, and started to no human tones – Eppie was a creature of endless claims and ever-growing desires, seeking and loving sunshine, and living sounds, and living movements; making trial of everything, with trust in new joy, and stirring the human kindness in all eyes that looked on her.

As the child's mind was growing into knowledge, his mind was growing into memory: as her life unfolded, his soul, long stupefied in a cold narrow prison, was unfolding too, and trembling gradually into full consciousness.

By the time Eppie was three years old, she developed a fine capacity for mischief, and for devising ingenious ways of being troublesome, which found much exercise, not only for Silas's patience, but for his watchfulness and penetration. Sorely was poor Silas puzzled on such occasions by the incompatible demands of love. Dolly Winthrop told him that punishment was good for Eppie, and that, as for rearing a child without making it tingle a little in soft and safe places now and then, it was not to be done.

For example. He had wisely chosen a broad strip of linen as a means of fastening her to his loom when he was busy: it made a broad belt round her waist, and was long enough to allow of her reaching the truckle-bed and sitting down on it, but not long enough for her to attempt any dangerous climbing. One bright summer's morning Silas had been more engrossed than usual in 'setting up' a new piece of work, an occasion on which his scissors were in requisition. These scissors, owing to an especial warning of Dolly's, had been kept carefully out of Eppie's reach. Silas had seated himself in his loom, and the noise of weaving had begun; but he had left his scissors on a ledge which Eppie's arm was long enough to reach; and now, like a small mouse, watching her opportunity, she stole quietly from her corner, secured the scissors, and toddled to the bed again, setting up her back as a mode of concealing the fact. She had a distinct intention as to the use of the scissors; and having cut the linen strip in a jagged but effectual manner, in two moments she had run out at the open door where the sunshine was inviting her, while poor Silas believed her to be a better child than usual. It was not until he happened to need his scissors that the terrible fact burst upon him: Eppie had run out by herself – had perhaps fallen into the Stone-pit. Silas, shaken by the worst fear that could have befallen him, rushed out, calling 'Eppie!' and ran eagerly about the unenclosed space, exploring the dry cavities into which she might have fallen, and then gazing with questioning dread at the smooth red surface of the water. The cold drops stood on his brow. How long had she been out? There was one hope – that she had crept through the stile and got into the fields, where he habitually took her to stroll. But the grass was high in the meadow, and there was no descrying her. He got over the stile into the next field, looking with dying hope towards a small pond which was now reduced to its summer shallowness, so as to leave a wide margin of good adhesive mud. Here, however, sat Eppie, discoursing cheerfully to her own small boot, which she was using as a bucket to convey the water into a deep hoof-mark, while her little naked foot was planted comfortably on a cushion of olive-green mud. A red-headed calf was observing her with alarmed doubt through the opposite hedge.

Silas, overcome with convulsive joy at finding his treasure again, could do nothing but snatch her up, and cover her with half-sobbing kisses. It was not until he had carried her home, and had begun to think of the necessary washing, that he recollected the need that he should punish Eppie, and 'make her remember'. The idea that she might run away again and come to harm, gave him unusual resolution, and for the first time he determined to try the coal-hole – a small closet near the hearth.

'Naughty, naughty Eppie,' he suddenly began, holding her on his knee, and pointing to her muddy feet and clothes – 'naughty to cut with the scissors and run away. Eppie must go into the coal-hole for being naughty. Daddy must put her in the coal-hole.'

He half-expected that this would be shock enough, and that Eppie would begin to cry. But instead of that, she began to shake herself on his knee, as if the proposition opened a pleasing novelty. Seeing that he must proceed to extremities, he put her into the coal-hole, and held the door closed, with a trembling sense that he was using a strong measure. For a moment there was silence, but then came a little cry, 'Opy, opy!' and Silas let her out again, saying, 'Now Eppie 'ull never be naughty again, else she must go in the coal-hole – a black naughty place.'

The weaving must stand still a long while this morning, for now Eppie must be washed, and have clean clothes on; but it was to be hoped that this punishment would have a lasting effect, and save time in future – though, perhaps, it would have been better if Eppie had cried more.

In half an hour she was clean again, and Silas having turned his back to see what he could do with the linen band, threw it down again, with the reflection that Eppie would be good without fastening for the rest of the morning. He turned round again, and was going to place her in her little chair near the loom, when she peeped out at him with black face and hands again, and said, 'Eppie in de toal-hole!'

This total failure of the coal-hole discipline shook Silas's belief in the efficacy of punishment. 'She'd take it all for fun,' he observed to Dolly, 'if I didn't hurt her, and that I can't do, Mrs Winthrop. If she makes me a bit o' trouble, I can bear it. And she's got no tricks but what she'll grow out of.'

'Well, that's partly true, Master Marner,' said Dolly, sympathetically; 'and if you can't bring your mind to frighten her off touching things, you must do what you can to keep 'em out of her way. That's what I do wi' the pups as the lads are allays a-rearing.'

So Eppie was reared without punishment, the burden of her misdeeds being borne vicariously by father Silas. The stone hut was made a soft nest for her, lined with downy patience: and also in the world that lay beyond the stone hut she knew nothing of frowns and denials.

Notwithstanding the difficulty of carrying her and his yarn or lined at the same time, Silas took her with him in most of his journeys to the farmhouses. Everywhere he must sit a little and talk about the child, and words of interest were always ready for him. No child was afraid of approaching Silas when Eppie was near him: there was no repulsion around him now, either for young or old; for the little child had come to link him once more with the whole world.

Silas began now to think of Raveloe life entirely in relation to Eppie: she must have everything that was a good in Raveloe; and he listened docilely, that he might come to understand better what this life was, from which, for fifteen years, he had stood aloof as from a strange thing, with which he could have no communion. The disposition to hoard had been utterly crushed at the very first by the loss of his long-stored gold. And now something had come to replace his hoard which gave a growing purpose to the earnings, drawing his hope and joy continually onward beyond the money.

In old days there were angels who came and took men by the hand and led them away from the city of destruction. We see no white-winged angels now. But yet men are led away from threatening destruction: a hand is put into theirs, which leads them forth gently towards a calm and bright land, so that they look no more backward; and the hand may be a little child's.

A PARENTAL ODE TO MY SON
AGED 3 YEARS AND 5 MONTHS
Thomas Hood

Thou happy, happy elf!
(But stop, – first let me kiss away that tear) –
Thou tiny image of myself!
(My love, he's poking peas into his ear!)
Thou merry, laughing sprite!
With spirits feather-light,
Untouched by sorrow, and unsoiled by sin –
(Good Heavens! the child is swallowing a pin!)

Thou little tricksy Puck!
With antic toys so funnily bestuck,
Light as the singing bird that wings the air –
(The door! the door! he'll tumble down the stair!)
Thou darling of thy sire!
(Why, Jane, he'll set his pinafore a-fire!)
Thou imp of mirth and joy!
In Love's dear chain, so strong and bright a link,
Thou idol of thy parents – (Drat the boy!
There goes my ink!)

Thou cherub – but of earth;
Fit playfellow for Fays, by moonlight pale,
In harmless sport and mirth,
(That dog will bite him if he pulls its tail!)

Thou human humming-bee, extracting honey
From every blossom in the world that blows,
        Singing in Youth's Elysium ever sunny,
(Another tumble! – that's his precious nose!)

        Thy father's pride and hope!
(He'll break the mirror with that skipping-rope!)
With pure heart newly stamped from Nature's mint –
(Where did he learn that squint!)
        Thou young domestic dove!
(He'll have that jug off with another shove!)
        Dear nurseling of the Hymeneal nest!
        (Are those torn clothes his best?)
        Little epitome of man!
(He'll climb upon the table, that's his plan!)
Touch'd with the beauteous tints of dawning life –
        (He's got a knife!)

        Thou enviable being!
No storms, no clouds, in thy blue sky foreseeing,
        Play on, play on,
        My elfin John!
Toss the light ball – bestride the stick –
(I knew so many cakes would make him sick!)
With fancies, buoyant as the thistle-down,
Prompting the face grotesque, and antic brisk,
        With many a lamb-like frisk,
(He's got the scissors, snipping at your gown!)

Thou pretty opening rose!
(Go to your mother, child, and wipe your nose!)
Balmy and breathing music like the South,
(He really brings my heart into my mouth!)
Fresh as the morn, and brilliant as its star –
(I wish that window had an iron bar!)
Bold as the hawk, yet gentle as the dove, –
    (I'll tell you what, my love,
I cannot write, unless he's sent above!)

READING NOTES

After reading Chapter 12 in which the baby comes to Silas Marner, the young mothers group badly wanted to know if they stayed together. They wanted to read on and find out. They enjoyed the descriptions of Silas's cluelessness about babies – 'Just like my partner' said one. There was much amicable disagreement about whether it is necessary to smack children. Then one mum told how terrifying it had been when she had once lost her toddler on a busy beach. They discussed modern forms of discipline and enjoyed remembering being put in the corner or made to sit on the naughty chair at infant school. Some time was spent on the meaning of the final paragraph.

The poem could almost be about Eppie, even down to the scissors. Everyone told of ways their children got into mischief and someone commented that she found it oddly comforting to think that years ago, parents had the same sort of trouble with naughty children as she experienced with hers today.

Shame On Me

🍂

THE SNOB
Morley Callaghan

(approximate reading time 12 minutes)

It was at the book counter in the department store that John Harcourt, the student, caught a glimpse of his father. At first he could not be sure in the crowd that pushed along the aisle, but there was something about the colour of the back of the elderly man's neck, something about the faded felt hat, that he knew very well. Harcourt was standing with the girl he loved, buying a book for her. All afternoon he had been talking to her, eagerly, but with an anxious diffidence, as if there still remained in him an innocent wonder that she should be delighted to be with him. From underneath her wide-brimmed straw hat, her face, so fair and beautifully strong with its expression of cool independence, kept turning up to him and sometimes smiled at what he said. That was the way they always talked, never daring to show much full, strong feeling. Harcourt had just bought the book, and had reached into his pocket for the money with a free, ready gesture to make it appear that he was accustomed to buying books for young ladies, when the white-haired man in the faded felt hat, at the other end of the counter, turned half toward him, and Harcourt knew he was standing only a few feet away from his father.

The young man's easy words trailed away and his voice became little more than a whisper, as if he were afraid that everyone in the store might recognize it. There was rising in him a dreadful uneasiness; something very precious that he wanted to hold seemed close to destruction. His father, standing at the end of the bargain counter, was planted squarely on his two feet, turning a book over thoughtfully in his hands. Then he took out his glasses from an old, worn leather case and adjusted them on the end of his nose, looking down over them at the book. His coat was thrown open, two buttons on his vest were undone, his gray hair was too long, and in his rather shabby clothes he looked very much like a working-man, a carpenter perhaps. Such resentment rose in young Harcourt that he wanted to cry out bitterly, 'Why does he dress as if he never owned a decent suit in his life? He doesn't care what the whole world thinks of him. He never did. I've told him a hundred times he ought to wear his good clothes when he goes out. Mother's told him the same thing. He just laughs. And now Grace may see him. Grace will meet him.'

So young Harcourt stood still, with his head down, feeling that something very painful was impending. Once he looked anxiously at Grace, who had turned to the bargain counter. Among those people drifting aimlessly by with hot red faces, getting in each other's way, using their elbows but keeping their faces detached and wooden, she looked tall and splendidly alone. She was so sure of herself, her relation to the people in the aisles, the clerks behind the counter, the books on the shelves, and everything around her. Still keeping his head down and moving close, he whispered uneasily, 'Let's go and have tea somewhere, Grace.'

'In a minute, dear,' she said.

'Let's go now.'

'In just a minute, dear,' she repeated absently.

'There's not a breath of air in here. Let's go now.'

'What makes you so impatient?'

'There's nothing but old books on that counter.'

'There may be something here I've wanted all my life,' she said, smiling at him brightly and not noticing the uneasiness in his face.

So Harcourt had to move slowly behind her, getting closer to his father all the time. He could feel the space that separated them narrowing. Once he looked up with a vague, sidelong glance. But his father, red-faced and happy, was still reading the book, only now there was a meditative expression on his face, as if something in the book had stirred him and he intended to stay there reading for some time.

Old Harcourt had lots of time to amuse himself, because he was on a pension after working hard all his life. He had sent John to the university and he was eager to have him distinguish himself. Every night when John came home, whether it was early or late, he used to go into his father's and mother's bedroom and turn on the light and talk to them about the interesting things that had happened to him during the day. They listened and shared this new world with him. They both sat up in their night-clothes and, while his mother asked all the questions, his father listened attentively with his head cocked on one side and a smile or a frown on his face. The memory of all this was in John now, and there was also a desperate longing and a pain within him growing harder to bear as he glanced fearfully at his father, but he thought stubbornly, 'I can't introduce him. It'll be easier for everybody if he doesn't see us. I'm not ashamed. But it will be easier. It'll be more sensible. It'll only embarrass him to see Grace.' By this time he knew he was ashamed, but he felt that his shame was justified, for Grace's father had the smooth, confident manner of a man who had lived all his life among people who were rich and sure of themselves. Often when he had been in Grace's home talking politely to her mother, John had kept on thinking of the plainness of his own home and of his parents' laughing, good-natured untidiness, and he resolved desperately that he must make Grace's people admire him.

He looked up cautiously, for they were about eight feet away from his father, but at that moment his father, too, looked up and John's glance shifted swiftly far over the aisle, over the counters, seeing nothing. As his father's blue, calm eyes stared steadily over the glasses, there was an instant when their glances might have met. Neither one could have been certain, yet John, as he turned away and began to talk to Grace hurriedly, knew surely that his father had seen him. He knew it by the steady calmness in his father's blue eyes. John's shame grew, and then humiliation sickened him as he waited and did nothing.

His father turned away, going down the aisle, walking erectly in his shabby clothes, his shoulders very straight, never once looking back. His father would walk slowly along the street, he knew, with that meditative expression deepening and becoming grave.

Young Harcourt stood beside Grace, brushing against her soft shoulder, and made faintly aware again of the delicate scent she used. There, so close beside him, she was holding within her everything he wanted to reach out for, only now he felt a sharp hostility that made him sullen and silent.

'You were right, John,' she was drawling in her soft voice. 'It does get unbearable in here on a hot day. Do let's go now. Have you ever noticed that department stores after a time can make you really hate people?' But she smiled when she spoke, so he might see that she really hated no one.

'You don't like people, do you?' he said sharply.

'People? What people? What do you mean?'

'I mean,' he went on irritably, 'you don't like the kind of people you bump into here, for example.'

'Not especially. Who does? What are you talking about?'

'Anybody could see you don't,' he said recklessly, full of a savage eagerness to hurt her. 'I say you don't like simple, honest people, the kind of people you meet all over the city.' He blurted the words out as if he wanted to shake her, but he was longing to say, 'You wouldn't like my family. Why couldn't I take you home to have dinner with them? You'd turn up your nose at them, because they've no pretensions. As soon as my father saw you, he knew you wouldn't want to meet him. I could tell by the way he turned.'

His father was on his way home now, he knew, and that evening at dinner they would meet. His mother and sister would talk rapidly, but his father would say nothing to him, or to anyone. There would only be Harcourt's memory of the level look in the blue eyes, and the knowledge of his father's pain as he walked away.

Grace watched John's gloomy face as they walked through the store, and she knew he was nursing some private rage, and so her own resentment and exasperation kept growing, and she said crisply, 'You're entitled to your moods on a hot afternoon, I suppose, but if I feel I don't like it here, then I don't like it. You wanted to go yourself. Who likes to spend very much time in a department store on a hot afternoon? I begin to hate every stupid person that bangs into me, everybody near me. What does that make me?'

'It makes you a snob.'

'So I'm a snob now?' she said angrily.

'Certainly you're a snob,' he said. They were at the door and going out to the street. As they walked in the sunlight, in the crowd moving slowly down the street, he was groping for words to describe the secret thoughts he had always had about her. 'I've always known how you'd feel about people I like who didn't fit into your private world,' he said.

'You're a very stupid person,' she said. Her face was flushed now, and it was hard for her to express her indignation, so she stared straight ahead as she walked along.

They had never talked in this way, and now they were both quickly eager to hurt each other. With a flow of words, she started to argue with him, then she checked herself and said calmly, 'Listen, John, I imagine you're tired of my company. There's no sense in having tea together. I think I'd better leave you right here.'

'That's fine,' he said. 'Good afternoon.'

'Good-bye.'

'Good-bye.'

She started to go, she had gone two paces, but he reached out desperately and held her arm, and he was frightened, and pleading. 'Please don't go, Grace.'

All the anger and irritation had left him; there was just a desperate anxiety in his voice as he pleaded, 'Please forgive me. I've no right to talk to you like that. I don't know why I'm so rude or what's the matter. I'm ridiculous. I'm very, very ridiculous. Please, you must forgive me. Don't leave me.'

He had never talked to her so brokenly, and his sincerity, the depth of his feeling, began to stir her. While she listened, feeling all the yearning in him, they seemed to have been brought closer together, by opposing each other, than ever before, and she began to feel almost shy. 'I don't know what's the matter. I suppose we're both irritable. It must be the weather,' she said. 'But I'm not angry, John.'

He nodded his head miserably. He longed to tell her that he was sure she would have been charming to his father, but he had never felt so wretched in his life. He held her arm tight, as if he must hold it or what he wanted most in the world would slip away from him, yet he kept thinking, as he would ever think, of his father walking away quietly with his head never turning.

'WHAT DOES YOUR FATHER DO?'
Roger McGough

At university, how that artful question embarrassed me.
In the common-room, coffee cup balancing on cavalry
    twills
Some bright spark (usually Sociology) would want an
    answer.
Shame on me, as feigning lofty disinterest, I would
    hesitate.

Should I mumble 'docker' in the hope of being misheard?
('There he goes, a doctor's son, and every inch the
    medical man.')
Or should I pick up the hook and throw it down like a
    gauntlet?
'Docker. My dad's a docker.' A whistle of corduroy.

How about? 'He's a stevedore, from the Spanish
    "estibador"
Meaning a packer, or loader, as in ship.' No, sounds too
On the Waterfront, and Dad was no Marlon Brando.
Besides, it's the handle they want not the etymology.

'He's a foreman on the docks.' A hint of status? Possibly.
A touch of class? Hardly. Better go with the
    straightforward:
'He works on the docks in Liverpool,' which leaves it
    open.

Crane-driver? Customs and Excise Officer? Canteen
    manager?

Clerk? Chairman of the Mersey Docks and Harbour
    Board?
In dreams, I hear him naming the docks he knew and
    loved.
A mantra of gentle reproach: *Gladstone, Hornby,
    Alexandra,*
*Langton, Brocklebank, Canada, Huskisson, Sandon,
    Wellington,*

Bramley Moor, Nelson, Salisbury, Trafalgar, Victoria.

READING NOTES

'I hate snobs,' said one young male member of a group. 'People who think they are better than you just because they are posh or have more money.' Someone else answered, 'Yes, but who is the snob here? It is not the posh woman but the poorer lad. The group members talked about the way in which the young man betrays his father, then tries to justify it to himself. People felt sorry for the father but Sam wondered why the father did not just say hello. 'He's made it worse. Perhaps he feels ashamed or something, too.' There is so much going on between these three people, some of it spoken, some left unsaid. People in all sorts of groups have a similar reaction – they always want to talk about this real sense of damage and what it is going to do to the relationships after the story ends.

The poem helpfully carries on the theme and was a great success with a group of warehousemen. Conversation veered between opinions on the young, cavalry-twilled snobbish student and memories of Liverpool Docks; ships on the Mersey, and the famous scene with Marlon Brando and Rod Steiger in the back of the car in *On the Waterfront*. 'The sad thing is,' said Alan, going back to the readings, 'they both really love their fathers, don't they?'

Clamorous Wings

❧

I'LL TELL ME MA

(THE SWIMMER, CHAPTER 5)

Brian Keenan

(approximate reading time 13 minutes)

Brian Keenan is still best known as one of the Beirut hostages. He was born in 1951 into a working-class family in East Belfast. I'll Tell Me Ma *is his childhood memoir.*

Dad loved the outdoors. On summer mornings, he would boil the kettle until it steamed, then pour the hot water into a basin which he would carry with him into the yard. While he sat on a stool or chair, Dad would go about his daily ablutions with great enthusiasm, splashing water every-where. Occasionally he used a cut-throat blade to shave with. He loved to sing as the blade scraped across his face. I thought he simply needed a good scrub because his work was often dirty and smelly, but it was probably that Mum wanted to use the sink to wash dishes or clothes. Dad was happy to be relegated to the yard. He wasn't obsessed with dirt or cleanliness. It was more than that: Dad was like a child around water. Water cast a spell on him and transformed him.

I had my first encounter with this in Alexandra Park. After a sleepless night when my growing pains had subsided into a series of disturbing dreams I awoke to the sound of my father's singing and sluicing. The noises he made blew away the dreams at once. I came down the stairs more asleep than awake and stood in the doorway of our scullery and watched him. He was unaware of me for some minutes and I was content to stay and watch, attracted by the animal abandon with which he washed. After some minutes he turned to me, vigorously drying his ears by pushing the towel into them. 'Bad dreams again, son?' he said without making any fuss about the fact. I nodded, half afraid that the acknowledgement might bring the dreams flocking back. 'Well it's very early, but it's going to be a big bright day. So why don't me and you go off to the park and maybe the waterworks, just the two of us?' I was swept away by the suggestion. Most of the street was still asleep. The milkman hadn't even arrived, rattling us all awake with his empty bottles and aluminium crates. And I had never been outside the front door or beyond the yard at this hour of the morning. In no time we were gone. The empty streets were new to me, though I had made this walk hundreds of times. Dad was quiet too. He never did talk much unless I asked him something. So we stole through the streets like a couple of conspirators. It seemed like no one else in the world was awake.

When we arrived at the main gates of the park, they were locked. But there were plenty of bars missing in the wrought-iron railing that enclosed it so we squeezed ourselves through. Dad first, then I handed him the small army canvas bag he had brought with him and finally I stepped rather than squeezed myself into the forbidden parkland. I was afraid of the park keeper catching us but didn't say anything. Dad walked briskly across the grass and on to the pathway. His casual demeanour made me forget the keeper, but not my sense of being afraid. The park, like the streets we had walked through, had lost its familiarity. The lack of distant traffic noise and the absence of voices of other children shouting and playing made the place seem twice as big. The trees I had tried to climb seemed larger and the bushes and shrubs that I had played hide-and-seek in did not invite me at this unearthly hour.

Instinctively we headed to a natural embankment that was crested by several well-formed trees. One had great muscular branches that grew out over the sloping landfall. Years ago someone had climbed the tree and crawled out along one of these branches to attach a rope, which drooped down and dangled over the embankment. It provided hours of fun for local children who would swing out from the edge and then drop to the ground. It was a constant challenge to see who could swing out the furthest and drop from the greatest height. When I went to the park with my parents and sister, I would watch the other lads screaming in panic and delight as they flew out from the hilltop and then plunged like a shot bird to the ground. I watched from a safe distance, never daring to join them. But this day, Dad hoisted me on to the 'Tarzan swing' as it was called and pushed me out. I clung on like grim death as the ground beneath me receded further and further. I was dreading that Dad would push me out even more when the swinging rope turned back on its arc. I said nothing as his hands received me then launched me back even further and higher into the empty air. I clenched the rope but felt only the numbness of my hands. I was glad we were alone and desperately hoped my dad could not see me white with fear. Suddenly I thought of his plane crash into the mountains and simultaneously heard him call 'Drop'. The noise of the command blasted into me and I released my grip and fell to the earth.

I landed easily and rolled a few feet to where Dad stood waiting. I was dumbfounded by what I had done and the fact that I was still in one piece. 'You see, son, I knew you could do it,' Dad said. He was genuinely thrilled and it spilt over into me. I was amazed at my feat and was annoyed now that no one except Dad saw me fly. Something new bubbled up inside me. I felt tingly and unafraid. The park seemed less big and foreboding. 'Want to try again?' he asked. 'Yes,' I answered, surprised by my sudden confidence. For twenty minutes he pushed me then encouraged me to run with the rope in my hand, launch myself off the precipice and drop at the highest point of the swing's incline. 'You'd make a great parachuter,' he commented encouragingly as I completed another flight and fall. The remark brought me closer to him and our model aeroplanes and to his unspoken adventures during the war. Now I was glad no one else was here. I didn't mind that the rest of the screaming jumpers hadn't seen me. When he suggested that we go swimming my new-found confidence fell from me faster than my fall from the swing. I didn't want to say no, but my fear of water was so great that I couldn't speak. Part of me also felt that to say no or to make some other feeble excuse would erase the magic of the past hour. 'Come on,' he said, picking up his haversack.

Instead of walking in the direction of the waterworks, we walked quietly towards the lake in the centre of the park. Swimming here was forbidden. The lake was surrounded by a low iron fence which was only three feet high. So it was not meant to keep people away from the deep water, only to emphasise the prohibition. I had never seen anyone swim here, except a family of swans. I had heard that the lake was maybe forty feet deep. The banks down to the water's edge were steep and overgrown with tall weeds. One reason I think Dad liked this park was its informality. It was more like the countryside than the term 'park' suggested.

'You wait here and mind this stuff. I won't be long,' he said without looking at me. I was immediately relieved and immediately apprehensive. The edges of the lake had swathes of water reed growing and beyond that a film of algae that looked like green confetti. Only at the centre could you see the still black sheen of unmoving water. It looked pretty at first glance, especially when the swans moved across it. But the thought of it was ominous, and the swans scared me. They were not like the birds in the reservoir lakes who were used to the proximity of people with their toy boats and the fishermen and families who often fed them bait or breadcrumbs. The lake swans never got close to human beings because of the fence, the bank and the reeds. The lake was their home and they patrolled it with austere assurance.

Dad stepped over the fence with the rolled-up towel and swimming trunks he had brought in the small haversack. Within minutes, he had changed and was descending the bank. 'Daddy, Daddy, what about the swans?' I asked, becoming more fearful by the second. I had seen the water-works swans hissing and charging at dogs they thought were too near their nests. I had watched them stand up and spread their wings, flapping furiously. 'The swans won't come near me,' Dad assured me calmly as he slid down through the waist-high weeds and entered the water like a sea snake. He breasted the reeds and the water without a sound. A few water hens scurried out and skimmed to the far side of the lake. Other birds called out their warning at his alien presence in

the water. Everywhere else around us was complete silence.

But Dad was no alien here. He swam on through the algae into the middle of the lake. I saw his head and face crusted with the green scum and his black shiny hair sitting on top of the water. He looked like a seal that had suddenly emerged out of the black depths. Then he disappeared again, only to reappear a few seconds later. I watched him intensely and felt lonely and afraid. He moved across the water as if his head was fixed to a submerged stick and an invisible hand was moving it under the surface. He wasn't himself. There were no signs of movement of a body beneath the dull water. For a moment I hardly recognised the thing in the water. All I knew was an overwhelming sense of distance between him and me. His hand came up out of the water and made a slight wave. And then he was swallowed up by the lake again. I knew the wave was an encouragement for me to be unafraid; but it was a passing gesture, as if he was only half conscious of me or anything else. There in the middle of the lake he hardly made a splash or a ripple. He seemed so content. Water was his element and he melted into it. I didn't know him. I only knew the man who made aeroplanes and who brought home animals. This aquatic beast who looked back at me like a ponderous seal, rolled languorously as a beaver, shook his wet hair and snorted like a water buffalo, was from another world.

If anyone was the intruder there, it was me. I wasn't part of this man who an hour ago had encouraged me to fly and be unafraid. I recalled that he had only brought a towel and trunks for himself. Obviously his decision to come here was premeditated around this swim. Something more than wanting to bring me this early in the morning had called him here.

Then I saw the swans emerge and move across the lake like two patrolling gunboats. I wanted to shout a warning but was afraid. I watched as they bore down on him silently and swiftly. I knew that at any moment there would be an eruption of water and wings blasting around my dad. 'Daddy, come on, hurry up,' I urged. He didn't seem to hear me or notice the birds. Then he calmly swam away and ceded the centre of the lake to the swans. They accepted and their bodies sank a little in the water as they ceased their pursuit.

Dad remained a few feet away, watching the birds while they began preening each other. Then he swam to the bank and emerged slowly from the water. His face, shoulders and chest were clotted with algae. It was as if he had grown green scales on his skin. He dried and dressed himself quickly and I knew we would go home now. Something had been appeased. The elemental gods of air and water had touched us separately and it was time to leave.

THE WILD SWANS AT COOLE
W. B. Yeats

The trees are in their autumn beauty,
The woodland paths are dry,
Under the October twilight the water
Mirrors a still sky;
Upon the brimming water among the stones
Are nine-and-fifty swans.

The nineteenth autumn has come upon me
Since I first made my count;
I saw, before I had well finished,
All suddenly mount
And scatter wheeling in great broken rings
Upon their clamorous wings.

I have looked upon those brilliant creatures,
And now my heart is sore.
All's changed since I, hearing at twilight,
The first time on this shore,
The bell-beat of their wings above my head,
Trod with a lighter tread.

Unwearied still, lover by lover,
They paddle in the cold
Companionable streams or climb the air;
Their hearts have not grown old;

Passion or conquest, wander where they will,
Attend upon them still.

But now they drift on the still water,
Mysterious, beautiful;
Among what rushes will they build,
By what lake's edge or pool
Delight men's eyes when I awake some day
To find they have flown away?

READING NOTES

Both story and poem are about memories, and readers often want to talk about the difference in the way we might see the same thing in childhood and as an adult. Or the way that time leaves some things apparently untouched while irrevocably changing others. The poem is beautiful and about beauty so why is it so sad? 'Mysterious, beautiful', is the poet's description of the swans, but they are many other things too.

The boy in the story is seeing and experiencing something different. Readers have thought hard about the nervous, fearful child. They have talked of their own childhood nightmares as well as their relationships with their fathers and shared special memories of doing things with Dad. How difficult would it be to recall your childhood in order to write a memoir? Are *things* such as Tarzan ropes, watching your father shave, the park, easier to remember than *feelings*?

'I hardly recognised the thing in the water. All I knew was an overwhelming sense of distance between him and me.' The idea of the possibility of distance and separateness existing at the same time as close and loving feeling is something which has really interested readers.

Many readers have remembered Brian Keenan as one of the Beirut hostages and have talked about their own memories and thoughts of that time.

The Paths of Our Lives

DAVID SWAN
Nathaniel Hawthorne

(approximate reading time 14 minutes)

We can be but partially acquainted even with the events which actually influence our course through life, and our final destiny. There are innumerable other events – if such they may be called – which come close upon us, yet pass away without actual results, or even betraying their near approach, by the reflection of any light or shadow across our minds. Could we know all the vicissitudes of our fortunes, life would be too full of hope and fear, exultation or disappointment, to afford us a single hour of true serenity. This idea may be illustrated by a page from the secret history of David Swan.

We have nothing to do with David until we find him, at the age of twenty, on the high road from his native place to the city of Boston, where his uncle, a small dealer in the grocery line, was to take him behind the counter. Be it enough to say that he was a native of New Hampshire, born of respectable parents, and had received an ordinary school education, with a classic finish by a year at Gilmanton Academy. After journeying on foot from sunrise till nearly noon of a

summer's day, his weariness and the increasing heat determined him to sit down in the first convenient shade, and
await the coming up of the stage-coach. As if planted on
purpose for him, there soon appeared a little tuft of maples,
with a delightful recess in the midst, and such a fresh bubbling
spring that it seemed never to have sparkled for any wayfarer
but David Swan. Virgin or not, he kissed it with his thirsty
lips, and then flung himself along the brink, pillowing his
head upon some shirts and a pair of pantaloons, tied up in a
striped cotton handkerchief. The sunbeams could not reach
him; the dust did not yet rise from the road after the heavy
rain of yesterday; and his grassy lair suited the young man
better than a bed of down. The spring murmured drowsily
beside him; the branches waved dreamily across the blue sky
overhead; and a deep sleep, perchance hiding dreams within
its depths, fell upon David Swan. But we are to relate events
which he did not dream of.

While he lay sound asleep in the shade, other people were
wide awake, and passed to and fro, afoot, on horseback, and in
all sorts of vehicles, along the sunny road by his bedchamber.
Some looked neither to the right hand nor the left, and knew
not that he was there; some merely glanced that way, without
admitting the slumberer among their busy thoughts; some
laughed to see how soundly he slept; and several, whose hearts
were brimming full of scorn, ejected their venomous superfluity
on David Swan. A middle-aged widow, when nobody else was
near, thrust her head a little way into the recess, and vowed that
the young fellow looked charming in his sleep. A temperance
lecturer saw him, and wrought poor David into the texture of

his evening's discourse, as an awful instance of dead drunken-
ness by the roadside. But censure, praise, merriment, scorn, and
indifference were all one, or rather all nothing, to David Swan.

He had slept only a few moments when a brown carriage,
drawn by a handsome pair of horses, bowled easily along, and
was brought to a standstill nearly in front of David's resting-
place. A linchpin had fallen out, and permitted one of the
wheels to slide off. The damage was slight, and occasioned
merely a momentary alarm to an elderly merchant and his
wife, who were returning to Boston in the carriage. While the
coachman and a servant were replacing the wheel, the lady
and gentleman sheltered themselves beneath the maple-trees,
and there espied the bubbling fountain, and David Swan asleep
beside it. Impressed with the awe which the humblest sleeper
usually sheds around him, the merchant trod as lightly as the
gout would allow; and his spouse took good heed not to rustle
her silk gown, lest David should start up all of a sudden.

'How soundly he sleeps!' whispered the old gentleman.
'From what a depth he draws that easy breath! Such sleep as
that, brought on without an opiate, would be worth more to
me than half my income; for it would suppose health and an
untroubled mind.'

'And youth, besides,' said the lady. 'Healthy and quiet age
does not sleep thus. Our slumber is no more like his than our
wakefulness.'

The longer they looked the more did this elderly couple
feel interested in the unknown youth, to whom the wayside
and the maple shade were as a secret chamber, with the rich
gloom of damask curtains brooding over him. Perceiving that

a stray sunbeam glimmered down upon his face, the lady contrived to twist a branch aside, so as to intercept it. And having done this little act of kindness, she began to feel like a mother to him.

'Providence seems to have laid him here,' whispered she to her husband, 'and to have brought us hither to find him, after our disappointment in our cousin's son. Methinks I can see a likeness to our departed Henry. Shall we waken him?'

'To what purpose?' said the merchant, hesitating. 'We know nothing of the youth's character.'

'That open countenance!' replied his wife, in the same hushed voice, yet earnestly. 'This innocent sleep!'

While these whispers were passing, the sleeper's heart did not throb, nor his breath become agitated, nor his features betray the least token of interest. Yet Fortune was bending over him, just ready to let fall a burden of gold. The old merchant had lost his only son, and had no heir to his wealth except a distant relative, with whose conduct he was dissatisfied. In such cases, people sometimes do stranger things than to act the magician, and awaken a young man to splendor who fell asleep in poverty.

'Shall we not waken him?' repeated the lady persuasively.

'The coach is ready, sir,' said the servant, behind.

The old couple started, reddened, and hurried away, mutually wondering that they should ever have dreamed of doing anything so very ridiculous. The merchant threw himself back in the carriage, and occupied his mind with the plan of a magnificent asylum for unfortunate men of business. Meanwhile, David Swan enjoyed his nap.

The carriage could not have gone above a mile or two, when a pretty young girl came along, with a tripping pace, which showed precisely how her little heart was dancing in her bosom. Perhaps it was this merry kind of motion that caused – is there any harm in saying it? – her garter to slip its knot. Conscious that the silken girth – if silk it were – was relaxing its hold, she turned aside into the shelter of the maple-trees, and there found a young man asleep by the spring! Blushing as red as any rose that she should have intruded into a gentleman's bedchamber, and for such a purpose, too, she was about to make her escape on tiptoe. But there was peril near the sleeper. A monster of a bee had been wandering over-head – buzz, buzz, buzz – now among the leaves, now flashing through the strips of sunshine, and now lost in the dark shade, till finally he appeared to be settling on the eyelid of David Swan. The sting of a bee is sometimes deadly. As free-hearted as she was innocent, the girl attacked the intruder with her handkerchief, brushed him soundly, and drove him from beneath the maple shade. How sweet a picture! This good deed accomplished, with quickened breath, and a deeper blush, she stole a glance at the youthful stranger for whom she had been battling with a dragon in the air.

'He is handsome!' thought she, and blushed redder yet.

How could it be that no dream of bliss grew so strong within him, that, shattered by its very strength, it should part asunder, and allow him to perceive the girl among its phan-toms? Why, at least, did no smile of welcome brighten upon his face? She was come, the maid whose soul, according to the old and beautiful idea, had been severed from his own, and whom, in all his vague but passionate desires, he yearned to meet. Her, only, could he love with a perfect love; him, only, could she receive into the depths of her heart; and now her image was faintly blushing in the fountain, by his side; should it pass away, its happy lustre would never gleam upon his life again.

'How sound he sleeps!' murmured the girl.

She departed, but did not trip along the road so lightly as when she came.

Now, this girl's father was a thriving country merchant in the neighborhood, and happened, at that identical time, to be looking out for just such a young man as David Swan. Had David formed a wayside acquaintance with the daughter, he would have become the father's clerk, and all else in natural succession. So here, again, had good fortune – the best of fortunes – stolen so near that her garments brushed against him; and he knew nothing of the matter.

The girl was hardly out of sight when two men turned aside beneath the maple shade. Both had dark faces, set off by cloth caps, which were drawn down aslant over their brows. Their dresses were shabby, yet had a certain smartness. These were a couple of rascals who got their living by whatever the devil sent them, and now, in the interim of other business, had staked the joint profits of their next piece of villany on a game of cards, which was to have been decided here under the trees. But, finding David asleep by the spring, one of the rogues whispered to his fellow, 'Hist! – Do you see that bundle under his head?'

The other villain nodded, winked, and leered.

'I'll bet you a horn of brandy,' said the first, 'that the chap has either a pocket-book, or a snug little hoard of small change, stowed away amongst his shirts. And if not there, we shall find it in his pantaloons pocket.'

'But how if he wakes?' said the other.

His companion thrust aside his waistcoat, pointed to the handle of a dirk, and nodded.

'So be it!' muttered the second villain.

They approached the unconscious David, and, while one pointed the dagger towards his heart, the other began to search the bundle beneath his head. Their two faces, grim, wrinkled, and ghastly with guilt and fear, bent over their victim, looking horrible enough to be mistaken for fiends, should he suddenly awake. Nay, had the villains glanced aside into the spring, even they would hardly have known themselves as reflected there. But David Swan had never worn a more tranquil aspect, even when asleep on his mother's breast.

'I must take away the bundle,' whispered one.

'If he stirs, I'll strike,' muttered the other.

But, at this moment, a dog scenting along the ground, came in beneath the maple-trees, and gazed alternately at each of these wicked men, and then at the quiet sleeper. He then lapped out of the fountain.

'Pshaw!' said one villain. 'We can do nothing now. The dog's master must be close behind.'

'Let's take a drink and be off,' said the other

The man with the dagger thrust back the weapon into his bosom, and drew forth a pocket pistol, but not of that kind which kills by a single discharge. It was a flask of liquor, with a block-tin tumbler screwed upon the mouth. Each drank a comfortable dram, and left the spot, with so many jests, and such laughter at their unaccomplished wickedness, that they might be said to have gone on their way rejoicing. In a few hours they had forgotten the whole affair, nor once imagined that the recording angel had written down the crime of murder against their souls, in letters as durable as eternity. As for David Swan, he still slept quietly, neither conscious of the shadow of death when it hung over him, nor of the glow of renewed life when that shadow was withdrawn.

He slept, but no longer so quietly as at first. An hour's repose had snatched, from his elastic frame, the weariness with which many hours of toil had burdened it. Now he stirred – now, moved his lips, without a sound – now, talked, in an inward tone, to the noonday spectres of his dream. But a noise of wheels came rattling louder and louder along the road, until it dashed through the dispersing mist of David's slumber and there was the stage-coach. He started up with all his ideas about him.

'Halloo, driver! – Take a passenger?' shouted he.

'Room on top!' answered the driver.

Up mounted David, and bowled away merrily towards Boston, without so much as a parting glance at that fountain of dreamlike vicissitude. He knew not that a phantom of Wealth had thrown a golden hue upon its waters – nor that one of Love had sighed softly to their murmur – nor that one of Death had threatened to crimson them with his blood – all, in the brief hour since he lay down to sleep. Sleeping or waking, we hear not the airy footsteps of the strange things that almost happen. Does it not argue a superintending Providence that, while viewless and unexpected events thrust themselves continually athwart our path, there should still be regularity enough in mortal life to render foresight even partially available?

THE ROAD NOT TAKEN
Robert Frost

Two roads diverged in a yellow wood,
And sorry I could not travel both
And be one traveler, long I stood
And looked down one as far as I could
To where it bent in the undergrowth;

Then took the other, as just as fair,
And having perhaps the better claim,
Because it was grassy and wanted wear;
Though as for that, the passing there
Had worn them really about the same,

And both that morning equally lay
In leaves no step had trodden black.
Oh, I kept the first for another day!
Yet knowing how way leads on to way,
I doubted if I should ever come back.

I shall be telling this with a sigh
Somewhere ages and ages hence:
Two roads diverged in a wood, and I –
I took the one less traveled by,
And that has made all the difference.

READING NOTES

This poem always gets people talking and speculating: if I had not gone to a friend's party that day, I would never have met . . . Or more generally: what if you always caught the bus to work but one day for no reason you decided to walk and that was the day the bus was bombed? People often say that the poem is about choices, yet what sort of choice can you make based on little or no evidence or facts? One ninety-year-old said she was interested in the poem's last line: 'And that has made all the difference' and the group wondered about that final word and what exactly it meant. 'That's what I like about it,' she said, 'you can never really know what the difference might have been but you can still think about the possibilities.'

The slightly archaic language of the story sometimes bothers people but there is always much discussion of the element of chance or 'Providence' in our lives. One group talked about angels, good and bad. 'The thing is,' said Roy, 'we just get up in the morning and set off. We don't know what is going to happen for good or ill or if we will get back into our bed at night. You can't stay in bed all day worrying about what might or might not happen.'

Unjust Life

🌿

EDWARD MILLS AND GEORGE BENTON:
A TALE
Mark Twain

(approximate reading time 16 minutes)

These two were distantly related to each other – seventh cousins, or something of that sort. While still babies they became orphans, and were adopted by the Brants, a childless couple, who quickly grew very fond of them. The Brants were always saying: 'Be pure, honest, sober, industrious, and considerate of others, and success in life is assured.' The children heard this repeated some thousands of times before they understood it; they could repeat it themselves long before they could say the Lord's Prayer; it was painted over the nursery door, and was about the first thing they learned to read. It was destined to be the unswerving rule of Edward Mills's life. Sometimes the Brants changed the wording a little, and said: 'Be pure, honest, sober, industrious, considerate, and you will never lack friends.'

Baby Mills was a comfort to everybody about him. When he wanted candy and could not have it, he listened to reason, and contented himself without it. When Baby Benton wanted candy, he cried for it until he got it. Baby Mills took care of his toys; Baby Benton always destroyed his in a very brief time, and then made himself so insistently disagreeable that, in order to have peace in the house, little Edward was persuaded to yield up his play-things to him.

When the children were a little older, Georgie became a heavy expense in one respect: he took no care of his clothes; consequently, he shone frequently in new ones, which was not the case with Eddie. The boys grew apace. Eddie was an increasing comfort, Georgie an increasing solicitude. It was always sufficient to say, in answer to Eddie's petitions, 'I would rather you would not do it' – meaning swimming, skating, picnicking, berrying, circusing, and all sorts of things which boys delight in. But NO answer was sufficient for Georgie; he had to be humored in his desires, or he would carry them with a high hand. Naturally, no boy got more swimming, skating, berrying, and so forth than he; no body ever had a better time. The good Brants did not allow the boys to play out after nine in summer evenings; they were sent to bed at that hour; Eddie honorably remained, but Georgie usually slipped out of the window toward ten, and enjoyed himself until midnight. It seemed impossible to break Georgie of this bad habit, but the Brants managed it at last by hiring him, with apples and marbles, to stay in. The good Brants gave all their time and attention to vain endeavors to regulate Georgie; they said, with grateful tears in their eyes, that Eddie needed no efforts of theirs, he was so good, so considerate, and in all ways so perfect.

By and by the boys were big enough to work, so they were

apprenticed to a trade: Edward went voluntarily; George was coaxed and bribed. Edward worked hard and faithfully, and ceased to be an expense to the good Brants; they praised him, so did his master; but George ran away, and it cost Mr Brant both money and trouble to hunt him up and get him back. By and by he ran away again – more money and more trouble. He ran away a third time – and stole a few things to carry with him. Trouble and expense for Mr Brant once more; and, besides, it was with the greatest difficulty that he succeeded in persuading the master to let the youth go unprosecuted for the theft.

Edward worked steadily along, and in time became a full partner in his master's business. George did not improve; he kept the loving hearts of his aged benefactors full of trouble, and their hands full of inventive activities to protect him from ruin. Edward, as a boy, had interested himself in Sunday-schools, debating societies, penny missionary affairs, anti-tobacco organizations, anti-profanity associations, and all such things; as a man, he was a quiet but steady and reliable helper in the church, the temperance societies, and in all movements looking to the aiding and uplifting of men. This excited no remark, attracted no attention – for it was his 'natural bent.'

Finally, the old people died. The will testified their loving pride in Edward, and left their little property to George – because he 'needed it'; whereas, 'owing to a bountiful Providence,' such was not the case with Edward. The property was left to George conditionally: he must buy out Edward's partner with it; else it must go to a benevolent organization called the Prisoner's Friend Society. The old people left a letter, in which they begged their dear son Edward to take their place and watch over George, and help and shield him as they had done.

Edward dutifully acquiesced, and George became his partner in the business. He was not a valuable partner: he had been meddling with drink before; he soon developed into a constant tippler now, and his flesh and eyes showed the fact unpleasantly. Edward had been courting a sweet and kindly spirited girl for some time. They loved each other dearly, and . . . But about this period George began to haunt her tearfully and imploringly, and at last she went crying to Edward, and said her high and holy duty was plain before her – she must not let her own selfish desires interfere with it: she must marry 'poor George' and 'reform him.' It would break her heart, she knew it would, and so on; but duty was duty. So she married George, and Edward's heart came very near breaking, as well as her own. However, Edward recovered, and married another girl – a very excellent one she was, too.

Children came to both families. Mary did her honest best to reform her husband, but the contract was too large. George went on drinking, and by and by he fell to misusing her and the little ones sadly. A great many good people strove with George – they were always at it, in fact – but he calmly took such efforts as his due and their duty, and did not mend his ways. He added a vice, presently – that of secret gambling. He got deeply in debt; he borrowed money on the firm's credit, as quietly as he could, and carried this system so far and so successfully that one morning the sheriff took possession of the establishment, and the two cousins found themselves penniless.

Times were hard, now, and they grew worse. Edward moved his family into a garret, and walked the streets day and night, seeking work. He begged for it, but it was really not to be had. He was astonished to see how soon his face became unwelcome; he was astonished and hurt to see how quickly the ancient interest which people had had in him faded out and disappeared. Still, he MUST get work; so he swallowed his chagrin, and toiled on in search of it. At last he got a job of carrying bricks up a ladder in a hod, and was a grateful man in consequence; but after that NOBODY knew him or cared anything about him. He was not able to keep up his dues in the various moral organizations to which he belonged, and had to endure the sharp pain of seeing himself brought under the disgrace of suspension.

But the faster Edward died out of public knowledge and interest, the faster George rose in them. He was found lying, ragged and drunk, in the gutter one morning. A member of the Ladies' Temperance Refuge fished him out, took him in hand, got up a subscription for him, kept him sober a whole week, then got a situation for him. An account of it was published.

General attention was thus drawn to the poor fellow, and a great many people came forward and helped him toward reform with their countenance and encouragement. He did not drink a drop for two months, and meantime was the pet of the good. Then he fell – in the gutter; and there was general sorrow and lamentation. But the noble sisterhood rescued him again. They cleaned him up, they fed him, they listened to the mournful music of his repentances, they got him his situation again. An account of this, also, was published, and the town was drowned in happy tears over the re-restoration of the poor beast and struggling victim of the fatal bowl. A grand temperance revival was got up, and after some rousing speeches had been made the chairman said, impressively: 'We are not about to call for signers; and I think there is a spectacle in store for you which not many in this house will be able to view with dry eyes.' There was an eloquent pause, and then George Benton, escorted by a red-sashed detachment of the Ladies of the Refuge, stepped forward upon the platform and signed the pledge. The air was rent with applause, and everybody cried for joy. Everybody wrung the hand of the new convert when the meeting was over; his salary was enlarged next day; he was the talk of the town, and its hero. An account of it was published.

George Benton fell, regularly, every three months, but was faithfully rescued and wrought with, every time, and good situations were found for him. Finally, he was taken around the country lecturing, as a reformed drunkard, and he had great houses and did an immense amount of good.

He was so popular at home, and so trusted – during his sober intervals – that he was enabled to use the name of a principal citizen, and get a large sum of money at the bank. A mighty pressure was brought to bear to save him from the consequences of his forgery, and it was partially successful – he was 'sent up' for only two years. When, at the end of a year, the tireless efforts of the benevolent were crowned with success, and he emerged from the penitentiary with a pardon in his pocket, the Prisoner's Friend Society met him at the door with a situation and a comfortable salary, and all the other benevolent people came forward and gave him advice, encouragement and help. Edward Mills had once applied to the Prisoner's Friend Society for a situation, when in dire need, but the question, 'Have you been a prisoner?' made brief work of his case.

While all these things were going on, Edward Mills had been quietly making head against adversity. He was still poor, but was in receipt of a steady and sufficient salary, as the respected and trusted cashier of a bank. George Benton never came near him, and was never heard to inquire about him. George got to indulging in long absences from the town; there were ill reports about him, but nothing definite.

One winter's night some masked burglars forced their way into the bank, and found Edward Mills there alone. They commanded him to reveal the 'combination,' so that they could get into the safe. He refused. They threatened his life. He said his employers trusted him, and he could not be traitor to that trust. He could die, if he must, but while he lived he would be faithful; he would not yield up the 'combination.' The burglars killed him.

The detectives hunted down the criminals; the chief one proved to be George Benton. A wide sympathy was felt for the widow and orphans of the dead man, and all the newspapers in the land begged that all the banks in the land would testify their appreciation of the fidelity and heroism of the murdered cashier by coming forward with a generous contribution of money in aid of his family, now bereft of support. The result was a mass of solid cash amounting to upward of five hundred dollars – an average of nearly three-eights of a cent for each bank in the Union. The cashier's own bank testified its gratitude by endeavoring to show (but humiliatingly failed in it) that the peerless servant's accounts were not square, and that he himself had knocked his brains out with a bludgeon to escape detection and punishment.

George Benton was arraigned for trial. Then everybody seemed to forget the widow and orphans in their solicitude for poor George. Everything that money and influence could do was done to save him, but it all failed; he was sentenced to death. Straightway the Governor was besieged with petitions for commutation or pardon; they were brought by tearful young girls; by sorrowful old maids; by deputations of pathetic widows; by shoals of impressive orphans. But no, the Governor – for once – would not yield.

Now George Benton experienced religion. The glad news flew all around. From that time forth his cell was always full of girls and women and fresh flowers; all the day long there was prayer, and hymn-singing, and thanksgiving, and homilies, and tears, with never an interruption, except an occasional five-minute intermission for refreshments.

This sort of thing continued up to the very gallows, and George Benton went proudly home, in the black cap, before a wailing audience of the sweetest and best that the region could produce. His grave had fresh flowers on it every day, for a while, and the head-stone bore these words, under a hand pointing aloft: 'He has fought the good fight.'

The brave cashier's head-stone has this inscription: 'Be pure, honest, sober, industrious, considerate, and you will never—'

Nobody knows who gave the order to leave it that way, but it was so given.

The cashier's family are in stringent circumstances, now, it is said; but no matter; a lot of appreciative people, who were not willing that an act so brave and true as his should go unrewarded, have collected forty-two thousand dollars – and built a Memorial Church with it.

THOU ART INDEED JUST, LORD, IF I CONTEND

Gerard Manley Hopkins

Justus quidem tu es, Domine, si disputem tecum:
verumtamen justa loquar ad te: Quare via impiorum
prosperatur? &c.

Thou art indeed just, Lord, if I contend
With thee; but, sir, so what I plead is just.
Why do sinners' ways prosper? and why must
Disappointment all I endeavour end?

Wert thou my enemy, O thou my friend,
How wouldst thou worse, I wonder, than thou dost
Defeat, thwart me? Oh, the sots and thralls of lust
Do in spare hours more thrive than I that spend,

Sir, life upon thy cause. See, banks and brakes
Now, leavèd how thick! lacèd they are again
With fretty chervil, look, and fresh wind shakes

Them; birds build – but not I build; no, but strain,
Time's eunuch, and not breed one work that wakes.
Mine, O thou lord of life, send my roots rain.

READING NOTES

Puzzling over the meaning of the poem, two women in a women's centre reading group found authenticity in the speaker's voice. 'That pain sounds real to me,' said Jo. 'I can't understand a lot of it, but when he says, "send my roots rain", that's a real cry from the heart; I know what that state of mind feels like.' Each member of the group looked for phrases they understood – some from experience. Then they each picked out a phrase they found particularly difficult. Working on the difficulties together was like unpicking knots in string and gradually quite a few straight inches were gained. Two big questions prompted much debate, if no final answers: Why do sinners' ways prosper? Why does God sometimes seem to treat humanity as if he were our enemy?

The group decided that the story was meant to sound like a morality tale; the characters were not exactly real but the questions the story raised were real questions: Why are bad people sometimes rewarded? Why do bad things happen to very good people? Jo told the group that her aunt had been badly burgled and one of the things that most upset her was that when the case came to court, it seemed as if the criminal was better looked after than the victim.

How much truth do you think there is in the Mark Twain story? Was it wrong of the Brants to teach the boys: 'Be pure, honest, sober, industrious, and considerate of others, and *success* in life is assured'? Should life be fair? The questions could go on and on.

Courage and Endeavour

❧

MY LEFT FOOT

(THE LETTER 'A', CHAPTER 1)

Christy Brown

(approximate reading time 17 minutes)

*Irish author, poet and painter, Christy Brown was born in 1932
with cerebral palsy.* My Left Foot *is his autobiography.*

I was born in the Rotunda Hospital, on June 5th, 1932.
There were nine children before me and twelve after me, so
I myself belong to the middle group. Out of this total of
twenty-two, seventeen lived, four died in infancy, leaving thir-
teen still to hold the family fort.

Mine was a difficult birth, I am told. Both mother and son
almost died. A whole army of relations queued up outside the
hospital until the small hours of the morning, waiting for
news and praying furiously that it would be good.

After my birth mother was sent to recuperate for some weeks
and I was kept in the hospital while she was away. I remained
there for some time, without name, for I wasn't baptised until
my mother was well enough to bring me to church.

It was mother who first saw that there was something wrong with me. I was about four months old at the time. She noticed that my head had a habit of falling backwards whenever she tried to feed me. She attempted to correct this by placing her hand on the back of my neck to keep it steady. But when she took it away back it would drop again. That was the first warning sign. Then she became aware of other defects as I got older. She saw that my hands were clenched nearly all of the time and were inclined to twine behind my back; my mouth couldn't grasp the teat of the bottle because even at that early age my jaws would either lock together tightly, so that it was impossible for her to open them, or they would suddenly become limp and fall loose, dragging my whole mouth to one side. At six months I could not sit up without having a mountain of pillows around me; at twelve months it was the same.

Very worried by this, mother told my father her fears, and they decided to seek medical advice without any further delay. I was a little over a year old when they began to take me to hospitals and clinics, convinced that there was something definitely wrong with me, something which they could not understand or name, but which was very real and disturbing.

Almost every doctor who saw and examined me, labelled me a very interesting but also a hopeless case. Many told mother very gently that I was mentally defective and would remain so. That was a hard blow to a young mother who had already reared five healthy children. The doctors were so very sure of themselves that mother's faith in me seemed almost an impertinence. They assured her that nothing could be done for me.

She refused to accept this truth, the inevitable truth – as it then seemed – that I was beyond cure, beyond saving, even beyond hope. She could not and would not believe that I was an imbecile, as the doctors told her. She had nothing in the world to go by, not a scrap of evidence to support her conviction that, though my body was crippled, my mind was not. In spite of all the doctors and specialists told her, she would not agree. I don't believe she knew why – she just knew without feeling the smallest shade of doubt.

Finding that the doctors could not help in any way beyond telling her not to place her trust in me, or, in other words, to forget I was a human creature, rather to regard me as just something to be fed and washed and then put away again, mother decided there and then to take matters into her own hands. I was *her* child, and therefore part of the family. No matter how dull and incapable I might grow up to be, she was determined to treat me on the same plane as the others, and not as the 'queer one' in the back room who was never spoken of when there were visitors present.

That was a momentous decision as far as my future life was concerned. It meant that I would always have my mother on my side to help me fight all the battles that were to come, and to inspire me with new strength when I was almost beaten. But it wasn't easy for her because now the relatives and friends had decided otherwise. They contended that I should be taken kindly, sympathetically, but not seriously. That would be a mistake. 'For your own sake,' they told her, 'don't look to this boy as you would to the others; it would only break your heart in the end.' Luckily for me, mother and father held out against the lot of them. But mother wasn't content just to say that I was not an idiot, she set out to prove it, not because of any rigid sense of duty, but out of love. That is why she was so successful.

At this time she had the five other children to look after besides the 'difficult one', though as yet it was not by any means a full house. There were my brothers, Jim, Tony and Paddy, and my two sisters, Lily and Mona, all of them very young, just a year or so between each of them, so that they were almost exactly like steps of stairs.

Four years rolled by and I was now five, and still as help-less as a newly born baby. While my father was out at brick-laying earning our bread and butter for us, mother was slowly, patiently pulling down the wall, brick by brick, that seemed to thrust itself between me and the other children, slowly, patiently penetrating beyond the thick curtain that hung over my mind, separating it from theirs. It was hard, heart-breaking work, for often all she got from me in return was a vague smile and perhaps a faint gurgle. I could not speak or even mumble, nor could I sit up without support on my own, let alone take steps. But I wasn't inert or motionless. I seemed indeed to be convulsed with movement, wild, stiff, snake-like movement that never left me, except in sleep. My fingers twisted and twitched continually, my arms twined backwards and would often shoot out suddenly this way and that, and my head lolled and sagged sideways. I was a queer, crooked little fellow.

Mother tells me how one day she had been sitting with me for hours in an upstairs room, showing me pictures out of a great big storybook that I had got from Santa Claus last Christmas and telling me the names of the different animals and flowers that were in them, trying without success to get me to repeat them. This had gone on for hours while she talked and laughed with me. Then at the end of it she leaned over me and said gently into my ear:

'Did you like it, Chris? Did you like the bears and the monkeys and all the lovely flowers? Nod your head for yes, like a good boy.'

But I could make no sign that I had understood her. Her face was bent over mine, hopefully. Suddenly, involuntarily, my queer hand reached up and grasped one of the dark curls that fell in a thick cluster about her neck. Gently she loosened the clenched fingers, though some dark strands were still clutched between them.

Then she turned away from my curious stare and left the room, crying. The door closed behind her. It all seemed hopeless. It looked as though there was some justification for my relatives' contention that I was an idiot and beyond help.

They now spoke of an institution.

'Never!' said my mother almost fiercely, when this was suggested to her. 'I know my boy is not an idiot. It is his body that is shattered, not his mind. I'm sure of that.'

Sure? Yet inwardly, she prayed God would give her some proof of her faith. She knew it was one thing to believe but quite another thing to prove.

I was now five, and still I showed no real sign of intelligence. I showed no apparent interest in things except with my toes – more especially those of my left foot. Although my natural habits were clean I could not aid myself, but in this respect my father took care of me. I used to lie on my back all the time in the kitchen or, on bright warm days, out in the garden, a little bundle of crooked muscles and twisted nerves, surrounded by a family that loved me and hoped for me and that made me part of their own warmth and humanity. I was lonely, imprisoned in a world of my own, unable to communicate with others, cut off, separated from them as though a glass wall stood between my existence and theirs, thrusting me beyond the sphere of their lives and activities. I longed to run about and play with the rest, but I was unable to break loose from my bondage.

Then, suddenly, it happened! In a moment everything was changed, my future life moulded into a definite shape, my mother's faith in me rewarded and her secret fear changed into open triumph.

It happened so quickly, so simply after all the years of waiting and uncertainty that I can see and feel the whole scene as if it had happened last week. It was the afternoon of a cold, grey December day. The streets outside glistened with snow; the white sparkling flakes stuck and melted on the window-panes and hung on the boughs of the trees like molten silver. The wind howled dismally, whipping up little whirling columns of snow that rose and fell at every fresh gust. And over all, the dull, murky sky stretched like a dark canopy, a vast infinity of greyness.

Inside, all the family were gathered round the big kitchen fire that lit up the little room with a warm glow and made giant shadows dance on the walls and ceiling.

In a corner Mona and Paddy were sitting huddled together, a few torn school primers before them. They were writing down little sums on to an old chipped slate, using a bright piece of yellow chalk. I was close to them, propped up by a few pillows against the wall, watching.

It was the chalk that attracted me so much. It was a long, slender stick of vivid yellow. I had never seen anything like it before, and it showed up so well against the black surface of the slate that I was fascinated by it as much as if it had been a stick of gold.

Suddenly I wanted desperately to do what my sister was doing. Then – without thinking or knowing exactly what I was doing, I reached out and took the stick of chalk out of my sister's hand – *with my left foot.*

I do not know why I used my left foot to do this. It is a puzzle to many people as well as to myself, for, although I had displayed a curious interest in my toes at an early age, I had never attempted before this to use either of my feet in any way. They could have been as useless to me as were my hands. That day, however, my left foot, apparently on its own volition, reached out and very impolitely took the chalk out of my sister's hand.

I held it tightly between my toes, and, acting on an impulse, made a wild sort of scribble with it on the slate. Next moment I stopped, a bit dazed, surprised, looking down at the stick of yellow chalk stuck between my toes, not knowing what to do with it next, hardly knowing how it got there. Then I looked up and became aware that everyone had stopped talking and were staring at me silently. Nobody stirred. Mona, her black curls framing her chubby little face, stared at me with great big eyes and open mouth. Across the open hearth, his face lit by flames, sat my father, leaning forward, hands outspread on his knees, his shoulders tense. I felt the sweat break out on my forehead.

My mother came in from the pantry with a steaming pot in her hand. She stopped midway between the table and the fire, feeling the tension flowing through the room. She followed their stare and saw me, in the corner. Her eyes looked from my face down to my foot, with the chalk gripped between my toes. She put down the pot.

Then she crossed over to me and knelt down beside me, as she had done so many times before.

'I'll show you what to do with it, Chris,' she said, very slowly and in a queer, jerky way, her face flushed as if with some inner excitement.

Taking another piece of chalk from Mona, she hesitated, then very deliberately drew, on the floor in front of me, *the single letter 'A'.*

'Copy that,' she said, looking steadily at me. 'Copy it, Christy.'

I couldn't.

I looked about me, looked around at the faces that were turned towards me, tense, excited faces that were at that moment frozen, immobile, eager, waiting for a miracle in their midst.

The stillness was profound. The room was full of flame and shadow that danced before my eyes and lulled my taut nerves into a sort of waking sleep. I could hear the sound of the water-tap dripping in the pantry, the loud ticking of the

clock on the mantelshelf, and the soft hiss and crackle of the
logs on the open hearth.

I tried again. I put out my foot and made a wild jerking
stab with the chalk which produced a very crooked line and
nothing more. Mother held the slate steady for me.

'Try again, Chris,' she whispered in my ear. 'Again.'

I did. I stiffened my body and put my left foot out again,
for the third time. I drew one side of the letter. I drew half
the other side. Then the stick of chalk broke and I was left
with a stump. I wanted to fling it away and give up. Then I
felt my mother's hand on my shoulder. I tried once more. Out
went my foot. I shook, I sweated and strained every muscle.
My hands were so tightly clenched that my fingernails bit into
the flesh. I set my teeth so hard that I nearly pierced my lower
lip. Everything in the room swam till the faces around me
were mere patches of white. But – I drew it – *the letter 'A'.*
There it was on the floor before me. Shaky, with awkward,

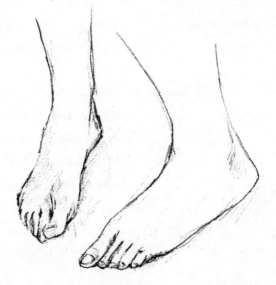

wobbly sides and a very uneven centre line. But it *was* the letter 'A'. I looked up. I saw my mother's face for a moment, tears on her cheeks. Then my father stooped down and hoisted me on to his shoulder.

I had done it! It had started – the thing that was to give my mind its chance of expressing itself. True, I couldn't speak with my lips, but now I would speak through something more lasting than spoken words – written words.

That one letter, scrawled on the floor with a broken bit of yellow chalk gripped between my toes, was my road to a new world, my key to mental freedom. It was to provide a source of relaxation to the tense, taut thing that was me which panted for expression behind a twisted mouth.

A NOISELESS PATIENT SPIDER
Walt Whitman

A noiseless patient spider,
I mark'd where on a little promontory it stood isolated;
Mark'd how to explore the vacant, vast surrounding,
It launched forth filament, filament, filament, out of
    itself,
Ever unreeling them, ever tirelessly speeding them.

And you O my Soul where you stand,
Surrounded, detached, in measureless oceans of space,
Ceaselessly musing, venturing, throwing, seeking the
    spheres to connect them,
Till the bridge you will need, be form'd, till the ductile
    anchor hold,
Till the gossamer thread you fling catch somewhere, O
    my Soul.

READING NOTES

Several members of a community reading group had seen the film
of the book with Daniel Day-Lewis playing Christy Brown and
talked briefly about that performance. David told us that his
brother had cerebral palsy. He spoke proudly about his brother's
achievements but confirmed how hard it had been for his parents
and indeed for the whole family. Everyone was moved by the
chapter and had nothing but praise for the mother. 'There are
times', said Patricia, 'when you need a strength that seems beyond
you and somehow you find it, like faith. Christy Brown's mother,'
she added, 'had nothing except faith and fierce love; this, not the
disability, is his inheritance.'

Coming after the powerful memoir, the poem takes on a special
resonance and prompts talk about the connections with the story
and about what the last words 'O my soul', might mean. Indeed,
how do you define the word soul? Some readers have remembered the story of Robert Bruce and the spider: how Bruce took
heart from the spider's refusal to give up trying. This is perhaps
another way of linking the poem to the story.

Theirs Not to Reason Why

🍃

BLACK BEAUTY

(AN OLD WAR HORSE, CHAPTER 34)

Anna Sewell

(approximate reading time 11 minutes)

This famous story, which was not originally written for children, is the autobiography of a horse. At this point in his life Black Beauty is sharing a stable with an old stallion who is a veteran of the Crimean War and the Charge of the Light Brigade . . .

Captain had been broken in and trained for an army horse; his first owner was an officer of cavalry going out to the Crimean War. He said he quite enjoyed the training with all the other horses, trotting together, turning together, to the right hand or the left, halting at the word of command, or dashing forward at full speed at the sound of the trumpet or signal of the officer. He was, when young, a dark, dappled iron grey, and considered very handsome. His master, a young, high-spirited gentleman, was very fond of him, and treated him from the first with the greatest care and kindness. He told me he thought the life of an army horse was very pleasant; but when it came to being sent abroad over the sea in a great ship, he almost changed his mind.

'That part of it,' said he, 'was dreadful! Of course we could not walk off the land into the ship; so they were obliged to put strong straps under our bodies, and then we were lifted off our legs in spite of our struggles, and were swung through the air over the water, to the deck of the great vessel. There we were placed in small close stalls, and never for a long time saw the sky, or were able to stretch our legs. The ship sometimes rolled about in high winds, and we were knocked about, and felt bad enough. However, at last it came to an end, and we were hauled up, and swung over again to the land; we were very glad, and snorted and neighed for joy, when we once more felt firm ground under our feet.

'We soon found that the country we had come to was very different from our own and that we had many hardships to endure besides the fighting; but many of the men were so fond of their horses that they did everything they could to make them comfortable in spite of snow, wet, and all things out of order.'

'But what about the fighting?' said I, 'was not that worse than anything else?'

'Well,' said he, 'I hardly know; we always liked to hear the trumpet sound, and to be called out, and were impatient to start off, though sometimes we had to stand for hours, waiting for the word of command; and when the word was given we used to spring forward as gayly and eagerly as if there were no cannon balls, bayonets, or bullets. I believe so long as we felt our rider firm in the saddle, and his hand steady on the bridle, not one of us gave way to fear, not even when the terrible bomb-shells whirled through the air and burst into a thousand pieces.

'I, with my noble master, went into many actions together without a wound; and though I saw horses shot down with bullets, pierced through with lances, and gashed with fearful sabre-cuts; though we left them dead on the field, or dying in the agony of their wounds, I don't think I feared for myself. My master's cheery voice, as he encouraged his men, made me feel as if he and I could not be killed. I had such perfect trust in him that while he was guiding me I was ready to charge up to the very cannon's mouth. I saw many brave men cut down, many fall mortally wounded from their saddles. I had heard the cries and groans of the dying, I had cantered over ground slippery with blood, and frequently had to turn aside to avoid trampling on wounded man or horse, but, until one dreadful day, I had never felt terror; that day I shall never forget.'

Here old Captain paused for awhile and drew a long breath; I waited, and he went on.

'It was one autumn morning, and as usual, an hour before daybreak our cavalry had turned out, ready caparisoned for the day's work, whether it might be fighting or waiting. The men stood by their horses waiting, ready for orders. As the light increased there seemed to be some excitement among the officers; and before the day was well begun we heard the firing of the enemy's guns.

'Then one of the officers rode up and gave the word for

the men to mount, and in a second every man was in his saddle, and every horse stood expecting the touch of the rein, or the pressure of his rider's heels, all animated, all eager; but still we had been trained so well that, except by the champing of our bits, and the restive tossing of our heads from time to time, it could not be said that we stirred.

'My dear master and I were at the head of the line, and as all sat motionless and watchful, he took a little stray lock of my mane which had turned over on the wrong side, laid it over on the right, and smoothed it down with his hand; then patting my neck, he said, 'We shall have a day of it to-day, Bayard, my beauty; but we'll do our duty as we have done.' He stroked my neck that morning more, I think, than he had ever done before; quietly on and on, as if he were thinking of something else. I loved to feel his hand on my neck, and arched my crest proudly and happily; but I stood very still, for I knew all his moods, and when he liked me to be quiet, and when gay.

'I cannot tell all that happened on that day, but I will tell of the last charge that we made together; it was across a valley right in front of the enemy's cannon. By this time we were well used to the roar of heavy guns, the rattle of musket fire, and the flying of shot near us; but never had I been under such a fire as we rode through on that day. From the right, from the left, and from the front, shot and shell poured in upon us. Many a brave man went down, many a horse fell, flinging his rider to the earth; many a horse without a rider ran wildly out of the ranks; then terrified at being alone, with no hand to guide him, came pressing in among his old companions, to gallop with them to the charge.

'Fearful as it was, no one stopped, no one turned back. Every moment the ranks were thinned, but as our comrades fell, we closed in to keep them together; and instead of being shaken or staggered in our pace our gallop became faster and faster as we neared the cannon.

'My master, my dear master! was cheering on his comrades with his right arm raised on high, when one of the balls whizzing close to my head struck him. I felt him stagger with the shock, though he uttered no cry; I tried to check my speed, but the sword dropped from his right hand, the rein fell loose from the left, and sinking backward from the saddle he fell to the earth; the other riders swept past us, and by the force of their charge I was driven from the spot where he fell.

'I wanted to keep my place by his side and not leave him under that rush of horses' feet, but it was in vain; and now without a master or a friend I was alone on that great slaughter ground; then fear took hold on me, and I trembled as I had never trembled before; and I too, as I had seen other horses do, tried to join in the ranks and gallop with them; but I was beaten off by the swords of the soldiers. Just then a soldier whose horse had been killed under him caught at my bridle and mounted me, and with this new master I was again going forward; but our gallant company was cruelly overpowered, and those who remained alive after the fierce fight for the guns came galloping back over the same ground. Some of the horses had been so badly wounded that they could scarcely move from the loss of blood; other noble creatures were trying on three legs to drag themselves along, and others were struggling to rise on their fore feet, when their hind legs had been shattered by shot. After the battle the wounded men were brought in and the dead were buried.'

'And what about the wounded horses?' I said; 'were they left to die?'

'No, the army farriers went over the field with their pistols and shot all that were ruined; some that had only slight wounds were brought back and attended to, but the greater part of the noble, willing creatures that went out that morning never came back! In our stables there was only about one in four that returned.

'I never saw my dear master again. I believe he fell dead from the saddle. I never loved any other master so well. I went into many other engagements, but was only once wounded, and then not seriously; and when the war was over I came back again to England, as sound and strong as when I went out.'

I said, 'I have heard people talk about war as if it was a very fine thing.'

'Ah!' said he, 'I should think they never saw it. No doubt it is very fine when there is no enemy, when it is just exercise and parade and sham fight. Yes, it is very fine then; but when thousands of good brave men and horses are killed or crippled for life, it has a very different look.'

'Do you know what they fought about?' said I.

'No,' he said, 'that is more than a horse can understand, but the enemy must have been awfully wicked people, if it was right to go all that way over the sea on purpose to kill them.'

THE CHARGE OF THE LIGHT BRIGADE
Alfred Tennyson

Half a league, half a league,
Half a league onward,
All in the valley of Death
    Rode the six hundred.
    'Forward, the Light Brigade!
Charge for the guns!' he said;
Into the valley of Death
    Rode the six hundred.

'Forward, the Light Brigade!'
Was there a man dismayed?
Not though the soldier knew
    Some one had blundered:
Their's not to make reply,
Their's not to reason why,
Their's but to do and die:
Into the valley of Death
    Rode the six hundred.

Cannon to right of them,
Cannon to left of them,
Cannon in front of them
    Volleyed and thundered;
Stormed at with shot and shell,
Boldly they rode and well,
Into the jaws of Death,

Into the mouth of Hell
    Rode the six hundred.

Flashed all their sabres bare,
Flashed as they turned in air
Sabring the gunners there,
Charging an army, while
    All the world wondered:
Plunged in the battery-smoke
Right through the line they broke;
Cossack and Russian
Reeled from the sabre-stroke
    Shattered and sundered.
Then they rode back, but not,
    Not the six hundred.

Cannon to right of them,
Cannon to left of them,
Cannon behind them
    Volleyed and thundered;
Stormed at with shot and shell,
While horse and hero fell,
They that had fought so well
Came through the jaws of Death,
Back from the mouth of Hell,
All that was left of them,
    Left of six hundred.

When can their glory fade?
O the wild charge they made!
All the world wondered.
Honour the charge they made!
Honour the Light Brigade,
Noble six hundred!

READING NOTES

In a day centre for the elderly, most of the group remembered *Black Beauty* from childhood. Discussion ranged from Florence Nightingale to the horror of horses in battle, to memories of going riding. The group thought it was a good anti-war story and were particularly struck by the final few lines: 'Do you know what they fought about?' said I. 'No,' he said, 'that is more than a horse can understand, but the enemy must have been awfully wicked people, if it was right to go all that way over the sea on purpose to kill them.'

Although not many group members remembered any historical details of the actual Charge of the Light Brigade, they found the poem very descriptive and the session finished with everyone reading the poem aloud and together, making quite a din.

Men Were Deceivers Ever

THE HANDBAG
Dorothy Whipple

(approximate reading time 19 minutes)

Mrs West had been alone for the weekend, but there was nothing new in that. William was often away. He didn't tell her where he was going and she would not ask. He merely said he wouldn't be at home on Tuesday, or Wednesday, or at the weekend, or whenever it was.

But Mrs West generally managed to find out where he had gone by going through the papers in his desk. He meant to keep the desk locked, but he often forgot and his wife took every advantage of that.

William had plenty of opportunity of getting away. He was a Councillor; probably he would shortly be an Alderman, the youngest Alderman, and probably, too, the Leader of his Party. He was very anxious to secure these honours and his wife knew he was being careful to keep in with everybody.

As a Councillor and a member of the Health, Education, Gas and other committees, William attended many Conferences. His wife used to go with him and she enjoyed them very much. They were always held at such pleasant places, at

Brighton, Harrogate, Bournemouth for instance, and they stayed at the best hotels. The Corporation paid William's first-class expenses and he used to manage to make those do for the both of them.

That was all over now. William first took to making excuses for not taking her, then he went without her without making excuses, and now he did not even tell her when or where he was going. The higher William rose in public life, the further he pushed her into the background.

She had discovered lately that he was making her out to be an invalid. People stopped her in the street to ask with sympathy how she was.

'Such a pity you weren't well enough to come to the Ball the other night,' someone would say, and Mrs West was obliged to smile and accept her imaginary illness because she would not let it be known that William had never told her about the Ball.

Dinners, luncheons, receptions, prize-distributions, William went to them all without her. She knew nothing of them until she saw an account of them in the paper, with Councillor William West prominently mentioned, or until such time as she found the desk unlocked and went through the discarded invitations. All of them were inscribed for Councillor and Mrs West, yet he never told her of them and she was too proud to charge him with them.

She didn't know precisely why he behaved in this way. She thought there must be several reasons. William had always been a vain man, but the older he got the vainer he became. He was forty-eight – she was the same age, but looked older

– he was handsome in a dark, increasingly florid way and he fancied himself considerably on a platform. He liked to show off, but not before his wife. He felt she judged him. She cramped his style, she knew when he was not telling the truth. He felt freer without her.

Mrs West also surmised that William was ashamed of her. She was plain, she had no taste in dress. She had done her own housework and economised for years, though they had maids and were prosperous now. There were no frills about her, she admitted, but she had made William very comfortable and had borne with his exacting, uncertain, often foolish behaviour for more than twenty years. She surmised, shrewdly, that William valued his comfortable home, his good food, but no longer wished to be seen about with the one who secured these things for him. He was ashamed of her. She wasn't smart enough for him.

If she had been Mrs Wintersley, now, it would have been different, thought Mrs West, sitting alone over the weekend. Mrs Wintersley was a youngish widow who had lately entered public affairs and taken her place on the Council. Mrs Wintersley was smart, there was no doubt about that. She had made quite a commotion on the Council and was in enormous demand at public functions: Prize Distributions, Women's Luncheon Clubs, the openings of schools, bazaars and so on.

Mrs West had seen Mrs Wintersley many a time, though Mrs Wintersley did not know who she was. Mrs Wintersley would probably have been astonished, thought Mrs West, to discover that the plain little woman sitting at the next table at the Rosebowl Tea Rooms the other day was the wife of the resplendent William West.

Mrs Wintersley had heard Mrs West's voice, because Mrs West often answered the telephone when Mrs Wintersley rang William up. Mrs Wintersley was always ringing William up. Mrs West supposed it was all right; they were both on the Council.

At the Rosebowl Tea Rooms, Mrs West had enjoyed her obscurity and had taken the opportunity of observing Mrs Wintersley very closely. She didn't like her, she decided. She was very well dressed and very well made-up, but she had a hard mouth and restless eyes, eyes always seeking for an audience. A person, Mrs West concluded, who could not live without limelight. She was afraid William was also like that.

Mrs Wintersley, when Mrs West had seen her before, had generally been in black, but on this particular afternoon she wore becoming blue-green tweeds. Everything about her toilet was carefully chosen as usual and Mrs West noticed that even her handbag exactly matched her suit. It was made of the same blue-green tweed and as it lay on the table while Mrs Wintersley had tea, Mrs West observed it, as she observed everything else about Mrs Wintersley.

Going through William's desk in his absence over the weekend, Mrs West had come upon an invitation for Tuesday evening to the Speech Day at the Girls' Grammar School. The Address and the Prizes, the paste-board announced, would be given by Councillor Mrs Wintersley and the invitation was inscribed as usual: 'Councillor and Mrs West. Platform.'

At the beginning of William's public career, Mrs West had

often been asked to give prizes and she had managed, she thought, rather well. At any rate, William used to congratulate her in those days, when they were both new to the platform together. But of course, Mrs West thought diffidently, William had left her far behind long ago.

The invitation was for Tuesday and it was Tuesday now. On the previous day William had returned from wherever it was he had been; Mrs West had not been able to find out where this was, since there was no reference to any conference in his desk.

William was now seated at the breakfast table, buried behind the paper. Mrs West had finished breakfast and was just about to leave the table when the maid brought in the morning post. William lowered the paper long enough to see that there was nothing for him before disappearing behind it again. For Mrs West, however, there was a parcel. She wondered what it could be. She rarely received parcels unless she sent for something from the London shops. Holding the parcel on her knee, out of the way of the breakfast things, she undid the wrappings.

Within them lay, of all unexpected things, a green tweed bag.

Mrs West stared uncomprehendingly. A green tweed bag?

Then, glancing towards William and observing that he was still buried behind the paper and had seen nothing, Mrs West bundled the bag back into its wrappings and took it swiftly out of the room. She hurried upstairs, stumbling in her haste, and gained her bedroom. Locking the door, she tumbled the bag from its wrappings again. There was a letter with it. With shaking fingers she drew the sheet of notepaper from the envelope. It was headed: The Troutfishers Inn, Patondale, and was addressed to Mrs West, 3 The Mount, Lynchester.

Dear Madam,
We have pleasure in returning to you a handbag found in room number sixteen after you had left this morning . . .

Mrs West went slowly to her bed and sat down upon it. The bag was Mrs Wintersley's. She would have known it anywhere. But why had it been sent to her? Why addressed to *Mrs West*, at 3 The Mount?

It took Mrs West several minutes to grasp the truth. William and Mrs Wintersley had spent the weekend at the Troutfishers Inn together. A flush of anger, humiliation and hurt rose in Mrs West's faded cheek. She knew William was foolish, vain, unkind, but she had never thought, she told herself, that he would do this kind of thing. Never.

She sat on the bed, her head low.

What a fool he was! He was endangering the very thing he cared most about – his public career. Aldermen were not allowed moral lapses; at least they must never be found out. But William, fool that he was, had registered at the inn in his own name. He had done that, she knew, because of his fixed idea that everybody knew him everywhere. He would think it useless to attempt to hide his importance under an assumed name. But he would suppose, and rightly, that no one knew his wife. No one did know her. He had seen to that. It would therefore be quite safe, he would think, for Mrs Wintersley to pose as Mrs West. But she had left this bag behind – there was nothing in it but a handkerchief and a lipstick with no incriminating mark of ownership on either – and they had sent it to the address William had given in the book.

Mrs West sat on the bed, the bag beside her, turning things over in her mind.

'William,' she said at lunch. 'I think I shall go to the Speech Day at the Girls' Grammar School tonight.'

William looked up.

'I haven't accepted for you,' he said.

'That's all right,' said Mrs West equably. 'I rang up the Headmistress this morning to say I should be there.'

William frowned.

'Why should you go?' he said. 'It will be very boring.'

'All the same,' she said calmly. 'I think I shall go.'

And at eight o'clock she was there, in a moleskin coat and a straw hat with a blue rose in it, waiting in an ante-room with the rest of the 'platform' for the arrival of Mrs Wintersley. William looked put out. Mrs West knew it was because she was there, but she didn't mind. She felt quite easy and comfortable; it was someone else's turn to be humiliated now, she told herself.

Mrs Wintersley arrived, beautifully dressed in black with a tiny hat, a floating veil and a bunch of lilies of the valley pinned under her chin. She was effusively greeted by everybody, including William. Mrs West stood apart, but when the Headmistress, in her Oxford hood, reading out the names of the guests and their places on the platform came to the name of Mrs West, that lady saw Mrs Wintersley turn sharply in astonishment. Mrs West felt her prolonged stare of amused surprise, but she herself continued to smile imperturbably from under her straw hat. Let Mrs Wintersley smile while she could, she thought.

Mrs West found that she had been given a place of honour next to Mrs Wintersley, with William beside her. Nothing could have been more convenient to her purpose.

'Shall we go?' said the Headmistress.

As they filed out, Mrs Wintersley fell back to speak to William West.

'I left my bag behind at the inn,' she said in an undertone.

'Good Lord,' he exclaimed. 'How did that happen? I thought women never moved without their bags.'

'It wasn't the one I ordinarily use. It was the one that matches my tweed suit. There was nothing in it.'

'That's better,' said William. 'Well, I'll write and ask them to return it to the office.'

Mrs Wintersley's face cleared. She advanced, amidst a burst of handclapping, to her place on the platform.

Mrs West followed her. It was quite pleasant, she thought, to be at one of these affairs again. She liked the rows of young faces below her, the palms beside her, the flowers, the long table covered with a ceremonial cloth and piled with suitable literature, silver cups, shields and medals.

Behind the front row of the platform there were other rows containing people of less importance, minor councillors, mistresses, and so on.

The Press took flashlight photographs of Mrs Wintersley with Mrs West small beside her and William towering beyond.

The platform then sat down and the school sang its opening song.

The Headmistress came behind William and asked him, in the absence of the Mayor, to propose the vote of thanks to Mrs Wintersley later. William nodded importantly, exchanged a glance with Mrs Wintersley and began to make notes on a small card concealed in the palm of his hand.

After the song, the Headmistress announced that she would read her report.

While she read, Mrs Wintersley sat gracefully, conning her notes or smiling at the girls. Mrs West rather grimly regarded her. She did not hear a word of the report. It was over before she realised it and she had to hasten to join in the applause.

There was another song. Mrs Wintersley received a few whispered instructions from the Headmistress. The address, Mrs West had long ago noted on her programme, was to be given next, before the distribution of the prizes.

The song ended; the school sat down again. The Headmistress rose to announce that she had the greatest pleasure in asking Mrs Wintersley to give her address. A few words in eulogy of Mrs Wintersley and the admirable work she was doing in the city followed and amid great applause, Mrs Wintersley rose.

She stood there, waiting for the clapping to die down and Mrs West looking up at her, saw the confident smile and the sparkle in her eyes. Mrs Wintersley was collecting her audience; she was enjoying herself.

At a sign from the Headmistress, the applause ceased. There was silence, a hush of expectancy. Mrs Wintersley, with a slight cough, laid one finely-gloved hand on the table and in her ringing voice began:

'Ladies and gentlemen. Girls.'

She inhaled a long breath.

'I am very glad . . .' she said.

As if she were tired of holding it, Mrs West brought from under her voluminous moleskin sleeve a wholly unsuitable green tweed bag and laid it on the table beside the prizes.

'I am very honoured,' Mrs Wintersley was saying, 'to have been asked to come here tonight . . .'

Distracted by the movement on the table under her eyes, Mrs Wintersley, frowning in annoyance, glanced down. She came to a dead stop. Her voice dying on the listening air, Mrs Wintersley stared in as much horror at the green tweed bag as Macbeth at the apparition of the dagger.

With an audible gasp, she put out a shaking hand towards it. The platform, the school craned in amazement to see what it was that had so affected her. The Headmistress stood with a petrified stare. William West half-rose to his feet, watching the approach of Mrs Wintersley's hand towards the green tweed bag. But on the very point of touching it, Mrs Wintersley suddenly snatched back her hand as if something had burnt it. With a hoarse exclamation, she turned on Mrs West. But the sight of that lady smiling imperturbably from under her straw hat seemed to complete Mrs Wintersley's strange collapse. She whipped round, turning her back on the school, presenting a convulsed face to the platform.

'I . . . I . . .' she stammered. 'I can't go on . . . Something . . . I'm not well. I'm . . . Let me pass, please.'

Plunging through the chairs, the occupants of which got hurriedly up to make way for her, tripping clumsily over the red drugget laid down in her honour, Mrs Wintersley rushed headlong from the platform. In the staring silence, her smart hat awry, her veil flying, her high heels rattling loudly over the wooden floor, Mrs Wintersley fled down the length of the hall, followed, to the astonishment of all, by Councillor William West.

As they made their amazing exit through the door at the end of the hall, uproar broke out. Five hundred girls, their parents and the occupants of the platform burst into excited comment. The Headmistress, stern, drawn to her full height, struck on her bell. But silence did not follow. Confusion continued to reign. The Headmistress advanced to the front of the platform and with lips compressed struck the bell again and again and again. She struck until the tongues were still and all eyes upon her. Then calmly and coldly she spoke:

'Mrs Wintersley is evidently indisposed,' she said. 'But she will be adequately taken care of and our programme must go on. There will be no address. We shall proceed at once to the distribution of the prizes. Er . . .' The Headmistress faltered in her turn. She looked uncertainly behind and around her. Who could give the prizes now? Who was there important enough? She stood there, at a loss. Mrs West leaned forward from her place, smiling helpfully. 'Shall I give the prizes?' she said.

SIGH NO MORE

William Shakespeare

(FROM *MUCH ADO ABOUT NOTHING*, ACT 2, SCENE iii)

Sigh no more, ladies, sigh no more,
    Men were deceivers ever;
One foot in sea, and one on shore,
    To one thing constant never.
Then sigh not so, but let them go,
    And be you blithe and bonny,
Converting all your sounds of woe
    Into Hey nonny, nonny.

Sing no more ditties, sing no more
    Of dumps so dull and heavy;
The fraud of men was ever so,
    Since summer first was leavy.
Then sigh not so, but let them go,
    And be you blithe and bonny,
Converting all your sounds of woe
    Into Hey nonny, nonny.

READING NOTES

At the point in the story when Mrs West brings out the green handbag and places it on the table, a woman in a carers' group stood up and cheered. Although the story is told in an amusing style, the group talked seriously about faithfulness in marriage which led on to an appraisal of the ways in which marriage has changed over the last hundred years. By the time it came to the poem, the lone male in the group said he was beginning to feel himself 'thoroughly got at'.

The Trouble with Pleasures

🌿

A PAIR OF SILK STOCKINGS
Kate Chopin

(approximate reading time 12 minutes)

Little Mrs Sommers one day found herself the unexpected possessor of fifteen dollars. It seemed to her a very large amount of money, and the way in which it stuffed and bulged her worn old *porte-monnaie* gave her a feeling of importance such as she had not enjoyed for years.

The question of investment was one that occupied her greatly. For a day or two she walked about apparently in a dreamy state, but really absorbed in speculation and calculation. She did not wish to act hastily, to do anything she might afterward regret. But it was during the still hours of the night when she lay awake revolving plans in her mind that she seemed to see her way clearly toward a proper and judicious use of the money.

A dollar or two should be added to the price usually paid for Janie's shoes, which would insure their lasting an appreciable time longer than they usually did. She would buy so and so many yards of percale for new shirt waists for the boys and Janie and Mag. She had intended to make the old ones do by skilful patching. Mag should have another gown. She had seen some beautiful patterns, veritable bargains in the shop windows. And still there would be left enough for new stockings – two pairs apiece – and what darning that would save for a while! She would get caps for the boys and sailor-hats for the girls. The vision of her little brood looking fresh and dainty and new for once in their lives excited her and made her restless and wakeful with anticipation.

The neighbors sometimes talked of certain 'better days' that little Mrs Sommers had known before she had ever thought of being Mrs Sommers. She herself indulged in no such morbid retrospection. She had no time – no second of time to devote to the past. The needs of the present absorbed her every faculty. A vision of the future like some dim, gaunt monster sometimes appalled her, but luckily to-morrow never comes.

Mrs Sommers was one who knew the value of bargains; who could stand for hours making her way inch by inch toward the desired object that was selling below cost. She could elbow her way if need be; she had learned to clutch a piece of goods and hold it and stick to it with persistence and determination till her turn came to be served, no matter when it came.

But that day she was a little faint and tired. She had swallowed a light luncheon – no! when she came to think of it, between getting the children fed and the place righted, and preparing herself for the shopping bout, she had actually forgotten to eat any luncheon at all!

She sat herself upon a revolving stool before a counter that was comparatively deserted, trying to gather strength and courage to charge through an eager multitude that was besieging breastworks of shirting and figured lawn. An all-gone limp feeling had come over her and she rested her hand aimlessly upon the counter. She wore no gloves. By degrees she grew aware that her hand had encountered something very soothing, very pleasant to touch. She looked down to see that her hand lay upon a pile of silk stockings. A placard near by announced that they had been reduced in price from two dollars and fifty cents to one dollar and ninety-eight cents; and a young girl who stood behind the counter asked her if she wished to examine their line of silk hosiery. She smiled, just as if she had been asked to inspect a tiara of diamonds with the ultimate view of purchasing it. But she went on feeling the soft, sheeny luxurious things – with both hands now, holding them up to see them glisten, and to feel them glide serpent-like through her fingers.

Two hectic blotches came suddenly into her pale cheeks. She looked up at the girl.

'Do you think there are any eights-and-a-half among these?'

There were any number of eights-and-a-half. In fact, there were more of that size than any other. Here was a light-blue pair; there were some lavender, some all black and various shades of tan and gray. Mrs Sommers selected a black pair and looked at them very long and closely. She pretended to be examining their texture, which the clerk assured her was excellent.

'A dollar and ninety-eight cents,' she mused aloud. 'Well, I'll take this pair.' She handed the girl a five-dollar bill and waited for her change and for her parcel. What a very small parcel it was! It seemed lost in the depths of her shabby old shopping-bag.

Mrs Sommers after that did not move in the direction of the bargain counter. She took the elevator, which carried her to an upper floor into the region of the ladies' waiting-rooms. Here, in a retired corner, she exchanged her cotton stockings for the new silk ones which she had just bought. She was not going through any acute mental process or reasoning with herself, nor was she striving to explain to her satisfaction the motive of her action. She was not thinking at all. She seemed for the time to be taking a rest from that laborious and fatiguing function and to have abandoned herself to some mechanical impulse that directed her actions and freed her of responsibility.

How good was the touch of the raw silk to her flesh! She felt like lying back in the cushioned chair and reveling for a while in the luxury of it. She did for a little while. Then she replaced her shoes, rolled the cotton stockings together and thrust them into her bag. After doing this she crossed straight over to the shoe department and took her seat to be fitted.

She was fastidious. The clerk could not make her out; he could not reconcile her shoes with her stockings, and she was not too easily pleased. She held back her skirts and turned her feet one way and her head another way as she glanced down at the polished, pointed-tipped boots. Her foot and ankle looked very pretty. She could not realize that they belonged to her and were a part of herself. She wanted an excellent and stylish fit, she told the young fellow who served her, and she did not mind the difference of a dollar or two more in the price so long as she got what she desired.

It was a long time since Mrs Sommers had been fitted with gloves. On rare occasions when she had bought a pair they were always 'bargains', so cheap that it would have been preposterous and unreasonable to have expected them to be fitted to the hand.

Now she rested her elbow on the cushion of the glove counter, and a pretty, pleasant young creature, delicate and deft of touch, drew a long-wristed 'kid' over Mrs Sommers's hand. She smoothed it down over the wrist and buttoned it neatly, and both lost themselves for a second or two in admiring contemplation of the little symmetrical gloved hand. But there were other places where money might be spent.

There were books and magazines piled up in the window of a stall a few paces down the street. Mrs Sommers bought two high-priced magazines such as she had been accustomed to read in the days when she had been accustomed to other pleasant things. She carried them without wrapping. As well as she could she lifted her skirts at the crossings. Her stockings and boots and well fitting gloves had worked marvels in her bearing – had given her a feeling of assurance, a sense of belonging to the well-dressed multitude.

She was very hungry. Another time she would have stilled the cravings for food until reaching her own home, where she would have brewed herself a cup of tea and taken a snack of anything that was available. But the impulse that was guiding her would not suffer her to entertain any such thought.

There was a restaurant at the corner. She had never entered

its doors; from the outside she had sometimes caught glimpses of spotless damask and shining crystal, and soft-stepping waiters serving people of fashion.

When she entered her appearance created no surprise, no consternation, as she had half feared it might. She seated herself at a small table alone, and an attentive waiter at once approached to take her order. She did not want a profusion; she craved a nice and tasty bite – a half dozen blue-points, a plump chop with cress, a something sweet – a crème-frappée, for instance; a glass of Rhine wine, and after all a small cup of black coffee.

While waiting to be served she removed her gloves very leisurely and laid them beside her. Then she picked up a magazine and glanced through it, cutting the pages with a blunt edge of her knife. It was all very agreeable. The damask was even more spotless than it had seemed through the window, and the crystal more sparkling. There were quiet ladies and gentlemen, who did not notice her, lunching at the small tables like her own. A soft, pleasing strain of music could be heard, and a gentle breeze, was blowing through the window. She tasted a bite, and she read a word or two, and she sipped the amber wine and wiggled her toes in the silk stockings. The price of it made no difference. She counted the money out to the waiter and left an extra coin on his tray, whereupon he bowed before her as before a princess of royal blood.

There was still money in her purse, and her next temptation presented itself in the shape of a matinée poster.

It was a little later when she entered the theatre, the play had begun and the house seemed to her to be packed. But there were vacant seats here and there, and into one of them she was ushered, between brilliantly dressed women who had gone there to kill time and eat candy and display their gaudy attire. There were many others who were there solely for the play and acting. It is safe to say there was no one present who bore quite the attitude which Mrs Sommers did to her surroundings. She gathered in the whole – stage and players and people in one wide impression, and absorbed it and enjoyed it. She laughed at the comedy and wept – she and the gaudy woman next to her wept over the tragedy. And they talked a little together over it. And the gaudy woman wiped her eyes and sniffled on a tiny square of filmy, perfumed lace and passed little Mrs Sommers her box of candy.

The play was over, the music ceased, the crowd filed out. It was like a dream ended. People scattered in all directions. Mrs Sommers went to the corner and waited for the cable car.

A man with keen eyes, who sat opposite to her, seemed to like the study of her small, pale face. It puzzled him to decipher what he saw there. In truth, he saw nothing – unless he were wizard enough to detect a poignant wish, a powerful longing that the cable car would never stop anywhere, but go on and on with her forever.

ARE THEY SHADOWS
Samuel Daniel

Are they shadows that we see?
And can shadows pleasure give?
Pleasures only shadows be,
Cast by bodies we conceive,
And are made the things we deem
In those figures which they seem.

But these pleasures vanish fast,
Which by shadows are expressed;
Pleasures are not, if they last;
In their passing is their best.
Glory is most bright and gay
In a flash, and so away.

Feed apace then, greedy eyes
On the wonder you behold;
Take it sudden as it flies,
Though you take it not to hold.
When your eyes have done their part,
Thought must length it in the heart.

READING NOTES

A reading group in a hostel wanted to read the poem through two or three times. As one member put it: 'the meaning is a bit slippery'. People have enjoyed talking about the nature of real pleasure: do we spoil it if we think about it? Is it true 'Pleasures are not, if they last'? Is it right to 'Take it sudden as it flies'? In the story Mrs Sommers does just this but readers will have different opinions as to whether it was the right thing for her. Some people might feel that it was worth it, while others that at the end of her day, 'It was like a dream ended'. When she goes back to the reality of her day-to-day life, will feelings of guilt at the extravagance spoil the memory and pleasure of the dream? Nowadays we often hear and read about 'making time for me', or 'me time'. Is this an excuse to be selfish or self-indulgent, or an important necessity?

Desire

🍃

THE NECKLACE
Guy De Maupassant

(approximate reading time 19 minutes)

The girl was one of those pretty and charming young creatures who sometimes are born, as if by a slip of fate, into a family of clerks. She had no dowry, no expectations, no way of being known, understood, loved, married by any rich and distinguished man; so she let herself be married to a little clerk of the Ministry of Public Instruction.

She dressed plainly because she could not dress well, but she was unhappy as if she had really fallen from a higher station; since with women there is neither caste nor rank, for beauty, grace and charm take the place of family and birth. Natural ingenuity, instinct for what is elegant, a supple mind are their sole hierarchy, and often make of women of the people the equals of the very greatest ladies.

Mathilde suffered ceaselessly, feeling herself born to enjoy all delicacies and all luxuries. She was distressed at the poverty of her dwelling, at the bareness of the walls, at the shabby chairs, the ugliness of the curtains. All those things, of which another woman of her rank would never even have been conscious, tortured her and made her angry. The sight of the little Breton peasant who did her humble housework aroused in her despairing regrets and bewildering dreams. She thought of silent antechambers hung with Oriental tapestry, illumined by tall bronze candelabra, and of two great footmen in knee breeches who sleep in the big armchairs, made drowsy by the oppressive heat of the stove. She thought of long reception halls hung with ancient silk, of the dainty cabinets containing priceless curiosities and of the little coquettish perfumed reception rooms made for chatting at five o'clock with intimate friends, with men famous and sought after, whom all women envy and whose attention they all desire.

When she sat down to dinner, before the round table covered with a tablecloth in use three days, opposite her husband, who uncovered the soup tureen and declared with a delighted air, 'Ah, the good soup! I don't know anything better than that,' she thought of dainty dinners, of shining silverware, of tapestry that peopled the walls with ancient personages and with strange birds flying in the midst of a fairy forest; and she thought of delicious dishes served on marvellous plates and of the whispered gallantries to which you listen with a sphinxlike smile while you are eating the pink meat of a trout or the wings of a quail.

She had no gowns, no jewels, nothing. And she loved nothing but that. She felt made for that. She would have liked so much to please, to be envied, to be charming, to be sought after.

She had a friend, a former schoolmate at the convent, who was rich, and whom she did not like to go to see any more because she felt so sad when she came home.

But one evening her husband reached home with a triumphant air and holding a large envelope in his hand.

'There,' said he, 'there is something for you.'

She tore the paper quickly and drew out a printed card which bore these words:

The Minister of Public Instruction and Madame Georges Ramponneau request the honour of M. and Madame Loisel's company at the palace of the Ministry on Monday evening, January 18th.

Instead of being delighted, as her husband had hoped, she threw the invitation on the table crossly, muttering:

'What do you wish me to do with that?'

'Why, my dear, I thought you would be glad. You never go out, and this is such a fine opportunity. I had great trouble to get it. Every one wants to go; it is very select, and they are not giving many invitations to clerks. The whole official world will be there.'

She looked at him with an irritated glance and said impatiently:

'And what do you wish me to put on my back?'

He had not thought of that. He stammered:

'Why, the gown you go to the theatre in. It looks very well to me.'

He stopped, distracted, seeing that his wife was weeping. Two great tears ran slowly from the corners of her eyes toward the corners of her mouth.

'What's the matter? What's the matter?' he answered.

By a violent effort she conquered her grief and replied in a calm voice, while she wiped her wet cheeks:

'Nothing. Only I have no gown, and, therefore, I can't go to this ball. Give your card to some colleague whose wife is better equipped than I am.'

He was in despair. He resumed:

'Come, let us see, Mathilde. How much would it cost, a suitable gown, which you could use on other occasions – something very simple?'

She reflected several seconds, making her calculations and wondering also what sum she could ask without drawing on herself an immediate refusal and a frightened exclamation from the economical clerk.

Finally she replied hesitating:

'I don't know exactly, but I think I could manage it with four hundred francs.'

He grew a little pale, because he was laying aside just that amount to buy a gun and treat himself to a little shooting next summer on the plain of Nanterre, with several friends who went to shoot larks there of a Sunday.

But he said:

'Very well. I will give you four hundred francs. And try to have a pretty gown.'

The day of the ball drew near and Madame Loisel seemed sad, uneasy, anxious. Her frock was ready, however. Her husband said to her one evening:

'What is the matter? Come, you have seemed very queer these last three days.'

And she answered:

'It annoys me not to have a single piece of jewellery, not a single ornament, nothing to put on. I shall look poverty-stricken. I would almost rather not go at all.'

'You might wear natural flowers,' said her husband. 'They're very stylish at this time of year. For ten francs you can get two or three magnificent roses.'

She was not convinced.

'No; there's nothing more humiliating than to look poor among other women who are rich.'

'How stupid you are!' her husband cried. 'Go look up your friend, Madame Forestier, and ask her to lend you some jewels. You're intimate enough with her to do that.'

She uttered a cry of joy:

'True! I never thought of it.'

The next day she went to her friend and told her of her distress.

Madame Forestier went to a wardrobe with a mirror, took out a large jewel box, brought it back, opened it and said to Madame Loisel:

'Choose, my dear.'

She saw first some bracelets, then a pearl necklace, then a Venetian gold cross set with precious stones, of admirable workmanship. She tried on the ornaments before the mirror, hesitated and could not make up her mind to part with them, to give them back. She kept asking:

'Haven't you any more?'

'Why, yes. Look further; I don't know what you like.'

Suddenly she discovered, in a black satin box, a superb diamond necklace, and her heart throbbed with an immoderate desire. Her hands trembled as she took it. She fastened it round her throat, outside her high-necked waist, and was lost in ecstasy at her reflection in the mirror.

Then she asked, hesitating, filled with anxious doubt:

'Will you lend me this, only this?'

'Why, yes, certainly.'

She threw her arms round her friend's neck, kissed her passionately, then fled with her treasure.

The night of the ball arrived. Madame Loisel was a great success. She was prettier than any other woman present, elegant, graceful, smiling and wild with joy. All the men looked at her, asked her name, sought to be introduced. All the attachés of the Cabinet wished to waltz with her. She was remarked by the minister himself.

She danced with rapture, with passion, intoxicated by pleasure, forgetting all in the triumph of her beauty, in the glory of her success, in a sort of cloud of happiness comprised of all this homage, admiration, these awakened desires and of that sense of triumph which is so sweet to woman's heart.

She left the ball about four o'clock in the morning. Her husband had been sleeping since midnight in a little deserted anteroom with three other gentlemen whose wives were enjoying the ball.

He threw over her shoulders the wraps he had brought, the modest wraps of common life, the poverty of which contrasted with the elegance of the ball dress. She felt this and wished to escape so as not to be remarked by the other women, who were enveloping themselves in costly furs.

Loisel held her back, saying: 'Wait a bit. You will catch cold outside. I will call a cab.'

But she did not listen to him and rapidly descended the stairs. When they reached the street they could not find a carriage and began to look for one, shouting after the cabmen passing at a distance.

They went toward the Seine in despair, shivering with cold. At last they found on the quay one of those ancient night cabs which, as though they were ashamed to show their shabbiness during the day, are never seen round Paris until after dark.

It took them to their dwelling in the Rue des Martyrs, and sadly they mounted the stairs to their flat. All was ended for her. As to him, he reflected that he must be at the ministry at ten o'clock that morning.

She removed her wraps before the glass so as to see herself once more in all her glory. But suddenly she uttered a cry. She no longer had the necklace around her neck!

'What is the matter with you?' demanded her husband, already half-undressed.

She turned distractedly toward him.

'I have – I have – I've lost Madame Forestier's necklace,' she cried.

He stood up, bewildered.

'What! – how? Impossible!'

They looked among the folds of her skirt, of her cloak, in her pockets, everywhere, but did not find it.

'You're sure you had it on when you left the ball?' he asked.

'Yes, I felt it in the vestibule of the minister's house.'

'But if you had lost it in the street we should have heard it fall. It must be in the cab.'

'Yes, probably. Did you take his number?'

'No. And you – didn't you notice it?'

'No.'

They looked, thunderstruck, at each other. At last Loisel put on his clothes.

'I shall go back on foot,' said he, 'over the whole route, to see whether I can find it.'

He went out. She sat waiting on a chair in her ball dress, without strength to go to bed, overwhelmed, without any fire, without a thought.

Her husband returned about seven o'clock. He had found nothing.

He went to the police headquarters, to the newspaper offices to offer a reward; he went to the cab companies – everywhere, in fact, whither he was urged by the least spark of hope.

She waited all day, in the same condition of mad fear before this terrible calamity.

Loisel returned at night with a hollow, pale face. He had discovered nothing.

'You must write to your friend,' said he, 'that you have broken the clasp of her necklace and that you are having it mended. That will give us time to turn round.'

She wrote at his dictation.

At the end of a week they had lost all hope. Loisel, who had aged five years, declared:

'We must consider how to replace that ornament.'

The next day they took the box that had contained it and

went to the jeweller whose name was found within. He consulted his books.

'It was not I, madame, who sold that necklace; I must simply have furnished the case.'

Then they went from jeweller to jeweller, searching for a necklace like the other, trying to recall it, both sick with chagrin and grief.

They found, in a shop at the Palais Royal, a string of diamonds that seemed to them exactly like the one they had lost. It was worth forty thousand francs. They could have it for thirty-six.

So they begged the jeweller not to sell it for three days yet. And they made a bargain that he should buy it back for thirty-four thousand francs, in case they should find the lost necklace before the end of February.

Loisel possessed eighteen thousand francs which his father had left him. He would borrow the rest.

He did borrow, asking a thousand francs of one, five hundred of another, five louis here, three louis there. He gave notes, took up ruinous obligations, dealt with usurers and all the race of lenders. He compromised all the rest of his life, risked signing a note without even knowing whether he could meet it; and, frightened by the trouble yet to come, by the black misery that was about to fall upon him, by the prospect of all the physical privations and moral tortures that he was to suffer, he went to get the new necklace, laying upon the jeweller's counter thirty-six thousand francs.

When Madame Loisel took back the necklace Madame Forestier said to her with a chilly manner:

'You should have returned it sooner; I might have needed it.'

She did not open the case, as her friend had so much feared. If she had detected the substitution, what would she have thought, what would she have said? Would she not have taken Madame Loisel for a thief?

Thereafter Madame Loisel knew the horrible existence of the needy. She bore her part, however, with sudden heroism. That dreadful debt must be paid. She would pay it. They dismissed their servant; they changed their lodgings; they rented a garret under the roof.

She came to know what heavy housework meant and the odious cares of the kitchen. She washed the dishes, using her dainty fingers and rosy nails on greasy pots and pans. She washed the soiled linen, the shirts and the dishcloths, which she dried upon a line; she carried the slops down to the street every morning and carried up the water, stopping for breath at every landing. And dressed like a woman of the people, she went to the fruiterer, the grocer, the butcher, a basket on her arm, bargaining, meeting with impertinence, defending her miserable money, sou by sou.

Every month they had to meet some notes, renew others, obtain more time.

Her husband worked evenings, making up a tradesman's accounts, and late at night he often copied manuscript for five sous a page.

This life lasted ten years.

At the end of ten years they had paid everything, everything, with the rates of usury and the accumulations of the compound interest.

Madame Loisel looked old now. She had become the woman of impoverished households – strong and hard and rough. With frowsy hair, skirts askew and red hands, she talked loud while washing the floor with great swishes of water. But sometimes, when her husband was at the office, she sat down near the window and she thought of that gay evening of long ago, of that ball where she had been so beautiful and so admired.

What would have happened if she had not lost that necklace? Who knows? Who knows? How strange and changeful is life! How small a thing is needed to make or ruin us!

But one Sunday, having gone to take a walk in the Champs Elysées to refresh herself after the labours of the week, she suddenly perceived a woman who was leading a child. It was Madame Forestier, still young, still beautiful, still charming.

Madame Loisel felt moved. Should she speak to her? Yes, certainly. And now that she had paid, she would tell her all about it. Why not?

She went up.

'Good-day, Jeanne.'

The other, astonished to be familiarly addressed by this plain good-wife, did not recognise her at all and stammered:

'But – madame! – I do not know— You must have mistaken.'

'No. I am Mathilde Loisel.'

Her friend uttered a cry.

'Oh, my poor Mathilde! How you are changed!'

'Yes, I have had a pretty hard life, since I last saw you, and great poverty – and that because of you!'

'Of me! How so?'

'Do you remember that diamond necklace you lent me to wear at the ministerial ball?'

'Yes. Well?'

'Well, I lost it.'

'What do you mean? You brought it back.'

'I brought you back another exactly like it. And it has taken us ten years to pay for it. You can understand that it was not easy for us, for us who had nothing. At last it is ended, and I am very glad.'

Madame Forestier had stopped.

'You say that you bought a necklace of diamonds to replace mine?'

'Yes. You never noticed it, then! They were very similar.'

And she smiled with a joy that was at once proud and ingenuous.

Madame Forestier, deeply moved, took her hands.

'Oh, my poor Mathilde! Why, my necklace was paste! It was worth at most only five hundred francs!'

OVERHEARD ON A SALTMARSH
Harold Monro

Nymph, nymph, what are your beads?
Green glass, goblin. Why do you stare at them?
Give them me.

>   No.

Give them me. Give them me.

>   No.

Then I will howl all night in the reeds,
Lie in the mud and howl for them.

Goblin, why do you love them so?

They are better than stars or water,
Better than voices of winds that sing,
Better than any man's fair daughter,
Your green glass beads on a silver ring.

Hush, I stole them out of the moon.

Give me your beads, I want them.

>   No.

I will howl in the deep lagoon
For your green glass beads, I love them so.
Give them me. Give them.

>   No.

READING NOTES

At the end of the story, do you feel sorry for Mathilde or did she get her just reward? Members of a drop-in reading group thought she paid a high price because her life was ruined. 'On the other hand,' said one reader, 'what sort of selfish existence might she have lived if she had not lost the necklace?' Most people felt for the husband as the victim of her envious discontent both before and after the ball. There was much talk about what else they could have done about the missing necklace and why Mathilde 'bore her part with sudden heroism'. Someone else wondered how far the observation, 'with women there is neither caste nor rank, for beauty, grace and charm take the place of family and birth' could still be said to be true today.

The poem takes up the themes of envy and greed. This group enjoyed taking parts and reading it aloud and, while comparing the goblin to Gollum, noticed that it is the nymph who has stolen the beads while the goblin merely desires them. The atmosphere of the poem, the voices, the passionate desire were all investigated.

Trouble

✦

FAR FROM THE MADDING CROWD

(ON CASTERBRIDGE HIGHWAY, CHAPTER 40)

Thomas Hardy

(approximate reading time 16 minutes)

Bathsheba Everdene is married to the dashing Sergeant Troy. What she does not know is that Troy's heart secretly belongs to Fanny Robin, Bathsheba's former servant, who is pregnant with Troy's child.

One evening Bathsheba and Troy, out riding in their carriage, come across Fanny, now destitute and making her way on foot to the workhouse at Casterbridge. Bathsheba does not recognise her and Troy makes an excuse so that he can return hurriedly to Fanny and give her some money, promising to come to her later . . .

For a considerable time the woman walked on. Her steps became feebler, and she strained her eyes to look afar upon the naked road, now indistinct amid the penumbrae of night. At length her onward walk dwindled to the merest totter, and she opened a gate within which was a haystack. Underneath this she sat down and presently slept.

When the woman awoke it was to find herself in the depths of a moonless and starless night. A heavy unbroken crust of cloud stretched across the sky, shutting out every speck of heaven; and a distant halo which hung over the town of Casterbridge was visible against the black concave, the luminosity appearing the brighter by its great contrast with the circumscribing darkness. Towards this weak, soft glow the woman turned her eyes.

'If I could only get there!' she said. 'Meet him the day after tomorrow: God help me! Perhaps I shall be in my grave before then.'

A manor-house clock from the far depths of shadow struck the hour, one, in a small, attenuated tone. After midnight the voice of a clock seems to lose in breadth as much as in length, and to diminish its sonorousness to a thin falsetto.

Afterwards a light – two lights – arose from the remote shade, and grew larger. A carriage rolled along the road, and passed the gate. It probably contained some late diners-out. The beams from one lamp shone for a moment upon the crouching woman, and threw her face into vivid relief. The face was young in the groundwork, old in the finish; the general contours were flexuous and childlike, but the finer lineaments had begun to be sharp and thin.

The pedestrian stood up, apparently with revived determination, and looked around. The road appeared to be familiar to her, and she carefully scanned the fence as she slowly walked along. Presently there became visible a dim white shape; it was another milestone. She drew her fingers across its face to feel the marks.

'Two more!' she said.

She leant against the stone as a means of rest for a short interval, then bestirred herself, and again pursued her way. For a slight distance she bore up bravely, afterwards flagging as before. This was beside a lone copsewood, wherein heaps of white chips strewn upon the leafy ground showed that woodmen had been faggoting and making hurdles during the day. Now there was not a rustle, not a breeze, not the faintest clash of twigs to keep her company. The woman looked over the gate, opened it, and went in. Close to the entrance stood a row of faggots, bound and unbound, together with stakes of all sizes.

By the aid of the Casterbridge aurora, and by feeling with her hands, the woman selected two sticks from the heaps. These sticks were nearly straight to the height of three or four feet, where each branched into a fork like the letter Y. She sat down, snapped off the small upper twigs, and carried the remainder with her into the road. She placed one of these forks under each arm as a crutch, tested them, timidly threw her whole weight upon them – so little that it was – and swung herself forward. The girl had made for herself a material aid.

The crutches answered well. The pat of her feet, and the tap of her sticks upon the highway, were all the sounds that came from the traveller now. She had passed the last mile-stone by a good long distance, and began to look wistfully towards the bank as if calculating upon another milestone soon. The crutches, though so very useful, had their limits of power. Mechanism only transfers labour, being powerless to supersede it, and the original amount of exertion was not cleared away; it was thrown into the body and arms. She was exhausted, and each swing forward became fainter. At last she swayed sideways, and fell.

Here she lay, a shapeless heap, for ten minutes and more. The morning wind began to boom dully over the flats, and to move afresh dead leaves which had lain still since yesterday. The woman desperately turned round upon her knees, and next rose to her feet. Steadying herself by the help of one crutch, she essayed a step, then another, then a third, using the crutches now as walking-sticks only. Thus she progressed till descending Mellstock Hill another milestone appeared, and soon the beginning of an iron-railed fence came into view. She staggered across to the first post, clung to it, and looked around.

The Casterbridge lights were now individually visible. It was getting towards morning, and vehicles might be hoped for, if not expected soon. She listened. There was not a sound of life save that acme and sublimation of all dismal sounds, the bark of a fox, its three hollow notes being rendered at intervals of a minute with the precision of a funeral bell.

'Less than a mile!' the woman murmured. 'No; more,' she added, after a pause. 'The mile is to the county hall, and my resting-place is on the other side Casterbridge. A little over a mile, and there I am!' After an interval she again spoke. 'Five or six steps to a yard – six perhaps. I have to go seventeen hundred yards. A hundred times six, six hundred. Seventeen times that. O pity me, Lord!'

Holding to the rails, she advanced, thrusting one hand

forward upon the rail, then the other, then leaning over it whilst she dragged her feet on beneath.

This woman was not given to soliloquy; but extremity of feeling lessens the individuality of the weak, as it increases that of the strong. She said again in the same tone, 'I'll believe that the end lies five posts forward, and no further, and so get strength to pass them.'

This was a practical application of the principle that a half-feigned and fictitious faith is better than no faith at all.

She passed five posts and held on to the fifth.

'I'll pass five more by believing my longed-for spot is at the next fifth. I can do it.'

She passed five more.

'It lies only five further.'

She passed five more.

'But it is five further.'

She passed them.

'That stone bridge is the end of my journey,' she said, when the bridge over the Froom was in view.

She crawled to the bridge. During the effort each breath of the woman went into the air as if never to return again.

'Now for the truth of the matter,' she said, sitting down. 'The truth is, that I have less than half a mile.' Self-beguilement with what she had known all the time to be false had given her strength to come over half a mile that she would have been powerless to face in the lump. The artifice showed that the woman, by some mysterious intuition, had grasped the paradoxical truth that blindness may operate more vigorously than prescience, and the short-sighted effect more than the far-seeing; that limitation, and not comprehensiveness, is needed for striking a blow.

The half-mile stood now before the sick and weary woman like a stolid Juggernaut. It was an impassive King of her world. The road here ran across Durnover Moor, open to the road on either side. She surveyed the wide space, the lights, herself, sighed, and lay down against a guard-stone of the bridge.

Never was ingenuity exercised so sorely as the traveller here exercised hers. Every conceivable aid, method, stratagem, mechanism, by which these last desperate eight hundred yards could be overpassed by a human being unperceived, was revolved in her busy brain, and dismissed as impracticable. She thought of sticks, wheels, crawling – she even thought of rolling. But the exertion demanded by either of these latter two was greater than to walk erect. The faculty of contrivance was worn out. Hopelessness had come at last.

'No further!' she whispered, and closed her eyes.

From the stripe of shadow on the opposite side of the bridge a portion of shade seemed to detach itself and move into isolation upon the pale white of the road. It glided noiselessly towards the recumbent woman.

She became conscious of something touching her hand; it was softness and it was warmth. She opened her eyes, and the substance touched her face. A dog was licking her cheek.

He was a huge, heavy, and quiet creature, standing darkly against the low horizon, and at least two feet higher than the present position of her eyes. Whether Newfoundland, mastiff, bloodhound, or what not, it was impossible to say. He seemed to be of too strange and mysterious a nature to belong to any variety among those of popular nomenclature. Being thus assignable to no breed, he was the ideal embodiment of canine greatness – a generalisation from what was common to all. Night, in its sad, solemn, and benevolent aspect, apart from its stealthy and cruel side, was personified in this form. Darkness endows the small and ordinary ones among mankind with poetical power, and even the suffering woman threw her idea into figure.

In her reclining position she looked up to him just as in earlier times she had, when standing, looked up to a man. The animal, who was as homeless as she, respectfully withdrew a step or two when the woman moved, and, seeing that she did not repulse him, he licked her hand again.

A thought moved within her like lightning. 'Perhaps I can make use of him – I might do it then!'

She pointed in the direction of Casterbridge, and the dog seemed to misunderstand: he trotted on. Then, finding she could not follow, he came back and whined.

The ultimate and saddest singularity of woman's effort and invention was reached when, with a quickened breathing, she rose to a stooping posture, and, resting her two little arms upon the shoulders of the dog, leant firmly thereon, and murmured stimulating words. Whilst she sorrowed in her heart she cheered with her voice, and what was stranger than that the strong should need encouragement from the weak was that cheerfulness should be so well stimulated by such utter dejection. Her friend moved forward slowly, and she with small mincing steps moved forward beside him, half her weight being thrown upon the animal. Sometimes she sank as she had sunk from walking erect, from the crutches, from the rails. The dog, who now thoroughly understood her desire and her incapacity, was frantic in his distress on these occasions; he would tug at her dress and run forward. She always called him back, and it was now to be observed that the woman listened for human sounds only to avoid them. It was evident that she had an object in keeping her presence on the road and her forlorn state unknown.

Their progress was necessarily very slow. They reached the bottom of the town, and the Casterbridge lamps lay before them like fallen Pleiads as they turned to the left into the dense shade of a deserted avenue of chestnuts, and so skirted the borough. Thus the town was passed, and the goal was reached.

On this much-desired spot outside the town rose a picturesque building. Originally it had been a mere case to hold people. The shell had been so thin, so devoid of excrescence, and so closely drawn over the accommodation granted, that the grim character of what was beneath showed through it, as the shape of a body is visible under a winding-sheet.

Then Nature, as if offended, lent a hand. Masses of ivy grew up, completely covering the walls, till the place looked like an abbey; and it was discovered that the view from the front, over the Casterbridge chimneys, was one of the most magnificent in the county. A neighbouring earl once said that he would give up a year's rental to have at his own door the view enjoyed by the inmates from theirs – and very probably the inmates would have given up the view for his year's rental.

This stone edifice consisted of a central mass and two wings, whereon stood as sentinels a few slim chimneys, now gurgling sorrowfully to the slow wind. In the wall was a gate, and by the gate a bellpull formed of a hanging wire. The woman raised herself as high as possible upon her knees, and could just reach the handle. She moved it and fell forwards in a bowed attitude, her face upon her bosom.

It was getting on towards six o'clock, and sounds of movement were to be heard inside the building which was the haven of rest to this wearied soul. A little door by the large one was opened, and a man appeared inside. He discerned the panting heap of clothes, went back for a light, and came again. He entered a second time, and returned with two women.

These lifted the prostrate figure and assisted her in through the doorway. The man then closed the door.

'How did she get here?' said one of the women.

'The Lord knows,' said the other.

'There is a dog outside,' murmured the overcome traveller. 'Where is he gone? He helped me?'

'I stoned him away,' said the man.

The little procession then moved forward – the man in front bearing the light, the two bony women next, supporting between them the small and supple one. Thus they entered the house and disappeared.

IN MEMORIAM
Alfred Tennyson
(FROM *IN MEMORIAM*, SECTION 50)

Be near me when my light is low,
    When the blood creeps, and the nerves prick
    And tingle; and the heart is sick,
And all the wheels of Being slow.

Be near me when the sensuous frame
    Is rack'd with pangs that conquer trust;
    And Time, a maniac scattering dust,
And Life, a Fury slinging flame.

Be near me when my faith is dry,
    And men the flies of latter spring,
    That lay their eggs, and sting and sing
And weave their petty cells and die.

Be near me when I fade away,
    To point the term of human strife,
    And on the low dark verge of life
The twilight of eternal day.

READING NOTES

Do you think the woman in the story is a victim or a survivor? In one group, this question produced a very lively discussion. People admired not only her courage but her instinct for survival. How does she find the strength to keep on going? 'In times of trouble,' said one reader, 'we say one day at a time, just as Fanny says "I'll believe that the end lies five posts forward."' The story is a sad one, the incident with the dog upsetting, but what else do you get out of the story as a reader? Why do we read stories of suffering and hardship? In times of trouble would you want fiction and poetry to cheer you up, or to deal with the matter of pain and sorrow? One reader put it like this, 'The poem describes just what it is like at the very lowest times of my life.' The group went on to talk about the big matter in the poem – faith and trust – and whom they felt the speaker of the poem was addressing: 'Be near me'. The poem almost seems to dissolve in the final verse. Is something lost or held onto? What are your thoughts at the end of the poem?

Phases of Love

🌿

JANE EYRE

(EXTRACT FROM CHAPTER 15)

Charlotte Brontë

(approximate reading time 15 minutes)

Jane, an unloved orphan, grew up in Lowood Institution, a charity boarding school, where she survived hardship and cruelty. Now she has come to Thornfield Hall as governess to Adele, the young ward of Mr Rochester. Rochester's wife is mad and, unknown to Jane, is living locked away in the attic of the house, under the care of an unreliable servant, Grace Poole. Despite her plain appearance and modest position, Rochester is intrigued by Jane and she in turn finds herself becoming more and more drawn to him . . .

And was Mr Rochester now ugly in my eyes? No, reader: gratitude, and many associations, all pleasurable and genial, made his face the object I best liked to see; his presence in a room was more cheering than the brightest fire. Yet I had not forgotten his faults; indeed, I could not, for he brought them frequently before me. He was proud, sardonic, harsh to inferiority of every description: in my secret soul I knew that his great kindness to me was balanced by unjust severity to many others. He was moody, too; unaccountably so; I more than once, when sent for to read to him, found him sitting in his library alone, with his head bent on his folded arms; and, when he looked up, a morose, almost a malignant, scowl blackened his features. But I believed that his moodiness, his harshness, and his former faults of morality (I say *former*, for now he seemed corrected of them) had their source in some cruel cross of fate. I believed he was naturally a man of better tendencies, higher principles, and purer tastes than such as circumstances had developed, education instilled, or destiny encouraged. I thought there were excellent materials in him; though for the present they hung together somewhat spoiled and tangled. I cannot deny that I grieved for his grief, whatever that was, and would have given much to assuage it.

Though I had now extinguished my candle and was laid down in bed, I could not sleep for thinking of his look when he paused in the avenue, and told how his destiny had risen up before him, and dared him to be happy at Thornfield.

'Why not?' I asked myself. 'What alienates him from the house? Will he leave it again soon? Mrs Fairfax said he seldom stayed here longer than a fortnight at a time; and he has now been resident eight weeks. If he does go, the change will be doleful. Suppose he should be absent spring, summer, and autumn: how joyless sunshine and fine days will seem!'

I hardly know whether I had slept or not after this musing; at any rate, I started wide awake on hearing a vague murmur, peculiar and lugubrious, which sounded, I thought, just above me. I wished I had kept my candle burning: the night was drearily dark; my spirits were depressed. I rose and sat up in bed, listening. The sound was hushed.

I tried again to sleep; but my heart beat anxiously: my inward tranquillity was broken. The clock, far down in the hall, struck two. Just then it seemed my chamber-door was touched; as if fingers had swept the panels in groping a way along the dark gallery outside. I said, 'Who is there?' Nothing answered. I was chilled with fear.

All at once I remembered that it might be Pilot, who, when the kitchen-door chanced to be left open, not unfrequently found his way up to the threshold of Mr Rochester's chamber: I had seen him lying there myself in the mornings. The idea calmed me somewhat: I lay down. Silence composes the nerves; and as an unbroken hush now reigned again through the whole house, I began to feel the return of slumber. But it was not fated that I should sleep that night. A dream had scarcely approached my ear, when it fled affrighted, scared by a marrow-freezing incident enough.

This was a demoniac laugh – low, suppressed, and deep – uttered, as it seemed, at the very keyhole of my chamber door. The head of my bed was near the door, and I thought at first the goblin-laughter stood at my bedside – or rather, crouched by my pillow: but I rose, looked round, and could see nothing; while, as I still gazed, the unnatural sound was reiterated: and I knew it came from behind the panels. My first impulse was to rise and fasten the bolt; my next, again to cry out, 'Who is there?'

Something gurgled and moaned. Ere long, steps retreated up the gallery towards the third-storey staircase: a door had lately been made to shut in that staircase; I heard it open and close, and all was still.

'Was that Grace Poole? and is she possessed with a devil?' thought I. Impossible now to remain longer by myself: I must go to Mrs Fairfax. I hurried on my frock and a shawl; I withdrew the bolt and opened the door with a trembling hand. There was a candle burning just outside, and on the matting in the gallery. I was surprised at this circumstance: but still more was I amazed to perceive the air quite dim, as if filled with smoke; and, while looking to the right hand and left, to find whence these blue wreaths issued, I became further aware of a strong smell of burning.

Something creaked: it was a door ajar; and that door was Mr Rochester's, and the smoke rushed in a cloud from thence. I thought no more of Mrs Fairfax; I thought no more of Grace Poole, or the laugh: in an instant, I was within the chamber. Tongues of flame darted round the bed: the curtains were on fire. In the midst of blaze and vapour, Mr Rochester lay stretched motionless, in deep sleep.

'Wake! wake!' I cried. I shook him, but he only murmured and turned: the smoke had stupefied him. Not a moment could be lost: the very sheets were kindling, I rushed to his basin and ewer; fortunately, one was wide and the other deep, and both were filled with water. I heaved them up, deluged the bed and its occupant, flew back to my own room, brought my own water-jug, baptised the couch afresh, and, by God's aid, succeeded in extinguishing the flames which were devouring it.

The hiss of the quenched element, the breakage of a pitcher which I flung from my hand when I had emptied it, and, above all, the splash of the shower-bath I had liberally bestowed, roused Mr Rochester at last. Though it was now dark, I knew he was awake; because I heard him fulminating strange anathemas at finding himself lying in a pool of water.

'Is there a flood?' he cried.

'No, sir,' I answered; 'but there has been a fire: get up, do; you are quenched now; I will fetch you a candle.'

'In the name of all the elves in Christendom, is that Jane Eyre?' he demanded. 'What have you done with me, witch, sorceress? Who is in the room besides you? Have you plotted to drown me?'

'I will fetch you a candle, sir; and, in Heaven's name, get up. Somebody has plotted something: you cannot too soon find out who and what it is.'

'There! I am up now; but at your peril you fetch a candle yet: wait two minutes till I get into some dry garments, if any dry there be – yes, here is my dressing-gown. Now run!'

I did run; I brought the candle which still remained in the gallery. He took it from my hand, held it up, and surveyed the bed, all blackened and scorched, the sheets drenched, the carpet round swimming in water.

'What is it? and who did it?' he asked.

I briefly related to him what had transpired: the strange laugh I had heard in the gallery: the step ascending to the third storey; the smoke, – the smell of fire which had conducted me to his room; in what state I had found matters there, and how I had deluged him with all the water I could lay hands on.

He listened very gravely; his face, as I went on, expressed more concern than astonishment; he did not immediately speak when I had concluded.

'Shall I call Mrs Fairfax?' I asked.

'Mrs Fairfax? No; what the deuce would you call her for? What can she do? Let her sleep unmolested.'

'Then I will fetch Leah, and wake John and his wife.'

'Not at all: just be still. You have a shawl on. If you are not warm enough, you may take my cloak yonder; wrap it about you, and sit down in the arm-chair: there, – I will put it on. Now place your feet on the stool, to keep them out of the wet. I am going to leave you a few minutes. I shall take the candle. Remain where you are till I return; be as still as a mouse. I must pay a visit to the second storey. Don't move, remember, or call any one.'

He went: I watched the light withdraw. He passed up the gallery very softly, unclosed the staircase door with as little noise as possible, shut it after him, and the last ray vanished. I was left in total darkness. I listened for some noise, but heard nothing. A very long time elapsed. I grew weary: it was cold, in spite of the cloak; and then I did not see the use of staying, as I was not to rouse the house. I was on the point of risking Mr Rochester's displeasure by disobeying his orders, when the light once more gleamed dimly on the gallery wall, and I heard his unshod feet tread the matting. 'I hope it is he,' thought I, 'and not something worse.'

He re-entered, pale and very gloomy. 'I have found it all out,' said he, setting his candle down on the washstand; 'it is as I thought.'

'How, sir?'

He made no reply, but stood with his arms folded, looking on the ground. At the end of a few minutes he inquired in rather a peculiar tone –

'I forget whether you said you saw anything when you opened your chamber door.'

'No, sir, only the candlestick on the ground.'

'But you heard an odd laugh? You have heard that laugh before, I should think, or something like it?'

'Yes, sir: there is a woman who sews here, called Grace Poole, – she laughs in that way. She is a singular person.'

'Just so. Grace Poole – you have guessed it. She is, as you say, singular – very. Well, I shall reflect on the subject. Meantime, I am glad that you are the only person, besides myself, acquainted with the precise details of to-night's incident. You are no talking fool: say nothing about it. I will account for this state of affairs' (pointing to the bed): 'and now return to your own room. I shall do very well on the sofa in the library for the rest of the night. It is near four – in two hours the servants will be up.'

'Good-night, then, sir,' said I, departing.

He seemed surprised – very inconsistently so, as he had just told me to go.

'What!' he exclaimed, 'are you quitting me already, and in that way?'

'You said I might go, sir.'

'But not without taking leave; not without a word or two of acknowledgment and good-will: not, in short, in that brief, dry fashion. Why, you have saved my life! – snatched me from a horrible and excruciating death! and you walk past me as if we were mutual strangers! At least shake hands.'

He held out his hand; I gave him mine: he took it first in one, then in both his own.

'You have saved my life: I have a pleasure in owing you so immense a debt. I cannot say more. Nothing else that has being would have been tolerable to me in the character of creditor for such an obligation: but you: it is different; – I feel your benefits no burden, Jane.'

He paused; gazed at me: words almost visible trembled on his lips, – but his voice was checked.

'Good-night again, sir. There is no debt, benefit, burden, obligation, in the case.'

'I knew,' he continued, 'you would do me good in some way, at some time; – I saw it in your eyes when I first beheld you: their expression and smile did not' – (again he stopped) – 'did not' (he proceeded hastily) 'strike delight to my very inmost heart so for nothing. People talk of natural sympathies; I have heard of good genii: there are grains of truth in the wildest fable. My cherished preserver, goodnight!'

Strange energy was in his voice, strange fire in his look.

'I am glad I happened to be awake,' I said: and then I was going.

'What! you *will* go?'

'I am cold, sir.'

'Cold? Yes, – and standing in a pool! Go, then, Jane; go!' But he still retained my hand, and I could not free it. I bethought myself of an expedient.

'I think I hear Mrs Fairfax move, sir,' said I.

'Well, leave me:' he relaxed his fingers, and I was gone.

I regained my couch, but never thought of sleep. Till morning dawned I was tossed on a buoyant but unquiet sea, where billows of trouble rolled under surges of joy. I thought sometimes I saw beyond its wild waters a shore, sweet as the hills of Beulah; and now and then a freshening gale, wakened by hope, bore my spirit triumphantly towards the bourne: but I could not reach it, even in fancy – a counteracting breeze blew off land, and continually drove me back. Too feverish to rest, I rose as soon as day dawned.

TO ANTHEA,
WHO MAY COMMAND HIM ANYTHING
Robert Herrick

Bid me to live, and I will live
    Thy Protestant to be:
Or bid me love, and I will give
    A loving heart to thee.

A heart as soft, a heart as kind,
    A heart as sound and free
As in the whole world thou canst find,
    That heart I'll give to thee.

Bid that heart stay, and it will stay
    To honour thy decree:
Or bid it languish quite away,
    And 't shall do so for thee.

Bid me to weep, and I will weep
    While I have eyes to see:
And, having none, yet I will keep
    A heart to weep for thee.

Bid me despair, and I'll despair,
    Under that cypress tree:
Or bid me die, and I will dare
    E'en death to die for thee.

Thou art my life, my love, my heart,
 The very eyes of me,
And hast command of every part,
 To live and die for thee.

READING NOTES

Most members of a young mothers' group were moved by the full-blown, passionate love poem and compared this state with what seemed to be just the first stirring of love between Jane and Rochester in the chapter from *Jane Eyre*. 'They don't really know they are in love,' Emma thought, and everyone then looked for evidence of something more than ordinary concern for each other. Emma wished someone would write her a love poem like Herrick's and one or two members said that they had tried to write poetry, though never love poetry. The group took turns to read out their favourite verse, the final verse proving the most popular, though one mother thought it was 'over-emotional and embarrassing'. Discussion then turned back to the story and in particular to what Rochester meant when he said, 'I feel your benefits no burden, Jane.' One person had seen a film version; no one had read the book; and there was speculation on who might have set fire to the bed and to what happened next.

Loving

❦

THE FIGHT IN THE PLOUGH AND OX
George Mackay Brown

(approximate reading time 16 minutes)

1

The farmers in the parish were peaceable men, and they drank on market days in an alehouse, the Plough and Ox kept by a lady called Madge Brims.

The fishermen's pub was called the Arctic Whaler. There the fishermen drank when they came in cold from the lobster fishing.

The men from the farms – the ploughmen and the shepherds – got on quite well with the fishermen. They met and mingled on the Hamnavoe street at the weekends, and sometimes exchanged a few bantering words. Once or twice a fight threatened, when the young ones fell to arguing, mostly about girls; but then the older men would come between the spitters and snarlers, and patch things up, and there was rarely ill-feeling.

But the country men never darkened the door of the Arctic Whaler, nor did the lobster men stand outside the door of Madge Brims's, the wall of which was studded with horseshoes, and think for one moment of going in there for a glass of Old Orkney whisky, price threepence.

The men from the land and the men from the sea segregated themselves strictly, when it came to refreshments at the end of a day's hard work.

In the Arctic Whaler, you would hear talk of smuggled tobacco from a Dutch ship, whales, halibut so big they broke the nets, shipwrecks, seal-women.

There was none of that kind of talk in Mistress Brims's – it was all about horse and ox, the best way to train a sheepdog, oats and barley, whether it was better to grind one's own grain or to take it in a cart to the scoundrel of a miller. Often, of course, the young men spoke about the lasses. The bonniest lass in the parish that year was said to be Jenny of Furss, the one daughter of a very poor crofter called Sam Moorfea of Furss. Sam was so poor he couldn't even afford to drink in Madge's place, where the ale was a penny the pewter mug. Sam Moorfea had to sit beside the fire at home and drink the ale he brewed himself, poured out for him by his beautiful daughter Jenny.

'Oh, but she's a right bonny lass, Jenny!' said Will the blacksmith who, by reason of his calling, always drank with the farm men. 'I would like well to have Jenny take me a mug of buttermilk, every day when I stand wiping sweat from me between the forge and anvil.'

'No, Jenny deserves better than that,' said John Greenay, whose father owned a big farm. 'I can see Jenny with her arms full of sheaves at harvest time, and her long hair blowing brighter above them in the wind.'

The young countrymen seemed to vie with each other, that summer, in praise of Jenny Moorfea. Their faces shone, with joy and beer. The old men shook their heads in the hostelry, as much as to say, '*We* thought that way once, too, before the sweet-mouthed lasses we married began to nag and rage at us . . .' They winked at each other, the old men. 'Ah well, but they'll find out in time, the young fools that they are . . .'

2

It so happened that Sam Moorfea had such a poor croft, and three young boys to feed, that he kept a small fishing-boat on the beach, and fished inshore for haddocks whenever he had a moment to spare from ploughing and threshing. His wife was six years dead, and so Jenny did all the housework and brought up her three brothers well, and whenever her father caught a basket of fish, Jenny took them to Hamnavoe to sell to the housewives there.

And so, Jenny got to know the fishing folk well too. And that summer, when Jenny had arrived at her full beauty, some of the young fishermen looked at her, and they thought they had never in their lives seen such a lovely creature.

That first night, in the Arctic Whaler, the young men's talk was all of Jenny of Furss. 'My grandfather,' said Tom Swanbister, 'saw a mermaid on the Kirk Rocks and he was never done speaking about her beauty, but – poor old man – he died without setting eyes on Jenny Moorfea . . .'

'I'm saving up for a new boat,' said Alec Houton, 'I have twelve sovereigns now in the jar in my mother's cupboard. I would pour them singing into Jenny's hands for one kiss . . .'

Stephen Hoy said, 'I'm going to call my new boat *Jenny*. I was going to call her the *Annie* after the lass next door, that I thought I might marry some day. But now I've settled for *Jenny*. I'll get good catches with the *Jenny*.'

There was a young fisherman called Bertie Ness. At the mention of the name *Jenny*, a look of purest joy came on his face. But he said nothing.

The old fishermen at the bar counter shook their heads and turned pitying looks on the young fishermen. They had thought things like that too, in their youth, and they were still poor men, and they were nagged and raged at when they came in from the west with half-empty baskets.

3

It happened that year, that there was a very good harvest in Orkney, the most bountiful for twenty years. Even the poor croft of Furss was studded with golden stooks.

It was far otherwise on the sea. From horizon to horizon, the sea was barren. It seemed that the lobsters had gone in their blue armour to fight in distant underseas wars. It seemed that haddock and cod had been drawn by that enchantress, the moon, to far-away trystings.

It was a very hard summer along the waterfront of Hamnavoe.

Week after week the boats returned empty from the west, to the shrieking of gulls and the mewling of cats and – worse – the tongue-tempests of the womenfolk.

No wonder it drove the men, after sunset, to the Arctic Whaler, where they sat silent and brooding for the most part.

One evening Stephen Hoy and Alec Houton quarrelled with each other in the Arctic Whaler as to which of their boats could sail furthest west. It began mildly enough, but soon they were snarling at each other. Other fishermen, young and old, joined in the dispute, voices were raised, old half-forgotten ancestral disputes were aired; it reached such a stage of anger that Walter Groat the landlord told them all to leave, get out, come back when they had some money to spend (for lately they had been sitting at the tables till midnight over one mug of thin beer, all they could afford).

Out they trooped, like sullen churlish chidden dogs. The old men went home to their many-worded wives. The young men drifted by twos and threes along the street. At last they found themselves outside Madge Brims's hostelry. Inside, merry rustic voices were raised. Tomorrow was Harvest Home; they were getting in good voice for it.

The young fishermen did a thing never heard of before: they entered the tavern of the hill men, the farmers, the shepherds.

A sudden silence fell. It was as if a troop of wretched penniless outcast beachcombers had trooped up from the shore, bringing the coldness of the ebb with them – and that was pretty much the way things stood that night, in fact, with the fishermen.

But soon the country men returned to their drams and their stories and their loud bothy songs.

One or two went so far as to walk across to where the bitter fishermen stood against the wall and give them a welcome. Will the blacksmith offered to buy them all a dram. 'You look that miserable,' he said.

The fishermen looked at him coldly.

'Can I do anything for you gentlemen?' said Madge Brims to the young men from the salt piers. They answered her never a word.

From then on, the boys from the farms, the crofts, and the sheepfolds ignored those boors of fishermen.

They began to talk about girls. It was the high mark of every discussion or debate or flyting or boasting in Madge Brims's hostelry – it was inevitable – it ended up with praise of bonny lasses.

At last John Greenay, son and heir of the wealthiest farmer in the parish, his face flushed like sunset with whisky, said, 'We all know fine who is the bonniest lass hereabouts, and that's Jenny Moorfea of Furss. And now I'm going to tell you men something – I'm going to marry Jenny in October. I'm going to take her home to Netherquoy. She'll be mistress there, some day.'

Hardly was the last boastful word out of his mouth than it was silenced by the impact of a pewter mug. The mug had been seized from a table by Stephen Hoy the fisherman and hurled with full force.

And at the same time Alec Houton yelled, 'You yokel! You dung-spreader! Jenny Moorfea is coming to our pier to be my wife!'

A trickle of blood came from John Greenay's split lip. The pewter mug rolled about on the flagstone floor, clattering. That was the only sound to be heard for fully five seconds.

Then the young farm men leapt to the defence of their companion. They didn't like John Greenay all that much –

he boasted overmuch about his gear and goods – and besides, they loved Jenny Moorfea more than he did (or so they supposed). But those young fishermen had challenged and insulted the whole race of farmers.

It was the worse fight ever known in a Hamnavoe hostelry since the days of the whaling men a century before. There was a flinging and thudding of fists – there were shouts of rage, contempt, fear, and pain – glasses splintered against the wall – heavy pewter mugs rang like armour on the stone floor – noses were broken, eyes looked like thunder clouds. Will Laird the blacksmith spat out a tooth. Hands closed about throats. There was the flash of a fishing knife. A table was knocked over and twelve glasses and mugs and half a bottle of Old Man of Hoy whisky fell in ruins.

It was the knife-flash that finally unlocked the petrified mouth of Madge Brims. 'Police!' she shouted from the open door of the hostelry. 'Help! Murder! My walls are splashed with whisky and beer and blood!'

What did our heroes care about the law and the disturbance of the Queen's peace? The shouts of battle grew louder. It seemed, in fact, as if an element of joy had entered into the affray. Frankie Stenhouse the young shepherd kicked the sea knife out of Ronald the fisherman's hand. It was to be a fair fist-fight – no heart-stabbings – no hangings for murder.

And still the wounded fighters (for not one of them now but had a broken nose or a thunder-loaded eye or a fractured jaw) melled bloodily on the floor, and raged louder against each other (with, it seemed to some, a mounting access of joy and delight).

Madge Brims had abandoned her tavern to go to the police station in the south end of Hamnavoe, a mile away, to summon the solitary policeman, Constable Bunahill.

A cunning lazy rouge of a fisherman, Simon Readypenny, seized his chance when the battle was at its height to slip behind the counter and put a bottle of brandy into one sea pocket and a bottle of Jamaica into another. And he disappeared into the night, leaving the tumult and the shouting to the fools. (He was found, grey in the face, in a cave, the next morning.)

The tumult and the shouting! It had now reached such a pitch that it could be heard in the granite houses of the respectable merchants and magistrates at the back of the town; and the shopkeepers got out of their beds and double-locked their doors. Indeed, a Graemsay man claimed to have heard the din in his island across Hoy Sound.

Then, a sudden silence fell.

The combatants disengaged themselves. They got to their feet, they made some semblance of wiping the blood from their faces with their shirt sleeves. Will Laird the blacksmith took a splinter of a whisky glass out of his beard.

They would not look at each other. They shuffled their feet like naughty boys chidden by the headmaster.

They were all on their feet now, in the wrecked hostelry, except young Bertie Ness the fisherman, whose kneecap had been cracked by a random kick.

The warriors had become aware of a presence in the pub door. All the snarling heads had turned at once. Jenny Moorfea of Furss was standing there, looking lovelier than any of them had ever seen her before.

Jenny Moorfea pushed her way through the wounds and the dishevelment, and she knelt down beside Bertie Ness, the stricken one, the poorest of all the poor fishermen there, and she kissed him.

4

That is all that needs to be said about the celebrated battle in Madge Brims's bar.

Six men – three from the farms, three from the fishing-boats – appeared at the Burgh court the following week and were fined half-a-crown each for disturbing the peace.

Then all six of them went from the courthouse into a neutral bar and pledged each other like battle-scarred comrades.

The following April, Jenny and Bertie Ness were married in the kirk.

They rented a little house at the end of a stone pier. Bertie Ness went to the fishing to begin with, with Stephen Hoy in his new boat, the *Annie*.

They had such good fishing that summer, and for the two succeeding summers, that Bertie was able to buy a second-hand fishing-boat for himself, the *Madge Brims*, and also to buy their cottage.

Now they have three children, and the two boys are as winsome as their mother, and the youngest – the daughter – is a delight to all the folk that live along that waterfront.

MY LOVE IS LIKE A RED, RED ROSE
Robert Burns

O my Luve's like a red, red rose,
    That's newly sprung in June;
Oh my Luve's like the melodie,
    That's sweetly play'd in tune.

As fair art thou, my bonie lass,
    So deep in luve am I;
And I will love thee still, my Dear,
    Till a' the seas gang dry.

Till a' the seas gang dry, my Dear,
    And the rocks melt wi' the sun:
And I will love thee still, my Dear,
    While the sands o' life shall run.

And fare thee weel, my only Luve!
    And fare thee weel, a while!
And I will come again, my Luve,
    Tho' it were ten thousand mile!

READING NOTES

Most people, if they know this poem, will know it as a song. In a home for the elderly the group sang it together and there were not many dry eyes by the end. Someone remembered her mother singing the song and others remembered with fondness the Scottish singer Kenneth McKellar who sang it 'so that it broke your heart'. Robert Burns, visits to Scotland and, of course, roses were other topics of conversation.

George Mackay Brown's story is set in Orkney. The people in the story are poor and hard working and a lot of readers have been moved by the thought that much of the way of life for those people will have now disappeared. There is much in the story that seems far away and strange yet human nature seems not to change – love, jealousy, fights in pubs, fights between gangs, all of those are still with us. Readers have often compared the fight in the story to the fight in the John Wayne film *The Quiet Man*. The story feels as if it might be told at a fireside and has been described as 'enchanting', 'tender' and 'robust'. Do you share this opinion?

Love and Marriage

❧

MADAME BOVARY

(PART I, CHAPTER 4)

Gustave Flaubert

(approximate reading time 12 minutes)

The story is set in nineteenth-century northern France. Charles Bovary is decent, dull and unimaginative. His parents, however, are determined that he should be a successful doctor. He makes a poor student, eventually scraping a pass in the necessary exams. His mother persuades him to marry a much older wealthy widow with whom he is unhappy. One day he is called to a farm to treat the farmer. He meets the farmer's daughter Emma to whom he is immediately attracted. Following the death of Heloise, his wife, Charles asks Farmer Roualt for Emma's hand in marriage. Emma thinks Charles will be the answer to her romantic dreams . . .

The guests arrived early in carriages, in one-horse chaises, two-wheeled cars, old open gigs, wagonettes with leather hoods, and the young people from the nearer villages in carts, in which they stood up in rows, holding on to the sides so as not to fall, going at a trot and well shaken up. Some came from a distance of thirty miles, from Goderville, from Normanville, and from Cany.

All the relatives of both families had been invited, quarrels between friends arranged, acquaintances long since lost sight of written to.

From time to time one heard the crack of a whip behind the hedge; then the gates opened, a chaise entered. Galloping up to the foot of the steps, it stopped short and emptied its load. They got down from all sides, rubbing knees and stretching arms. The ladies, wearing bonnets, had on dresses in the town fashion, gold watch chains, pelerines with the ends tucked into belts, or little coloured fichus fastened down behind with a pin, and that left the back of the neck bare. The lads, dressed like their papas, seemed uncomfortable in their new clothes (many that day hand-sewed their first pair of boots), and by their sides, speaking never a word, wearing the white dress of their first communion lengthened for the occasion were some big girls of fourteen or sixteen, cousins or elder sisters no doubt, rubicund, bewildered, their hair greasy with rose pomade, and very much afraid of dirtying their gloves. As there were not enough stable-boys to unharness all the carriages, the gentlemen turned up their sleeves and set about it themselves. According to their different social positions they wore tail-coats, overcoats, shooting jackets, cutaway-coats; fine tail-coats, redolent of family respectability, that only came out of the wardrobe on state occasions; overcoats with long tails flapping in the wind and round capes and pockets like sacks; shooting jackets of coarse cloth, generally worn with a cap with a brass-bound peak; very short cutaway-coats with two small buttons in the back, close together like a pair of eyes, and the tails of which seemed cut out of one piece by a carpenter's hatchet. Some, too (but these, you may be sure, would sit at the bottom of the table), wore their best blouses – that is to say, with collars turned down to the shoulders, the back gathered into small plaits and the waist fastened very low down with a worked belt.

And the shirts stood out from the chests like cuirasses! Everyone had just had his hair cut; ears stood out from the heads; they had been close-shaved; a few, even, who had had to get up before daybreak, and not been able to see to shave, had diagonal gashes under their noses or cuts the size of a three-franc piece along the jaws, which the fresh air en route had enflamed, so that the great white beaming faces were mottled here and there with red dabs.

The mairie was a mile and a half from the farm, and they went thither on foot, returning in the same way after the ceremony in the church. The procession, first united like one long coloured scarf that undulated across the fields, along the narrow path winding amid the green corn, soon lengthened out, and broke up into different groups that loitered to talk. The fiddler walked in front with his violin, gay with ribbons at its pegs. Then came the married pair, the relations, the friends, all following pell-mell; the children stayed behind amusing themselves plucking the bell-flowers from oat-ears, or playing amongst themselves unseen. Emma's dress, too long, trailed a little on the ground; from time to time she stopped to pull it up, and then delicately, with her gloved hands, she picked off the coarse grass and the thistledowns, while Charles, empty-handed, waited till she had finished. Old Rouault, with a new silk hat and the cuffs of his black coat covering his hands up to the nails, gave his arm to Madame Bovary senior. As to Monsieur Bovary senior, who, heartily despising all these folk, had come simply in a frock-coat of military cut with one row of buttons – he was passing compliments of the bar to a fair young peasant. She bowed, blushed, and did not know what to say. The other wedding guests talked of their business or played tricks behind each other's backs, egging one another on in advance to be jolly. Those who listened could always catch the squeaking of the fiddler, who went on playing across the fields. When he saw that the rest were far behind he stopped to take breath, slowly rosined his bow, so that the strings should sound more shrilly, then set off again, by turns lowering and raising his neck, the better to mark time for himself. The noise of the instrument drove away the little birds from afar.

The table was laid under the cart-shed. On it were four sirloins, six chicken fricassees, stewed veal, three legs of mutton, and in the middle a fine roast suckling pig, flanked by four chitterlings with sorrel. At the corners were decanters of brandy. Sweet bottled-cider frothed round the corks, and all the glasses had been filled to the brim with wine beforehand. Large dishes of yellow cream, that trembled with the least shake of the table, had designed on their smooth surface the initials of the newly wedded pair in nonpareil arabesques. A confectioner of Yvetot had been entrusted with the tarts and sweets. As he had only just set up on the place, he had taken a lot of trouble, and at dessert he himself brought in a set dish that evoked loud cries of wonderment. To begin with, at its base there was a square of blue cardboard, representing a temple with porticoes, colonnades, and stucco statuettes all round, and in the niches constellations of gilt paper stars; then on the second stage was a dungeon of Savoy cake, surrounded by many fortifications in candied angelica, almonds, raisins, and quarters of oranges; and finally, on the upper platform a green field with rocks set in lakes of jam, nutshell boats, and a small Cupid balancing himself in a chocolate swing whose two uprights ended in real roses for balls at the top.

Until night they ate. When any of them were too tired of sitting, they went out for a stroll in the yard, or for a game with corks in the granary, and then returned to table. Some towards the finish went to sleep and snored. But with the coffee everyone woke up. Then they began songs, showed off tricks, raised heavy weights, performed feats with their fingers, then tried lifting carts on their shoulders, made broad jokes, kissed the women. At night when they left, the horses, stuffed up to the nostrils with oats, could hardly be got into the shafts; they kicked, reared, the harness broke, their masters laughed or swore; and all night in the light of the moon along country roads there were runaway carts at full gallop plunging into the ditches, jumping over yard after yard of stones, clambering up the hills, with women leaning out from the tilt to catch hold of the reins.

Those who stayed at the Bertaux spent the night drinking in the kitchen. The children had fallen asleep under the seats.

The bride had begged her father to be spared the usual marriage pleasantries. However, a fishmonger, one of their cousins (who had even brought a pair of soles for his wedding present), began to squirt water from his mouth through the keyhole, when old Rouault came up just in time to stop him, and explain to him that the distinguished position of his son-in-law would not allow of such liberties. The cousin all the same did not give in to these reasons readily. In his heart he accused old Rouault of being proud, and he joined four or five other guests in a corner, who having, through mere chance, been several times running served with the worst helps of meat, also were of opinion they had been badly used, and were whispering about their host, and with covered hints hoping he would ruin himself.

Madame Bovary, senior, had not opened her mouth all day. She had been consulted neither as to the dress of her daughter-in-law nor as to the arrangement of the feast; she went to bed early. Her husband, instead of following her, sent to Saint-Victor for some cigars, and smoked till daybreak, drinking kirsch-punch, a mixture unknown to the company. This added greatly to the consideration in which he was held.

Charles, who was not of a facetious turn, did not shine at the wedding. He answered feebly to the puns, doubles entendres, compliments, and chaff that it was felt a duty to let off at him as soon as the soup appeared.

The next day, on the other hand, he seemed another man. It was he who might rather have been taken for the virgin of the evening before, whilst the bride gave no sign that revealed anything. The shrewdest did not know what to make of it, and they looked at her when she passed near them with an unbounded concentration of mind. But Charles concealed nothing. He called her 'my wife', tutoyed* her, asked for her of everyone, looked for her everywhere, and often he dragged her into the yards, where he could be seen from far between the trees, putting his arm around her waist, and walking half-bending over her, ruffling the chemisette of her bodice with his head.

Two days after the wedding the married pair left. Charles, on account of his patients, could not be away longer. Old Rouault had them driven back in his cart, and himself accompanied them as far as Vassonville. Here he embraced his daughter for the last time, got down, and went his way. When he had gone about a hundred paces he stopped, and as he saw the cart disappearing, its wheels turning in the dust, he gave a deep sigh. Then he remembered his wedding, the old times, the first pregnancy of his wife; he, too, had been very happy the day when he had taken her from her father to his home, and had carried her off on a pillion, trotting through the snow, for it was near Christmas-time, and the country was all white. She held him by one arm, her basket hanging from the other; the wind blew the long lace of her Cauchois headdress so that it sometimes flapped across his mouth, and when he turned his head he saw near him, on his shoulder, her little rosy face, smiling silently under the gold bands of her cap. To warm her hands she put them from time to time in his breast. How long ago it all was! Their son would have been thirty by now.

* Used the familiar form of address.

Then he looked back and saw nothing on the road. He felt dreary as an empty house; and tender memories mingling with the sad thoughts in his brain, addled by the fumes of the feast, he felt inclined for a moment to take a turn towards the church. As he was afraid, however, that this sight would make him yet more sad, he went right away home.

Monsieur and Madame Charles arrived at Tostes about six o'clock.

The neighbours came to the windows to see their doctor's new wife.

The old servant presented herself, curtsied to her, apologised for not having dinner ready, and suggested that madame, in the meantime, should look over her house.

SONNET 116
William Shakespeare

Let me not to the marriage of true minds
Admit impediments. Love is not love
Which alters when it alteration finds,
Or bends with the remover to remove:
O no, it is an ever-fixèd mark,
That looks on tempests and is never shaken;
It is the star to every wandering bark,
Whose worth's unknown, although his height be taken.
Love's not Time's fool, though rosy lips and cheeks
Within his bending sickle's compass come;
Love alters not with his brief hours and weeks,
But bears it out even to the edge of doom.
  If this be error and upon me proved,
   I never writ, nor no man ever loved.

READING NOTES

Here is an opportunity for people to remember their own wedding
or family weddings. In a nursing home for the elderly everyone in
the group brought along their wedding photographs and carers
and residents alike shared memories, admired beautiful brides
and handsome grooms, recalled happy times and celebrated
young love.

The simple country wedding in France, 150 years ago invites
comparison with twenty-first century extravaganzas. Some things
are so different – weddings on the beach, long, expensive hen
and stag parties – and some things never change – the feast; the
cake; the difficult mother-in-law; the practical jokes; the sentimental father.

Shakespeare's line 'love is not love which alters when it alteration finds' prompted talk of the effect of time on different attitudes to the seriousness of marriage vows. What advice would
the old give to the young on their wedding day? And can it be
true that love 'looks on tempests and is never shaken'? This group
had plenty to say.

Little Acts of Kindness

❦

LITTLE WOMEN
(BETH FINDS THE PALACE BEAUTIFUL, CHAPTER 6)
Louisa May Alcott

(approximate reading time 17 minutes)

The little women of the book title are the four March sisters. Meg is the beauty, Jo the tomboy, Amy is precocious and Beth is the shy one with a deep love of music. The family have fallen on hard times while the girls' father is away serving as a Union chaplain in the American Civil War. The rather grand house next door is newly occupied by the elderly Mr Laurence and his grandson Laurie . . .

The big house did prove a Palace Beautiful, though it took some time for all to get in, and Beth found it very hard to pass the lions. Old Mr Laurence was the biggest one, but after he had called, said something funny or kind to each one of the girls, and talked over old times with their mother, nobody felt much afraid of him, except timid Beth. The other lion was the fact that they were poor and Laurie rich, for this made them shy of accepting favors which they could not return. But, after a while, they found that he considered them the benefactors, and could not do enough to show how grateful he was for Mrs March's motherly welcome, their cheerful society, and the comfort he took in that humble home of theirs. So they soon forgot their pride and interchanged kindnesses without stopping to think which was the greater.

All sorts of pleasant things happened about that time, for the new friendship flourished like grass in spring. Everyone liked Laurie, and he privately informed his tutor that 'the Marches were regularly splendid girls.' With the delightful enthusiasm of youth, they took the solitary boy into their midst and made much of him, and he found something very charming in the innocent companionship of these simple-hearted girls. Never having known mother or sisters, he was quick to feel the influences they brought about him, and their busy, lively ways made him ashamed of the indolent life he led. He was tired of books, and found people so interesting now that Mr Brooke was obliged to make very unsatisfactory reports, for Laurie was always playing truant and running over to the Marches'.

'Never mind, let him take a holiday, and make it up afterward,' said the old gentleman. 'The good lady next door says he is studying too hard and needs young society, amusement, and exercise. I suspect she is right, and that I've been coddling the fellow as if I'd been his grandmother. Let him do what he likes, as long as he is happy. He can't get into mischief in that little nunnery over there, and Mrs March is doing more for him than we can.'

What good times they had, to be sure. Such plays and tableaux, such sleigh rides and skating frolics, such pleasant evenings in the old parlor, and now and then such gay little parties at the great house. Meg could walk in the conservatory whenever she liked and revel in bouquets, Jo browsed over the new library voraciously, and convulsed the old gentleman with her criticisms, Amy copied pictures and enjoyed beauty to her heart's content, and Laurie played 'lord of the manor' in the most delightful style.

But Beth, though yearning for the grand piano, could not pluck up courage to go to the 'Mansion of Bliss', as Meg called it. She went once with Jo, but the old gentleman, not being aware of her infirmity, stared at her so hard from under his heavy eyebrows, and said 'Hey!' so loud, that he frightened her so much her 'feet chattered on the floor', she never told her mother, and she ran away, declaring she would never go there any more, not even for the dear piano. No persuasions or enticements could overcome her fear, till, the fact coming to Mr Laurence's ear in some mysterious way, he set about mending matters. During one of the brief calls he made, he artfully led the conversation to music, and talked away about great singers whom he had seen, fine organs he had heard, and told such charming anecdotes that Beth found it impossible to stay in her distant corner, but crept nearer and nearer, as if fascinated. At the back of his chair she stopped and stood listening, with her great eyes wide open and her cheeks red with excitement of this unusual performance. Taking no more notice of her than if she had been a fly, Mr Laurence talked on about Laurie's lessons and teachers. And presently, as if the idea had just occurred to him, he said to Mrs March ...

'The boy neglects his music now, and I'm glad of it, for

he was getting too fond of it. But the piano suffers for want of use. Wouldn't some of your girls like to run over, and practice on it now and then, just to keep it in tune, you know, ma'am?'

Beth took a step forward, and pressed her hands tightly together to keep from clapping them, for this was an irresistible temptation, and the thought of practicing on that splendid instrument quite took her breath away. Before Mrs March could reply, Mr Laurence went on with an odd little nod and smile . . .

'They needn't see or speak to anyone, but run in at any time. For I'm shut up in my study at the other end of the house, Laurie is out a great deal, and the servants are never near the drawing room after nine o'clock.'

Here he rose, as if going, and Beth made up her mind to speak, for that last arrangement left nothing to be desired. 'Please, tell the young ladies what I say, and if they don't care to come, why, never mind.' Here a little hand slipped into his, and Beth looked up at him with a face full of gratitude, as she said, in her earnest yet timid way . . .

'Oh sir, they do care, very very much!'

'Are you the musical girl?' he asked, without any startling 'Hey!' as he looked down at her very kindly.

'I'm Beth. I love it dearly, and I'll come, if you are quite sure nobody will hear me, and be disturbed,' she added, fearing to be rude, and trembling at her own boldness as she spoke.

'Not a soul, my dear. The house is empty half the day, so come and drum away as much as you like, and I shall be obliged to you.'

'How kind you are, sir!'

Beth blushed like a rose under the friendly look he wore, but she was not frightened now, and gave the hand a grateful squeeze because she had no words to thank him for the precious gift he had given her. The old gentleman softly stroked the hair off her forehead, and, stooping down, he kissed her, saying, in a tone few people ever heard . . .

'I had a little girl once, with eyes like these. God bless you, my dear! Good day, madam.' And away he went, in a great hurry.

Beth had a rapture with her mother, and then rushed up to impart the glorious news to her family of invalids, as the girls were not home. How blithely she sang that evening, and how they all laughed at her because she woke Amy in the

night by playing the piano on her face in her sleep. Next day, having seen both the old and young gentleman out of the house, Beth, after two or three retreats, fairly got in at the side door, and made her way as noiselessly as any mouse to the drawing room where her idol stood. Quite by accident, of course, some pretty, easy music lay on the piano, and with trembling fingers and frequent stops to listen and look about, Beth at last touched the great instrument, and straightway forgot her fear, herself, and everything else but the unspeakable delight which the music gave her, for it was like the voice of a beloved friend.

She stayed till Hannah came to take her home to dinner, but she had no appetite, and could only sit and smile upon everyone in a general state of beatitude.

After that, the little brown hood slipped through the hedge nearly every day, and the great drawing room was haunted by a tuneful spirit that came and went unseen. She never knew that Mr Laurence opened his study door to hear the old-fashioned airs he liked. She never saw Laurie mount guard in the hall to warn the servants away. She never suspected that the exercise books and new songs which she found in the rack were put there for her especial benefit, and when he talked to her about music at home, she only thought how kind he was to tell things that helped her so much. So she enjoyed herself heartily, and found, what isn't always the case, that her granted wish was all she had hoped. Perhaps it was because she was so grateful for this blessing that a greater was given her. At any rate she deserved both. 'Mother, I'm going to work Mr Laurence a pair of slippers. He is so kind to me, I must thank

him, and I don't know any other way. Can I do it?' asked
Beth, a few weeks after that eventful call of his.

'Yes, dear. It will please him very much, and be a nice way
of thanking him. The girls will help you about them, and I
will pay for the making up,' replied Mrs March, who took
peculiar pleasure in granting Beth's requests because she so
seldom asked anything for herself.

After many serious discussions with Meg and Jo, the
pattern was chosen, the materials bought, and the slippers
begun. A cluster of grave yet cheerful pansies on a deeper
purple ground was pronounced very appropriate and pretty,
and Beth worked away early and late, with occasional lifts
over hard parts. She was a nimble little needlewoman, and
they were finished before anyone got tired of them. Then
she wrote a short, simple note, and with Laurie's help, got
them smuggled onto the study table one morning before the
old gentleman was up.

When this excitement was over, Beth waited to see what
would happen. All day passed and a part of the next before any
acknowledgement arrived, and she was beginning to fear she
had offended her crotchety friend. On the afternoon of the
second day, she went out to do an errand, and give poor Joanna,
the invalid doll, her daily exercise. As she came up the street,
on her return, she saw three, yes, four heads popping in and
out of the parlor windows, and the moment they saw her, several
hands were waved, and several joyful voices screamed . . .

'Here's a letter from the old gentleman! Come quick, and
read it!'

'Oh, Beth, he's sent you . . .' began Amy, gesticulating with unseemly energy, but she got no further, for Jo quenched her by slamming down the window.

Beth hurried on in a flutter of suspense. At the door her sisters seized and bore her to the parlor in a triumphal procession, all pointing and all saying at once, 'Look there! Look there!' Beth did look, and turned pale with delight and surprise, for there stood a little cabinet piano, with a letter lying on the glossy lid, directed like a sign board to 'Miss Elizabeth March.'

'For me?' gasped Beth, holding onto Jo and feeling as if she should tumble down, it was such an overwhelming thing altogether.

'Yes, all for you, my precious! Isn't it splendid of him? Don't you think he's the dearest old man in the world? Here's the key in the letter. We didn't open it, but we are dying to know what he says,' cried Jo, hugging her sister and offering the note.

'You read it! I can't, I feel so queer! Oh, it is too lovely!' and Beth hid her face in Jo's apron, quite upset by her present.

Jo opened the paper and began to laugh, for the first words she saw were . . .

'Miss March: Dear Madam –'

'How nice it sounds! I wish someone would write to me so!' said Amy, who thought the old-fashioned address very elegant.

'"I have had many pairs of slippers in my life, but I never had any that suited me so well as yours,"' continues Jo.

'"Heartsease is my favorite flower, and these will always remind me of the gentle giver. I like to pay my debts, so I know you will allow 'the old gentleman' to send you something which once belonged to the little grand-daughter he lost. With hearty thanks and best wishes, I remain Your grateful friend and humble servant, James Laurence."'

'There, Beth, that's an honor to be proud of, I'm sure! Laurie told me how fond Mr Laurence used to be of the child who died, and how he kept all her little things carefully. Just think, he's given you her piano. That comes of having big blue eyes and loving music,' said Jo, trying to soothe Beth, who trembled and looked more excited than she had ever been before.

'See the cunning brackets to hold candles, and the nice green silk, puckered up, with a gold rose in the middle, and the pretty rack and stool, all complete,' added Meg, opening the instrument and displaying its beauties.

'"Your humble servant, James Laurence"'. Only think of his writing that to you. I'll tell the girls. They'll think it's splendid,' said Amy, much impressed by the note.

'Try it, honey. Let's hear the sound of the baby pianny,' said Hannah, who always took a share in the family joys and sorrows.

So Beth tried it, and everyone pronounced it the most remarkable piano ever heard. It had evidently been newly tuned and put in apple-pie order, but, perfect as it was, I think the real charm lay in the happiest of all happy faces which leaned over it, as Beth lovingly touched the beautiful black and white keys and pressed the bright pedals.

'You'll have to go and thank him,' said Jo, by way of a joke, for the idea of the child's really going never entered her head.

'Yes, I mean to. I guess I'll go now, before I get frightened thinking about it.' And, to the utter amazement of the assembled family, Beth walked deliberately down the garden, through the hedge, and in at the Laurences' door.

'Well, I wish I may die if it ain't the queerest thing I ever see! The pianny has turned her head! She'd never have gone in her right mind,' cried Hannah, staring after her, while the girls were rendered quite speechless by the miracle.

They would have been still more amazed if they had seen what Beth did afterward. If you will believe me, she went and knocked at the study door before she gave herself time to think, and when a gruff voice called out, 'come in!' she did go in, right up to Mr Laurence, who looked quite taken aback, and held out her hand, saying, with only a small quaver in her voice, 'I came to thank you, sir, for . . .' But she didn't finish, for he looked so friendly that she forgot her speech and, only remembering that he had lost the little girl he loved, she put both arms round his neck and kissed him.

If the roof of the house had suddenly flown off, the old gentleman wouldn't have been more astonished. But he liked it. Oh, dear, yes, he liked it amazingly! And was so touched and pleased by that confiding little kiss that all his crustiness vanished, and he just set her on his knee, and laid his wrinkled cheek against her rosy one, feeling as if he had got his own little grand-daughter back again. Beth ceased to fear him from that moment, and sat there talking to him as cozily as if she had known him all her life, for love casts out fear, and gratitude can conquer pride. When she went home, he walked with her to her own gate, shook hands cordially, and touched his hat as he marched back again, looking very stately and erect, like a handsome, soldierly old gentleman, as he was.

When the girls saw that performance, Jo began to dance a jig, by way of expressing her satisfaction, Amy nearly fell out of the window in her surprise, and Meg exclaimed, with up-lifted hands, 'Well, I do believe the world is coming to an end.'

'AMONG ALL LOVELY THINGS MY LOVE HAD BEEN' [THE GLOW-WORM]
William Wordsworth

Among all lovely things my Love had been;
Had noted well the stars, all flowers that grew
About her home; but she had never seen
A Glow-worm, never one, and this I knew.

While riding near her home one stormy night
A single Glow-worm did I chance to espy;
I gave a fervent welcome to the sight,
And from my Horse I leapt; great joy had I.

Upon a leaf the Glow-worm did I lay,
To bear it with me through the stormy night:
And, as before, it shone without dismay;
Albeit putting forth a fainter light.

When to the Dwelling of my Love I came,
I went into the Orchard quietly;
And left the Glow-worm, blessing it by name,
Laid safely by itself, beneath a Tree.

The whole next day, I hoped, and hoped with fear;
At night the Glow-worm shone beneath the Tree;
I led my Lucy to the spot, 'Look here!'
Oh! joy it was for her, and joy for me!

READING NOTES

The chapter from *Little Women* brought back memories of childhood reading for some members of an afternoon reading group. John said he had enjoyed the chapter but had never read the novel which he'd considered a girl's book. There was much thought given to the line from the story: 'the fact that they were poor and Laurie rich, [for this] made them shy of accepting favors which they could not return.' Why is it that giving and receiving is not always straightforward?

Joyce said the chapter had made her cry as she remembered how much she had loved her grandfather. Grandfathers then became the topic of conversation before the group moved on to other books and films that might be described as weepies. Finally, there was talk of best presents ever received; playing the piano; and how families used to sing round the piano.

The group then had a long talk about kindness and how much we depend on it and the importance of acting kindly towards others; how easy it is to be kind and to be thoughtlessly unkind and the difference between charity and kindness. Bill regretted never having seen a glow-worm but thought the poem was saying that being kind to others was the best way of achieving happiness for yourself: 'joy it was for her, and joy for me!' And joy for Beth and the old man too.

Faces of Friendship

🍂

THE RAILWAY CHILDREN

(THE PRIDE OF PERKS, CHAPTER 9)

Edith Nesbit

(approximate reading time 22 minutes)

Roberta (Bobbie), Peter and Phyllis have come to live in the country where, in much-reduced circumstances, their mother must write stories in order to make a living for them. Unbeknown to the children, their father has been falsely imprisoned on spying charges. The three Edwardian children become caught up in the world of the local railway and among their new friends is Perks, the station porter . . .

It was breakfast-time. Mother's face was very bright as she poured the milk and ladled out the porridge.

'I've sold another story, Chickies,' she said; 'the one about the King of the Mussels, so there'll be buns for tea. You can go and get them as soon as they're baked. About eleven, isn't it?'

Peter, Phyllis, and Bobbie exchanged glances with each other. Then Bobbie said: 'Mother, would you mind if we didn't have

the buns for tea to-night, but on the fifteenth? That's next Thursday.'

'I don't mind when you have them, dear,' said Mother, 'but why?'

'Because it's Perks's birthday,' said Bobbie; 'he's thirty-two, and he says he doesn't keep his birthday any more, because he's got other things to keep – not rabbits or secrets – but the kids and the missus.'

'You mean his wife and children,' said Mother.

'Yes,' said Phyllis; 'it's the same thing, isn't it?'

'And we thought we'd make a nice birthday for him. He's been so awfully jolly decent to us, you know, Mother,' said Peter.

'I see,' said Mother. 'Certainly. It would be nice to put his name on the buns with pink sugar, wouldn't it?'

'Perks,' said Peter, 'it's not a pretty name.'

'His other name's Albert,' said Phyllis; 'I asked him once.'

'We might put A. P.,' said Mother; 'I'll show you how when the day comes.'

This was all very well as far as it went. But even fourteen halfpenny buns with A. P. on them in pink sugar do not of themselves make a very grand celebration.

'But there must be something to trim besides buns,' said Bobbie.

'Let's all be quiet and think,' said Phyllis; 'no one's to speak until it's thought of something.'

'Hooray!' cried Peter, suddenly, 'I've got it. Perks is so nice to everybody. There must be lots of people in the village who'd like to help to make him a birthday. Let's go round and ask everybody.'

'Mother said we weren't to ask people for things,' said Bobbie, doubtfully.

'For ourselves, she meant, silly, not for other people.'

'Let's ask Mother first,' said Bobbie.

'Oh, what's the use of bothering Mother about every little thing?' said Peter, especially when she's busy. Come on. Let's go down to the village now and begin.'

So they went. The old lady at the Post-office said she didn't see why Perks should have a birthday any more than anyone else.

'No,' said Bobbie, 'I should like everyone to have one. Only we know when his is.'

'Mine's to-morrow,' said the old lady, 'and much notice anyone will take of it. Go along with you.'

So they went.

And some people were kind, and some were crusty. And some would give and some would not. It is rather difficult work asking for things.

When the children got home and counted up what had been given and what had been promised, they felt that for the first day it was not so bad. Peter wrote down the lists of the things in the little pocket-book where he kept the numbers of his engines. These were the lists:

GIVEN. A tobacco pipe from the sweet shop. Half a pound of tea from the grocer's. A woollen scarf slightly faded from the draper's, which was the other side of the grocer's. A stuffed squirrel from the Doctor.
PROMISED. A piece of meat from the butcher. Six fresh eggs from the woman who lived in the old turn-pike cottage. A piece of honeycomb and six bootlaces from the cobbler, and an iron shovel from the black-smith's.

Very early next morning Bobbie got up and woke Phyllis. This had been agreed on between them.

They cut a big bunch of roses, and put it in a basket with

the needle-book that Phyllis had made for Bobbie on her birthday, and a very pretty blue necktie of Phyllis's. Then they wrote on a paper: 'For Mrs Ransome, with our best love, because it is her birthday,' and they put the paper in the basket, and they took it to the Post Office, and went in and put it on the counter and ran away before the old woman at the Post-office had time to get into her shop.

When they got home Peter had grown confidential over helping Mother to get the breakfast and had told her their plans.

'There's no harm in it,' said Mother, 'but it depends *how* you do it. I only hope he won't be offended and think it's *charity*. Poor people are very proud, you know.'

'It isn't because he's poor,' said Phyllis; 'it's because we're fond of him.'

'I'll find some things that Phyllis has outgrown,' said Mother, 'if you're quite sure you can give them to him without his being offended. What are you writing, Bobbie?'

'Nothing particular,' said Bobbie, who had suddenly begun to scribble. 'I'm sure he'd like the things, Mother.'

The morning of the fifteenth was spent very happily in getting the buns and watching Mother make A. P. on them with pink sugar.

Afterwards the children went up to the village to collect the honey and the shovel and the other promised things.

The old lady at the Post-office was standing on her doorstep. The children said 'Good morning,' politely, as they passed.

'Here, stop a bit,' she said.

So they stopped.

'Those roses,' said she.

'Did you like them?' said Phyllis; 'they were as fresh as fresh. I made the needle-book, but it was Bobbie's present.' She skipped joyously as she spoke.

'Here's your basket,' said the Post-office woman. She went in and brought out the basket. It was full of fat, red gooseberries.

'I dare say Perks's children would like them,' said she.

'You *are* an old dear,' said Phyllis, throwing her arms around the old lady's fat waist. 'Perks *will* be pleased.'

'He won't be half so pleased as I was with your needlebook and the tie and the pretty flowers and all,' said the old lady, patting Phyllis's shoulder. 'You're good little souls, that you are. Look here. I've got a pram round the back in the wood-lodge. It was got for my Emmie's first, that didn't live but six months, and she never had but that one. I'd like Mrs Perks to have it. It 'ud be a help to her with that great boy of hers. Will you take it along?'

'*Oh!*' said all the children together. 'Oh, *isn't* it nice to think there is going to be a real live baby in it again!'

'Yes,' said Mrs Ransome, sighing, and then laughing; 'here, I'll give you some peppermint cushions for the little ones, and then you run along before I give you the roof off my head and the clothes off my back.'

All the things that had been collected for Perks were packed into the perambulator, and at half-past three Peter and Bobbie and Phyllis wheeled it down to the little yellow house where Perks lived.

The house was very tidy. On the window ledge was a jug

of wildflowers, big daisies, and red sorrel, and feathery, flowery grasses.

There was a sound of splashing from the wash-house, and a partly washed boy put his head round the door.

'Mother's a-changing of herself,' he said.

'Down in a minute,' a voice sounded down the narrow, freshly scrubbed stairs.

The children waited. Next moment the stairs creaked and Mrs Perks came down, buttoning her bodice. Her hair was brushed very smooth and tight, and her face shone with soap and water.

'I'm a bit late changing, Miss,' she said to Bobbie, 'owing to me having had a extry clean-up to-day, along o' Perks happening to name its being his birthday. I don't know what put it into his head to think of such a thing. We keeps the children's birthdays, of course; but him and me – we're too old for such like, as a general rule.'

'We knew it was his birthday,' said Peter, 'and we've got some presents for him outside in the perambulator.'

As the presents were being unpacked, Mrs Perks gasped. When they were all unpacked, she surprised and horrified the children by sitting suddenly down on a wooden chair and bursting into tears.

'Oh, don't!' said everybody; 'oh, please don't!' And Peter added, perhaps a little impatiently, '*Don't* you like it?', while his sisters patted Mrs Perks on the back.

She stopped crying as suddenly as she had begun.

'There, there, don't you mind me. *I'm* all right!' she said. 'Like it? Why, it's a birthday such as Perks never 'ad, not even when 'e was a boy. And then she went on and said all kinds of nice things.

At last Peter said: 'Look here, we're glad you're pleased. But if you go on saying things like that, we must go home. And we did want to stay and see if Mr Perks is pleased, too. But we can't stand this.'

'I won't say another single word,' said Mrs Perks, with a beaming face.

'Can we have a plate for the buns?' Bobbie asked abruptly. And then Mrs Perks hastily laid the table for tea, and the buns and the honey and the gooseberries were displayed on plates, and the roses were put in two glass jam jars, and the tea-table looked, as Mrs Perks said, 'fit for a Prince. Oh Bless us! 'e *is* early!'

Perks had indeed unlatched the latch of the little front gate.

'Oh,' whispered Bobbie, 'let's hide in the back kitchen, and YOU tell him about it. But give him the tobacco first, because you got it for him. And when you've told him, we'll all come in and shout, "Many happy returns!"'

It was a very nice plan, but it did not quite come off. To begin with, there was only just time for Peter and Bobbie and Phyllis to rush into the wash-house, pushing the young and open-mouthed Perks children in front of them. There was not time to shut the door, so that, without at all meaning it, they had to listen to what went on in the kitchen.

'Hullo, old woman!' they heard Mr Perks's voice say; 'here's a pretty set-out!'

'It's your birthday tea, Bert,' said Mrs Perks, 'and here's a ounce of your extry particular. I got it o' Saturday along o' your happening to remember it was your birthday to-day.'

'Good old girl!' said Mr Perks, and there was a sound of a kiss.

'But what's that pram doing here? And what's all these bundles? And where did you get the sweetstuff, and –'

The children did not hear what Mrs Perks replied, because just then Bobbie gave a start, put her hand in her pocket, and all her body grew stiff with horror.

'Oh!' she whispered to the others, 'whatever shall we do? I forgot to put the labels on any of the things! He won't know what's from who. He'll think it's all *us*, and that we're trying to be grand or charitable or something horrid.'

'Hush!' said Peter.

And then they heard the voice of Mr Perks, loud and rather angry.

'I don't care,' he said; 'I won't stand it, and so I tell you straight.'

'But,' said Mrs Perks, 'it's them children you make such a fuss about – the children from the Three Chimneys.'

'I don't care,' said Perks, firmly, 'not if it was a angel from Heaven. We've got on all right all these years and no favours asked. I'm not going to begin these sort of charity goings-on at my time of life, so don't you think it, Nell.'

'Oh, hush!' said poor Mrs Perks; 'Bert, shut your silly tongue, for goodness' sake. The all three of 'ems in the wash-house a-listening to every word you speaks.'

'Then I'll give them something to listen to,' said the angry Perks, and he took two strides to the wash-house door, and flung it wide open.

'Come out,' said Perks, 'come out and tell me what you

mean by it. 'Ave I ever complained to you of being short, as you comes this charity lay over me?'

'*Oh!*' said Phyllis, 'I thought you'd be so pleased; I'll never try to be kind to anyone else as long as I live. No, I won't, not never.'

She burst into tears.

'We didn't mean any harm,' said Peter.

'It ain't what you means so much as what you does,' said Perks.

'Oh, *don't!*' cried Bobbie, trying hard to be braver than Phyllis, and to find more words than Peter had done for explaining in. 'We thought you'd love it. We always have things on our birthdays.'

'Oh, yes,' said Perks, 'your own relations; that's different.'

'Oh, no,' Bobbie answered. '*Not* our own relations. When it was my birthday Mother gave me the brooch like a buttercup, Mrs Viney gave me two lovely glass pots, and nobody thought she was coming the charity lay over us.'

'But they're not all from us –' said Peter, 'only we forgot to put the labels on. They're from all sorts of people in the village.'

'Who put 'em up to it, I'd like to know?' asked Perks.

'Why, we did,' sniffed Phyllis.

Perks sat down heavily in the elbow-chair and looked at them with what Bobbie afterwards described as withering glances of gloomy despair.

'So you've been round telling the neighbours we can't make both ends meet? Well, now you've disgraced us as deep as you can in the neighbourhood, you can just take the whole bag of tricks back w'ere it come from. Very much obliged, I'm sure. I don't doubt but what you meant it kind, but I'd rather not be acquainted with you any longer if it's all the same to you.' He deliberately turned the chair round so that his back was turned to the children. The legs of the chair grated on the brick floor, and that was the only sound that broke the silence.

Then suddenly Bobbie spoke.

'Look here,' she said, 'this is most awful.'

'That's what I says,' said Perks, not turning round.

'Look here,' said Bobbie, desperately, 'we'll go if you like – and you needn't be friends with us any more if you don't want, but—'

'*We* shall always be friends with *you*, however nasty you are to us,' sniffed Phyllis, wildly.

'Be quiet,' said Peter, in a fierce aside.

'But before we go,' Bobbie went on desperately, 'do let us show you the labels we wrote to put on the things.'

'I don't want to see no labels,' said Perks. 'Do you think I've kept respectable and outer debt on what I gets, and her having to take in washing, to be give away for a laughing-stock to all the neighbours?'

'Laughing?' said Peter; 'you don't know.'

'You're a very hasty gentleman,' whined Phyllis; 'do let Bobbie tell you about the labels!'

'Well. Go ahead!' said Perks, grudgingly.

'Well, then,' said Bobbie, fumbling miserably, yet not without hope, in her tightly stuffed pocket, 'we wrote down all the things everybody said when they gave us the things, with the people's names, because Mother said we ought to be careful – because – but I wrote down what she said – and you'll see.'

But Bobbie could not read the labels just at once. She had to swallow once or twice before she could begin.

'Mother's first. It says:

'"Little Clothes for Mrs Perks's children." Mother said, "I'll find some of Phyllis's things that she's grown out of if you're quite sure Mr Perks wouldn't be offended and think it's meant for charity. I'd like to do some little thing for him, because he's so kind to you. I can't do much because we're poor ourselves."'

Bobbie paused.

'That's all right,' said Perks, 'your Ma's a born lady. We'll keep the little frocks, and what not, Nell.'

'Then there's the perambulator and the gooseberries, and the sweets,' said Bobbie, 'they're from Mrs Ransome. She said: "I dare say Mr Perks's children would like the sweets. And the perambulator was got for my Emmie's first – it didn't live but six months. I'd like Mrs Perks to have it. It would be a help with her fine boy. I'd have given it before if I'd been sure she'd accept of it from me." She told me to tell you,' Bobbie added, 'that it was her Emmie's little one's pram.'

'I can't send that pram back, Bert,' said Mrs Perks, firmly, 'and I won't. So don't you ask me—'

'I'm not a-asking anything,' said Perks, gruffly.

'Then the shovel,' said Bobbie. 'Mr James made it for you himself. And he said – where is it? Oh, yes, here! He said, "You tell Mr Perks it's a pleasure to make a little trifle for a man as is so much respected," and then he said he wished he could shoe your children and his own children, like they do the horses, because, well, he knew what shoe leather was.'

'James is a good enough chap,' said Perks.

'Then the honey,' said Bobbie, in haste, 'and the boot-laces. *He* said he respected a man that paid his way – and the butcher said the same. And the old turnpike woman said many was the time you'd lent her a hand with her garden when you were a lad – and things like that came home to roost – I don't know what she meant. And everybody who gave anything said they liked you, and it was a very good idea of ours; and nobody said anything about charity or anything horrid like that. And the old gentleman gave Peter a gold pound for you, and said you were a man who knew your work. And I thought you'd *love* to know how fond people are of you, and I never was so unhappy in my life. Good-bye. I hope you'll forgive us some day –'

She could say no more, and she turned to go.

'Stop,' said Perks, still with his back to them; 'I take back every word I've said contrary to what you'd wish. Nell, set on the kettle.'

'We'll take the things away if you're unhappy about them,' said Peter; 'but I think everybody'll be most awfully disappointed, as well as us.'

'I'm not unhappy about them,' said Perks; 'I don't know,' he added, suddenly wheeling the chair round and showing a very odd-looking screwed-up face, 'I don't know as ever I was better pleased. Not so much with the presents – though they're an A1 collection – but the kind respect of our neighbours. That's worth having, eh, Nell?'

'I think it's all worth having,' said Mrs Perks, 'and you've made a most ridiculous fuss about nothing, Bert, if you ask me.'

'No, I ain't,' said Perks, firmly; 'if a man didn't respect hisself, no one wouldn't do it for him.'

'But everyone respects you,' said Bobbie; 'they all said so.'

'I knew you'd like it when you really understood,' said Phyllis, brightly.

'Humph! You'll stay to tea?' said Mr Perks.

Later on Peter proposed Mr Perks's health. And Mr Perks proposed a toast, also honoured in tea, and the toast was, 'May the garland of friendship be ever green,' which was much more poetical than anyone had expected from him.

FRIENDSHIP
Elizabeth Jennings

Such love I cannot analyse;
It does not rest in lips or eyes,
Neither in kisses nor caress.
Partly, I know, it's gentleness

And understanding in one word
Or in brief letters. It's preserved
By trust and by respect and awe.
These are the words I'm feeling for.

Two people, yes, two lasting friends.
The giving comes, the taking ends.
There is no measure for such things.
For this all Nature slows and sings.

READING NOTES

After the poem was read out loud, an elderly woman in a library group became rather quiet. Later she explained that her best friend now lived in Canada and they had not seen each other for nearly twenty years. The poem reminded her how much she missed their old, easy, day-to-day friendship. 'This poem says everything,' she said: 'It's preserved / By trust and by respect and awe.' She stayed behind to copy it out and send to Vancouver. The group talked about what makes a great friendship; about what happens when friends fall out and about how you have to work at keeping a friendship going. They wondered about the word 'awe'. Was it an appropriate word in this context? In the end, most thought it was.

In *The Railway Children*, Phyllis says to Perks: 'We shall always be friends with you, however nasty you are to us.' Even though Phyllis is rather silly, the group wondered about the truth of this remark and also considered how easy it is for good intentions to be taken the wrong way.

In the Eye of the Beholder

A WORK OF ART
Anton Chekhov

(approximate reading time 9 minutes)

Sasha Smirnov, the only son of his mother, holding under his arm, something wrapped up in No. 223 of the Financial News, assumed a sentimental expression, and went into Dr Koshelkov's consulting-room.

'Ah, dear lad!' was how the doctor greeted him. 'Well! How are we feeling? What good news have you for me?'

Sasha blinked, laid his hand on his heart and said in an agitated voice: 'Mamma sends her greetings to you, Ivan Nikolaevitch, and told me to thank you . . . I am the only son of my mother and you have saved my life . . . you have brought me through a dangerous illness and . . . we do not know how to thank you.'

'Nonsense, lad!' said the doctor, highly delighted. 'I only did what anyone else would have done in my place.'

'I am the only son of my mother . . . we are poor people and cannot of course repay you, and . . . we are quite ashamed, doctor, although, however, mamma and I . . . the only son of my mother, earnestly beg you to accept in token of our gratitude . . . this object, which . . . An object of great value, an antique bronze . . . A rare work of art.'

'You shouldn't!' said the doctor, frowning. 'What's this for!'

'No, please do not refuse,' Sasha went on muttering as he unpacked the parcel. 'You will wound mamma and me by refusing . . . It's a fine thing . . . an antique bronze . . . It was left us by my deceased father and we have kept it as a precious souvenir. My father used to buy antique bronzes and sell them to connoisseurs . . . Mamma and I keep on the business now . . .'

Sasha undid the object and put it solemnly on the table. It was a not very tall candelabra of old bronze and artistic workmanship. It consisted of a group: on the pedestal stood two female figures in the costume of Eve and in attitudes for the description of which I have neither the courage nor the fitting temperament. The figures were smiling coquettishly and altogether looked as though, had it not been for the necessity of supporting the candlestick, they would have skipped off the pedestal and have indulged in an orgy such as is improper for the reader even to imagine.

Looking at the present, the doctor slowly scratched behind his ear, cleared his throat and blew his nose irresolutely.

'Yes, it certainly is a fine thing,' he muttered, 'but . . . how shall I express it? . . . it's . . . h'm . . . it's not quite for family reading. It's not simply decolleté but beyond anything, dash it all . . .'

'How do you mean?'

'The serpent-tempter himself could not have invented anything worse . . . Why, to put such a phantasmagoria on the table would be defiling the whole flat.'

'What a strange way of looking at art, doctor!' said Sasha, offended. 'Why, it is an artistic thing, look at it! There is so much beauty and elegance that it fills one's soul with a feeling of reverence and brings a lump into one's throat! When one sees anything so beautiful one forgets everything earthly . . . Only look, how much movement, what an atmosphere, what expression!'

'I understand all that very well, my dear boy,' the doctor interposed, 'but you know I am a family man, my children run in here, ladies come in.'

'Of course if you look at it from the point of view of the crowd,' said Sasha, 'then this exquisitely artistic work may appear in a certain light . . . But, doctor, rise superior to the crowd, especially as you will wound Mamma and me by refusing it. I am the only son of my mother, you have saved my life . . . We are giving you the thing most precious to us and . . . and I only regret that I have not the pair to present to you . . .'

'Thank you, my dear fellow, I am very grateful . . . Give my respects to your mother but really consider, my children, run in here, ladies, come . . . However, let it remain! I see there's no arguing with you.'

'And there is nothing to argue about,' said Sasha, relieved. 'Put the candlestick here, by this vase. What a pity we have not the pair to it! It is a pity! Well, good-bye, doctor.'

After Sasha's departure the doctor looked for a long time at the candelabra, scratched behind his ear and meditated.

'It's a superb thing, there's no denying it,' he thought, 'and it would be a pity to throw it away . . . But it's impossible for me to keep it . . . H'm! . . . Here's a problem! To whom can I make a present of it, or to what charity can I give it?'

After long meditation he thought of his good friend, the lawyer Uhov, to whom he was indebted for the management of legal business.

'Excellent,' the doctor decided, 'it would be awkward for him as a friend to take money from me, and it will be very suitable for me to present him with this. I will take him the devilish thing! Luckily he is a bachelor and easy-going.'

Without further procrastination the doctor put on his hat and coat, took the candelabra and went off to Uhov's.

'How are you, friend!' he said, finding the lawyer at home. 'I've come to see you . . . to thank you for your efforts . . . You won't take money so you must at least accept this thing here . . . See, my dear fellow . . . The thing is magnificent!'

On seeing the bronze the lawyer was moved to indescribable delight.

'What a specimen!' he chuckled. 'Ah, deuce take it, to think of them imagining such a thing, the devils! Exquisite! Ravishing! Where did you get hold of such a delightful thing?'

After pouring out his ecstasies the lawyer looked timidly towards the door and said: 'Only you must carry off your present, my boy . . . I can't take it . . .'

'Why?' cried the doctor, disconcerted.

'Why . . . because my mother is here at times, my clients . . . besides I should be ashamed for my servants to see it.'

'Nonsense! Nonsense! Don't you dare to refuse!' said the doctor, gesticulating. 'It's piggish of you! It's a work of art! . . .

What movement . . . what expression! I won't even talk of it! You will offend me!'

'If one could plaster it over or stick on fig-leaves . . .'

But the doctor gesticulated more violently than before, and dashing out of the flat went home, glad that he had succeeded in getting the present off his hands.

When he had gone away the lawyer examined the candelabra, fingered it all over, and then, like the doctor, racked his brains over the question what to do with the present.

'It's a fine thing,' he mused, 'and it would be a pity to throw it away and improper to keep it. The very best thing would be to make a present of it to someone . . . I know what! I'll take it this evening to Shashkin, the comedian. The rascal is fond of such things, and by the way it is his benefit tonight.'

No sooner said than done. In the evening the candelabra, carefully wrapped up, was duly carried to Shashkin's. The whole evening the comic actor's dressing-room was besieged by men coming to admire the present; the dressing-room was filled with the hum of enthusiasm and laughter like the neighing of horses. If one of the actresses approached the door and asked: 'May I come in?' the comedian's husky voice was heard at once: 'No, no, my dear, I am not dressed!'

After the performance the comedian shrugged his shoulders, flung up his hands and said: 'Well what am I to do with the horrid thing? Why, I live in a private flat! Actresses come and see me! It's not a photograph that you can put in a drawer!'

'You had better sell it, sir,' the hairdresser who was disrobing the actor advised him. 'There's an old woman living about here who buys antique bronzes. Go and enquire for Madame Smirnov . . . everyone knows her.'

The actor followed his advice . . . Two days later the doctor was sitting in his consulting-room, and with his finger to his brow was meditating on the acids of the bile. All at once the door opened and Sasha Smirnov flew into the room. He was smiling, beaming, and his whole figure was radiant with happiness. In his hands he held something wrapped up in newspaper.

'Doctor!' he began breathlessly, 'imagine my delight! Happily for you we have succeeded in picking up the pair to your candelabra! Mamma is so happy . . . I am the only son of my mother, you saved my life . . .'

And Sasha, all of a tremor with gratitude, set the candelabra before the doctor. The doctor opened his mouth, tried to say something, but said nothing: he could not speak.

'A THING OF BEAUTY'

(FROM *ENDYMION*)

John Keats

A thing of beauty is a joy for ever:
Its loveliness increases, it will never
Pass into nothingness; but still will keep
A bower quiet for us, and a sleep
Full of sweet dreams, and health, and quiet breathing.
Therefore, on every morrow, are we wreathing
A flowery band to bind us to the earth,
Spite of despondence, of the inhuman dearth
Of noble natures, of the gloomy days,
Of all the unhealthy and o'er-darkened ways
Made for our searching: yes, in spite of all,
Some shape of beauty moves away the pall
From our dark spirits.

READING NOTES

'This poem,' thought one reader, 'says we are "wreathing a flowery band to bind us to the earth". I suppose it is saying that beautiful things cheer you up and on the whole, I agree with that,' he said. Among the lines and phrases that people have found particularly thought-provoking are 'it will never pass into nothingness' and 'some shape of beauty moves away the pall/From our dark spirits.'

The story will often prompt talk about what is considered to be beautiful and how much value people should or do place in it. Everyone has some experience of unwanted gifts, especially at Christmas, and what to do about them without giving offence is a real dilemma. Similarly, Sasha's work of art leads naturally on to the subject of art and in particular, modern art, on which contentious subject most people have something to say.

After Dark

❦

MY ADVENTURE IN NORFOLK
A. J. Alan

(approximate reading time 19 minutes)

I don't know how it is with you, but during February *my* wife generally says to me: 'Have you thought at all about what we are going to do for August?' And, of course, I say 'No', and then she begins looking through the advertisements of bungalows to let.

Well, this happened last year, as usual, and she eventually produced one that looked possible. It said: 'Norfolk – Hickling Broad – Furnished Bungalow – Garden – Garage, Boathouse', and all the rest of it – Oh! – *and* plate and linen. It also mentioned an exorbitant rent. I pointed out the bit about the rent, but my wife said: 'Yes, you'll have to go down and see the landlord, and get him to come down. They always do.' As a matter of fact, they always don't, but that's a detail.

Anyway, I wrote off to the landlord and asked if he could arrange for me to stay the night in the place to see what it was really like. He wrote back and said: 'Certainly', and that he was engaging Mrs So-and-so to come in and 'oblige me', and make up the beds and so forth.

I tell you, we do things thoroughly in our family – I have to sleep in all the beds, and when I come home my wife counts the bruises and decides whether they will do or not.

At any rate, I arrived, in a blinding snowstorm, at about *the* most desolate spot on God's earth. I'd come to Potter Heigham by train, and been driven on – it was a good five miles from the station. Fortunately, Mrs Selston, the old lady who was going to 'do' for me, was there, and she'd lighted a fire, and cooked me a steak, for which I was truly thankful.

I somehow think the cow, or whatever they get steaks off, had only died that morning. It was very – er – obstinate. While I dined, she talked to me. She *would* tell me all about an operation her husband had just had. *All* about it. It was almost a lecture on surgery. The steak was rather underdone, and it sort of made me feel I was illustrating her lecture. Anyway, she put me clean off my dinner, and then departed for the night.

I explored the bungalow and just had a look outside. It was, of course, very dark, but not snowing quite so hard. The garage stood about fifteen yards from the back door. I walked round it but didn't go in. I also went down to the edge of the broad, and verified the boathouse. The whole place looked as though it might be all right in the summertime, but just then it made one wonder why people ever wanted to go to the North Pole.

Anyhow, I went indoors and settled down by the fire. You've no idea how quiet it was; even the water-fowl had taken a night off – at least, they weren't working.

At a few minutes to eleven I heard the first noise there'd

been since Mrs What's-her-name – Selston – had cleared out. It was the sound of a car. If it had gone straight by I probably shouldn't have noticed it at all, only it didn't go straight by; it seemed to stop farther up the road, before it got to the house. Even that didn't make much impression. After all, cars *do* stop.

It must have been five or ten minutes before it was borne in on me that it hadn't gone on again. So I got up and looked out of the window. It had left off snowing, and there was a glare through the gate that showed that there were headlamps somewhere just out of sight. I thought I might as well stroll out and investigate.

I found a fair-sized limousine pulled up in the middle of the road about twenty yards short of my gate. The light was rather blinding, but when I got close to it I found a girl with the bonnet open, tinkering with the engine. Quite an attractive young female, from what one could see, but she was so muffled up in furs that it was rather hard to tell.

I said: 'Er – good evening – anything I can do?'

She said she didn't know what was the matter. The engine had just stopped, and wouldn't start again. And it *had*! It wouldn't even turn, either with the self-starter or the handle. The whole thing was awfully hot, and I asked her whether there was any water in the radiator. She didn't see why there shouldn't be, there always had been. This didn't strike me as entirely conclusive. I said we'd better put some in, and see what happened. She said, why not use snow? But I thought not. There was an idea at the back of my mind that there was some reason why it was unwise to use melted snow, and it wasn't until I arrived back with a bucketful that I remembered what it was. Of course – goitre.

When I got back to her she'd got the radiator cap off, and inserted what a Danish friend of mine called a 'funeral'. We poured a little water in . . . Luckily I'd warned her to stand clear. The first tablespoonful that went in came straight out again, red-hot, and blew the 'funeral' sky-high. We waited a few minutes until things had cooled down a bit, but it was no go. As fast as we poured water in it simply ran out again into the road underneath. It was quite evident that she'd been driving with the radiator bone dry, and that her engine had seized right up.

I told her so.

She said: 'Does that mean I've got to stop here all night?'

I explained that it wasn't as bad as all that; that is, if she cared to accept the hospitality of my poor roof (and it *was* a poor roof – it let the wet in). But she wouldn't hear of it. By the by, she didn't know the – er – circumstances, so it wasn't that. No, she wanted to leave the car where it was and go on on foot.

I said: 'Don't be silly, it's miles to anywhere.'

However, at that moment we heard a car coming along the road, the same way as she'd come. We could see its lights, too, although it was a very long way off. You know how flat Norfolk is – you can see a terrific distance.

I said: 'There's the way out of all your troubles. This thing, whatever it is, will give you a tow to the nearest garage, or at any rate a lift to some hotel.'

One would have expected her to show some relief, but she

didn't. I began to wonder what she jolly well *did* want. She wouldn't let me help her to stop where she was, and she didn't seem anxious for any one to help her to go anywhere else.

She was quite peculiar about it. She gripped hold of my arm, and said: 'What do you think this is that's coming?'

I said: 'I'm sure I don't know, being a stranger in these parts, but it sounds like a lorry full of milk-cans.'

I offered to lay her sixpence about it (this was before the betting-tax came in). She'd have had to pay, too, because it *was* a lorry full of milk-cans. The driver had to pull up because there wasn't any room to get by.

He got down and asked if there was anything he could do to help. We explained the situation. He said he was going to Norwich, and was quite ready to give her a tow if she wanted it. However, she wouldn't do that, and it was finally decided to shove her car into my garage for the night, to be sent for next day, and the lorry was to take her along to Norwich.

Well, I managed to find the key of the garage, and the lorry-driver – Williams, his name was – and I ran the car in and locked the door. This having been done (ablative absolute) I suggested that it was a very cold night. Williams agreed, and said he didn't mind if he did. So I took them both indoors and mixed them a stiff whisky and water each. There wasn't any soda. And, naturally, the whole thing had left *me* very cold, too. I hadn't an overcoat on.

Up to now I hadn't seriously considered the young woman. For one thing it had been dark, *and* there had been a seized engine to look at. Er – I'm afraid that's not a very gallant remark. What I mean is that to anyone with a mechanical mind a motor car in that condition is much more interesting than – er – well it *is* very interesting – but why labour the point? However, in the sitting-room, in the lamplight, it was possible to get more of an idea. She was a little older than I'd thought, and her eyes were too close together.

Of course, she wasn't a – how shall I put it? Her manners weren't quite easy and she was careful with her English. *You* know. But that wasn't it. She treated us with a lack of friendliness which was – well, we'd done nothing to deserve it. There was a sort of vague hostility and suspicion, which seemed rather hard lines, considering. Also, she was so anxious to keep in the shadow that if I hadn't moved the lamp away she'd never have got near the fire at all.

And the way she hurried the wretched Williams over his drink was quite distressing; and foolish, too, as *he* was going to drive, but that was her – funnel. When he'd gone out to start up his engine I asked her if she was all right for money, and she apparently was. Then they started off, and I shut up the place and went upstairs.

There happened to be a local guide-book in my bedroom, with maps in it. I looked at these and couldn't help wondering where the girl in the car had come from; I mean my road seemed so very unimportant. The sort of road one might use if one wanted to avoid people. If one were driving a stolen car, for instance. This was quite a thrilling idea. I thought it might be worth while having another look at the car. So I once more unhooked the key from the kitchen dresser and sallied forth into the snow. It was as black as pitch, and so still that my candle hardly flickered. It wasn't a large garage, and the car nearly filled it. By the by, we'd backed it in so as to make it easier to tow it out again.

The engine I'd already seen, so I squeezed past along the wall and opened the door in the body part of the car. At least, I only turned the handle, and the door was pushed open from the inside and – something – fell out on me. It pushed me quite hard, and wedged me against the wall. It also knocked the candle out of my hand and left me in the dark – which was a bit of a nuisance. I wondered what on earth the thing was, barging into me like that, so I felt it, rather gingerly, and found it was a man – a dead man – with a moustache. He'd evidently been sitting propped up against the door. I managed to put him back, as decorously as possible, and shut the door again.

After a lot of grovelling about under the car I found the candle and lighted it, and opened the opposite door and switched on the little lamp in the roof – and then – oo-er!

Of course, I had to make some sort of examination. He was an extremely tall and thin individual. He must have been well over six feet three. He was dark and very cadaverous-looking. In fact, I don't suppose he'd ever looked so cadaverous in his life. He was wearing a trench-coat.

It wasn't difficult to tell what he'd died of. He'd been shot through the back. I found the hole just under the right scrofula, or scalpel – what is shoulder-blade, anyway? Oh, clavicle – stupid of me – well, that's where it was, and the bullet had evidently gone through into the lung. I say 'evidently', and leave it at that.

There were no papers in his pockets, and no tailor's name

on his clothes, but there was a note-case, with nine pounds in it. Altogether a most unpleasant business. Of course, it doesn't do to question the workings of Providence, but one couldn't help wishing it hadn't happened. It was just a little mysterious, too – er – who had killed him? It wasn't likely that the girl had or she wouldn't have been joy-riding about the country with him; and if someone else had murdered him why hadn't she mentioned it? Anyway, she hadn't and she'd gone, so one couldn't do anything for the time being. No telephone, of course. I just locked up the garage and went to bed. That was two o'clock.

Next morning I woke early, for some reason or other, and it occurred to me as a good idea to go and have a look at things – by daylight, and before Mrs Selston turned up. So I did. The first thing that struck me was that it had snowed heavily during the night, because there were no wheel-tracks or footprints, and the second was that I'd left the key in the garage door. I opened it and went in. The place was completely empty. No car, no body, no nothing. There was a patch of grease on the floor where I'd dropped the candle, otherwise there was nothing to show I'd been there before. One of two things must have happened: either some people had come along during the night and taken the car away, or else I'd fallen asleep in front of the fire and dreamt the whole thing.

Then I remembered the whisky glasses.

They should still be in the sitting-room. I went back to look, and they were, all three of them. So it *hadn't* been a dream and the car *had* been fetched away, but they must have been jolly quiet over it.

The girl had left her glass on the mantelpiece, and it showed several very clearly defined finger-marks. Some were mine, naturally, because I'd fetched the glass from the kitchen and poured out the drink for her, but hers, her finger-marks, were clean and mine were oily, so it was quite easy to tell them apart. It isn't necessary to point out that this glass was very important. There'd evidently been a murder, or something of that kind, and the girl must have known all about it, even if she hadn't actually done it herself, so anything she had left in the way of evidence ought to be handed over to the police; and this was all she *had* left. So I packed it up with meticulous care in an old biscuit-box out of the larder.

When Mrs Selston came, I settled up with her and came back to town. Oh, I called on the landlord on the way and told him I'd 'let him know' about the bungalow. Then I caught my train, and in due course drove straight to Scotland Yard. I went up and saw my friend there. I produced the glass and asked him if his people could identify the marks. He said: 'Probably not,' but he sent it down to the finger-print department and asked me where it came from. I said: 'Never mind; let's have the identification first.' He said: 'All right.'

They're awfully quick, these people – the clerk was back in three minutes with a file of papers. They knew the girl all right. They told me her name and showed me her photograph; not flattering. Quite an adventurous lady, from all accounts. In the early part of her career she'd done time twice for shop-lifting, chiefly in the book department. Then she'd what they call 'taken up with' a member of one of those race-gangs one sometimes hears about.

My pal went on to say that there'd been a fight between two of these gangs, in the course of which her friend had got shot. She'd managed to get him away in a car, but it had broken down somewhere in Norfolk. So she'd left it and the dead man in someone's garage, and had started off for Norwich in a lorry. Only she never got there. On the way the lorry had skidded, and both she and the driver – a fellow called Williams – had been thrown out, and they'd rammed their heads against a brick wall, which every one knows is a fatal thing to do. At least, it was in their case.

I said: 'Look here, it's all very well, but you simply can't know all this; there hasn't been time – it only happened last night.'

He said: 'Last night be blowed! It all happened in February, nineteen-nineteen. The people you've described have been dead for years.'

I said: 'Oh!'

And to think that I might have stuck to that nine pounds!

SILVER
Walter de la Mare

Slowly, silently, now the moon
Walks the night in her silver shoon;
This way, and that, she peers, and sees
Silver fruit upon silver trees;
One by one the casements catch
Her beams beneath the silvery thatch;
Couched in his kennel, like a log,
With paws of silver sleeps the dog;
From their shadowy cote the white breasts peep
Of doves in a silver feathered sleep;
A harvest mouse goes scampering by,
With silver claws, and silver eye;
And moveless fish in the water gleam,
By silver reeds in a silver stream.

READING NOTES

The first thing a group in a day centre for the elderly wanted to talk about after hearing this story was the unreliability of old cars. There was much amusement remembering the pains of starting handles, double-declutching and having to push a car that would not start.

Dorothy liked the fact that this was a partly humorous ghost story as she did not believe in ghosts but was able to enjoy the story because of its comedy. There was plenty of general talk about ghosts. While not many actually believed in them, everyone felt that houses retain something, a spirit perhaps, of the people who have lived and died in them.

'Silver' is a well-loved poem and many will know it by heart. Readers have enjoyed choosing favourite lines and images in an effort to understand what makes the poem so atmospheric. Darkness and moonlight change the way we experience our surroundings and there is much to say about the part the moon plays in our lives, both scientifically and emotionally.

Dark Stairs and Empty Halls

$\mathscr{J}$

THE DEMON LOVER
Elizabeth Bowen

(approximate reading time 17 minutes)

Toward the end of her day in London Mrs Drover went round to her shut-up house to look for several things she wanted to take away. Some belonged to herself, some to her family, who were by now used to their country life. It was late August; it had been a steamy, showery day: at the moment the trees down the pavement glittered in an escape of humid yellow afternoon sun. Against the next batch of clouds, already piling up ink-dark, broken chimneys and parapets stood out. In her once familiar street, as in any unused channel, an unfamiliar queerness had silted up; a cat wove itself in and out of railings, but no human eye watched Mrs Drover's return. Shifting some parcels under her arm, she slowly forced round her latchkey in an unwilling lock, then gave the door, which had warped, a push with her knee. Dead air came out to meet her as she went in.

The staircase window having been boarded up, no light

came down into the hall. But one door, she could just see, stood ajar, so she went quickly through into the room and unshuttered the big window in there. Now the prosaic woman, looking about her, was more perplexed than she knew by everything that she saw, by traces of her long former habit of life – the yellow smoke stain up the white marble mantelpiece, the ring left by a vase on the top of the escritoire, the bruise in the wallpaper where, on the door being thrown open widely, the china handle had always hit the wall. The piano, having gone away to be stored, had left what looked like claw marks on its part of the parquet. Though not much dust had seeped in, each object wore a film of another kind; and, the only ventilation being the chimney, the whole drawing room smelled of the cold hearth. Mrs Drover put down her parcels on the escritoire and left the room to proceed upstairs; the things she wanted were in a bedroom chest.

She had been anxious to see how the house was – the part-time caretaker she shared with some neighbours was away this week on his holiday, known to be not yet back. At the best of times he did not look in often, and she was never sure that she trusted him. There were some cracks in the structure, left by the last bombing, on which she was anxious to keep an eye. Not that one could do anything –

A shaft of refracted daylight now lay across the hall. She stopped dead and stared at the hall table – on this lay a letter addressed to her.

She thought first – then the caretaker *must* be back. All the same, who, seeing the house shuttered, would have dropped a letter in at the box? It was not a circular, it was not a bill.

And the post office redirected, to the address in the country, everything for her that came through the post. The caretaker (even if he *were* back) did not know she was due in London today – her call here had been planned to be a surprise – so his negligence in the manner of this letter, leaving it to wait in the dust, annoyed her. Annoyed, she picked up the letter, which bore no stamp. But it cannot be important, or they would know . . . She took the letter rapidly upstairs with her, without a stop to look at the writing till she let in light. The room looked over the garden and sharpened and lowered, the trees and rank lawns seemed already to smoke with dark. Her reluctance to look again at the letter came from the fact that she felt intruded upon – and by someone contemptuous of her ways. However, in the tenseness preceding the fall of rain she read it: it was a few lines.

Dear Kathleen: You will not have forgotten that today is our anniversary, and the day we said. The years have gone by at once slowly and fast. In view of the fact that nothing has changed, I shall rely upon you to keep your promise. I was sorry to see you leave London, but was satisfied that you would be back in time. You may expect me, therefore, at the hour arranged. Until then . . .
K.

Mrs Drover looked for the date: It was today's. She dropped the letter onto the bedsprings, then picked it up to see the writing again – her lips, beneath the remains of lipstick, beginning to go white. She felt so much the change in her own face that she sent to the mirror, polished a clear patch in it, and looked at once urgently and stealthily in. She was confronted by a woman of forty-four, with eyes starting out under a hat brim that had been rather carelessly pulled down. She had not put on any more powder since she left the shop where she ate her solitary tea. The pearls her husband had given her on their marriage hung loose round her now rather thinner throat, slipping in the V of the pink wool jumper her sister knitted last autumn as they sat round the fire. Mrs Drover's most normal expression was one of controlled worry but of assent. Since the birth of the third of her little boys, attended by a quite serious illness, she had had an intermittent muscular flicker to the left of her mouth, but in spite of this she could always sustain a manner that was at once energetic and calm.

Turning from her own face as precipitously as she had gone to meet it, she went to the chest where the things were, unlocked it, threw up the lid, and knelt to search. But as rain began to come crashing down she could not keep from looking over her shoulder at the stripped bed on which the letter lay. Behind the blanket of rain the clock of the church that still stood struck six – with rapidly heightening apprehension she counted each of the slow strokes. 'The hour arranged . . . My God,' she said, '*what* hour? How should I . . .? After twenty-five years . . .'

The young girl talking to the soldier in the garden had not ever completely seen his face. It was dark; they were saying goodbye under a tree. Now and then – for it felt, from not seeing him at this intense moment, as though she had never seen him at all – she verified his presence for these few moments longer by putting out a hand, which he each time pressed, without very much kindness, and painfully, on to one of the breast buttons of his uniform. That cut of the button on the palm of her hand was, principally, what she was to carry away. This was so near the end of a leave from France that she could only wish him already gone. It was August 1916. Being not kissed, being drawn away from and looked at intimidated Kathleen till she imagined spectral glitters in the place of his eyes.

Turning away and looking back up the lawn she saw, through branches of trees, the drawing-room window alight: she caught a breath for the moment when she could go running back there into the safe arms of her mother and sister, and cry: 'What shall I do, what shall I do? He has gone.'

Hearing her catch her breath, her fiancé said, without feeling: 'Cold?'

'You're going away such a long way.'

'Not so far as you think.'

'I don't understand?'

'You don't have to,' he said. 'You will. You know what we said.'

'But that was – suppose you – I mean, suppose.'

'I shall be with you,' he said, 'sooner or later. You won't forget that. You need do nothing but wait.'

Only a little more than a minute later she was free to run up the silent lawn. Looking in through the window at her mother and sister, who did not for the moment perceive her, she already felt that unnatural promise drive down between her and the rest of all humankind. No other way to having given herself could have made her feel so apart, lost and forsworn. She could not have plighted a more sinister troth.

Kathleen behaved well when, some months later, her fiancé was reported missing, presumed killed. Her family not only supported her but were able to praise her courage without stint because they could not regret, as a husband for her, the man they knew almost nothing about. They hoped she would, in a year or two, console herself – and had it been only a question of consolation things might have gone much straighter ahead. But her trouble, behind just a little grief, was a complete dislocation from everything. She did not reject other lovers, for these failed to appear. For years, she failed to attract men – and with the approach of her thirties she became natural enough to share her family's anxiousness on the score. She began to put herself out, to wonder, and at thirty-two she was very greatly relieved to find herself being courted by William Drover. She married him, and the two of them settled down in the quiet, arboreal part of Kensington: in this house the years piled up, her children were born, and they all lived till they were driven out by the bombs of the next war. Her movements as Mrs Drover were circumscribed, and she dismissed any idea that they were still watched.

As things were – dead or living the letter writer sent her only a threat. Unable, for some minutes, to go on kneeling with her back exposed to the empty room, Mrs Drover rose from the chest to sit on an upright chair whose back was firmly against the wall. The desuetude of her former bedroom, her married London home's whole air of being a cracked cup from which memory, with its reassuring power, had either evaporated or leaked away, made a crisis – and at just this crisis the letter writer had, knowledgeably, struck. The hollowness of the house this evening cancelled years on years of voices, habits and steps. Through the shut windows she only heard rain fall on the roofs around. To rally herself, she said she was in a mood – and for two or three seconds shutting her eyes, told herself that she had imagined the letter. But she opened them – there it lay on the bed.

On the supernatural side of the letter's entrance she was not permitting her mind to dwell. Who, in London, knew she meant to call at the house today? Evidently, however, that had been known. The caretaker, *had* he come back, had had no cause to expect her: he would have taken the letter in his pocket, to forward it, at his own time, through the post. There was no other sign that the caretaker had been in – but, if not? Letters dropped in at doors of deserted houses do not fly or walk to tables in halls. They do not sit on the dust of empty tables with the air of certainty that they will be found. There is needed some human hand – but nobody but the caretaker had a key. Under the circumstances she did not care to consider, a house can be entered without a key. It was possible that she was not alone now. She might be being waited for, down-stairs. Waited for – until when? Until 'the hour arranged'. At least that was not six o'clock: six has struck.

She rose from the chair and went over and locked the door.

The thing was, to get out. To fly? No, not that: she had to catch her train. As a woman whose utter dependability was the keystone of her family life, she was not willing to return to the country, to her husband, her little boys, and her sister, without the objects she had come up to fetch. Resuming her work at the chest she set about making up a number of parcels in a rapid, fumbling-decisive way. These, with her shopping parcels, would be too much to carry; these meant a taxi – at the thought of the taxi her heart went up and her normal breathing resumed. I will ring up the taxi; the taxi cannot come too soon: I shall hear the taxi out there running its engine, till I walk calmly down to it through the hall. I'll ring up – But no: the telephone is cut off . . . She tugged at a knot she had tied wrong.

The idea of flight . . . He was never kind to me, not really. I don't remember him kind at all. Mother said he never consid-ered me. He was set on me, that was what it was – not love. Not love, not meaning a person well. What did he do, to make me promise like that? I can't remember – But she found that she could.

She remembered with such dreadful acuteness that the twenty-five years since then dissolved like smoke and she instinctively looked for the weal left by the button on the palm of her hand. She remembered not only all that he said and did but the complete suspension of *her* existence during that August week. I was not myself – they all told me so at the time. She remembered – but with one white burning blank as where acid has dropped on a photograph: *under no conditions* could she remember his face.

So, wherever he may be waiting, I shall not know him. You have no time to run from a face you do not expect.

The thing was to get to the taxi before any clock struck what could be the hour. She would slip down the street and round the side of the square to where the square gave on the main road. She would return in the taxi, safe, to her own door, and bring the solid driver into the house with her to pick up the parcels from room to room. The idea of the taxi driver made her decisive, bold: she unlocked her door, went to the top of the staircase, and listened down.

She heard nothing – but while she was hearing nothing the *passé* air of the staircase was disturbed by a draught that travelled up to her face. It emanated from the basement: down where a door or window was being opened by someone who chose this moment to leave the house.

The rain had stopped; the pavements steamily shone as Mrs Drover let herself out by inches from her own front door into the empty street. The unoccupied houses opposite continued to meet her look with their damaged stare. Making toward the thoroughfare and the taxi, she tried not to keep looking behind. Indeed, the silence was so intense – one of those creeks of London silence exaggerated this summer by damage of war – that no tread could have gained on hers unheard. Where her street debouched on the square where people went on living, she grew conscious of, and checked, her unnatural pace. Across the open end of the square, two buses impassively passed each other: women, a perambulator, cyclists, a man wheeling a barrow signalised, once again, the ordinary flow of life. At the square's most populous corner should be – and was – the short taxi rank. This evening, only one taxi – but this, although it presented its blank rump, appeared already to be alertly waiting for her. Indeed, without looking round the driver started his engine as she panted up from behind and put her hand on the door. As she did so, the clock struck seven. The taxi faced the main road: to make the trip back to her house it would have to turn – she had settled back on the seat and the taxi *had* turned before she, surprised by its knowing movement, recollected that she had not 'said where'. She leaned forward to scratch at the glass panel that divided the driver's head from her own.

The driver braked to what was almost a stop, turned round, and slid the glass panel back: the jolt of this flung Mrs Drover forward till her face was almost into the glass. Through the aperture driver and passenger, not six inches between them, remained for an eternity eye to eye. Mrs Drover's mouth hung open for some seconds before she could issue her first scream. After that she continued to scream freely and to beat with her gloved hands on the glass all round as the taxi, accelerating without mercy, made off with her into the hinterland of deserted streets.

THE LISTENERS
Walter de la Mare

'Is there anybody there?' said the Traveller,
　　Knocking on the moonlit door;
And his horse in the silence champed the grasses
　　Of the forest's ferny floor:
And a bird flew up out of the turret,
　　Above the Traveller's head:
And he smote upon the door again a second time;
　　'Is there anybody there?' he said.
But no one descended to the Traveller;
　　No head from the leaf-fringed sill
Leaned over and looked into his grey eyes,
　　Where he stood perplexed and still.
But only a host of phantom listeners
　　That dwelt in the lone house then
Stood listening in the quiet of the moonlight
　　To that voice from the world of men:
Stood thronging the faint moonbeams on the dark stair,
　　That goes down to the empty hall,
Hearkening in an air stirred and shaken
　　By the lonely Traveller's call.
And he felt in his heart their strangeness,
　　Their stillness answering his cry,
While his horse moved, cropping the dark turf,
　　'Neath the starred and leafy sky;
For he suddenly smote on the door, even
　　Louder, and lifted his head:—

'Tell them I came, and no one answered,
    That I kept my word,' he said.
Never the least stir made the listeners,
    Though every word he spake
Fell echoing through the shadowiness of the still house
    From the one man left awake:
Ay, they heard his foot upon the stirrup,
    And the sound of iron on stone,
And how the silence surged softly backward,
    When the plunging hoofs were gone.

READING NOTES

A group of parents and guardians found much to talk about in this atmospheric story. Why had the woman become engaged to someone she hardly knew and seemed afraid of? The way the first two paragraphs create a sense of unease. Was the man evil? Was that why you could never fully see his face? What indeed is evil? Several people felt the story ended too abruptly. Would knowing what happened after the taxi drives off make it more or less frightening?

The poem is also intensely atmospheric and, like the story, leaves you with hundreds of questions: who is the Traveller; why has he come; to whom has he made a promise; who are the 'phantom listeners' and why is there no one there? Someone noticed the sounds and patterns of the words in the poem – 'the forest's ferny floor' or 'the silence surged softly backward' – and talked about what that added to the mood. Everyone had ideas about the story behind the poem. Do you think the poem succeeds because the mystery remains impenetrable or would you prefer to know?

The Call of the Wild

🌿

THE CALL OF THE WILD

(THE WAGER, CHAPTER 6)

Jack London

(approximate reading time 11 minutes)

The story is set in Alaska at the time of the Klondike gold rush. Buck is a cross between a St Bernard and a Scottish sheepdog. He has been stolen from his home in California and sold in Alaska to be trained as a sledge dog. Life is tough and brutal and Buck endures much cruelty and danger in the hands of bad owners. In this extract he is owned by a good master, John Thornton, to whom he is devoted . . .

That winter, at Dawson, Buck performed another exploit, not so heroic, perhaps, but one that put his name many notches higher on the totem-pole of Alaskan fame. This exploit was particularly gratifying to the three men; for they stood in need of the outfit which it furnished, and were enabled to make a long-desired trip into the virgin East, where miners had not yet appeared. It was brought about by a conversation in the Eldorado Saloon, in which men waxed boastful of their favorite dogs. Buck, because of his record, was the target for these men, and Thornton was driven stoutly to defend him. At the end of half an hour one man stated that his dog could start a sled with five hundred pounds and walk off with it; a second bragged six hundred for his dog; and a third, seven hundred.

'Pooh! pooh!' said John Thornton; 'Buck can start a thousand pounds.'

'And break it out? and walk off with it for a hundred yards?' demanded Matthewson, a Bonanza King, he of the seven hundred vaunt.

'And break it out, and walk off with it for a hundred yards,' John Thornton said coolly.

'Well,' Matthewson said, slowly and deliberately, so that all could hear, 'I've got a thousand dollars that says he can't. And there it is.' So saying, he slammed a sack of gold dust of the size of a bologna sausage down upon the bar.

Nobody spoke. Thornton's bluff, if bluff it was, had been called. He could feel a flush of warm blood creeping up his face. His tongue had tricked him. He did not know whether Buck could start a thousand pounds. Half a ton! The enormousness of it appalled him. He had great faith in Buck's strength and had often thought him capable of starting such a load; but never, as now, had he faced the possibility of it, the eyes of a dozen men fixed upon him, silent and waiting. Further, he had no thousand dollars; nor had Hans or Pete.

'I've got a sled standing outside now, with twenty fifty-pound sacks of flour on it,' Matthewson went on with brutal directness; 'so don't let that hinder you.'

Thornton did not reply. He did not know what to say. He glanced from face to face in the absent way of a man who has lost the power of thought and is seeking somewhere to find the thing that will start it going again. The face of Jim O'Brien, a Mastodon King and old-time comrade, caught his eyes. It was as a cue to him, seeming to rouse him to do what he would never have dreamed of doing.

'Can you lend me a thousand?' he asked, almost in a whisper.

'Sure,' answered O'Brien, thumping down a plethoric sack by the side of Matthewson's. 'Though it's little faith I'm having, John, that the beast can do the trick.'

The Eldorado emptied its occupants into the street to see the test. The tables were deserted, and the dealers and game-keepers came forth to see the outcome of the wager and to lay odds. Several hundred men, furred and mittened, banked around the sled within easy distance. Matthewson's sled, loaded with a thousand pounds of flour, had been standing for a couple of hours, and in the intense cold (it was sixty below zero) the runners had frozen fast to the hard-packed snow. Men offered odds of two to one that Buck could not budge the sled. A quibble arose concerning the phrase 'break out.' O'Brien contended it was Thornton's privilege to knock the runners loose, leaving Buck to 'break it out' from a dead stand-still. Matthewson insisted that the phrase included breaking the runners from the frozen grip of the snow. A majority of the men who had witnessed the making of the bet decided in his favor, whereat the odds went up to three to one against Buck.

There were no takers. Not a man believed him capable of the feat. Thornton had been hurried into the wager, heavy with doubt; and now that he looked at the sled itself, the concrete fact, with the regular team of ten dogs curled up in the snow before it, the more impossible the task appeared. Matthewson waxed jubilant.

'Three to one!' he proclaimed. 'I'll lay you another thousand at that figure, Thornton. What d'ye say?'

Thornton's doubt was strong in his face, but his fighting spirit was aroused – the fighting spirit that soars above odds, fails to recognize the impossible, and is deaf to all save the clamor for battle. He called Hans and Pete to him. Their sacks were slim, and with his own the three partners could rake together only two hundred dollars. In the ebb of their fortunes, this sum was their total capital; yet they laid it unhesitatingly against Matthewson's six hundred.

The team of ten dogs was unhitched, and Buck, with his own harness, was put into the sled. He had caught the contagion of the excitement, and he felt that in some way he must do a great thing for John Thornton. Murmurs of admiration at his splendid appearance went up. He was in perfect condition, without an ounce of superfluous flesh, and the one hundred and fifty pounds that he weighed were so many pounds of grit and virility. His furry coat shone with the sheen of silk. Down the neck and across the shoulders, his mane, in repose as it was, half bristled and seemed to lift with every movement, as though excess of vigor made each particular hair alive and active. The great breast and heavy fore legs were no more than in proportion with the rest of the body, where the muscles showed in tight rolls underneath the skin. Men felt these muscles and proclaimed them hard as iron, and the odds went down to two to one.

'Gad, sir! Gad, sir!' stuttered a member of the latest dynasty, a king of the Skookum Benches. 'I offer you eight hundred for him, sir, before the test, sir; eight hundred just as he stands.'

Thornton shook his head and stepped to Buck's side.

'You must stand off from him,' Matthewson protested. 'Free play and plenty of room.'

The crowd fell silent; only could be heard the voices of the gamblers vainly offering two to one. Everybody acknowledged Buck a magnificent animal, but twenty fifty-pound sacks of flour bulked too large in their eyes for them to loosen their pouch-strings.

Thornton knelt down by Buck's side. He took his head in his two hands and rested cheek on cheek. He did not playfully shake him, as was his wont, or murmur soft love curses; but he whispered in his ear. 'As you love me, Buck. As you love me,' was what he whispered. Buck whined with suppressed eagerness.

The crowd was watching curiously. The affair was growing mysterious. It seemed like a conjuration. As Thornton got to his feet, Buck seized his mittened hand between his jaws, pressing in with his teeth and releasing slowly, half-reluctantly. It was the answer, in terms, not of speech, but of love. Thornton stepped well back.

'Now, Buck,' he said.

Buck tightened the traces, then slacked them for a matter of several inches. It was the way he had learned.

'Gee!' Thornton's voice rang out, sharp in the tense silence.

Buck swung to the right, ending the movement in a plunge that took up the slack and with a sudden jerk arrested his one hundred and fifty pounds. The load quivered, and from under the runners arose a crisp crackling.

'Haw!' Thornton commanded.

Buck duplicated the manoeuvre, this time to the left. The crackling turned into a snapping, the sled pivoting and the runners slipping and grating several inches to the side. The sled was broken out. Men were holding their breaths, intensely unconscious of the fact.

'Now, MUSH!'

Thornton's command cracked out like a pistol-shot. Buck threw himself forward, tightening the traces with a jarring lunge. His whole body was gathered compactly together in the tremendous effort, the muscles writhing and knotting like live things under the silky fur. His great chest was low to the ground, his head forward and down, while his feet were flying like mad, the claws scarring the hard-packed snow in parallel grooves. The sled swayed and trembled, half-started forward. One of his feet slipped, and one man groaned aloud. Then the sled lurched ahead in what appeared a rapid succession of jerks, though it never really came to a dead stop again . . . half an inch . . . an inch . . . two inches . . . The jerks perceptibly diminished; as the sled gained momentum, he caught them up, till it was moving steadily along.

Men gasped and began to breathe again, unaware that for a moment they had ceased to breathe. Thornton was running behind, encouraging Buck with short, cheery words. The distance had been measured off, and as he neared the pile of firewood which marked the end of the hundred yards, a cheer began to grow and grow, which burst into a roar as he passed the firewood and halted at command. Every man was tearing himself loose, even Matthewson. Hats and mittens were flying in the air. Men were shaking hands, it did not matter with whom, and bubbling over in a general incoherent babel.

But Thornton fell on his knees beside Buck. Head was against head, and he was shaking him back and forth. Those who hurried up heard him cursing Buck, and he cursed him long and fervently, and softly and lovingly.

'Gad, sir! Gad, sir!' spluttered the Skookum Bench king. 'I'll give you a thousand for him, sir, a thousand, sir – twelve hundred, sir.'

Thornton rose to his feet. His eyes were wet. The tears were streaming frankly down his cheeks. 'Sir,' he said to the Skookum Bench king, 'no, sir. You can go to hell, sir. It's the best I can do for you, sir.'

Buck seized Thornton's hand in his teeth. Thornton shook him back and forth. As though animated by a common impulse, the onlookers drew back to a respectful distance; nor were they again indiscreet enough to interrupt.

SEA FEVER
John Masefield

I must go down to the seas again, to the lonely sea and
the sky,
And all I ask is a tall ship and a star to steer her by;
And the wheel's kick and the wind's song and the white
sail's shaking,
And a grey mist on the sea's face, and a grey dawn
breaking.

I must go down to the seas again, for the call of the
running tide
Is a wild call and a clear call that may not be denied;
And all I ask is a windy day with the white clouds flying,
And the flung spray and the blown spume, and the sea-
gulls crying.

I must go down to the seas again, to the vagrant gypsy
life,
To the gull's way and the whale's way where the wind's
like a whetted knife;
And all I ask is a merry yarn from a laughing fellow-rover,
And quiet sleep and a sweet dream when the long trick's
over.

READING NOTES

After listening to the story, an elderly man in a day centre reading group said that he had had dogs all his life and thought that a real dog lover would never have made his dog do such a dangerously hard task just for a bet. 'Thornton had doubts,' he said, 'he didn't think it was possible, yet he went ahead. That's not right.' Others had not thought of the story in this way; they had simply been impressed at how much the dog was prepared to go through for his master. Inevitably the talk centred on dogs: how to treat and train them. There was talk about Alaska: though no one in the group had been there, some had seen films about the gold rush and knew it to be a wild place and time. Questions about what the call of the wild might be led on to the reading of the poem which was familiar to quite a few. One woman was able to recite the first verse word-perfectly.

Why the poem is called 'Sea Fever'; and the ways in which the poem achieves a sense of urgency that seems to make you feel you too 'must' go down to the sea, necessitate a close look at the language of the poem. What are your feelings about the sea: fear, fascination? And are you drawn to wild places or do you prefer to read about them from the relative safety of suburban life?

Cats

❧

THE SUMMER BOOK

(THE CAT, CHAPTER 9)

Tove Jansson

(approximate reading time 10 minutes)

'The Cat' is a stand-alone chapter from The Summer Book. Following the death of her mother, six-year-old Sophia has come to spend the long summer with her grandmother on a very small island in the Gulf of Finland. The old lady and the young child must get to know and understand one another . . .

It was a tiny kitten when it came and could drink its milk only from a nipple. Fortunately, they still had Sophia's baby bottle in the attic. In the beginning, the kitten slept in a tea-cosy to keep warm, but when it found its legs they let it sleep in the cottage in Sophia's bed. It had its own pillow, next to hers.

It was a fisherman's cat and it grew fast. One day, it left the cottage and moved into the house, where it spent its nights under the bed in the box where they kept the dirty dishes. It had odd ideas of its own even then. Sophia carried the cat back to the cottage and tried as hard as she could to ingratiate herself,

but the more love she gave it, the quicker it fled back to the dish box. When the box got too full, the cat would howl and someone would have to wash the dishes. Its name was Ma Petite, but they called it Moppy.

'It's funny about love,' Sophia said. 'The more you love someone, the less he likes you back.'

'That's very true,' Grandmother observed. 'And so what do you do?'

'You go on loving,' said Sophia threateningly. 'You love harder and harder.'

Her grandmother sighed and said nothing.

Moppy was carried around to all the pleasant places a cat might like, but he only glanced at them and walked away. He was flattened with hugs, endured them politely and climbed back into the dish box. He was entrusted with burning secrets and merely averted his yellow gaze. Nothing in the world seemed to interest this cat but food and sleep.

'You know,' Sophia said, 'sometimes I think I hate Moppy. I don't have the strength to go on loving him, but I think about him all the time!'

Week after week, Sophia pursued the cat. She spoke softly and gave him comfort and understanding, and only a couple of times did she lose her patience and yell at him, or pull his tail. At such times Moppy would hiss and run under the house, and afterwards his appetite was better and he slept even longer than usual, curled up in unapproachable softness with one paw daintily across his nose.

Sophia stopped playing and started having nightmares. She couldn't think about anything but this cat who refused to be affectionate. Meanwhile Moppy grew into a lean and wild little animal, and one June night he didn't come back to his dish box. In the morning, he walked into the house and stretched – front legs first, with his rear end up in the air – then he closed his eyes and sharpened his claws on the rocking chair, after which he jumped up on the bed and went to sleep. The cat's whole being radiated calm superiority.

He's started hunting, Grandmother thought.

She was right. The very next morning, the cat came in and placed a small dusky yellow bird on the doorstep. Its neck had been deftly broken with one bite, and some bright red drops of blood lay prettily on the shiny coat of feathers. Sophia turned pale and stared fixedly at the murdered bird. She sidled past Moppy, the murderer, with small, forced steps, and then turned and rushed out.

Later, Grandmother remarked on the curious fact that wild

animals, cats for example, cannot understand the difference between a rat and a bird.

'Then they're dumb!' said Sophia curtly. 'Rats are hideous and birds are nice. I don't think I'll talk to Moppy for three days.' And she stopped talking to her cat.

Every night, the cat went into the woods, and every morning it killed its prey and carried it into the house to be admired, and every morning the bird was thrown into the sea. A little while later, Sophia would appear outside the window and shout, 'Can I come in? Have you taken out the body?' She punished Moppy and increased her own pain by means of a terrible coarseness. 'Have you cleaned up the blood?' she would yell, or, 'How many murdered today?' And morning coffee was no longer what it had been.

It was a great relief when Moppy finally learned to conceal his crimes. It is one thing to see a pool of blood and quite another thing only to know about it. Moppy probably grew tired of all the screaming and fussing, and perhaps he thought the family ate his birds. One morning when Grandmother was taking her first cigarette on the veranda, she dropped her holder and it rolled through a crack in the floor. She managed to raise one of the planks, and there was Moppy's handiwork – a row of small bird skeletons, all picked clean. Of course she knew that the cat had continued to hunt, and could not have stopped, but the next time he rubbed against her leg as he passed, she drew away and whispered, 'You sly bastard.' The cat dish stood untouched by the steps, and attracted flies.

'You know what?' Sophia said. 'I wish Moppy had never

been born. Or else that I'd never been born. That would have been better.'

'So you're still not speaking to each other?' Grandmother asked.

'Not a word,' Sophia said. 'I don't know what to do. And what if I do forgive him – what fun is that when he doesn't even care?' Grandmother couldn't think of anything to say.

Moppy turned wild and rarely came into the house. He was the same colour as the island – a light yellowish grey with striped shadings like granite, or like sunlight on a sand bottom. When he slipped across the meadow by the beach, his progress was like a stroke of wind through the grass. He would watch for hours in the thicket, a motionless silhouette, two pointed ears against the sunset, and then suddenly vanish . . . and some bird would chirp, just once. He would slink under the creeping pines, soaked by the rain and lean as a streak, and he would wash himself voluptuously when the sun came out. He was an absolutely happy cat, but he didn't share anything with anyone. On hot days, he would roll on the smooth rock, and sometimes he would eat grass and calmly vomit his own hair the way cats do. And what he did between times no one knew.

One Saturday, the Övergårds came for coffee. Sophia went down to look at their boat. It was big, full of bags and jerry cans and baskets, and in one of the baskets a cat was meowing. Sophia lifted the lid and the cat licked her hand. It was a big white cat with a broad face. It kept right on purring when she picked it up and carried it ashore.

'So you found the cat,' said Anna Övergård. 'It's a nice cat, but it's not a mouser, so we thought we'd give it to some friends.'

Sophia sat on the bed with the heavy cat on her lap. It never stopped purring. It was soft and warm and submissive.

They struck a bargain easily, with a bottle of rum to close the deal. Moppy was captured and never knew what was happening until the Övergårds' boat was on its way to town.

The new cat's name was Fluff. It ate fish and liked to be petted. It moved into Sophia's cottage and slept every night in her arms, and every morning it came in to morning coffee and slept some more in the bed beside the stove. If the sun was shining, it would roll on the warm granite.

'Not there!' Sophia yelled. 'That's Moppy's place!' She carried the cat a little farther off, and it licked her on the nose and rolled obediently in the new spot.

The summer grew prettier and prettier, a long series of calm blue summer days. Every night, Fluff slept against Sophia's cheek.

'It's funny about me,' Sophia said. 'I think nice weather gets to be boring.'

'Do you?' her grandmother said. 'Then you're just like your grandfather, he liked storms too.' But before she could say anything else about Grandfather, Sophia was gone.

And gradually the wind came up, sometime during the night, and by morning there was a regular south-wester spitting foam all over the rocks.

'Wake up,' Sophia whispered. 'Wake up, kitty, precious, there's a storm.'

Fluff purred and stretched warm sleepy legs in all directions. The sheet was covered with cat hair.

'Get up!' Sophia shouted. 'It's a storm!' But the cat just

turned over on its broad stomach. And suddenly Sophia was furious. She kicked open the door and threw the cat out in the wind and watched how it laid its ears back, and she screamed, 'Hunt! Do something! Be like a cat!' And then she started to cry and ran to the guest room and banged on the door.

'What's wrong now?' Grandmother said.

'I want Moppy back!' Sophia screamed.

'But you know how it'll be,' Grandmother said.

'It'll be awful,' said Sophia gravely. 'But it's Moppy I love.'

And so they exchanged cats again.

A CAT
Edward Thomas

She had a name among the children;
But no one loved though someone owned
Her, locked her out of doors at bedtime
And had her kittens duly drowned.

In Spring, nevertheless, this cat
Ate blackbirds, thrushes, nightingales,
And birds of bright voice and plume and flight,
As well as scraps from neighbours' pails.

I loathed and hated her for this;
One speckle on a thrush's breast
Was worth a million such; and yet
She lived long, till God gave her rest.

READING NOTES

'What I like about this story,' said a woman in a group of carers, 'is that it shows you can't choose who to love. You just love.' The child in the story thinks a lot about the nature of love and people have talked about the way in which animals can teach you life lessons. Not everyone likes cats and usually for the reasons the poem and story confirm. Cats are predatory; they will kill birds and mice and if you can't live with that then don't keep a cat or you will have to resign yourself to live as Sophia will have to live – in between loving and hating Moppy. The poem moves back and forth in feelings of pity and disgust. What is the last line saying, and is the writer a cat lover?

Something to Say

❧

TREES CAN SPEAK
Alan Marshall

I heard footsteps and I looked up. A man carrying a prospector's dish was clambering down the bank.

'This man never speaks,' the store-keeper in the town three miles away had told me. 'A few people have heard him say one word like "Hullo" or something. He makes himself understood by shaking or nodding his head.'

'Is there something wrong with him?' I asked.

'No. He can talk if he wants to. Silent Joe, they call him.'

When the man reached a spot where the creek widened into a pool he squatted on his heels and scooped some water into the dish. He stood up and, bending over the dish, began to wash the dirt it contained by swinging it in a circular motion.

I lifted my crutches from the ground and hopped along the pebbles till I stood opposite him across the pool.

'Good day,' I said. 'Great day.'

He raised his head and looked at me. His eyes were grey, the greenish grey of the bush. There was no hostility in his look, just a searching.

They suddenly changed their expression and said, as plainly as if he had spoken, 'Yes.'

I sat down and watched him. He poured the muddy water into the clear pool.

It rolled along the sandy bottom, twisting and turning in whorls and convolutions until it faded into a faint cloud, moving swiftly with the current.

He washed the residue many times.

I crossed over above the pool and walked down to him.

'Get anything?'

He held the dish towards me and pointed to three specks of gold resting on the outer edge of a layer of sand.

'So that's gold,' I said. 'Three specks, eh! Half the troubles of this world come from collections of specks like those.'

He smiled. It took a long time to develop. It moved over his face slowly and somehow I thought of an egret in flight, as if wings had come and gone.

He looked at me with kindliness and, for a moment, I saw the bush, not remote and pitying, but beckoning like a friend. He was akin to trees and they spoke through him.

If I could only understand him I would understand the bush, I thought.

But he turned away and like the gums, was remote again, removed from contact by his silence which was not the silence of absent speech, but the eloquent silence of trees.

'I am coming with you,' I said.

We walked side by side. He studied the track for my benefit. He kicked limbs aside, broke the branches of wattles drooping over the path that skirted the foot of the hill.

We moved into thicker timber. The sun pierced the canopy of branches and spangled our shoulders with leaf patterns. A cool, leaf-mould breath of earth rose from the foot-printed moss. The track dipped sharply down into a gully and ended in a small clearing.

Thin grass, spent with seeding, quivered hopelessly in a circle of trees.

In the centre of the clearing a mound of yellow clay rose from around the brink of a shaft. A windlass, erected on the top of the mound, spanned the opening.

A heavy iron bucket dangled from the roller.

'So this is your mine!' I said.

He nodded, looking at it with a pleased expression.

I climbed to the top of the mound and peered down into darkness. A movement of air, dank with the moisture from buried rocks and clay, welled up and broke coldly on my face. I pushed a small stone over the edge. It flashed silently from sight, speeding through a narrow darkness for a tense gap of time, then rang an ending from somewhere deep down in the earth.

'Cripes, that's deep!' I exclaimed.

He was standing beside me, pleased that I was impressed.

'Do you go down that ladder?' I asked. I pointed to a ladder of lashed saplings that was wired to a facing of timber.

He nodded.

'I can climb ladders,' I murmured, wondering how I could get down, 'but not that one.'

He looked at me questioningly, a sympathetic concern shading his face.

'Infantile paralysis,' I explained. 'It's a nuisance sometimes. Do you think you could lower me down in that bucket? I want to see the reef where you get the gold.'

I expected him to demur. It would be the natural reaction. I expected him to shake his head in an expressive communication of the danger involved.

But he didn't hesitate. He reached out across the shaft and drew the bucket to the edge. I placed my crutches on the ground and straddled it so that my legs hung down the sides and the handle lay between my knees. I grasped the rope and said, 'Righto,' then added, 'You're coming down the ladder, aren't you?'

He nodded and caught hold of the bucket handle. He lifted and I was swung out over the shaft. The bucket slowly revolved, then stopped and began a reversing movement. He grasped the windlass, removed a chock. I saw him brace himself against the strain. His powerful arms worked slowly like crank-shafts. I sank into the cold air that smelt of frogs.

'What the hell did I come down here for?' I thought. 'This is a damn silly thing to do.'

The bucket twisted slowly. A spiralling succession of jutting rock and layers of clay passed my eyes. I suddenly bumped the side. The shaft took a turn and continued down at an angle so that the opening was eclipsed and I was alone.

I pushed against the side to save my legs from being scraped against the rocks. The bucket grated downwards, sending a cascade of clay slithering before it, then stopped.

A heavy darkness pressed against me. I reached down and touched the floor of the shaft. I slid off the bucket and sat down on the ground beside it.

In a little while I heard the creak of a ladder. Gravel and small stones pattered beside me. I was conscious of someone near me in the dark, then a match flared and he lit a candle. A yellow stiletto of flame rose towards his face, then shrank back to the drooping wick. He sheltered it with his hand till the wax melted and the shadows moved away to a tunnel that branched from the foot of the shaft.

'I'm a fool,' I said. 'I didn't bring my crutches.'

He looked at me speculatively while candle shadows fluttered upon his face like moths. His expression changed to one of decision and I answered the unspoken intention as if it had been conveyed to me in words.

'Thanks very much. I'm not heavy.'

He bent down and lifted me onto his back. Beneath his faded blue shirt I could feel his shoulder muscles bunch then slip into movement.

He crouched low as he walked so that my head would not strike the rocks projecting from the roof of the tunnel. I rose and fell to each firm step.

The light from the candle moved ahead of us, cleansing the tunnel of darkness.

At the end of the drive he stopped and lowered me gently to the ground.

He held the candle close to the face and pointed a heavy finger at the narrow reef which formed a diagonal scar across the rock.

'So that's it!' I exclaimed.

I tried to break a piece out with my fingers. He lifted a small bar from the ground and drove it into the vein. I picked up some shattered pieces and searched them in the light of the candle. He bent his head near mine and watched the stone I was turning in my fingers. He suddenly reached out his hand and took it away. He licked it then smiled and held it towards me. With his thumb he indicated a speck of gold adhering to the surface.

I was excited at the find. I asked him many questions. He sat with his hands clasped around his drawn-up knees and answered with eloquent expressions and shakes of the head.

The candle flame began to flutter in a scooped stub of wax.

'I think it's time we left,' I said.

He rose and carried me back to the foot of the shaft, I tied my knees together with string and placed my legs in the bucket this time. I had no control over the right leg, which fell helplessly to one side if not bound to its stronger neighbour. I sat on the edge of the bucket clasping the windlass rope and waited. The candle welled into sudden brightness then fluttered and died. I could hear the creaks of the tortured ladder, then silence.

In all the world only I was alive. The darkness had texture and weight like a blanket of black. The silence had no expectancy. I sat brooding sombrely, drained of all sunlight and song. The world of birds and trees and laughter was as remote as a star.

Without reason, seemingly without object, I suddenly began to rise like a bubble. I swung in emptiness; I moved in a void, governed by planetary laws over which I had no control.

Then I crashed against the side and the lip of the bucket tipped as it caught in projecting tongues of stone. The bottom moved up and out then slumped heavily downwards as the edge broke free.

I scraped and bounced upwards till I emerged from a sediment of darkness into a growing light. Above my head the mouth of the shaft increased in size.

I suddenly burst into dazzling sunlight. An arm reached out; a hand grasped the handle of the bucket. There was a lift and I felt the solidity of earth beneath me. It was good to stand on something that didn't move, to feel the sun on your face.

He stood watching me, his outstretched arm bridging him to a grey box-tree that seemed strangely like himself.

I thanked him then sat down on the rubble for a yarn. I told him about myself and something about the people I had met. He listened without moving, but I felt the power of his interest drawing words from me as dry earth absorbs water.

'Goodbye,' I said before I left him, and I shook his hand.

I went away, but before I reached the trees I turned and waved to him.

He was still standing against the grey box like a kindred tree, but he straightened quickly and waved in return.

'Goodbye,' he called, and it was as if a tree had spoken.

MIRACLE ON ST DAVID'S DAY
Gillian Clarke

They flash upon that inward eye
Which is the bliss of solitude.
'Daffodils', William Wordsworth

An afternoon yellow and open-mouthed
with daffodils. The sun treads the path
among cedars and enormous oaks.
It might be a country house, guests strolling,
the rumps of gardeners between nursery shrubs.

I am reading poetry to the insane.
An old woman, interrupting, offers
as many buckets of coal as I need.
A beautiful chestnut-haired boy listens
entirely absorbed. A schizophrenic

on a good day, they tell me later.
In a cage of first March sun, a woman
sits not listening, not seeing, not feeling.
In her neat clothes, the woman is absent.
A big, mild man is tenderly led

to his chair. He has never spoken.
His labourer's hands on his knees, he rocks
gently to the rhythm of the poems.
I read to their presences, absences,
to the big, dumb labouring man as he rocks.

He is suddenly standing, silently,
huge and mild, but I feel afraid. Like slow
movement of spring water or the first bird
of the year in the breaking darkness,
the labourer's voice recites 'The Daffodils'.

The nurses are frozen, alert; the patients
seem to listen. He is hoarse but word-perfect.
Outside the daffodils are still as wax,
a thousand, ten thousand, their syllables
unspoken, their creams and yellows still.

Forty years ago, in a Valleys school,
the class recited poetry by rote.
Since the dumbness of misery fell
he has remembered there was a music
of speech and that once he had something to say.

When he's done, before the applause, we observe
the flowers' silence. A thrush sings,
and the daffodils are flame.

READING NOTES

This story rendered a usually vociferous library reading group, temporarily speechless. Firstly because no one was quite sure what had happened and secondly because of the story's strangely haunting quality. Two sentences in particular were looked at closely: 'He was akin to trees and they spoke through him' and 'his silence was not the silence of absent speech, but the eloquent silence of trees.' Conversation covered the effects of living close to nature; the grandeur and importance of trees; what trees say to us; the courage of the narrator – is it really his own fearless-ness or a sense of trust and confidence in Silent Joe that enables him to go down the shaft?

After listening to 'Miracle on St David's Day', what are your first feelings? Are they to do with loss – the years lost to illness; 'the dumbness of misery'; the sad 'absences' – or are you moved by the power of memory and the final vision of the daffodils as 'flame'? The quotation from Wordsworth's 'The Daffodils' invites attention both for itself and for its part in Gillian Clarke's poem.

Most people have learnt poetry at school. What do you have in your own inner anthology?

Letting Go

🍂

FLIGHT
Doris Lessing

(approximate reading time 12 minutes)

Above the old man's head was the dovecote, a tall wire-netted shelf on stilts, full of strutting, preening birds. The sunlight broke on their grey breasts into small rainbows. His ears were lulled by their crooning, his hands stretched up towards his favourite, a homing pigeon, a young plump-bodied bird which stood still when it saw him and cocked a shrewd bright eye.

'Pretty, pretty, pretty,' he said, as he grasped the bird and drew it down, feeling the cold coral claws tighten around his finger. Content, he rested the bird lightly on his chest, and leaned against a tree, gazing out beyond the dovecote into the landscape of a late afternoon. In folds and hollows of sunlight and shade, the dark red soil, which was broken into great dusty clods, stretched wide to a tall horizon. Trees marked the course of the valley; a stream of rich green grass the road.

His eyes travelled homewards along this road until he saw his grand-daughter swinging on the gate underneath a frangi-pani tree. Her hair fell down her back in a wave of sunlight, and her long bare legs repeated the angles of the frangipani stems, bare, shining-brown stems among patterns of pale blossoms.

She was gazing past the pink flowers, past the railway cottage, where they lived, along the road to the village.

His mood shifted. He deliberately held out his wrist for the bird to take flight, and caught it again at the moment it spread its wings. He felt the plump shape strive and strain under his fingers; and, in a sudden access of troubled spite, shut the bird into a small box and fastened the bolt. 'Now you stay there,' he muttered; and turned his back on the shelf of birds. He moved warily along the hedge, stalking his grand-daughter, who was now looped over the gate, her head loose on her arms, singing. The light happy sound mingled with the crooning of the birds, and his anger mounted.

'Hey!' he shouted; saw her jump, look back, and abandon the gate. Her eyes veiled themselves, and she said in a pert neutral voice: 'Hullo, Grandad.' Politely she moved towards him, after a lingering backward glance at the road.

'Waiting for Steven, hey?' he said, his fingers curling like claws into his palm.

'Any objection?' she asked lightly, refusing to look at him.

He confronted her, his eyes narrowed, shoulders hunched, tight in a hard knot of pain which included the preening birds, the sunlight, the flowers, herself. He said: 'Think you're old enough to go courting, hey?'

The girl tossed her head at the old-fashioned phrase and sulked, 'Oh, Grandad!'

'Think you want to leave home, hey? Think you can go running around the fields at night?'

Her smile made him see her, as he had every evening of this warm end-of-summer month, swinging hand in hand along the road to the village with that red-handed, red-throated, violent-bodied youth, the son of the postmaster. Misery went to his head and he shouted angrily: 'I'll tell your mother!'

'Tell away!' she said, laughing, and went back to the gate. He heard her singing, for him to hear:

'I've got you under my skin,
I've got you deep in the heart of . . .'

'Rubbish,' he shouted. 'Rubbish. Impudent little bit of rubbish!'

Growling under his breath he turned towards the dovecote, which was his refuge from the house he shared with his daughter and her husband and their children. But now the house would be empty. Gone all the young girls with their laughter and their squabbling and their teasing. He would be left, uncherished and alone, with that square-fronted, calm-eyed woman, his daughter.

He stooped, muttering, before the dovecote, resenting the absorbed cooing birds.

From the gate the girl shouted: 'Go and tell! Go on, what are you waiting for?'

Obstinately he made his way back to the house, with quick, pathetic persistent glances of appeal back at her. But she never looked around. Her defiant but anxious young body stung him into love and repentance. He stopped. 'But I never meant . . .' he muttered, waiting for her to turn round and run to him. 'I didn't mean . . .'

She did not turn. She had forgotten him. Along the road came the young man Steven, with something in his hand. A present for her? The old man stiffened as he watched the gate swing back, and the couple embrace. In the brittle shadows of the frangipani tree his grand-daughter, his darling, lay in the arms of the postmaster's son, and her hair flowed back over his shoulder.

'I see you!' shouted the old man spitefully. They did not move. He stumped into the little whitewashed house, hearing the wooden veranda creak angrily under his feet. His daughter was sewing in the front room, threading a needle held to the light.

He stopped again, looking back into the garden. The couple were now sauntering among the bushes, laughing. As he watched he saw the girl escape from the youth with a sudden mischievous movement, and run off through the flowers with him in pursuit. He heard shouts, laughter, a scream, silence.

'But it's not like that at all,' he muttered miserably. 'It's not like that. Why can't you see? Running and giggling, and kissing and kissing. You'll come to something quite different.'

He looked at his daughter with sardonic hatred, hating himself. They were caught and finished, both of them, but the girl was still running free.

'Can't you *see*?' he demanded of his invisible grand-daughter, who was at that moment lying in the thick green grass with the postmaster's son.

His daughter looked at him and her eyebrows went up in tired forbearance.

'Put your birds to bed?' she asked, humouring him.

'Lucy,' he said, urgently. 'Lucy . . .'

'Well what is it now?'

'She's in the garden with Steven.'

'Now you just sit down and have your tea.'

He stumped his feet alternately, thump, thump, on the hollow wooden floor and shouted: 'She'll marry him. I'm telling you, she'll be marrying him next!'

His daughter rose swiftly, brought him a cup, set him a plate.

'I don't want any tea. I don't want it, I tell you.'

'Now, now,' she crooned. 'What's wrong with it? Why not?'

'She's eighteen. Eighteen!'

'I was married at seventeen and I never regretted it.'

'Liar,' he said. 'Liar. Then you should regret it. Why do you make your girls marry? It's you who do it. What do you do it for? Why?'

'The other three have done fine. They've three fine husbands. Why not Alice?'

'She's the last,' he mourned. 'Can't we keep her a bit longer?'

'Come, now, dad. She'll be down the road, that's all. She'll be here everyday to see you.'

'But it's not the same.' He thought of the other three girls, transformed inside a few months from charming petulant spoiled children into serious young matrons.

'You never did like it when we married!' she said. 'Why not? Every time, it's the same. When I got married you made me feel like it was something wrong. And my girls the same. You get them all crying and miserable the way you go on. Leave Alice alone. She's happy.' She sighed, letting her eyes linger on the sun-lit garden. 'She'll marry next month. There's no reason to wait.'

'You've said they can marry?' he said incredulously.

'Yes, dad, why not?' she said coldly, and took up her sewing.

His eyes stung, and he went out on to the veranda. Wet spread down over his chin and he took out a handkerchief and mopped his whole face. The garden was empty.

From around a corner came the young couple; but their faces were no longer set against him. On the wrist of the postmaster's son balanced a young pigeon, the light gleaming on its breast.

'For me?' said the old man, letting the drops shake off his chin. 'For me?'

'Do you like it?' The girl grabbed his hand and swung on it. 'It's for you, Grandad. Steven brought it for you.' They hung about him, affectionate, concerned, trying to charm away his wet eyes and his misery. They took his arms and directed him to the shelf of birds, one on each side, enclosing him, petting him, saying wordlessly that nothing would be changed, nothing could change, and that they would be with him always. The bird was proof of it, they said, from their lying happy eyes, as they thrust it on him. 'There, Grandad, it's yours. It's for you.'

They watched him as he held it on his wrist, stroking its soft, sun-warmed back, watching the wings lift and balance.

'You must shut it up for a bit,' said the girl intimately. 'Until it knows this is its home.'

'Teach your grandmother to suck eggs,' growled the old man.

Released by his half-deliberate anger, they fell back, laughing at him. 'We're glad you like it.' They moved off, now serious and full of purpose to the gate, where they hung, backs to him, talking quietly. More than anything could, their grown-up seriousness shut him out, making him alone; also, it quietened him, took the sting out of their tumbling like puppies on the grass. They had forgotten him again. Well, so they should, the old man reassured himself, feeling his throat clotted with tears, his lips trembling. He held the new bird to his face, for the caress of its silken feathers. Then he shut it in a box and took out his favourite.

'*Now* you can go,' he said aloud. He held it poised, ready for flight, while he looked down the garden towards the boy and the girl. Then, clenched in the pain of loss, he lifted the bird on his wrist and watched it soar. A whirr and spatter of wings, and a cloud of birds rose into the evening from the dovecote.

At the gate Alice and Steven forgot their talk and watched the birds.

On the veranda, that woman, his daughter, stood gazing, her eyes shaded with a hand that still held her sewing.

It seemed to the old man that the whole afternoon had stilled to watch his gesture of self-command, that even the leaves of the trees had stopped shaking.

Dry-eyed and calm, he let his hands fall to his sides and stood erect, staring up into the sky.

The cloud of shining silver birds flew up and up, with a shrill cleaving of wings, over the dark ploughed land and the darker belts of trees, and the bright folds of grass, until they floated high in the sunlight, like a cloud of motes of dust.

They wheeled in a wide circle, tilting their wings so there was flash after flash of light, and one after another they dropped from the sunshine of the upper sky to shadow, one after another, returning to the shadowed earth over trees and grass and field, returning to the valley and the shelter of night.

The garden was all a fluster and a flurry of returning birds. Then silence, and the sky was empty.

The old man turned, slowly, taking his time; he lifted his

eyes to smile proudly down the garden at his grand-daughter. She was staring at him. She did not smile. She was wide-eyed, and pale in the cold shadow, and he saw the tears run shivering off her face.

EVERYONE SANG
Siegfried Sassoon

Everyone suddenly burst out singing;
And I was filled with such delight
As prisoned birds must find in freedom,
Winging wildly across the white
Orchards and dark-green fields; on – on – and out of
    sight.

Everyone's voice was suddenly lifted;
And beauty came like the setting sun:
My heart was shaken with tears; and horror
Drifted away . . . O, but Everyone
Was a bird; and the song was wordless; the singing will
    never be done.

READING NOTES

'Sometimes I think I understand this poem,' said a member of a hospital reading group, 'and then I lose it again.' The group spent some time talking about the mixed feelings of joy and sadness the poem seems to convey, and puzzled over the final words: 'O, but Everyone was a bird; and the song was wordless; the singing will never be done.'

The end of 'Flight' was found to be similarly enigmatic: what is the reason for the girl's tears? There was much to say about loving and letting go and the difficulty of coming to terms with your children becoming adults. Some knew the feeling of loneliness and redundancy when children grow up and leave home. For many parents, the time when children leave home coincides with their own parents becoming more dependent.

The poem and story are full of complexities and oppositions: love and hatred; captivity and release; youth and age; sounds and silence. Much food for thought here.

Where We Live

🌿

ON THE BLACK HILL
(CHAPTER 1)
Bruce Chatwin

(approximate reading time 13 minutes)

For forty-two years, Lewis and Benjamin Jones slept side by side, in their parents' bed, at their farm which was known as 'The Vision'.

The bedstead, an oak four-poster, came from their mother's home at Bryn-Draenog when she married in 1899. Its faded cretonne hangings, printed with a design of larkspur and roses, shut out the mosquitoes of summer, and the draughts in the winter. Calloused heels had worn holes in the linen sheets, and parts of the patchwork quilt had frayed. Under the goose-feather mattress, there was a second mattress, of horsehair, and this had sunk into two troughs, leaving a ridge between the sleepers.

The room was always dark and smelled of lavender and mothballs.

The smell of mothballs came from a pyramid of hatboxes piled up beside the washstand. On the bed-table lay a pincushion still stuck with Mrs Jones' hatpins; and on the end wall hung an engraving of Holman Hunt's 'Light of the World', enclosed in an ebonised frame.

One of the windows looked out over the green fields of England: the other looked back into Wales, past a clump of larches, at the Black Hill.

Both the brothers' hair was even whiter than the pillow-cases.

Every morning their alarm went off at six. They listened to the farmers' broadcast as they shaved and dressed. Downstairs, they tapped the barometer, lit the fire and boiled a kettle for tea. They did the milking and the foddering before coming back for breakfast.

The house had roughcast walls and a roof of mossy stone tiles and stood at the far end of the farmyard in the shade of an old Scots pine. Below the cowshed there was an orchard of wind-stunted apple-trees, and then the fields slanted down to the dingle, and there were birches and alders along the stream.

Long ago, the place had been called Ty-Cradoc – and Caractacus is still a name in these parts – but in 1737 an ailing girl called Alice Morgan saw the Virgin hovering over a patch of rhubarb, and ran back to the kitchen, cured. To celebrate the miracle, her father renamed his farm 'The Vision' and carved the initials A.M. with the date and a cross on the lintel above the porch. The border of Radnor and

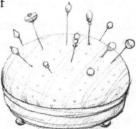

Hereford was said to run right through the middle of the staircase.

The brothers were identical twins.

As boys, only their mother could tell them apart: now age and accidents had weathered them in different ways.

Lewis was tall and stringy, with shoulders set square and a steady long-limbed stride. Even at eighty he could walk over the hills all day, or wield an axe all day, and not get tired.

He gave off a strong smell. His eyes – grey, dreamy and astigmatic – were set well back into the skull, and capped with thick round lenses in white metal frames. He bore the scar of a cycling accident on his nose and, ever since, its tip had curved downwards and turned purple in cold-weather.

His head would wobble as he spoke: unless he was fumbling with his watch-chain, he had no idea what to do with his hands. In company he always wore a puzzled look; and if anyone made a statement of fact, he'd say, 'Thank you!' or 'Very kind of you!' Everyone agreed he had a wonderful way with sheepdogs.

Benjamin was shorter, pinker, neater and sharper-tongued. His chin fell into his neck, but he still possessed the full stretch of his nose, which he would use in conversation as a weapon. He had less hair.

He did all the cooking, the darning and the ironing; and he kept the accounts. No one could be fiercer in a haggle over the stock-prices and he would go on, arguing for hours, until the dealer threw up his hands and said, 'Come off, you old skinflint!' and he'd smile and say, 'What can you mean by that?'

For miles around the twins had the reputation of being incredibly stingy – but this was not always so.

They refused, for example, to make a penny out of hay. Hay, they said, was God's gift to the farmer; and providing The Vision had hay to spare, their poorer neighbours were welcome to what they needed. Even in the foul days of January, old Miss Fifield the Tump had only to send a message with the postman, and Lewis would drive the tractor over with a load of bales.

Benjamin's favourite occupation was delivering lambs. All the long winter, he waited for the end of March, when the curlews started calling and the lambing began. It was he, not Lewis, who stayed awake to watch the ewes. It was he who would pull a lamb at a difficult birth. Sometimes, he had to thrust his forearm into the womb to disentangle a pair of twins; and afterwards, he would sit by the fireside, unwashed and contented, and let the cat lick the afterbirth off his hands.

In winter and summer, the brothers went to work in striped flannel shirts with copper studs to fasten them at the neck. Their jackets and waistcoats were made of brown whipcord, and their trousers were of darker corduroy. They wore their moleskin hats with the brims turned down; but since Lewis had the habit of lifting his to every stranger, his fingers had rubbed the nap off the peak.

From time to time, with a slow mock of solemnity, they consulted their silver watches – not to tell the hour but to see whose watch was beating faster. On Saturday nights they took turns to have a hip-bath in front of the fire; and they lived for the memory of their mother.

Because they knew each other's thoughts, they even quarrelled without speaking. And sometimes – perhaps after one of these silent quarrels, when they needed their mother to unite them – they would stand over her patchwork quilt and peer at the black velvet stars and the hexagons of printed calico that had once been her dresses. And without saying a word they could see her again – in pink, walking through the oatfield with a jug of draught cider for the reapers. Or in green, at a sheep-shearers' lunch. Or in a blue-striped apron bending over the fire. But the black stars brought back a memory of their father's coffin, laid out on the kitchen table, and the chalk-faced women, crying.

Nothing in the kitchen had changed since the day of his funeral. The wallpaper, with its pattern of Iceland poppies and russet fern, had darkened over with smoke-resin; and though the brass knobs shone as brightly as ever, the brown paint had chipped from the doors and skirting.

The twins never thought of renewing these threadbare decorations for fear of cancelling out the memory of that bright spring morning, over seventy years before, when they had helped their mother stir a bucket of flour-and-water paste, and watched the whitewash caking on her scarf.

Benjamin kept her flagstones scrubbed, the iron grate gleaming with black lead polish, and a copper kettle always hissing on the hob.

Friday was his baking day – as it had once been hers – and on Friday afternoons he would roll up his sleeves to make

Welsh cakes or cottage loaves, pummelling the dough so vigorously that the cornflowers on the oilcloth cover had almost worn away.

On the mantelpiece stood a pair of Staffordshire spaniels, five brass candlesticks, a ship-in-a-bottle and a tea-caddy painted with a Chinese lady. A glass-fronted cabinet – one pane repaired with Scotch tape – contained china ornaments, silver-plated teapots, and mugs from every Coronation and Jubilee. A flitch of bacon was rammed into a rack in the rafters. The Georgian pianoforte was proof of idler days and past accomplishments.

Lewis kept a twelve-bore shotgun propped up beside the grandfather clock: both the brothers were terrified of thieves and antique-dealers.

Their father's only hobby – in fact, his only interest apart from farming and the Bible – had been to carve wooden frames for the pictures and family photographs that covered every spare stretch of wall. To Mrs Jones it had been a miracle that a man of her husband's temper and clumsy hands should have had the patience for such intricate work. Yet, from the moment he took up his chisels, from the moment the tiny white shavings flew, all the meanness went out of him.

He had carved a 'gothic' frame for the religious colour print 'The Broad and Narrow Path'. He had invented some 'biblical' motifs for the watercolour of the Pool of Bethesda; and when his brother sent an oleograph from Canada, he smeared the surface with linseed oil to make it look like an Old Master, and spent a whole winter working up a surround of maple leaves.

And it was this picture, with its Red Indian, its birchbark, its pines and a crimson sky – to say nothing of its association with the legendary Uncle Eddie – that first awoke in Lewis a yearning for far-off places.

Apart from a holiday at the seaside in 1910, neither of the twins had ever strayed further than Hereford. Yet these restricted horizons merely inflamed Lewis's passion for geography. He would pester visitors for their opinions on 'them savages in Africky'; for news of Siberia, Salonika or Sri Lanka; and when someone spoke of President Carter's failure to rescue the Teheran hostages, he folded his arms and said, decisively, 'Him should'a gone to get 'em through Odessa.'

His image of the outside world derived from a Bartholomew's atlas of 1925 when the two great colonial empires were coloured pink and mauve, and the Soviet Union was a dull sage green. And it offended his sense of order to find that the planet was now full of bickering little countries with unpronounceable names. So, as if to suggest that real journeys only existed in the imagination – and perhaps to show off – he would close his eyes and chant the lines his mother taught him:

Westward, westward, Hiawatha
Sailed into the fiery sunset
Sailed into the purple vapours
Sailed into the dusk of evening.

Too often the twins had fretted at the thought of dying childless – yet they had only to glance at their wall of photographs to get rid of the gloomiest thoughts. They knew the names of all the sitters and never tired of finding likenesses between people born a hundred years apart.

Hanging to the left of their parents' wedding group was a picture of themselves at the age of six, gaping like baby barn-owls and dressed in identical page-boy collars from the fête in Lurkenhope Park. But the one that gave them the most pleasure was a colour snapshot of their great-nephew Kevin, also aged six, and got up in a wash-towel turban, as Joseph in a nativity play.

Since then, fourteen years had passed and Kevin had grown into a tall, black-haired young man with bushy eyebrows that met in the middle, and slaty grey-blue eyes. In a few months the farm would be his.

So now, when they looked at that faded wedding picture; when they saw their father's face framed in fiery red sideburns (even in a sepia photo you could tell he had bright red hair); when they saw the leg-o'-mutton sleeves of their mother's dress, the roses in her hat, and the ox-eye daisies in her bouquet; and when they compared her sweet smile with Kevin's, they knew that their lives had not been wasted and that time, in its healing circle, had wiped away the pain and anger, the shame and the sterility, and had broken into the future with the promise of new things.

THE SELF-UNSEEING
Thomas Hardy

Here is the ancient floor,
Footworn and hollowed and thin,
Here was the former door
Where the dead feet walked in.

She sat here in her chair,
Smiling into the fire;
He who played stood there,
Bowing it higher and higher.

Childlike, I danced in a dream;
Blessings emblazoned that day;
Everything glowed with a gleam;
Yet we were looking away!

READING NOTES

A group in a nursing home found the description of the farm-house in the story very evocative. References to washstands, 'The Light of the World', the Staffordshire spaniels, the glass-fronted cabinet and the family photographs on the wall retrieved many similar memories. They were interested in the fact that the old men were twins and wondered what it must have been like for the brothers to have spent their whole lives together. They talked about the men living 'for the memory of their mother', of family homes and of their need to know that their home would stay in the family. They found a lot to talk about in the final sentence – in particular the phrase 'the healing circle of time'.

George thought that the poem seemed easy enough when he first read it but 'got deeper' the more he thought about it and each line presented the group with food for thought. Someone else felt that the last line spoiled the thought of 'blessings embla-zoned that day' and they talked about whether happy memories must always be tinged with a certain sadness. Finally, each member of the group went on to describe the first house they could remember living in.

Senior Moments

❦

PICKWICK PAPERS

(EXTRACT FROM CHAPTER 22)

Charles Dickens

(approximate reading time 16 minutes)

*Samuel Pickwick Esq. is portly, affable and reasonably well off.
He is founder and president of the Pickwick Club. He and the
other members: Mr Nathaniel Winkle, Mr Augustus Snodgrass,
and Mr Tracy Tupman make journeys through England and
report their findings to the rest of the club members. Sam Weller
is Pickwick's personal servant and in this extract they are staying
at an inn in Ipswich where Samuel Pickwick has been sitting
up late after dinner talking to a fellow guest . . .*

Mr Pickwick sat himself down in a chair before the fire,
and fell into a train of rambling meditations. His mind
wandered and flew off at a tangent and then it came back to
The Great White Horse at Ipswich, with sufficient clearness
to convince Mr Pickwick that he was falling asleep. So he
roused himself, and began to undress, when he recollected he
had left his watch on the table downstairs.

Now this watch was a special favourite with Mr Pickwick, having been carried about, beneath the shadow of his waist-coat, for a greater number of years than we feel called upon to state at present. The possibility of going to sleep, unless it were ticking gently beneath his pillow, or in the watch-pocket over his head, had never entered Mr Pickwick's brain. So as it was pretty late now, and he was unwilling to ring his bell at that hour of the night, he slipped on his coat, of which he had just divested himself, and taking the japanned candlestick in his hand, walked quietly downstairs.

The more stairs Mr Pickwick went down, the more stairs there seemed to be to descend, and again and again, when Mr Pickwick got into some narrow passage, and began to congratulate himself on having gained the ground-floor, did another flight of stairs appear before his astonished eyes. At last he reached a stone hall, which he remembered to have seen when he entered the house. Passage after passage did he explore; room after room did he peep into; at length, as he was on the point of giving up the search in despair, he opened the door of the identical room in which he had spent the evening, and beheld his missing property on the table.

Mr Pickwick seized the watch in triumph, and proceeded to retrace his steps to his bedchamber. If his progress down-ward had been attended with difficulties and uncertainty, his journey back was infinitely more perplexing. Rows of doors, garnished with boots of every shape, make, and size, branched off in every possible direction. A dozen times did he softly turn the handle of some bedroom door which resembled his own, when a gruff cry from within of 'Who the devil's that?' or 'What do you want here?' caused him to steal away, on tiptoe, with a perfectly marvellous celerity. He was reduced to the verge of despair, when an open door attracted his attention. He peeped in. Right at last! There were the two beds, whose situation he perfectly remembered, and the fire still burning. His candle, not a long one when he first received it, had flickered away in the drafts of air through which he had passed and sank into the socket as he closed the door after him. 'No matter,' said Mr Pickwick, 'I can undress myself just as well by the light of the fire.'

The bedsteads stood one on each side of the door; and on the inner side of each was a little path, terminating in a rush-bottomed chair, just wide enough to admit of a person's getting into or out of bed, on that side, if he or she thought proper. Having carefully drawn the curtains of his bed on the outside, Mr Pickwick sat down on the rush-bottomed chair, and leisurely divested himself of his shoes and gaiters. He then took off and folded up his coat, waistcoat, and neck-cloth, and slowly drawing on his tasselled nightcap, secured it firmly on his head, by tying beneath his chin the strings which he always had attached to that article of dress. It was at this moment that the absurdity of his recent bewilderment struck upon his mind. Throwing himself back in the rush-bottomed chair, Mr Pickwick laughed to himself so heartily, that it would have been quite delightful to any man of well-constituted mind to have watched the smiles that expanded his amiable features as they shone forth from beneath the nightcap.

'It is the best idea,' said Mr Pickwick to himself, smiling till he almost cracked the nightcap strings – 'it is the best idea, my losing myself in this place, and wandering about these staircases, that I ever heard of. Droll, droll, very droll.' Here Mr Pickwick smiled again, a broader smile than before, and was about to continue the process of undressing, in the best possible humour, when he was suddenly stopped by a most unexpected interruption: to wit, the entrance into the room of some person with a candle, who, after locking the door, advanced to the dressing-table, and set down the light upon it.

The smile that played on Mr Pickwick's features was instantaneously lost in a look of the most unbounded and wonder-stricken surprise. The person, whoever it was, had come in so suddenly and with so little noise, that Mr Pickwick had had no time to call out, or oppose their entrance. Who could it

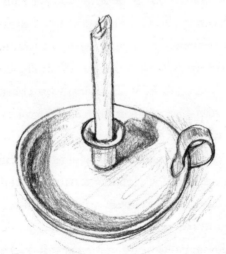

be? A robber? Some evil-minded person who had seen him come upstairs with a handsome watch in his hand, perhaps. What was he to do?

The only way in which Mr Pickwick could catch a glimpse of his mysterious visitor with the least danger of being seen himself, was by creeping on to the bed, and peeping out from between the curtains on the opposite side. To this manoeuvre he accordingly resorted. Keeping the curtains carefully closed with his hand, so that nothing more of him could be seen than his face and nightcap, and putting on his spectacles, he mustered up courage and looked out.

Mr Pickwick almost fainted with horror and dismay. Standing before the dressing-glass was a middle-aged lady, in yellow curl-papers, busily engaged in brushing what ladies call their 'back-hair.' However the unconscious middle-aged lady came into that room, it was quite clear that she contemplated remaining there for the night; for she had brought a rushlight and shade with her, which, with praiseworthy precaution against fire, she had stationed in a basin on the floor, where it was glimmering away, like a gigantic lighthouse in a particularly small piece of water.

'Bless my soul!' thought Mr Pickwick, 'what a dreadful thing!'

'Hem!' said the lady; and in went Mr Pickwick's head with automaton-like rapidity.

'I never met with anything so awful as this,' thought poor Mr Pickwick, the cold perspiration starting in drops upon his nightcap. 'Never. This is fearful.'

It was quite impossible to resist the urgent desire to see what was going forward. So out went Mr Pickwick's head again. The prospect was worse than before. The middle-aged lady had finished arranging her hair; had carefully enveloped it in a muslin nightcap with a small plaited border; and was gazing pensively on the fire.

'This matter is growing alarming,' reasoned Mr Pickwick with himself. 'I can't allow things to go on in this way. By the self-possession of that lady, it is clear to me that I must have come into the wrong room. If I call out she'll alarm the house; but if I remain here the consequences will be still more frightful.' Mr Pickwick, it is quite unnecessary to say, was one of the most modest and delicate-minded of mortals. The very idea of exhibiting his nightcap to a lady overpowered him, but he had tied those confounded strings in a knot, and, do what he would, he couldn't get it off. The disclosure must be made. There was only one other way of doing it. He shrunk behind the curtains, and called out very loudly—

'Ha-hum!'

That the lady started at this unexpected sound was evident, by her falling up against the rushlight shade; that she persuaded herself it must have been the effect of imagination was equally clear, for when Mr Pickwick, under the impression that she had fainted away stone-dead with fright, ventured to peep out again, she was gazing pensively on the fire as before.

'Most extraordinary female this,' thought Mr Pickwick, popping in again. 'Ha hum!'

These last sounds, so like those in which, as legends inform us, the ferocious giant Blunderbore was in the habit of expressing his opinion that it was time to lay the cloth, were too distinctly audible to be again mistaken for the workings of fancy.

'Gracious Heaven!' said the middle-aged lady, 'what's that?'
'It's–it's – only a gentleman, ma'am,' said Mr Pickwick, from behind the curtains.

'A gentleman!' said the lady, with a terrific scream.

'It's all over!' thought Mr Pickwick.

'A strange man!' shrieked the lady. Another instant and the house would be alarmed. Her garments rustled as she rushed towards the door.

'Ma'am,' said Mr Pickwick, thrusting out his head, in the extremity of his desperation, 'ma'am!'

Now, although Mr Pickwick was not actuated by any definite object in putting out his head, it was instantaneously productive of a good effect. The lady, as we have already stated, was near the door. She must pass it, to reach the staircase, and she would most undoubtedly have done so by this time, had not the sudden apparition of Mr Pickwick's nightcap driven her back into the remotest corner of the apartment, where she stood staring wildly at Mr Pickwick, while Mr Pickwick in his turn stared wildly at her.

'Wretch,' said the lady, covering her eyes with her hands, 'what do you want here?'

'Nothing, ma'am; nothing whatever, ma'am,' said Mr Pickwick earnestly.

'Nothing!' said the lady, looking up.

'Nothing, ma'am, upon my honour,' said Mr Pickwick, nodding his head so energetically, that the tassel of his nightcap danced again. 'I am almost ready to sink, ma'am, beneath the confusion of addressing a lady in my nightcap (here the lady hastily snatched off hers), but I can't get it off, ma'am (here

Mr Pickwick gave it a tremendous tug, in proof of the statement). It is evident to me, ma'am, now, that I have mistaken this bedroom for my own. I had not been here five minutes, ma'am, when you suddenly entered it.'

'If this improbable story be really true, Sir,' said the lady, sobbing violently, 'you will leave it instantly.'

'I will, ma'am, with the greatest pleasure,' replied Mr Pickwick.

'Instantly, sir,' said the lady.

'Certainly, ma'am,' interposed Mr Pickwick, very quickly. 'Certainly, ma'am. I–I–am very sorry, ma'am,' said Mr Pickwick, making his appearance at the bottom of the bed, 'to have been the innocent occasion of this alarm and emotion; deeply sorry, ma'am.'

The lady pointed to the door. One excellent quality of Mr Pickwick's character was beautifully displayed at this moment, under the most trying circumstances. Although he had hastily put on his hat over his nightcap, after the manner of the old patrol; although he carried his shoes and gaiters in his hand, and his coat and waistcoat over his arm; nothing could subdue his native politeness.

'I am exceedingly sorry, ma'am,' said Mr Pickwick, bowing very low.

'If you are, Sir, you will at once leave the room,' said the lady.

'Immediately, ma'am; this instant, ma'am,' said Mr Pickwick, opening the door, and dropping both his shoes with a crash in so doing.

'I trust, ma'am,' resumed Mr Pickwick, gathering up his shoes, and turning round to bow again – 'I trust, ma'am, that

my unblemished character, and the devoted respect I entertain for your sex, will plead as some slight excuse for this—'
But before Mr Pickwick could conclude the sentence, the lady
had thrust him into the passage, and locked and bolted the
door behind him.

Whatever grounds of self-congratulation Mr Pickwick
might have for having escaped so quietly from his late awkward
situation, his present position was by no means enviable. He
was alone, in an open passage, in a strange house in the
middle of the night, half dressed; it was not to be supposed
that he could find his way in perfect darkness to a room
which he had been wholly unable to discover with a light,
and if he made the slightest noise in his fruitless attempts to
do so, he stood every chance of being shot at, and perhaps
killed, by some wakeful traveller. He had no resource but to
remain where he was until daylight appeared. So after groping
his way a few paces down the passage, and, to his infinite
alarm, stumbling over several pairs of boots in so doing, Mr
Pickwick crouched into a little recess in the wall, to wait for
morning, as philosophically as he might.

He was not destined, however, to undergo this additional
trial of patience; for he had not been long ensconced in his
present concealment when, to his unspeakable horror, a man,
bearing a light, appeared at the end of the passage. His horror
was suddenly converted into joy, however, when he recognised
the form of his faithful attendant. It was indeed Mr Samuel
Weller, who after sitting up thus late, in conversation with
the boots, who was sitting up for the mail, was now about to
retire to rest.

'Sam,' said Mr Pickwick, suddenly appearing before him, 'where's my bedroom?'

Mr Weller stared at his master with the most emphatic surprise; and it was not until the question had been repeated three several times, that he turned round, and led the way to the long-sought apartment.

'Sam,' said Mr Pickwick, as he got into bed, 'I have made one of the most extraordinary mistakes to-night, that ever were heard of.'

'Wery likely, Sir,' replied Mr Weller drily.

RESOLUTIONS WHEN I COME TO BE OLD
Jonathan Swift

Not to marry a young Woman

Not to keep young Company unless they really desire it.

Not to be peevish, or morose, or suspicious.

Not to scorn present Ways, or Wits, or Fashions, or Men, or War, &c.

Not to be fond of Children, or let them come near me hardly.

Not to tell the same Story over and over to the same People.

Not to be covetous.

Not to neglect decency, or cleanliness, for fear of falling into Nastiness.

Not to be over severe with young People, but to give allowances for their youthful Follies and Weaknesses.

Not to be influenced by, or give ear to knavish tattling servants, or others.

Not to be too free of advice, not trouble any but those that desire it.

To desire some good Friends to inform me which of these Resolutions I break, or neglect, and wherein; and reform accordingly.

Not to talk much, nor of myself.

Not to boast of my former beauty, or strength, or favour with Ladies, &c.

Not to hearken to Flatteries, nor conceive I can be
    beloved by a young woman. Et eos qui hereditatem
    captant, odisse ac vitare.
Not to be positive or opiniative.
Not to set up for observing all these Rules, for fear that I
    should observe none.

READING NOTES

Groups of all ages have had fun with the poem. Everyone's list of things not to do when they are old always includes the line about not telling the same story over and over to the same people. The possible age of the poet when he wrote the poem and why he includes the resolution 'Not to be fond of children' are questions worth thinking about, as is the whole problem of the keeping of resolutions.

While not everyone has experienced Mr Pickwick's particular mistake, nearly everyone can recall a particularly embarrassing incident and you do not even have to be old to know the humiliation of a senior moment. Coaching inns; four poster beds; nightcaps; back-hair; real fires in the bedroom and manservants are things of the past and the cause of general amusement nowadays. How does this compare to a stay at a modern pub or B&B?

When Youth is Far Behind

✣

FAITH AND HOPE GO SHOPPING
Joanne Harris

(approximate reading time 25 minutes)

It's Monday, so it must be rice pudding again. It's not so much the fact that they're careful of our teeth, here at the Meadowbank Home, rather a general lack of imagination. As I told Claire the other day, there are lots of things you can eat without having to chew. Oysters. Foie gras. Avocado vinaigrette. Strawberries and cream. Crème brûlée with vanilla and nutmeg. Why then this succession of bland puddings and gummy meats? Claire – the sulky blonde, always chewing a wad of gum – looked at me as if I were mad. Fancy food, they claim, upsets the stomach. God forbid our remaining tastebuds should be over-stimulated. I saw Hope grinning round the last mouthful of ocean pie, and I knew she'd heard me. Hope may be blind, but she's no slouch.

Faith and Hope. With names like that we might be sisters. Kelly – that's the one with the exaggerated lip liner – thinks we're quaint. Chris sometimes sings to us when he's cleaning out the rooms. *Faith, Hope and Cha-ri-tee!* He's the best of them, I suppose. Cheery and irreverent, he's always in trouble for talking to us. He wears tight T-shirts and an earring. I tell him that the last thing we want is charity, and that makes him laugh. *Hinge and Bracket*, he calls us. *Butch and Sundance*.

I'm not saying it's a bad place here. It's just so *ordinary* – not the comfortable ordinariness of home, with its familiar grime and clutter, but that of waiting-rooms and hospitals, a pastel-detergent place with a smell of air freshener and distant bedpans. We don't get many visits, as a rule. I'm one of the lucky ones; my son Tom calls every fortnight with my magazines and a bunch of chrysanths – the last ones were yellow – and any news he thinks won't upset me. But he isn't much of a conversationalist. *Are you keeping well, then, Mam?* and a comment or two about the garden is about all he can manage, but he means well. As for Hope, she's been here five years – even longer than me – and she hasn't had a visitor yet. Last Christmas I gave her a box of my chocolates and told her they were from her daughter in California. She gave me one of her sardonic little smiles.

'If that's from Priscilla, sweetheart,' she said primly, 'then you're Ginger Rogers.'

I laughed at that. I've been in a wheelchair for twenty years, and the last time I did any dancing was just before men stopped wearing hats.

We manage, though. Hope pushes me around in my chair, and I direct her. Not that there's much directing to do in here; she can get around just by using the ramps. But the nurses like to see us using our resources. It fits in with their *Waste not, Want not* ethic. And of course, I read to her. Hope loves stories. In fact, she's the one who started me reading in the first place. We've had *Wuthering Heights*, and *Pride and Prejudice*, and *Doctor Zhivago*. There aren't many books here, but the library van comes round every four weeks, and we send Lucy out to get us something nice. Lucy's a college student on Work Experience, so she knows what to choose. Hope was furious when she wouldn't let us have *Lolita*, though. Lucy thought it wouldn't suit us.

'One of the greatest writers of the twentieth century, and you thought he wouldn't *suit* us!' Hope used to be a professor at Cambridge, and still has that imperious twang in her voice sometimes. But I could tell Lucy wasn't really listening. They get that look – even the brighter ones – that nursery-nurse smile which says *I know better. I know better because you're old.* It's the rice pudding all over again, Hope tells me. Rice pudding for the soul.

If Hope taught me to appreciate literature, it was I who introduced her to magazines. They've been my passion for years, fashion glossies and society pages, restaurant reviews and film releases. I started her out on book reviews, slyly taking her off-guard with an article here or a fashion page there. We found I had quite a talent for description, and now we wade deliciously together through the pages of bright ephemera, moaning over Cartier diamonds and Chanel lipsticks and lush, impossible clothes. It's strange, really. When I was young those things really didn't interest me. I think Hope was more elegant than I was – after all there were college balls and academy parties and summer picnics on the Backs. Of course now we're both the same. Nursing-home chic. Things tend to be communal here – some people forget what belongs to them, so there's a lot of pilfering. I carry my nicest things with me, in the rack under my wheelchair. I have my money and what's left of my jewellery hidden in the seat cushion.

I'm not supposed to have money here. There's nothing to spend it on, and we're not allowed out unaccompanied. There's a combination lock on the door, and some people try to slip out with visitors as they leave. Mrs McAllister – ninety-two, spry, and mad as a hatter – keeps escaping. She thinks she's going home.

It must have been the shoes that began it. Slick, patent, candy-apple red with heels which went on forever, I found them in one of my magazines and cut out the picture. Sometimes I brought it out and looked at it in private, feeling dizzy and a little foolish, I don't know why. It wasn't as if it were a picture of a man, or anything like that. They were only shoes. Hope and I wear the same kind of shoes; lumpy leatherette slip-ons in porridge beige, eminently, indisputably *suitable* – but in secret we moan over Manolo Blahniks with six-inch Perspex heels, or Gina mules in fuchsia suede, or Jimmy Choos in hand-painted silk. It was absurd, of course. But I *wanted* those shoes with a fierceness which almost frightened me. I wanted, just once, to step out into the glossy, gleeful pages of one of my magazines. To taste the recipes; see the films; read the books. To me the shoes represented all of that; their cheery, brazen redness; their frankly impossible heels. Shoes made for anything – lolling, lounging, prowling, strutting, *flying* – anything but walking.

I kept the picture in my purse, occasionally taking it out

and unfolding it like a map to secret treasure. It didn't take
Hope long to find out I was hiding something.

'I know it's stupid,' I said. 'Maybe I'm going peculiar. I'll
probably end up like Mrs Banerjee, wearing ten overcoats and
stealing people's underwear.'

Hope laughed at that. 'I don't think so, Faith. I understand
you perfectly well.' She felt on the table in front of her for
her teacup. I knew better than to guide her hand. 'You want
to do something unsuitable. I want a copy of *Lolita*. You want
a pair of red shoes. Both of those things are equally unsuitable for people like us.' She drew a little closer, lowering her
voice. 'Is there an address on the page?' she asked.

There was. I told her. A Knightsbridge address. It might
as well have been Australia.

'Hey! Butch and Sundance!' It was cheery Chris, who had
come to clean the windows. 'Planning a heist?'

Hope smiled. 'No, Christopher,' she said slyly. 'An escape.'

We planned it with the furtive cunning of prisoners-of-
war. We had one great advantage; the element of surprise. We
were not habitual escapees, like Mrs McAllister, but trusties,
nicely lucid and safely immobile. There would have to be a
diversion, I suggested. Something which would bring the duty
nurse away from the desk, leaving the entrance unguarded.
Hope took to waiting by the door, listening to the sound of
the keypads until she was almost certain she could duplicate
the combination. We timed it with the precision of old
campaigners. At nine minutes to nine on Friday morning I
picked up one of Mr Bannerman's cigarette-butts from the
common room and hid it in the paper-filled metal bin in my

room. At eight minutes to, Hope and I were in the lobby on our way to the breakfast-room. Ten seconds later, as expected, the sprinkler went off. On our corridor I could hear Mrs McAllister screaming *Fire! Fire!*

Kelly was on duty. Clever Lucy might have remembered to secure the doors. Thick Claire might not have left the desk at all. But Kelly grabbed the nearest fire extinguisher from the wall and ran towards the smoke. Hope pushed me towards the door, and felt for the keypad. It was seven minutes to nine.

'Hurry! She'll be back any moment!'

'Shh.' *Beep-beep-beep-beep*. 'Got it. I knew one day I'd find a use for those music lessons they gave me as a child.' The door slid open. We crunched out onto sunlit gravel.

This was where Hope would need my help. No ramps here, in the real world. I tried not to stare, mesmerised, at the sky, at the trees. Tom hadn't taken me out of the building for over six months.

'Straight ahead. Turn left. Stop. There's a pot hole in front of us. Take it easy. Left again.' I remembered a bus stop just in front of the gates. The buses were like clockwork. Five to and twenty-five past the hour. You could hear them from the common room, honking and ratcheting past like cranky pensioners. For a dreadful moment I was convinced the bus stop had gone. There were roadworks where it had once stood; bollards lined the kerb. Then I saw it, fifty yards further down, a temporary bus stop on a shortened metal post. The bus appeared at the brow of the hill, huffing.

'Quick! Full speed ahead!' Hope reacted quickly. Her legs

are long and still muscular; she did ballet as a child. I leaned forwards, clutching my purse tightly, and held out my hand. Behind us I heard a cry; glancing back at the windows of the Meadowbank Home I saw Kelly at my bedroom window, her mouth open, yelling something. For a second I wasn't sure the bus would even take an old lady in a wheelchair, but it was the Hospital Circular, and there was a special ramp. The driver gave us a look of indifference and waved us aboard. Then Hope and I were on the bus, clinging to each other like giddy school-girls, laughing. People looked at us, but mostly without suspi-cion. A little girl looked at me and smiled. I realised how long ago it must have been since I saw anyone young.

We got off at the railway station. With some of the money in the chair cushion I bought two tickets to London. I panicked for a moment when the ticket man asked for my pass, but Hope told him, in her Cambridge-professor's voice, that we would pay the full fare. The ticket man rubbed his head for a minute, and then shrugged.

'Please yourself,' he said.

The train was long and smelt of coffee and burnt rubber. I guided Hope to where the guard had let down a ramp.

'Going down to the smoke, are we, ladies?' The guard sounded a little like Chris, his cap pushed back cockily from his forehead. 'Let me take that for you, love,' he said to Hope, meaning the wheelchair, but Hope shook her head.

'I can manage, thank you.'

'Straight up, old girl,' I told her. I saw the guard noticing Hope's blind eyes, but he didn't say anything. I was glad. Neither of us can stand that kind of thing.

The piece of paper with the Knightsbridge address was still in my purse. As we sat in the guard's van (with coffee and scones brought to us by the cheery guard) I unfolded it again. Hope heard me doing it, and smiled.

'Is it ridiculous?' I asked her, looking at the shoes again, shiny and red as Lolita lollies. 'Are we ridiculous?'

'Of course we are,' she answered serenely, sipping her coffee. 'And isn't it *fun?*'

It only took three hours to get down to London. I was expecting much longer, but trains, like everything else, move faster nowadays. We drank coffee again, and talked to the guard (whose name was not Chris, I learned, but Barry), and I described what countryside I could see to Hope while it blurred past at top speed.

'It's all right,' Hope reassured me. 'You don't have to do it all now. Just see it first, and we'll go over it all together, in our own time, when we get back.'

It was nearly lunchtime when we arrived in London. King's Cross was much bigger than I'd imagined it, all glass and glorious grime. I tried to see it as well as I could, whilst directing Hope through the crowds of people of all colours and ages: for a few moments even Hope seemed disorientated, and we dithered on the platform, wondering where all the porters had gone. Everyone but us seemed to know exactly where they were going, and people with briefcases jostled against the chair as we stood trying to work out where to go. I began to feel some of my courage erode.

'Oh, Hope,' I whispered. 'I'm not sure I can do this any more.'

But Hope was undeterred.

'Rubbish,' she said bracingly. 'There'll be taxis – over *there*, where the draught is coming from.' She pointed to our left, where I did see a sign, high above our heads, which read *Way Out*. 'We'll do what everyone does here. We'll get a cab. Onwards!' And at that we pushed right through the mess of people on the platform, Hope saying *Excuse me* in her Cambridge voice, me remembering to direct her. I checked my purse again, and Hope chuckled. This time I wasn't looking at the picture, though. Two hundred pounds had seemed like inexpressible riches at the Meadowbank Home, but the train fare had taught me that prices, too, had speeded up during our years away from the world. I wondered if we'd have enough.

The taxi driver was surly and reluctant, lifting the chair into the black cab while Hope steadied me. I'm not as slim as I was, and it was almost too much for her, but we managed.

'How about lunch?' I suggested, too brightly, to take away the sour taste of the driver's expression. Hope nodded. 'Anywhere that doesn't do rice pudding,' she said wryly.

'Is Fortnum and Mason's still there?' I asked the driver.

'Yes, darling, *and* the British Museum,' he said, revving his engine impatiently. *Best place for you two*, I thought I heard him mutter. Unexpectedly, Hope chuckled. 'Maybe we'll go there next,' she suggested meekly. That set me off as well. The driver gave us both a suspicious glance and set off, still muttering.

There are some places which can survive anything. Fortnum's is one of these, a little antechamber of heaven, glittering with sunken treasures. When all civilisations have collapsed, Fortnum's will still be there, with its genteel doormen and glass chandeliers, the last, untouchable, legendary defender of the faith. We entered on the first floor, through mountains of chocolates and cohorts of candied fruits. The air was cool and creamy with vanilla and allspice and peach. Hope turned her head gently from side to side, breathing in the perfume. There were truffles and caviar and foie gras in tiny tins and giant demijohns of green plums in aged brandy and cherries the colour of my Knightsbridge shoes. There were quail's eggs and nougatines and *langues de chat* in rice-paper packets and champagne bottles in gleaming battalions. We took the lift to the top floor and the café, where Hope and I drank Earl Grey from china cups, remembering the Meadowbank Home's plastic tea service and giggling. I ordered recklessly for both of us, trying not to think of my diminishing savings: smoked salmon and scrambled eggs on muffins light as puffs of air, tiny canapés of rolled anchovy and sundried tomatoes, Parma ham with slices of pink melon, apricot and chocolate parfait like a delicate caress.

'If Heaven is anything like as nice as this,' murmured Hope, 'send me there right now.'

Even the obligatory bathroom stop was a revelation: clean, gleaming tiles, flowers, fluffy pink towels, scented hand cream, perfume. I sprayed Hope with freesias and looked at us both in one of the big shiny mirrors. I'd expected us to look drab, maybe even a little foolish, in our nursing-home cardies and sensible skirts. Maybe we did. But to me we looked changed, gilded: for the first time I could see Hope as she must have been; I could see myself.

We spent a long time in Fortnum's. We visited floors of hats and scarves and handbags and dresses. I imprinted them all into my memory, to bring out later with Hope. She wheeled me patiently through forests of lingerie and coats and evening frocks like a breath of summer air, letting her thin, elegant fingers trail over silks and furs. Reluctantly we left: the streets were marvellous, but lacked sparkle: looking at the people rushing past us, haughty or indifferent, once again I was almost afraid. We hailed a taxi.

I was getting nervous now; a prickle of stage fright ran up my spine and I unfolded the paper again, its folds whitened by much handling. Once more I felt drab and old. What if the shop assistant wouldn't let me in? What if they laughed at me? Worse still was the suspicion – the certainty – that the shoes would be too expensive, that already I'd overspent, that maybe I hadn't even had enough to begin with . . . Spotting a bookshop, glad of the diversion, I stopped the cab and, with the help of the driver, we got out and bought Hope a copy of *Lolita*.

No one said it might be unsuitable. Hope smiled and held the book, running her fingers over the smooth unbroken spine.

'How good it smells,' she said softly. 'I'd almost forgotten.'

The cab driver, a black man with long hair, grinned at us. He was obviously enjoying himself.

'Where to now, ladies?' he asked.

I could not answer him. My hands trembled as I handed over the magazine page with the Knightsbridge address. If he'd laughed I think I would have wept. I was close to it already. But the driver just grinned again and drove off into the blaring traffic.

It was a tiny shop, a single window with glass display shelves and a single pair of shoes on each. Behind them, I could see a light interior, all pale wood and glass, with tall vases of white roses on the floor.

'Stop,' I told Hope.

'What's wrong? Is it shut?'

'No.'

The shop was empty. I could see that. There was one assistant, a young man in black, with long, clean hair. The shoes in the window were pale green, tiny, like buds just about to open. There were no prices on any of them.

'Onwards!' urged Hope in her Cambridge voice.

'I can't. It's—' I couldn't finish. I saw myself again, old and colourless, untouched by magic.

'Unsuitable,' barked Hope scornfully, and wheeled me in anyway.

For a second I thought she was going to hit the vase of roses by the door.

'Left!' I yelled, and we missed them. Just.

The young man looked at us curiously. He had a clever, handsome face, but I was relieved to see that his eyes were smiling. I held up the picture.

'I'd like to see – a pair of these,' I told him, trying to copy Hope's imperious tone, but sounding old and quavery instead. 'Size four.'

His eyes widened a little, but he did not comment. Instead he turned and went into the back of the shop, where I could see shelves of boxes waiting. I closed my eyes.

'I thought I had a pair left.'

He was carrying them, carefully, all sucked-sweet shiny and red, red, red.

'Let me see them, please.'

They were like Christmas baubles, like rubies, like impossible fruit.

'Would you like to try them on?'

He did not comment on my wheelchair, my old and lumpy feet in their porridge-coloured slip-ons. Instead he knelt in front of me, his dark hair falling around his face. Gently he removed my shoes. I know he could see the veins worming up my ankles and smell the violet scent of the talc which Hope rubs into my feet at bedtime. With great care he slipped the shoes onto my feet; I felt my arches push up alarmingly as the shoes slid into place.

'May I show you?' Carefully he stretched out my leg so that I could see.

'Ginger Rogers,' whispered Hope.

Shoes for strutting, sashaying, striding, soaring. Anything but walking. I looked at myself for a long time, fists clenched, a hot fierce sweetness in my heart. I wondered what Tom would say if he saw me now. My head was spinning.

'How much?' I asked hoarsely.

The young man told me a price so staggering that at first I was sure I'd misheard, more than I'd paid for my first house. I felt the knowledge clang deep at my insides, like something falling down a well.

'I'm sorry,' I heard myself saying from a distance. 'That's a little too dear.'

From his expression I guessed he might have been expecting it.

'Oh, Faith,' said Hope softly.

'It's all right,' I told them both. 'They didn't really suit me.'

The young man shook his head.

'You're wrong, madam,' he told me, with a crooked smile. 'I think they did.'

Gently he put the shoes – Valentine, racing-car, candy-apple red – back into their box. The room, light as it was, seemed a little duller when they had gone.

'Are you just here for the day, madam?'

I nodded. 'Yes. We've enjoyed ourselves very much. But now it's time to go home.'

'I'm sorry.' He reached over to one of the tall vases by the door and removed a rose. 'Perhaps you'd like one of these?' He put it into my hand. It was perfect, highly scented, barely open. It smelt of summer evenings and *Swan Lake*. In that moment I forgot all about the red shoes. A man – one who was not my son – had offered me flowers.

I still have the white rose. I put it in a paper cup of water for the train journey home, and then transferred it to a vase. The yellow chrysanths were finished, anyway. When it fades I will press the petals – which are still unusually scented – and use them to mark the pages of *Lolita*, which Hope and I are reading. Unsuitable, it may be. But I'd like to see them try to take it away.

WHEN YOU ARE OLD
W. B. Yeats

When you are old and grey and full of sleep
And nodding by the fire, take down this book,
And slowly read, and dream of the soft look
Your eyes had once, and of their shadows deep;

How many loved your moments of glad grace,
And loved your beauty with love false or true,
But one man loved the pilgrim soul in you,
And loved the sorrows of your changing face;

And bending down beside the glowing bars,
Murmur, a little sadly, how Love fled
And paced upon the mountains overhead
And hid his face amid a crowd of stars.

READING NOTES

Reading this story in residential care homes for the elderly has always proved a delight. While no one has ever expressed a desire to escape and run off to London, many say they dream of being able to do something exciting for a change. As Maggie said, 'If I had the energy, I would love to go back to the Lake District and just walk.'

The poem made Amy feel sad. 'So much is behind you,' she said. 'It's amazing.' When asked why she said 'amazing' she replied: 'Because I say to myself, was that me? Did I really do all those things? Amazing!'

Residential care homes, the indignities of old age, the perks of old age, the way in which the young view the elderly, Jimmy Choo shoes, provide something serious and not so serious to think and talk about.

Love at Christmas

THE GIFT OF THE MAGI
O. Henry

(approximate reading time 13 minutes)

One dollar and eighty-seven cents. That was all. And sixty cents of it was in pennies. Pennies saved one and two at a time by bulldozing the grocer and the vegetable man and the butcher until one's cheeks burned with the silent imputation of parsimony that such close dealing implied. Three times Della counted it. One dollar and eighty-seven cents. And the next day would be Christmas.

There was clearly nothing to do but flop down on the shabby little couch and howl. So Della did it. Which instigates the moral reflection that life is made up of sobs, sniffles, and smiles, with sniffles predominating.

While the mistress of the home is gradually subsiding from the first stage to the second, take a look at the home. A furnished flat at $8 per week. It did not exactly beggar description, but it certainly had that word on the lookout for the mendicancy squad.

In the vestibule below was a letter-box into which no letter would go, and an electric button from which no mortal finger could coax a ring. Also appertaining thereunto was a card bearing the name 'Mr James Dillingham Young.'

The 'Dillingham' had been flung to the breeze during a former period of prosperity when its possessor was being paid $30 per week. Now, when the income was shrunk to $20, though, they were thinking seriously of contracting to a modest and unassuming D. But whenever Mr James Dillingham Young came home and reached his flat above he was called 'Jim' and greatly hugged by Mrs James Dillingham Young, already introduced to you as Della. Which is all very good.

Della finished her cry and attended to her cheeks with the powder rag. She stood by the window and looked out dully at a gray cat walking a gray fence in a gray backyard. Tomorrow would be Christmas Day, and she had only $1.87 with which to buy Jim a present. She had been saving every penny she could for months, with this result. Twenty dollars a week doesn't go far. Expenses had been greater than she had calculated. They always are. Only $1.87 to buy a present for Jim. Her Jim. Many a happy hour she had spent planning for something nice for him. Something fine and rare and sterling – something just a little bit near to being worthy of the honor of being owned by Jim.

There was a pier-glass between the windows of the room. Perhaps you have seen a pier-glass in an $8 flat. A very thin and very agile person may, by observing his reflection in a rapid sequence of longitudinal strips, obtain a fairly accurate conception of his looks. Della, being slender, had mastered the art.

Suddenly she whirled from the window and stood before

the glass. Her eyes were shining brilliantly, but her face had lost its color within twenty seconds. Rapidly she pulled down her hair and let it fall to its full length.

Now, there were two possessions of the James Dillingham Youngs in which they both took a mighty pride. One was Jim's gold watch that had been his father's and his grandfather's. The other was Della's hair. Had the queen of Sheba lived in the flat across the airshaft, Della would have let her hair hang out the window some day to dry just to depreciate Her Majesty's jewels and gifts. Had King Solomon been the janitor, with all his treasures piled up in the basement, Jim would have pulled out his watch every time he passed, just to see him pluck at his beard from envy.

So now Della's beautiful hair fell about her rippling and shining like a cascade of brown waters. It reached below her knee and made itself almost a garment for her. And then she did it up again nervously and quickly. Once she faltered for a minute and stood still while a tear or two splashed on the worn red carpet.

On went her old brown jacket; on went her old brown hat. With a whirl of skirts and with the brilliant sparkle still in her eyes, she fluttered out the door and down the stairs to the street.

Where she stopped the sign read: 'Mme. Sofronie. Hair Goods of All Kinds.' One flight up Della ran, and collected herself, panting. Madame, large, too white, chilly, hardly looked the 'Sofronie.'

'Will you buy my hair?' asked Della.

'I buy hair,' said Madame. 'Take yer hat off and let's have a sight at the looks of it.'

Down rippled the brown cascade.

'Twenty dollars,' said Madame, lifting the mass with a practised hand.

'Give it to me quick,' said Della.

Oh, and the next two hours tripped by on rosy wings. Forget the hashed metaphor. She was ransacking the stores for Jim's present.

She found it at last. It surely had been made for Jim and no one else. There was no other like it in any of the stores, and she had turned all of them inside out. It was a platinum fob chain simple and chaste in design, properly proclaiming its value by substance alone and not by meretricious ornamentation – as all good things should do. It was even worthy of The Watch. As soon as she saw it she knew that it must be Jim's. It was like him. Quietness and value – the description applied to both. Twenty-one dollars they took from her for it, and she hurried home with the 87 cents. With that chain on his watch Jim might be properly anxious about the time in any company. Grand as the watch was, he sometimes looked at it on the sly on account of the old leather strap that he used in place of a chain.

When Della reached home her intoxication gave way a little to prudence and reason. She got out her curling irons and lighted the gas and went to work repairing the ravages made by generosity added to love. Which is always a tremendous task, dear friends – a mammoth task.

Within forty minutes her head was covered with tiny, close-lying curls that made her look wonderfully like a truant schoolboy. She looked at her reflection in the mirror long, carefully, and critically.

'If Jim doesn't kill me,' she said to herself, 'before he takes a second look at me, he'll say I look like a Coney Island chorus girl. But what could I do – oh! what could I do with a dollar and eighty-seven cents?'

At 7 o'clock the coffee was made and the frying-pan was on the back of the stove hot and ready to cook the chops.

Jim was never late. Della doubled the fob chain in her hand and sat on the corner of the table near the door that he always entered. Then she heard his step on the stair away down on the first flight, and she turned white for just a moment. She had a habit for saying little silent prayer about the simplest everyday things, and now she whispered: 'Please God, make him think I am still pretty.'

The door opened and Jim stepped in and closed it. He looked thin and very serious. Poor fellow, he was only twenty-two – and to be burdened with a family! He needed a new overcoat and he was without gloves.

Jim stopped inside the door, as immovable as a setter at

the scent of quail. His eyes were fixed upon Della, and there was an expression in them that she could not read, and it terrified her. It was not anger, nor surprise, nor disapproval, nor horror, nor any of the sentiments that she had been prepared for. He simply stared at her fixedly with that peculiar expression on his face.

Della wriggled off the table and went for him.

'Jim, darling,' she cried, 'don't look at me that way. I had my hair cut off and sold because I couldn't have lived through Christmas without giving you a present. It'll grow out again – you won't mind, will you? I just had to do it. My hair grows awfully fast. Say "Merry Christmas!" Jim, and let's be happy. You don't know what a nice – what a beautiful, nice gift I've got for you.'

'You've cut off your hair?' asked Jim, laboriously, as if he had not arrived at that patent fact yet even after the hardest mental labor.

'Cut it off and sold it,' said Della. 'Don't you like me just as well, anyhow? I'm me without my hair, ain't I?'

Jim looked about the room curiously.

'You say your hair is gone?' he said, with an air almost of idiocy.

'You needn't look for it,' said Della. 'It's sold, I tell you – sold and gone, too. It's Christmas Eve, boy. Be good to me, for it went for you. Maybe the hairs of my head were numbered,' she went on with sudden serious sweetness, 'but nobody could ever count my love for you. Shall I put the chops on, Jim?'

Out of his trance Jim seemed quickly to wake. He enfolded

his Della. For ten seconds let us regard with discreet scrutiny some inconsequential object in the other direction. Eight dollars a week or a million a year – what is the difference? A mathematician or a wit would give you the wrong answer. The magi brought valuable gifts, but that was not among them. This dark assertion will be illuminated later on.

Jim drew a package from his overcoat pocket and threw it upon the table.

'Don't make any mistake, Dell,' he said, 'about me. I don't think there's anything in the way of a haircut or a shave or a shampoo that could make me like my girl any less. But if you'll unwrap that package you may see why you had me going a while at first.'

White fingers and nimble tore at the string and paper. And then an ecstatic scream of joy; and then, alas! a quick feminine change to hysterical tears and wails, necessitating the immediate employment of all the comforting powers of the lord of the flat.

For there lay The Combs – the set of combs, side and back, that Della had worshipped long in a Broadway window. Beautiful combs, pure tortoiseshell, with jewelled rims – just the shade to wear in the beautiful vanished hair. They were expensive combs, she knew, and her heart had simply craved and yearned over them without the least hope of possession. And now, they were hers, but the tresses that should have adorned the coveted adornments were gone.

But she hugged them to her bosom, and at length she was able to look up with dim eyes and a smile and say: 'My hair grows so fast, Jim!'

And then Della leaped up like a little singed cat and cried, 'Oh, oh!'

Jim had not yet seen his beautiful present. She held it out to him eagerly upon her open palm. The dull precious metal seemed to flash with a reflection of her bright and ardent spirit.

'Isn't it a dandy, Jim? I hunted all over town to find it. You'll have to look at the time a hundred times a day now. Give me your watch. I want to see how it looks on it.'

Instead of obeying, Jim tumbled down on the couch and put his hands under the back of his head and smiled.

'Dell,' said he, 'let's put our Christmas presents away and keep 'em a while. They're too nice to use just at present. I sold the watch to get the money to buy your combs. And now suppose you put the chops on.'

The magi, as you know, were wise men – wonderfully wise men – who brought gifts to the Babe in the manger. They invented the art of giving Christmas presents. Being wise, their gifts were no doubt wise ones, possibly bearing the privilege of exchange in case of duplication. And here I have lamely related to you the uneventful chronicle of two foolish children in a flat who most unwisely sacrificed for each other the greatest treasures of their house. But in a last word to the wise of these days let it be said that of all who give gifts these two were the wisest. O all who give and receive gifts, such as they are wisest. Everywhere they are wisest. They are the magi.

CHRISTMAS CAROL
Eleanor Farjeon

God bless your house this Holy night,
  And all within it:

God bless the candle that you light,
  To midnight's minute;

The board at which you break your bread,
  The cup you drink of:

And as you raise it, the unsaid
  Name that you think of:

The warming fire, the bed of rest,
  The ringing laughter:

These things and all things else be blest
  From floor to rafter

This Holy night, from dark to light,
  Even more than other:

And if you have no house tonight,
  God bless you, brother.

READING NOTES

In a reading of 'The Gift of the Magi', someone nearly always guesses what is going to happen. Reading it with a group of people who all cared for ill or disabled relatives, was particularly moving, as it was generally agreed that the gift of love is the greatest of all. They all felt that their experience as carers had caused them to set less store by material things. Puzzling out what the author means when he says 'They are the magi', led to talk, not only about religion, but also about what it would be like if there were no Christmas Day. Although two of the people in the group were atheists, they still wanted 'an ideal day to aim for', a day when people can all at least try to bring the gift of love to each other – 'like playing football in no-man's land,' one man said.

Bringing the gift of love is the message of Eleanor Farjeon's poem but the real talking point is usually the final line with its reminder not only of the homeless at Christmas but of the many who face Christmas alone.

Christmas Eve

❧

A CHILD'S CHRISTMAS IN WALES
Dylan Thomas

(approximate reading time 20 minutes)

One Christmas was so much like another, in those years around the sea-town corner now and out of all sound except the distant speaking of the voices I sometimes hear a moment before sleep, that I can never remember whether it snowed for six days and six nights when I was twelve or whether it snowed for twelve days and twelve nights when I was six.

All the Christmases roll down toward the two-tongued sea, like a cold and headlong moon bundling down the sky that was our street; and they stop at the rim of the ice-edged fish-freezing waves, and I plunge my hands in the snow and bring out whatever I can find. In goes my hand into that wool-white bell-tongued ball of holidays resting at the rim of the carol-singing sea, and out come Mrs Prothero and the firemen.

It was on the afternoon of the day of Christmas Eve, and I was in Mrs Prothero's garden, waiting for cats, with her son Jim. It was snowing. It was always snowing at Christmas. December, in my memory, is white as Lapland, though there were no reindeers. But there were cats. Patient, cold and callous, our hands wrapped in socks, we waited to snowball the cats. Sleek and long as jaguars and horrible-whiskered, spitting and snarling, they would slink and sidle over the white back-garden walls, and the lynx-eyed hunters, Jim and I, fur-capped and moccasined trappers from Hudson Bay, off Mumbles Road, would hurl our deadly snowballs at the green of their eyes. The wise cats never appeared.

We were so still, Eskimo-footed arctic marksmen in the muffling silence of the eternal snows – eternal, ever since Wednesday – that we never heard Mrs Prothero's first cry from her igloo at the bottom of the garden. Or, if we heard it at all, it was, to us, like the far-off challenge of our enemy and prey, the neighbour's polar cat. But soon the voice grew louder.

'Fire!' cried Mrs Prothero, and she beat the dinner-gong.

And we ran down the garden, with the snowballs in our arms, toward the house; and smoke, indeed, was pouring out of the dining-room, and the gong was bombilating, and Mrs Prothero was announcing ruin like a town crier in Pompeii. This was better than all the cats in Wales standing on the wall in a row. We bounded into the house, laden with snowballs, and stopped at the open door of the smoke-filled room.

Something was burning all right; perhaps it was Mr Prothero, who always slept there after midday dinner with a newspaper over his face. But he was standing in the middle of the room, saying, 'A fine Christmas!' and smacking at the smoke with a slipper.

'Call the fire brigade,' cried Mrs Prothero as she beat the gong.

'They won't be there,' said Mr Prothero, 'it's Christmas.'

There was no fire to be seen, only clouds of smoke and Mr Prothero standing in the middle of them, waving his slipper as though he were conducting.

'Do something,' he said. And we threw all our snowballs into the smoke – I think we missed Mr Prothero – and ran out of the house to the telephone box.

'Let's call the police as well,' Jim said.

'And the ambulance.'

'And Ernie Jenkins, he likes fires.'

But we only called the fire brigade, and soon the fire engine came and three tall men in helmets brought a hose into the house and Mr Prothero got out just in time before they turned it on. Nobody could have had a noisier Christmas Eve. And when the firemen turned off the hose and were standing in the wet, smoky room, Jim's Aunt, Miss Prothero, came downstairs and peered in at them. Jim and I waited, very quietly, to hear what she would say to them. She said the right thing, always. She looked at the three tall firemen in their shining helmets, standing among the smoke and cinders and dissolving snowballs, and she said, 'Would you like anything to read?'

Years and years ago, when I was a boy, when there were wolves in Wales, and birds the colour of red-flannel petticoats whisked past the harp-shaped hills, when we sang and wallowed all night and day in caves that smelt like Sunday afternoons in damp front farmhouse parlours, and we chased, with the jawbones of deacons, the English and the bears, before the motor car, before the wheel, before the duchess-faced horse, when we rode the daft and happy hills bareback, it snowed and it snowed. But here a small boy says: 'It snowed last year, too. I made a snowman and my brother knocked it down and I knocked my brother down and then we had tea.'

'But that was not the same snow,' I say. 'Our snow was not only shaken from white wash buckets down the sky, it came shawling out of the ground and swam and drifted out of the arms and hands and bodies of the trees; snow grew overnight on the roofs of the houses like a pure and grandfather moss, minutely – ivied the walls and settled on the postman, opening the gate, like a dumb, numb thunder-storm of white, torn Christmas cards.'

'Were there postmen then, too?'

'With sprinkling eyes and wind-cherried noses, on spread, frozen feet they crunched up to the doors and mittened on them manfully. But all that the children could hear was a ringing of bells.'

'You mean that the postman went rat-a-tat-tat and the doors rang?'

'I mean that the bells the children could hear were inside them.'

'I only hear thunder sometimes, never bells.'

'There were church bells, too.'

'Inside them?'

'No, no, no, in the bat-black, snow-white belfries, tugged by bishops and storks. And they rang their tidings over the bandaged town, over the frozen foam of the powder and ice-cream hills, over the crackling sea. It seemed that all the churches boomed for joy under my window; and the weathercocks crew for Christmas, on our fence.'

'Get back to the postmen.'

'They were just ordinary postmen, fond of walking and dogs and Christmas and the snow. They knocked on the doors with blue knuckles . . .'

'Ours has got a black knocker . . .'

'And then they stood on the white Welcome mat in the little, drifted porches and huffed and puffed, making ghosts with their breath, and jogged from foot to foot like small boys wanting to go out.'

'And then the Presents?'

'And then the Presents, after the Christmas box. And the cold postman, with a rose on his button-nose, tingled down the tea-tray-slithered run of the chilly glinting hill. He went in his ice-bound boots like a man on fishmonger's slabs. He wagged his bag like a frozen camel's hump, dizzily turned the corner on one foot, and, by God, he was gone.'

'Get back to the Presents.'

'There were the Useful Presents: engulfing mufflers of the old coach days, and mittens made for giant sloths; zebra scarfs of a substance like silky gum that could be tug-o'-warred down to the galoshes; blinding tam-o'-shanters like patchwork tea cozies and bunny-suited busbies and balaclavas for victims of head-shrinking tribes; from aunts who always wore wool next to the skin there were mustached and rasping vests that made you wonder why the aunts had any skin left at all; and once I had a little crocheted nose bag from an aunt now, alas, no longer whinnying with us. And pictureless books in which small boys, though warned with quotations not to, would skate on Farmer Giles' pond and did and drowned; and books that told me everything about the wasp, except why.'

'Go on the Useless Presents.'

'Bags of moist and many-coloured jelly babies and a folded flag and a false nose and a tram-conductor's cap and a machine that punched tickets and rang a bell; never a catapult; once, by mistake that no one could explain, a little hatchet; and a celluloid duck that made, when you pressed it, a most unducklike sound, a mewing moo that an ambitious cat might make who wished to be a cow; and a painting book in which I could make the grass, the trees, the sea and the animals any colour I pleased, and still the dazzling sky-blue sheep are grazing in the red field under the rainbow-billed and pea-green birds. Hardboileds, toffee, fudge and allsorts, crunches, cracknels, humbugs, glaciers, marzipan, and butter-welsh for the Welsh. And troops of bright tin soldiers who, if they could not fight, could always run. And Snakes-and-Families and Happy Ladders. And Easy Hobbi-Games for Little Engineers, complete with instructions. Oh, easy for Leonardo! And a whistle to make the dogs bark to wake up the old man next door to make him beat on the wall with his stick to shake our picture off the wall. And a packet of cigarettes: you put one in your mouth and you stood at the corner of the street and you waited for hours, in vain, for an old lady to scold you for smoking a cigarette, and then with a smirk you ate it. And then it was breakfast under the balloons.'

*

'Were there Uncles like in our house?'

'There are always Uncles at Christmas. The same Uncles. And on Christmas morning, with dog-disturbing whistle and sugar fags, I would scour the swatched town for the news of the little world, and find always a dead bird by the Post Office or by the white deserted swings; perhaps a robin, all but one of his fires out. Men and women wading or scooping back from chapel, with taproom noses and wind-bussed cheeks, all albinos, huddles their stiff black jarring feathers against the irreligious snow. Mistletoe hung from the gas brackets in all the front parlours; there was sherry and walnuts and bottled beer and crackers by the dessertspoons; and cats in their fur-abouts watched the fires; and the high-heaped fire spat, all ready for the chestnuts and the mulling pokers. Some few large men sat in the front parlours, without their collars, Uncles almost certainly, trying their new cigars, holding them out judiciously at arms' length, returning them to their mouths, coughing, then holding them out again as though waiting for the explosion; and some few small aunts, not wanted in the kitchen, nor anywhere else for that matter, sat on the very edge of their chairs, poised and brittle, afraid to break, like faded cups and saucers.'

Not many those mornings trod the piling streets: an old man always, fawn-bowlered, yellow-gloved and, at this time of year, with spats of snow, would take his constitutional to the white bowling green and back, as he would take it wet or fire on Christmas Day or Doomsday; sometimes two hale young men, with big pipes blazing, no overcoats and wind blown scarfs, would trudge, unspeaking, down to the forlorn sea, to work up an appetite, to blow away the fumes, who knows, to walk into the waves until nothing of them was left but the two furling smoke clouds of their inextinguishable briars. Then I would be slap-dashing home, the gravy smell of the dinners of others, the bird smell, the brandy, the pudding and mince, coiling up to my nostrils, when out of a snow-clogged side lane would come a boy the spit of myself, with a pink-tipped cigarette and the violet past of a black eye, cocky as a bullfinch, leering all to himself.

I hated him on sight and sound, and would be about to put my dog whistle to my lips and blow him off the face of Christmas when suddenly he, with a violet wink, put his whistle to his lips and blew so stridently, so high, so exquisitely loud, that gobbling faces, their cheeks bulged with goose, would press against their tinsled windows, the whole length of the white echoing street. For dinner we had turkey and blazing pudding, and after dinner the Uncles sat in front of the fire, loosened all buttons, put their large moist hands over their watch chains, groaned a little and slept. Mothers, aunts and sisters scuttled to and fro, bearing tureens. Auntie Bessie, who had already been frightened, twice, by a clockwork mouse, whimpered at the sideboard and had some elderberry wine. The dog was sick. Auntie Dosie had to have three aspirins, but Auntie Hannah, who liked port, stood in the middle of the snowbound back yard, singing like a big-bosomed thrush. I would blow up balloons to see how big they would blow up to; and, when they burst, which they all did, the Uncles jumped and rumbled. In the rich and heavy afternoon, the

Uncles breathing like dolphins and the snow descending, I would sit among festoons and Chinese lanterns and nibble dates and try to make a model man-o'-war, following the Instructions for Little Engineers, and produce what might be mistaken for a sea-going tramcar.

Or I would go out, my bright new boots squeaking, into the white world, on to the seaward hill, to call on Jim and Dan and Jack and to pad through the still streets, leaving huge footprints on the hidden pavements.

'I bet people will think there's been hippos.'

'What would you do if you saw a hippo coming down our street?'

'I'd go like this, bang! I'd throw him over the railings and roll him down the hill and then I'd tickle him under the ear and he'd wag his tail.'

'What would you do if you saw two hippos?'

Iron-flanked and bellowing he-hippos clanked and battered through the scudding snow toward us as we passed Mr Daniel's house.

'Let's post Mr Daniel a snow-ball through his letter box.'

'Let's write things in the snow.'

'Let's write, "Mr Daniel looks like a spaniel" all over his lawn.'

Or we walked on the white shore. 'Can the fishes see it's snowing?'

The silent one-clouded heavens drifted on to the sea. Now we were snow-blind travellers lost on the north hills, and vast dewlapped dogs, with flasks round their necks, ambled and shambled up to us, baying 'Excelsior'. We returned home through the poor streets where only a few children fumbled with bare red fingers in the wheel-rutted snow and cat-called after us, their voices fading away, as we trudged uphill, into the cries of the dock birds and the hooting of ships out in the whirling bay. And then, at tea the recovered Uncles would be jolly; and the ice cake loomed in the centre of the table like a marble grave. Auntie Hannah laced her tea with rum, because it was only once a year.

Bring out the tall tales now that we told by the fire as the gaslight bubbled like a diver. Ghosts whooed like owls in the long nights when I dared not look over my shoulder; animals lurked in the cubbyhole under the stairs and the gas meter ticked. And I remember that we went singing carols once, when there wasn't the shaving of a moon to light the flying streets. At the end of a long road was a drive that led to a large house, and we stumbled up the darkness of the drive that night, each one of us afraid, each one holding a stone in his hand in case, and all of us too brave to say a word. The wind through the trees made noises as of old and unpleasant and maybe webfooted men wheezing in caves. We reached the black bulk of the house. 'What shall we give them? Hark the Herald?'

'No,' Jack said, 'Good King Wenceslas. I'll count three.' One, two, three, and we began to sing, our voices high and seemingly distant in the snow-felted darkness round the house that was occupied by nobody we knew. We stood close together, near the dark door. Good King Wenceslas looked out On the

Feast of Stephen . . . And then a small, dry voice, like the voice of someone who has not spoken for a long time, joined our singing: a small, dry, eggshell voice from the other side of the door: a small dry voice through the keyhole. And when we stopped running we were outside our house; the front room was lovely; balloons floated under the hot-water-bottle-gulping gas; everything was good again and shone over the town.

'Perhaps it was a ghost,' Jim said.

'Perhaps it was trolls,' Dan said, who was always reading.

'Let's go in and see if there's any jelly left,' Jack said. And we did that.

Always on Christmas night there was music. An uncle played the fiddle, a cousin sang 'Cherry Ripe', and another uncle sang 'Drake's Drum'. It was very warm in the little house. Auntie Hannah, who had got on to the parsnip wine, sang a song about Bleeding Hearts and Death, and then another in which she said her heart was like a Bird's Nest; and then everybody laughed again; and then I went to bed. Looking through my bedroom window, out into the moonlight and the unending smoke-coloured snow, I could see the lights in the windows of all the other houses on our hill and hear the music rising from them up the long, steady falling night. I turned the gas down, I got into bed. I said some words to the close and holy darkness, and then I slept.

THE OXEN
Thomas Hardy

Christmas Eve, and twelve of the clock.
  'Now they are all on their knees,'
An elder said as we sat in a flock
  By the embers in hearthside ease.

We pictured the meek mild creatures where
  They dwelt in their strawy pen,
Nor did it occur to one of us there
  To doubt they were kneeling then.

So fair a fancy few would weave
  In these years! Yet, I feel,
If someone said on Christmas Eve,
  'Come; see the oxen kneel,

'In the lonely barton by yonder coomb
  Our childhood used to know,'
I should go with him in the gloom,
  Hoping it might be so.

READING NOTES

'This story is full of the smell and feel of my childhood Christmases,' said one elderly man. There is so much here to talk about: snow; small boys making nuisances of themselves; the ordinary postman, who seems extraordinary compared to today's postal service. Games; dreadful hand-knitted presents; Christmas dinner; jelly; relatives; carol singing then and now and finally there is the pure delight and pleasure of the language. As someone said, 'I have read this before but it is only when I hear it read out loud that it truly comes to life.'

Another man in the group thought the poem reminded him of believing in Father Christmas: 'You begin to realise it is all made up, but it does not stop you hoping that perhaps it is true, like the story of the animals kneeling.' People often talk about the atmosphere that both story and poem create; the meaning of the final line; and whether our fondest memories are true or coloured by nostalgia and how we would like things to have been.

Read On

The aim of this section is to offer information, suggestions and enthusiasm for further stories, extracts and poems to read aloud – and where to find them.

Fleur Adcock (1934–)
Other poems: 'Things', 'For Andrew'. See: *Selected Poems* (OUP, 1983), *Dragon Talk* (Bloodaxe, 2010).

A. J. Alan (1883–1941)
His work is out of print now but try amazon.co.uk or abe.co.uk. for used copies. For further ghost stories try M. R. James, published by Penguin, OUP, Wordsworth and BBC Audio.

Louisa M. Alcott (1832–88)
Also try: Chapter 8, *Little Women* – in a fit of pique at not being allowed to go to the theatre, Amy burns the book Jo has been writing.

Hilaire Belloc (1870–1953)
Also try: 'Matilda', 'Tarantella'. See: *Cautionary Tales for Children* (Harcourt Brace, 2002).

Laurence Binyon (1869–1943)
Also try: 'For the Fallen'.

Elizabeth Bowen (1899–1973)
Also try: 'The Visitor', 'Maria', 'Summer Night'. See: *Collected Stories* (Vintage Classics, 1999).

Charlotte Brontë (1816–55)
Also try: Chapter 26, *Jane Eyre* – the wedding day of Jane and Edward Rochester.

Christy Brown (1932–81)
Also try: Christy Brown's autobiographical novel *Down All the Days* (Minerva, 1994).

George Mackay Brown (1921–96)
Also try: *Winter Tales* (Polygon, 2006), *The Sun's Net* (Polygon, 2010).

Robert Burns (1759–96)
Also try: 'To a Mouse', 'John Anderson, My Jo'. Collections of Burns' poems and songs are published by Canongate, Wordsworth, and on audio CD by HarperCollins.

Morley Callaghan (1903–90)
Morley Callaghan is not in print in the UK except for individual stories in anthologies. See: *Oxford Book of Short Stories* (OUP, 1981), *Best Canadian Short Stories* (Seal Books, Toronto).

Bruce Chatwin (1940–89)
Also try: Chatwin's account of his travels in South America, *In Patagonia* (Vintage Classics, 1999).

Anton Chekhov (1860–1904)
Also try: 'The Lottery Ticket', 'The Lady With the Little Dog', 'The Student'. See: Penguin, OUP, Vintage Classics and Wordsworth who all have collections of Chekhov stories in print.

Kate Chopin (1850–1904)
Also try: 'Désirée's Baby', set in Louisiana, about a woman who marries a slave owner and who is rejected when it is discovered that their baby is not white. See: *The Awakening and Other Stories* (Penguin, 2003).

Gillian Clarke (1937–)
Also try: 'Overheard in County Sligo', 'Hay-making'. See: *Collected Poems* (Carcanet, 1997), *Recipe for Water* (Carcanet, 2009).

Samuel Daniel (1562–1619)
Also try: 'Care-charmer Sleep', from *Delia*.

Walter de la Mare (1873–1956)
Also try: 'Fare Well', 'Autumn', 'Winter Dusk', 'The Ghost'. See: *Selected Poems* (Faber, 2006), and his very dark short stories, such as 'Seaton's Aunt', from *Short Stories, Volume One 1895–1926* (Giles de la Mare, 1996).

Charles Dickens (1812–70)
Also try: Chapter 1, *Great Expectations*, in which Pip, visiting
his parents' grave, is surprised and terrified by the appearance
of a desperate escaped convict.

George Eliot (1819–80)
Also try: Chapter 5, *The Mill on the Floss*. Young Maggie
Tulliver has been left in charge of her beloved brother's pet
rabbits while he is away at school, but she has forgotten about
them and they have all died.

Eleanor Farjeon (1881–1965)
Also try: 'Morning Has Broken'. See: *Kings and Queens*,
by Eleanor and Herbert Farjeon (Jane Nissen Books, 2002). A
poem for each of the British monarchs – brilliant!

Penny Feeny (1950–)
Also try: 'Voiceless', on summersetreview.org/06summer/
voiceless.htm, 'Falling Out of the Sky' (*Bracket*, Comma Press,
2005)

Gustave Flaubert (1821–80)
Also try: Flaubert's epic novel of love and revolution,
Sentimental Education. Penguin, OUP and Wordsworth all
have editions in print.

Robert Frost (1874–1963)
Also try: 'Stopping by Woods on a Snowy Evening', 'Mending
Wall', 'My November Guest'. See: *The Road Not Taken and
Other Poems* (Dover Thrift, 2009).

Thomas Hardy (1840–1928)

Also try: 'The Minute Before Meeting', 'I Look into My Glass', 'Heredity'. And also Chapter 5, *Far From the Madding Crowd* – Bathsheba has turned down a marrriage proposal from the farmer, Gabriel Oak. A few days later he suffers another blow.

Joanne Harris (1964–)

Also try: 'Tea With the Birds', from *Jigs and Reels* (Black Swan, 2005). See: *Chocolat* (Black Swan, 2000).

Nathaniel Hawthorne (1804–64)

Also try: *Young Goodman Brown and Other Tales* (OUP, 2008), *The Scarlet Letter*, a novel set in the harsh puritanical community of seventeenth-century Boston, about a young woman, Hester Prynne, who gives birth to an illegitimate baby. Penguin, OUP, Vintage Classics and Wordsworth have editions in print.

Robert Hayden (1913–80)

Also try: 'Frederick Douglass'. See: *Collected Poems* (W.W. Norton, 1997).

Seamus Heaney (1939–)

Also try: 'A Call', 'Postscript', 'Mossbawn Sunlight', 'Markings'. See: *The Spirit Level* (Faber, 2001), *Seeing Things* (Faber, 2002), *District and Circle* (Faber, 2008).

O. Henry (1862–1910)

Also try: 'The Ransom of Red Chief', the story of two kidnappers who, having kidnapped a loathsome boy, resort to paying the father to take him back, readbookonline.net/stories/Henry/108.

Robert Herrick (1591–1674)

Also try: 'To Daffodils', 'Corinna's Going A-Maying', 'Gather Ye Rosebuds'.

Thomas Hood (1799–1845)

Also try: 'I Remember, I Remember', 'November'.

Gerard Manley Hopkins (1844–89)

Also try: 'Heaven-Haven', 'Binsey Poplars', 'Pied Beauty', 'I Wake and Feel'. See: *Poems and Prose* (Penguin, 2008).

Tove Jansson (1914–2001)

Also try: *The Winter Book* (Sort of Books, 2006) – a collection of the best of her short stories.

Elizabeth Jennings (1926–2001)

Also try: 'Fragment for the Dark', 'A Little More', 'Delay', 'For My Sister'. See: *Collected Poems* (Carcanet, 1986).

John Keats (1795–1821)

Also try: 'Bright Star', 'To Autumn', 'To Sleep'.

Brian Keenan (1951–)
Also try: *An Evil Cradling* (Vintage, 1993) – his powerful
account of his time as a hostage in Beirut.

Doris Lessing (1919–)
Also try: 'Through the Tunnel'. See: *The Grass is Singing*
(Harper Perennial, 2008). In Doris Lessing's first novel, set in
Rhodesia, Mary, who hates the African bush where she lives, is
trapped in a loveless marriage to a failing farmer.

Jack London (1876–1916)
Also try: the short story 'To Build a Fire', and *White Fang*, a
novel about a wild wolf-dog in nineteenth-century Canada, in
The Call of the Wild, White Fang and Other Stories (OUP,
2009).

Katherine Mansfield (1888–1923)
Also try: 'The Garden Party', 'The Voyage', 'Life of Ma Parker'.
See: *Selected Stories* (OUP, 2002).

Alan Marshall (1902–84)
Alan Marshall has writen many short stories, mostly set in the
Australian bush, but he is not in print in the UK. The story in
this book comes from the *Oxford Book of Australian Short
Stories* (OUP, 1994).

John Masefield (1878–1967)
Also try: 'Cargoes', extracts from 'Reynard the Fox'. See: *Sea
Fever: Selected Poems of John Masefield* (Fyfield Books, 2005).

Guy de Maupassant (1850–93)
Also try: 'Boule de Suif', set in the Franco-Prussian War (possibly his most famous story), also 'Happiness', which is short, gentle and moving. See: *The Best Stories of Guy de Maupassant* (Wordsworth, 1997).

Roger McGough (1937–)
Also try: 'Cinders', 'Funicular Railway', 'Nine to Five'. See: *Collected Poems* (Penguin, 2004).

Harold Monro (1879–1932)
Also try: 'Living', 'At Home', 'Dog'.

Edith Nesbit (1858–1924)
Also try: *The Story of the Treasure Seekers* (Puffin, 1995), *The New Treasure Seekers* (Puffin, 1986). Also, her delightful poem 'Song', in which a new mother sings to her baby.

Saki (1870–1916)
Also try: 'Sredni Vashtar', 'The Bull', 'The Open Window'. See: *Collected Stories of Saki* (Wordsworth, 1993).

Siegfried Sassoon (1886–1967)
Also try: 'The Child at the Window', 'The Heart's Journey', 'XI', 'Invocation'. See: *The War Poems* (Faber, 1983), *Collected Poems* (Faber, 2002).

Vernon Scannell (1922–2007)

Also try: 'Walking Wounded', 'No Sense of Direction', 'Nettles'. No collections in print.

Anna Sewell (1820–78)

Also try: Chapters 7 and 8, *Black Beauty*. Black Beauty's stablemate, Ginger, tells his life story.

William Shakespeare (1564–1616)

Also try: 'Fear No More the Heat o' the Sun', sonnets 18, 29, 30, 73 and others.

Jonathan Swift (1667–1745)

Also try: *Gulliver's Travels*, which follows the travels and adventures of Lemuel Gulliver. Penguin, OUP, Vintage Classics and Wordsworth all have editions in print.

Alfred Tennyson (1809–92)

Also try: 'Crossing the Bar', 'Tears, Idle Tears', 'The Lady of Shallott'. Also *In Memoriam* – Tennyson's series of poems written after the death of his best friend left him with no more certainty that life had any meaning or purpose.

Dylan Thomas (1914–53)

Also try: 'Holiday Memory', a short recollection of an August Bank Holiday at the seaside. See: *Collected Stories* (Phoenix, 2000).

Edward Thomas (1878–1917)
Also try: 'Old Man', 'March', 'Adlestrop'. See: *Collected Poems* (Faber, 2004).

R. S. Thomas (1913–2000)
Also try: 'A Blackbird Singing', 'The Bright Field', 'A Day in Autumn'. See: *R. S. Thomas: Everyman Poetry 7* (Phoenix, 1996).

Mark Twain (1835–1910)
Also try: *The Best Stories of Mark Twain* (Modern Library Inc., 2004).

John Wain (1925–94)
All John Wain's fiction is out of print. Try secondhand bookshops, amazon.co.uk and abebooks.co.uk for used copies of his novel *Hurry On Down*.

Dorothy Whipple (1893–1966)
Also try: 'Saturday Afternoon'. See: *The Closed Door and Other Stories* (Persephone Books, 2007).

Walt Whitman (1819–92)
Also try: 'O Captain! My Captain!', 'When I Heard the Learn'd Astronomer', 'O Me! O Life!'. See: *The Works of Walt Whitman* (Wordsworth, 1995).

Tobias Wolff (1945–)
Also try: 'Firelight', 'Flyboys'. See: *The Night in Question* (Bloomsbury, 1997), *Our Story Begins: New and Selected Stories* (Bloomsbury, 2009).

William Wordsworth (1770–1850)
Also try: 'Stepping Westward', 'She Dwelt Among the Untrodden Ways', 'Old Man Travelling'. Longer poems: 'Michael', 'Lines Composed a Few Miles Above Tintern Abbey', 'Intimations of Immortality'. Penguin, OUP, Wordsworth all have editions of Wordsworth's poetry in print.

W. B. Yeats (1865–1939)
Also try: 'The Lake Isle of Innisfree', 'The Song of Wandering Aengus', 'He Wishes For the Cloths of Heaven'. See: *Collected Poems of W. B. Yeats* (Wordsworth, 2000).

Acknowledgements

Every effort has been made to trace and contact all copyright holders. If there are any inadvertent omissions or errors we will be pleased to correct these at the earliest opportunity.

Fleur Adock: 'For a Five-Year-Old', from *Poems 1960–2000* (Bloodaxe Books, 2000). Reprinted by permission of the publisher.

Hilaire Belloc: 'Rebecca', from *Cautionary Tales for Children* (Harcourt Brace, 2002). Copyright © Hilaire Belloc, 1907. Reprinted by permission of PFD (www.pfd.co.uk) on behalf of The Estate of Hilaire Belloc.

Laurence Binyon: 'The Little Dancers', from *Modern Verse 1900 –1940* (Oxford University Press, 1940). Reprinted by permission of The Society of Authors as the Literary Representatives of the Estate of Laurence Binyon.

Elizabeth Bowen: 'The Demon Lover', from *Collected Stories of Elizabeth Bowen* (Vintage, 1999). Copyright © The Estate of Elizabeth Bowen, 1945. Reprinted by permission of Curtis Brown Group Ltd, London, on behalf of the Estate of Elizabeth Bowen.

Christy Brown: 'The Letter A', from *My Left Foot* (Vintage, 2008). Reprinted by permission of The Random House Group Ltd.

George Mackay Brown: 'The Fight in the Plough and Ox', from *Winter Tales* (Polygon, 2006). Reprinted by permission of Polygon, an imprint of Birlinn Ltd.

Morley Callaghan: 'All the Years of Her Life', from *The Complete Stories, Volume One*, pages 1–8, published by Exile Editions © 2003. 'The Snob', from *The Complete Stories, Volume Two*, pages 16–22, published by Exile Editions © 2003.

Bruce Chatwin: extract from *On the Black Hill* (Vintage, 1999). Reprinted by permission of The Random House Group Ltd.

Anton Chekhov: 'A Work of Art', from *Love and Other Stories* (Dodo Press, 2006). Reprinted by permission of A. P. Watt Ltd on behalf of the Executor of the Estate of Constance Garnett.

Gillian Clarke: 'Miracle On St David's Day', from *Selected Poems* (Carcanet Press Ltd, 1996). Reprinted by permission of the publisher.

Walter de la Mare: 'The Listeners' and 'Silver', from *The Complete Poems of Walter de la Mare* (Faber, 1975). Reprinted by permission of The Literary Trustees of Walter de la Mare and the Society of Authors as their representative.

Eleanor Farjeon: 'A Christmas Carol', from *Sing for Your Supper* (Michael Joseph, 1938); 'It Was Long Ago', from *One Hundred Years of Poetry for Children*, edited by Michael Harrison and Christopher Stuart-Clark (OUP, 2000). Reprinted by permission of David Higham Associates Ltd.

Penny Feeny: 'At the End of the Line', first published in *The Reader* (issue 15, 2004). Reprinted by permission of the author.

Robert Frost: 'The Road Not Taken', from *The Poetry of Robert Frost*, edited by Edward Connery Lathem. (Jonathan Cape,1971). Reprinted by permission of The Random House Group Ltd.

Joanne Harris: 'Faith and Hope Go Shopping', from *Jigs and Reels* (Doubleday, 2004). Reprinted by permission of The Random House Group Ltd.

Robert Hayden: 'Those Winter Sundays', from *Collected Poems of Robert Hayden*, edited by Frederick Glaysher (Liveright, 1985). Copyright © 1966 by Robert Hayden. Reprinted by permission of Liveright Publishing Corporation.

Seamus Heaney: 'Digging', from *Opened Ground: Selected Poems, 1966–1996* (Faber, 2002). Reprinted by permission of the publisher.

Tove Jansson: 'The Cat', from *The Summer Book* (Sort Of Books, 2003). Copyright © 1972 by Tove Jansson. First Published in Swedish (as *Sommarboken*) by Schildts Förlags Ab, Finland. English translation by Thomas Teal. All rights reserved.

Elizabeth Jennings: 'Friendship', from *New Collected Poems* (Carcanet Press, 2002). Reprinted by permission of David Higham Associates Ltd.

Brian Keenan: 'The Swimmer', from *I'll Tell Me Ma* (Jonathan Cape, 2003). Reprinted by permission of the author.

Doris Lessing: 'Flight', from *The Habit of Loving* (MacGibbon and Kee, 1957). Copyright © 1957 by Doris Lessing. Reprinted by kind permission of Jonathan Clowes Ltd, London, on behalf of Doris Lessing.

Alan Marshall: 'Trees Can Speak', from *How's Andy Going?* (F.W. Cheshire, 1956). Reprinted by permission of Pearson Australia.

Roger McGough: 'What Does Your Father Do?', from *Everyday Eclipses* (Viking, 2002). Copyright © Roger McGough 2002. Reproduced by permission of PFD on behalf of Roger McGough.

Siegfried Sassoon: ' Everyone Sang', from *Collected Poems* (Faber, 1984). Reprinted by kind permission of Barbara Levy Literary Agency.

Vernon Scannell: 'Incendiary', from *Of Love and War*: *New and Selected Poems* (Robson Books, 2002). Reprinted by permission of the publisher.

Dylan Thomas: 'A Child's Christmas in Wales' (Orion, 1986). Reprinted by permission of David Higham Associates Ltd.

R.S. Thomas: 'Rich' from *Collected Later Poems 1988–2000* (Bloodaxe Books, 2004). Reprinted by permission of the publisher.

John Wain: 'Message for The Pig-man', from *Nuncle* (Macmillan, 1960). Reprinted by permission of The Estate of John Wain.

Dorothy Whipple: 'The Handbag', from *The Closed Door and Other Stories* (Persephone Books, 2007). Reprinted by permission of David Higham Associates Ltd.

Tobias Wolff: 'Powder', from *Our Story Begins* (Bloomsbury, 2009). Reprinted by permission of the publisher.

THANKS

The Reader Organisation is extremely grateful to all copyright holders who so big-heartedly waived or reduced their fee because they knew that all royalties for the book would go to the charity.

We should like to offer our thanks and appreciation to Emma Hayward for her dedicated hard work in pursuit of permissions.

Many thanks to Lisa Spurgin for all the hours she spent typing up the stories.

Sincere thanks to Mary Lundquist for her charming illustrations, so generously donated.

We are indebted to Becky Hardie at Chatto and Windus for her guidance and expertise as well as her belief and support for the whole project.

Finally, thanks and cheers to the great readers in the Get Into Reading groups; in particular those at Hoylake Cottage and Granville Court, Wallasey. Their sense of adventure, courage, application and enthusiasm over the past three years has been the inspiration for this anthology.